"Sometimes you want nothing more demanding than a brisk thriller with a supernatural edge to it. In which case, F. Paul Wilson's *The Haunted Air*, the latest entry in the Repairman Jack series, is just the ticket." —*San Francisco Chronicle*

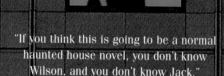

"If you think this is going to be a normal haunted house novel, you don't know Wilson, and you don't know Jack."
—*Fangoria*

"*The Haunted Air* is the best Repairman Jack novel since *Legacies* . . . and that's saying something. In Jack, F. Paul Wilson has created one of the most memorable—and most admirable—characters in modern fiction."
—*Laissez-Faire Electronic Times*

"Jack is righteous!" —Andrew Vachss

"Repairman Jack is one of the most original and intriguing characters to arise out of contemporary fiction in ages. His adventures are hugely entertaining."
—Dean Koontz

Jack is back, for 2004. F. Paul Wilson's engaging, self-employed, off-the-books fixer, Repairman Jack, returns for another intense, action-packed adventure just a little over the border into the weird, in *The Haunted Air*. First introduced years ago in the bestseller *The Tomb*, Jack has been the hero of a series of exciting novels set in and around New York City, including *Legacies*, *Conspiracies*, *All the Rage*, and *Hosts*.

"A brisk thriller with a supernatural edge to it. . . . F. Paul Wilson's *The Haunted Air*, the latest entry in the Repairman Jack series, is just the ticket. . . . *The Haunted Air* gives Wilson and Jack plenty of opportunity to do what they do best. There's some intriguing background on con games, some rousing action set pieces and a lot of snappy banter."
—*San Francisco Chronicle*

"If you think this is going to be a normal haunted house-novel, you don't know Wilson, and you don't know Jack. . . . as with all the Repairman Jack novels, *The Haunted Air* stands alone . . . Wilson's work is a lesson on how to do horror series fiction *right*."
—*Fangoria*

"*The Haunted Air* is the best Repairman Jack novel since *Legacies* . . . and that's saying something. In Jack, F. Paul Wilson has created one of the most memorable — and most admirable — characters in modern fiction."
—*Laissez-Faire Electronic Times*.

"*The Tomb* is one of the best all-out adventure stories I've read in years."
—Stephen King (President of the Repairman Jack fan club)

also by F. Paul Wilson

Repairman Jack
The Tomb
Legacies
Conspiracies
All the Rage
Hosts
The Haunted Air
Gateways

The Adversary Circle:
The Keep
The Tomb
The Touch
Reborn
Reprisal
Nightworld

Other Novels
Healer
Wheels Within Wheels
An Enemy of The State
Black Wind
Dydeetown World
The Tery
Sibs
The Select

Implant
Deep as the Marrow
Mirage
(with Matthew J. Costello)
Nightkill
(with Steven Spruill)
Masque
(with Matthew J. Costello)
The Christmas Thingy
Sims
The Fifth Harmonic
Midnight Mass

Short Fiction
Soft & Others
The Barrens & Others

Editor:
Freak Show
Diagnosis: Terminal

F. PAUL WILSON

THE HAUNTED AIR

A Repairman Jack novel

TOR®

A TOM DOHERTY ASSOCIATES BOOK
NEW YORK

This is a work of fiction. All the characters and events portrayed in this book are either products of the author's imagination or are used fictitiously.

THE HAUNTED AIR: A REPAIRMAN JACK NOVEL

Copyright © 2002 by F. Paul Wilson

A Tor Book
Published by Tom Doherty Associates, LLC
175 Fifth Avenue
New York, NY 10010

www.tor.com

Tor® is a registered trademark of Tom Doherty Associates, LLC.

ISBN 0-812-55731-X
EAN 978-0812-55731-2

First edition: September 2004
First mass market edition: April 2004

Printed in the United States of America

0 9 8 7 6 5 4 3 2 1

for two MIAs

Poul Anderson
Richard Laymon

ACKNOWLEDGMENTS

I owe a debt to works by James Randi (*An Encyclopedia of Claims, Frauds, and Hoaxes of the Occult and Supernatural, The Psychic Healers,* and *Flim-Flam!*) and M. Lamar Keene (*The Psychic Mafia*). These acted as invaluable guidebooks on what to look for on my visits to Spiritualist churches and psychic mediums.

Thanks to the usual crew for their editorial help on the manuscript: my wife Mary; my editor David Hartwell; his assistant Moshe Feder; Elizabeth Monteleone; Steven Spruill; and my agent Albert Zuckerman. And thanks to Blake Dollens, typo master, for his help with this edition.

FRIDAY

1

The bride wore white.

Only she wasn't a bride and the dress—two sizes too small at least—had faded to beige.

"Can I ask again," Jack said, leaning toward Gia, "why our hostess is wearing her wedding dress?"

Gia, seated next to him on the tattered, thirdhand-store sofa, sipped from her plastic cup of white wine. "You may."

A casual little get-together, Gia had told him. Some of her artist friends were going to gather at a loft in a converted warehouse on the fringe of the old Brooklyn Army Terminal, throw a little party for one of their clan who'd started to make it big. Come on, she'd said. It'll be fun.

Jack wasn't in a fun mood. Hadn't been for some time now. But he'd agreed to go. For Gia.

Maybe twenty people wandering about the space while Pavement's last album pounded from a boom box, echoing off the high ceilings, huge windows, and stripped-to-the-brick walls. The occupants sported hair colors that spanned the visible spectrum, skin that was either pierced or tattooed or both, and clothes that redlined the garishometer.

And Halloween was better than two months away.

Jack took a pull from his bottle of beer. He'd brought his own, opting to forego his usual Rolling Rock long necks for a six-pack of Harp. Good thing, too. The bridal-bedecked hostess had stocked Bud Light. He'd never tasted watered-down cow pee, but he imagined it tasted better than Bud Light.

"All right. Why is our hostess wearing her wedding dress?"

"Gilda's never been married. She's an artist, Jack. She's making a statement."

"What statement? I mean, besides *Look at me*?"

"I'm sure she'd tell you that it's up to the individual to decide."

"Okay. I've decided she just wants attention."

"Is that so bad? Just because you're frightened to death of attention doesn't make it wrong for other people to court it."

"Not frightened to death of it," Jack grumbled, not wanting to concede the point.

A tall, slim woman passed by then, a dead-white streak running along the side of her frizzy black swept-back hair.

He cocked his head toward her. "I know her statement: her husband's a monster."

"Karyn's not married."

A guy with gelled neon yellow hair slid by, each eyebrow pierced by at least a dozen gold rings.

"Hi, Gia," he said with a wave and kept moving.

"Hi, Nick."

"Let me guess," Jack muttered. "As a child Nick was frightened by a curtain rod."

"My, aren't we the cranky one tonight," Gia said, giving him a look.

Cranky barely touched it. He'd been alternating between bouts of rage and the way-down dumps for a couple of months now. Ever since Kate's death. Couldn't seem to pull himself out. He'd been finding it hard to get out of bed in the morning, and once he was up, there didn't seem to be anything he wanted to do. So he'd drag himself to Abe's or Julio's or Gia's and pretend he was fine. Same old Jack, just not working on anything at the moment.

The angry voice mail messages from his father, ragging on him for not showing up at Kate's wake or funeral, hadn't helped. *"Don't tell me you had something more important to do. She was your* sister, *damn it!"*

Jack knew that. After fifteen years of separation, Kate had come back into his life for one week during which he'd gotten to know her again, love her again, and now she was gone. Forever.

The facts said it wasn't Jack's fault, but the facts didn't keep Jack from blaming himself. And one other person . . .

He'd searched for the man he'd suspected of being in some way responsible, a man whose real name he didn't know but who'd called himself Sal Roma once, and maybe Ms. Aralo too. He'd put the word out but no one knew anything. Never heard of him. Jack wound up with a taste of his own medicine—Sal Roma didn't seem to exist.

Kate . . . she might still be alive if only he'd done things his way instead of listening to . . .

Stop. No point in traveling that well-worn trail again. He hadn't returned his father's calls. After a while they stopped.

He forced a smile for Gia. "Sorry. Pseudo-weirdos crank me off."

"Can't be much weirder than the people you spend most of your day with."

"Those are different. They're real. Their weirdness comes from inside. They wake up weird. They dress weird because they reach out a hand and whatever it touches first is what they wear that day. These people here spend hours in front of a mirror making themselves look weird. My weirdos have hair that spikes out in twenty directions because that's the way it was when they rolled out of bed this morning; these folks use herbal shampoo, half a gallon of gel, and a special comb to achieve their unwashed bed-head look. My weirdos don't belong; these people seem to want desperately to belong, but don't want anyone to know, so they try to outdo each other to look like outsiders."

Gia's lips twisted. "And the biggest outsider of them all is sitting right here in a short-sleeve plaid shirt, jeans, and work boots."

"And spending the evening watching pretensions collide with affectations. Present company excluded, of course."

One of the many things he loved about Gia was her lack of affectation. Her hair was blond by nature and short for convenience. Tonight she was wearing beige slacks and a sleeveless turquoise top that heightened the blue of her eyes. Her makeup consisted of a touch of lipstick. She didn't need anything more. She looked clean and healthy, a very untrendy look in this subculture.

But the subculture had percolated into the overculture, the fringe had become mainstreamed. Years ago construction workers threw bricks at longhairs and called them faggots, now the building trades were packed with ponytails and earrings.

"Maybe it's time I got myself adorned," Jack said.

Gia's eyebrows shot up. "You mean pierced? You?"

"Well, yeah. Sometimes I feel like I stand out because I'm not bejeweled and be-inked."

"Be-inked?"

"You know—tattooed."

Everyone seemed into it, and if he wanted to remain invisible, he'd have to follow the crowd.

"But nothing permanent," he added. Didn't want to lose his chameleon capabilities. "Maybe a clip-on earring and one or two of those temporary tattoos."

"Didn't you do something like that to your fingers once?"

"You remember those?" Phony prison tats. With indelible ink. A one-time thing for a hairy job that left a couple of toughs from a Brighton Beach gang blazing mad and combing the five boroughs for a guy with HELL BENT tats on his knuckles. He hadn't been able to wash those off soon enough. "No, I think I need something big and colorful."

"How about a heart encircled with rose vines and GIA in its center?"

"I was thinking more on the order of a green skull with orange flames roaring out of its eye sockets."

"Oh, how cool," Gia said, and sipped her wine.

"Yeah. Slap that on one deltoid, maybe get a bright red Hot Stuff devil for the other, put on a tank top, and I'll be set."

"Don't forget the earring."

"Right. One of those dangly ones, maybe with the Metallica logo."

"That's you, Jack. A speedmetal dude."

Jack sighed. "Adorned . . . accessorized . . . I was brought up thinking that real men didn't bother with fashion."

"So was I," Gia said. "But I have an excuse: I grew up in semi-rural Iowa. You . . . you're a northeasterner."

"True, but all the adult males I knew as a kid—my father and the men he knew—were plain dressers. Most had fought in Korea. They dressed up for things like weddings and funerals, but mostly they wore functional clothes. Nobody accessorized. You stayed in front of the mirror long enough to shave and comb the hair out of your eyes. Anything more and you were some sort of peacock."

"Welcome to twenty-first-century Peacockville," Gia said.

Nick drifted by again.

"What's Nick paint?" Jack asked.

"He doesn't paint. He's a performance artist. His stage name is Harry Adamski."

"Swell." Jack hated performance art. "What's his performance?"

Gia bit her upper lip. "He calls it stool art. Let's just say it's a very personal form of sculpture and, um, let it go at that."

Jack stared at her. What was Gia—?

"Oh, jeez. Really . . . ?"

She nodded.

"Christ," he said, letting loose, "is there anything out there that *can't* claim it's an art? There's the art of war, the art of the deal, the art of the shoe shine, the Artist Formerly Known As Prince—"

"I think he's back to calling himself Prince now."

"—the art of motorcycle maintenance. Smearing yourself with chocolate is art, hanging a toilet on a wall is art—"

"Come on, Jack. Lighten up. I was hoping a night out would lift your spirits. You've got to rejoin the living.

Lately your life's consisted of eating, sleeping, and watching movies. You haven't worked out or taken a job or even returned calls. I'm sure Kate wouldn't want you to spend the rest of your life moping around."

Jack knew Gia was right and looked away. He saw a willowy blonde in her mid twenties swaying in their direction. She carried a martini glass filled with reddish fluid, probably a cosmo. The bottom of her short, zebra-striped blouse did not meet the top of her low riding, skintight leopard miniskirt; in the interval a large diamond stud gleamed from her navel.

"Maybe I should pierce my navel," Jack said.

"Fine, but don't show me until you've shaved your belly."

"How about a pierced tongue?"

Gia gave him a sidelong glance and a sultry smile. "Now *that* could be interesting." She looked up and saw the blonde. "Oh, here comes Junie Moon, the guest of honor."

"That her real name?"

"Not sure. But that's the one she's used since I've known her. She was struggling along just like the rest of us until Nathan Lane bought one of her abstracts last year and started talking her up. Now she's about as hot as you can get."

"What's a Junie Moon original go for?"

"Twenty and up."

Jack blinked. "Twenty thou? She's that good?"

"Big difference between hot and good, but I like Junie's work. She creates this unique mix of hot and cold. Sort of a cross between De Kooning and Mondrian, if you can imagine such a thing."

Jack couldn't, because he couldn't recall any works by either.

"You sound happy for her."

"I am. She's a good kid. I've got almost ten years on her and she sort of adopted me as a surrogate mother over the past few years. Phones me a couple of times a week to chat, asks advice."

"And no hard feelings that she hit it and you haven't?"

"Not a bit. I won't say I don't wish it were me instead, but if it had to happen to someone else, I'm glad it was Junie. She's ditzy but she's got talent, and I like her."

That was Gia. The nurturer without a jealous bone in her body. Another of the many reasons he loved her. But even if it didn't bother her, it rankled Jack to see the crap that hung in the galleries and exhibits she was always dragging him to, while her own canvases remained stacked in her studio.

"Bet her stuff's not half as good as yours."

"Mine are different."

Gia made her living in commercial art. She did a lot of advertising work, but over the years she'd developed a reputation among the art directors at the city's publishing houses as a talented and reliable artist. She'd walked Jack through a Barnes and Noble last week, pointing out her work on half a dozen hardcovers and trade paperbacks.

Nice stuff, but nothing like the paintings Gia did for herself. Jack loved those. He didn't know a lot about art, but he'd picked up a little following Gia around, and her urban roofscapes reminded him of Edward Hopper, one of the few artists he'd pay to see.

Junie dropped into the narrow space next to Gia on the couch, spilling a few drops of her drink. Her blue-shadowed lids drooped slightly. He wondered how many she'd had.

"Hey," she said, and kissed Gia on the cheek.

Gia introduced her to Jack and they shook hands across Gia. She looked about as down in the dumps as Jack felt.

Gia nudged her. "Why so glum? This party's for you."

"Yeah, I'd better enjoy it now." She took a gulp of her cosmopolitan. "My fifteen minutes are so over."

"What are you talking about?"

"My lucky bracelet. It's gone. It's the whole reason for my success."

"You think it was stolen?" Jack said, glancing at her bare wrists and then at the partygoers. No shortage of jealousy here, he'd bet. "When did you last see it?"

"Tuesday. I remember taking it off after finishing a painting. I took a shower, then went out shopping. Next morning I went to put it on before starting a new work, and it was gone."

"Anything else missing?" Jack said.

"Not a thing." She tossed back the rest of her drink. "And it's not valuable. It's an old piece of junk jewelry I picked up at a secondhand store. It looks homemade—I mean, it's set with a cat's eye marble, of all things—but I liked it. And as soon as I started wearing it, my paintings began to sell. The bracelet made it happen."

"Is that so?" Jack said. He felt Gia's hand grip the top of his thigh and begin to squeeze, trying to head off what she knew he was going to say, but he spoke anyway. "So it's got nothing to do with talent."

Junie shook her head and shrugged. "I never changed my style, but I started wearing the bracelet while I worked, and the first painting I finished with it was the one Nathan Lane bought. After that, everything started happening for me. It changed my luck. I've so got to find it."

"You've looked for it, I presume," Gia said.

"Turned my place upside down. But tomorrow I'm getting professional help."

"A bloodhound?" Jack offered, which earned him another squeeze.

"No. I've got an appointment with my psycho." She giggled. "I mean my psychic."

Gia's fingers became a vise, so Jack decided to heed her. "I'm sure he'll be a big help."

"Oh, I know he will! He's wonderful! I left my old seer for Ifasen a couple of months ago and am I ever glad. The man's absolutely incredible."

"Ifasen?" Jack knew most of the major players in the local psychic racket, if not personally, at least by rep, and the name Ifasen didn't ring a bell.

"He's new. Just moved into Astoria and—oh, my God! I just realized! That's just up the road from here! Maybe I can see him tonight!"

."It's pretty late, Junie. Will he—?"

"This is an emergency! He's got to see me!"

She pulled out her cell phone and speed-dialed a number, listened for a moment, then snapped it closed.

"Damn! His answering service! So what. I'm going up there anyway." She pushed herself up from the couch and staggered a step. "Gotta find a cab."

Gia glanced at Jack, concern in her eyes, then back to Junie. "You'll never get one around here."

She grinned and hiked her miniskirt from mid-thigh to her hip. "Sure I will. Just like what's-her-name in that movie."

"Claudette Colbert in *It Happened One Night*," Jack said automatically as he wondered when the last time was a cab had cruised the Brooklyn Army Terminal area at this hour. "And someone'll think you're looking for more than a ride if you do that. We'll call you a cab."

"They never come," she said, heading for the door.

Again that concerned look from Gia. "Jack, we can't let her go. She's in no condition—"

"She's a grown-up."

"Only nominally. Jack?"

She cocked her head and looked at him with big, Girl Scout cookie-selling eyes. Refusing Gia anything was difficult, but when she did that . . .

"Oh, all right." Donning a put-upon expression, he rose and offered a hand to help Gia to her feet; in truth he was delighted for an excuse to bail this party. "I'll give her a ride. But it's not 'just up the road.' It's on the upper end of Queens."

Gia smiled, and it touched Jack right down to the base of his spine.

Somehow, between saying good-bye to the hostess bride and reaching the sidewalk, they picked up two extra passengers: Karyn—the Bride of Frankenstein—and her friend Claude, an anorexic-looking six footer with a flattop haircut that jutted out over his forehead, making his head look like

an anvil from the side. They both thought a jaunt to a psychic's house would be moby cool.

Plenty of room in Jack's Crown Vic. If he'd come alone,
he probably would have traveled by subway. But Gia's
presence demanded the security of a car. With Gia in the
passenger seat, and the other three in the back, Jack
wheeled the big black Ford up a ramp onto the Brooklyn-
Queens Expressway and headed north along the elevated
roadway. He said he hoped no one minded but he was
opening all the windows, and he did, without waiting for
answers. His car; they didn't like it, they could walk.

This kind of summer night, not too humid, not terribly
hot, brought him back to his teens when he drove a beat-
up old Corvair convertible that he got for a song because
too many people had listened to Ralph Nader and dumped
one of the best cars ever made. On nights like this he'd
drive with no destination, always with the top down, letting
the wind swirl around him.

Not much swirling tonight. Even at this hour the BQE
was crowded, but Junie made the creeping traffic seem even
slower by rattling on and on about her psychic guru: Ifasen
talked to the dead, and Ifasen let the dead talk to you, and
Ifasen knew your deepest, darkest secrets and could do the
most amazing, impossible, *incredible* things.

Not amazing or impossible to Jack. He was familiar with
all the amazing, impossible, *incredible* things Ifasen did,
and even had a pretty good idea how the man was going
to get back Junie's bracelet for her.

Yeah, Junie was a ditz, but a lovable ditz.

Maybe some music would slow her Ifasen chatter. He
stuck one of his homemade CDs in the player. John Lennon's voice filled the car.

"This happened once before . . ."

"The Beatles?" Claude said from the back. "I didn't think
anyone listened to them anymore."

"Think again," Jack said. He turned up the volume. "Listen to that harmony."

". . . I saw the light! . . ."

"Lennon and McCartney were born to sing together."

"You have to realize," Gia said, "that Jack doesn't like anything modern."

"How can you say that?"

"How?" She was smiling. "Look at your apartment, your favorite buildings"—she pointed to the CD player—"the music you listen to. You don't own a song recorded after the eighties."

"Not true."

Karyn piped up. "What's a current group or singer you listen to?"

Jack didn't want to tell her that he had Tenacious D's last disc in the glove compartment. Time for some fun.

"I like Britney Spears a lot."

"I'm sure you like to *look* at her at lot," Gia said, "but name one of her songs. Just one."

"Well . . ."

"Got him!" Karyn laughed.

"I like some of Eminem's stuff."

"Never," Gia said.

"It's true. I liked that conscience song he did, you know where he's got a good voice talking in one ear and a bad voice in the other. That was neat."

"Enough to buy it?"

"Well, no . . ."

"Got him again," Karyn said. "You want to try the nineties? Can you name one song from the nineties you listened to?"

"Hey, maybe I wasn't exactly a Spice Girls fan, but I was one hell of a nineties kinda guy."

"Prove it. One nineties group—name one you bought and listened to."

"Easy. The Traveling Willburys."

Claude burst out laughing as Karyn groaned. "I give up!"

"Hey, the Willburys formed in the nineties, so that makes them a nineties group. I also liked World Party's 'Goodbye Jumbo.' "

"Retro!"

"And hey, Counting Crows. I liked that 'Mr. Jones' song they did."

"That's because it sounded like Van Morrison!"

"That's not my fault. And you can't say Counting Crows weren't nineties. So there. A nineties guy, that was I."

"I'm getting a headache."

"Some Beatles will fix that," Jack said. "This disc is all pre-Pepper, before they got self-conscious. Good stuff."

The double-tracked guitar intro from "And Your Bird Can Sing" filled the car as Jack followed the BQE's meandering course along the Brooklyn waterfront, running either two or three stories above or one or two stories below street level. A bumpy ride over pavement with terminal acne. As they ran under the Brooklyn Heights overhang a magnificent vista of lower Manhattan, all lights ablaze, slid into view.

"I feel like I'm in *Moonstruck*," Karyn said.

"Except in *Moonstruck* the Trade Towers were there," Claude added.

The car fell silent as they passed under the neighboring on-ramps of the Brooklyn and Manhattan Bridges.

Jack had never liked the Trade Towers, had never thought he'd miss those soulless silver-plated Twix bars. But he did, and still felt a stab of fury when he noticed the hole in his sky where they'd been. The terrorists, like most outsiders to the city, probably had viewed the twins as some sort of crown on the skyline, so they'd aimed for the head. But Jack wondered how the city would have reacted if the Empire State and the Chrysler Buildings had been targeted instead. They were more part of the city's heart and soul and history. King Kong—the *real* King Kong—had climbed the Empire State Building.

Brooklyn turned into Queens at the Kosciusko Bridge and the highway wandered past Long Island City, then the equally unspectacular Jackson Heights.

Astoria sits on the northwest shoulder of Queens along the East River. Jack visited frequently, but rarely by car. One of his mail drops was on Steinway Street. As he drove he debated a side trip to pick up his mail, but canned the idea. His passengers might start asking questions. He'd subway back next week.

Following Junie's somewhat disjointed directions—she usually cabbed here so she wasn't exactly sure of all her landmarks—he jumped off the BQE onto Astoria Boulevard and turned north, running a seamless gauntlet of row houses.

"If this Ifasen's so good," Jack said, "what's he doing out here in the sticks?"

Junie said, "Queens isn't the sticks!"

"Is to me. Too open. Too much sky. Makes me nervous. Like I'm going to have a panic attack or something." He swerved the car. "Whoa!"

"What's wrong?" Junie cried.

"Just saw a herd of buffalo. Thought they were going to stampede in front of the car. Told you this was the sticks."

As the back seat laughed, Gia gave his thigh one of those squeezes.

They passed a massive Greek Orthodox church but the people passing along the sidewalk out front were dressed in billowy pantaloons and skull caps and saris. Astoria used to be almost exclusively Greek; now it housed sizable Indian, Korean, and Bangladeshi populations. A polyglotopolis.

They cruised into the commercial district along Ditmars Boulevard where they passed the usual boutiques, nail salons, travel agencies, pet shops, and pharmacies, plus the ubiquitous KFCs, Dunkin Donuts, and McDonald's, interspersed with gyro, souvlaki, and kabab houses. They passed a Pakistani-Bangladeshi restaurant; its front, like a fair number of others, sported signs written not just in foreign languages but foreign script. The Greek influence was still strong, though—Greek coffee shops, Greek bakeries, even the pizzerias sported the Acropolis or one of the Greek gods on their awnings.

"There!" Junie cried, leaning forward and pointing through the windshield at a produce shop with a yellow

awning inscribed with English and what looked like San-
skrit. "I recognize that place! Make a right at the corner
here."

Jack complied and turned into a quiet residential neighborhood. This street was lined with duplexes, a relief from
the row houses. A train rumbled along a trestle looming
above them.

"He's number 735," Junie said. "You can't miss it. It's
the only detached single-family home on the block."

"Might be the only one in Astoria," Jack said.

"Should be on the right somewhere along—" Her arm
lanced ahead again. "Here! Here it is! Awriiight!" Jack
heard the slap of a high five somewhere behind him. "Told
you I'd get us here!"

Jack found an empty spot and pulled into the curb.

Junie was out the door before he'd put the car in PARK.
"Come on, guys! Let's go talk to dead folks!"

Karyn and Claude piled out, but Jack stayed put. "I think
we'll pass."

"Aw, no," Junie said, leaning toward the passenger window. "Gia, you've got to come meet him. You've got to
see what he can do!"

Gia looked at him. "What do you say?"

Jack lowered his voice. "I know this game. It's not—"

"You were a psychic?"

"No. I just helped one once."

"Great! Then you can explain it all afterwards." She
smiled and tugged on his arm. "Come on. This could be
fun."

"Fun like that party?" Gia gave him a look so Jack
shrugged his acquiescence. "All right. Let's see if this guy
lives up to Junie's press release."

Junie cheered and led Karyn and Claude toward the house
while Jack closed up the car. He joined Gia at the curb. He
started toward the house but stopped when he saw it.

"What's wrong?" Gia said.

He stared at the house. "Look at this place."

Jack couldn't say why, but he immediately disliked the house. It was colonial in shape, with an attached garage, but made of some sort of dark brown stone. It probably looked better during the day. Jack could make out a well-trimmed lawn and impatiens and marigolds in bloom among the foundation plantings along the front porch. But here in the dark it seemed to squat on its double-size lot like some huge, glowering toad edging hungrily toward the sidewalk. He could imagine a snakelike tongue uncoiling through the front door and snagging some unwary passerby.

"Definitely creepy looking," Gia said. "Probably by design."

"Don't go in there," said an accented voice from his left.

Jack turned and saw a slim, dark Indian woman in a royal blue sari, strolling her way along the sidewalk, being led by a big German shepherd on a leash.

"Excuse me?" Jack said.

"Very bad place," the woman said, closer now. Her dark hair was knitted into a long thick braid that trailed over her right shoulder; a fine golden ring pierced her right nostril. "Bad past. Worse future. Stay away." She didn't slow her pace as she came abreast of them. Her black eyes flashed at Jack—"Stay away"—then at Gia—"especially you."

Then she walked on. The dog looked back over his shoulder, but the woman did not.

"Now *that's* creepy," Gia said as an uncertain smile wavered across her lips.

Jack had always believed that in confronting a fear and facing it down, you weakened it. Recent events had given him second thoughts about the wisdom of that belief. And with Gia along . . .

"Maybe we should listen to her."

Gia laughed. "Oh, come *on!* She probably works for this guy; he sends her out to get us in the mood. Or maybe she's just a local wacko. You're not taking her seriously, are you?"

Jack looked after the retreating saried figure, now barely visible in the shadows. After what he'd been through lately, he was taking a lot more things seriously, things he'd laughed at before.

"I don't know."

"Oh, let's go," she said, tugging him up the front walk. "Junie's been seeing him for a couple of months and nothing bad's happened to her."

Jack put an arm around Gia's back and together they approached the house. They joined the others on the front porch where Junie had been jabbing at the bell button with no results.

She jabbed it again. "Where is he?"

"Maybe he's not home," Jack said.

"He's got to be! I can't—"

Just then the front door eased open a crack. Jack saw an eye and a sliver of dark cheek.

"Ifasen! It's me! Junie! Thank God you're here!"

The door opened wider, revealing a tall, lean black man, maybe thirty. He wore a white T-shirt and gray slacks; his hair was woven into neat, tight dreads that brushed his wide shoulders. Ifasen reminded Jack of Lenny Kravitz in his dreadlock days.

"Ms. Moon," he said with an unplaceable accent. "It's late."

Jack hid a smile at the obvious statement. This guy was experienced. The normal response would be, *What are you doing here at this hour?* But if you're supposed to be someone who knows all—or maybe not all, but a helluva lot more than ordinary people—you don't ask questions. You make statements.

But he wondered at the man's expression when he'd opened the door. He'd looked . . . relieved. Who had he been expecting?

"I know. And I know my appointment's tomorrow, but I had to come."

"You couldn't wait," he said, his tone calm, exuding confidence and assurance.

"Yes! Right! I need your help! I lost my good luck bracelet! You've got to find it for me!"

As he considered her plea, his gaze roamed among Jack and Gia and the others on the porch.

"I see you've brought company."

"I told them all about you and they're dying to meet you. Can we come in? Please?"

"Very well," Ifasen said. He stepped back and opened the door the rest of the way. "But only for a few minutes. I have to be rested for my early clients tomorrow."

That's right, Jack remembered. Weekends are busy times for psychics.

Junie led the way, followed by Karyn and Claude. Jack and Gia were just stepping over the threshold when a deep rumble filled the air, vibrating through their bones and shaking the house.

"Bomb!" Ifasen yelled. "Out! Everybody out!"

Then another sound, a deafening, high-pitched, echoing scream—whether of pain, fear, or joy, Jack couldn't say—filled the air.

Didn't sound like a bomb to Jack but he wasn't taking any chances. He grabbed Gia and hauled her back across the porch and onto the lawn. Junie, Claude, and a shrieking Karyn scurried behind them.

Ifasen was still at the front door, calling for someone named Charlie.

Jack kept moving, pushing Gia ahead of him up the walk toward the car. Then he noticed something.

He stopped. "Wait. Feel that?"

Gia looked into his eyes, and then at her feet. "The ground . . ."

"Right. It's shaking."

"Oh, my God!" Junie cried. "It's an earthquake!"

Just as suddenly as the tremors had started, they stopped.

Jack looked around. Across the street, up and down the block, lights were on and people were spilling out into their yards, standing around in all states of dress and undress, some crying, some looking simply bewildered.

Gia was staring at him. "Jack. An earthquake? In New York?"

"Don't you remember that one on the Upper East Side back in '01?"

"I read about it, but I never felt it. I felt *this*. And I didn't like it!"

Neither had Jack. Maybe people in places like LA got used to something like this, but feeling the solid granite bedrock of good old New York City rolling and trembling under his feet . . . pretty damn unsettling.

"What about that other sound? Like a scream? Did you hear that?"

Gia nodded as she moved closer and clutched his arm. "Like a damned soul."

"Probably just some old nails tearing free in the quake."

"If you say so. Sure sounded like a voice though."

Sure did, Jack thought. But he didn't want to add to her unease.

He looked around and saw Ifasen approaching with another, younger black man who bore a family resemblance. Both had similar builds and features, but instead of dreads the newcomer's hair was cut in a neat fade. He wore black slacks, black sneakers, and a lightweight long-sleeve turtleneck, also black.

"An earthquake, Ifasen!" Junie said. "Can you believe it?"

"I knew something was going to happen," Ifasen said. "But impending seismic activity interferes with psychic transmission, so I couldn't get a clear message."

Jack nodded approval. The guy ad-libbed well.

Close up now, Jack noticed a horizontal scar along Ifasen's left cheek; his milk chocolate skin was otherwise flawless except for the stipple of whiskers shadowing his jaw.

"Can we go back inside now?" Junie said.

Ifasen shook his head. "I don't know . . ."

"Please?"

He sighed. "Very well. But only briefly." He put a hand on the younger man's shoulder. "This, by the way, is my brother Kehinde. He lives in Menelaus Manor with me."

Menelaus Manor? Jack thought, staring at the old house. This place has a name?

Kehinde led the way back to the house. Jack hung back with Gia so he could talk to Ifasen.

"Why'd you think it was a bomb?"

Ifasen blinked but his onyx eyes remained unreadable. "What gives you that idea?"

"Oh, I don't know. Maybe the fact that you yelled 'Bomb!' when the house started to shake."

"I'm not sure. Perhaps I was startled and it was the first thought that came to mind. The pre-seismic vibrations—"

Jack held up a hand. "Yeah. You told us."

Jack sensed Ifasen was telling the truth, and that bothered him. When your house starts to shake, rattle, and roll, it could be a lot of things, but *bomb* should not be first on your guess list.

Unless you were expecting one.

"And where's Charlie?"

Ifasen stiffened. "Who?"

"I heard you calling for someone named Charlie while we were evacuating."

"You must have misheard me, sir. I was calling for my brother Kehinde."

Jack turned to Gia. "Let's split. I don't think this is a good idea."

Before Gia could answer, Ifasen said, "Please. There's nothing to fear. Really."

"Let's do it, Jack." She glanced at Ifasen. "It'll take us, what—half an hour?"

"At most." Ifasen smiled. "As I said, I need my rest."

Half an hour, Jack thought. Okay. What could happen in half an hour?

2

"This is my channeling room," Ifasen said with a sweeping gesture.

Impressive, Jack thought as he looked around.

Ifasen had decked out the high-ceilinged first-floor room with a wide array of spiritualist and New Age paraphernalia along with some unique touches. Most striking were the host of statues—some looked like the real deal—from churches and Indian temples and Mayan pyramids: Mary, Saint Joseph, Kali, Shiva, a totem pole, a snake-headed god, cathedral gargoyles, and a ten-foot stone Ganesha holding a gold scepter in his coiled elephant trunk. Drapes covered the windows. The oak-paneled walls were festooned with paintings of spiritualist icons. Jack recognized Madame Blatavsky, the Mona Lisa of this Louvre of phonies.

At the far end of the room sat a round table surrounded by chairs; an ornate, pulpitlike podium upon a two-foot dais dominated the near end; Ifasen took his place behind it while Jack, Gia, Junie, Karyn, and Claude seated themselves among the chairs clustered before it.

"I am Ifasen," he said, "and I have been blessed with a gift that allows me to communicate with the spirit world. I cannot speak directly with the dead, but with the aid of Ogunfiditimi, an ancient Nigerian wise man who has been my spirit guide since I was a child, I can bring revelations and messages of peace and hope to our world from the place beyond.

"Ms. Moon's sitting with me was scheduled for tomorrow, but due to her dire need, I have moved it up to tonight. In gratitude, she has made a generous donation to the Menelaus Manor Foundation on behalf of you, her friends, to allow you to become part of her sitting."

Karyn and Claude clapped; Junie, alone in the front row, turned and waved.

"I will answer her question and yours in the form of a billet reading," Ifasen said. "My brother Kehinde is passing among you with billets, envelopes, and pens."

The billets turned out to be index cards. Jack took a couple from Kehinde for Gia and himself. He knew this game but decided to play along.

Ifasen said, "Please write your question on the billet, sign it, fold it, and seal it in the envelope. I will then contact Ogunfiditimi and ask him if he can find the answers in the spirit world. This is not a time for prank questions, or schemes to test the spirit world. Do not waste Ogunfiditimi's time by asking a question to which you already know the answer. And realize this: the mere fact that you have asked a question does not obligate the spirits to answer. They pick and choose. The worthier the question, the more likely it will be answered."

Great hedge, Jack thought. The perfect out.

"May I ask a question?" Gia said, raising her hand like a schoolgirl.

"Of course."

"Why do we have to seal the question in an envelope? Why can't we simply hand you the card and get the answer?"

Ifasen smiled. "Excellent question. Communication with the spirit world is not like a long-distance call. Words sometimes filter through, but often the communication is in the form of hints and feelings. To open the clearest channel, I need to empty my mind. If I'm thinking about the question, I'll muddy the waters with my own opinions and prejudices. But if I don't know the question, then my own thoughts can't get in the way. What comes through then is pure Spirit Truth."

"Smooth," Jack whispered. "Silky smooth."

Jack scribbled *How is my sister?* on his card and showed it to Gia.

"Is that fair?" she said.

"It's something I'd like to know."

Before he folded the card he tore a piece off the top left corner. As he slipped it inside the envelope he glanced at Gia and saw her sealing hers.

"What did you ask?"

She smiled. "That's between me and Ogunfiditimi."

He was about to press her when a soft musical chime filtered through the room. He looked up and saw Ifasen holding what appeared to be a large bowl of beaten brass on the tips of his fingers.

"This is a ceremonial bell from a temple deep in the jungles of Thailand. It is said that if properly mounted it will ring an entire day from a single stroke." He flicked a fingernail against the shiny surface and again the soft chime sounded. "But tonight we will be using it as a bowl to collect your billets."

He handed the bell to Kehinde who passed among them, collecting the envelopes. Jack kept an eye on him, watching closely as the younger brother placed the bell behind the base of the podium. He fiddled with something out of sight, then shook out a white cloth. The bell reappeared, covered with the cloth, and was handed up to Ifasen.

Jack leaned back, nodding. *Gotcha.*

Kehinde walked off and the lighting changed, the room growing dark while an overhead spot brightened, leaving Ifasen towering above them, bathed in a glow from heaven. He whipped off the white cloth and stared down into the bowl. After a moment he reached in and removed an envelope. He held it before him.

"I have the first question," he intoned. He lowered his head and raised the envelope on high where it gleamed like a star in the brilliant light. "Ogunfiditimi, hear me. These supplicants come before me, seeking knowledge, knowledge that only you can provide. Heed their requests and furnish the answers they seek."

He shuddered once, twice, then spoke in a flat, sepulchral tone.

"You are not yet ready. You must work harder, hone your craft, and above all, be patient. It will come."

Ifasen looked up and blinked. He lowered the envelope and picked up a slim gold-plated letter opener. He slit the top of the envelope and pulled the card from within. He unfolded it and, to Jack's chagrin, held it by the upper left corner. After reading it he smiled down at Karyn. "Does that answer your question, Karyn?"

She nodded enthusiastically.

Clause said, "What did you ask?"

"I wanted to know when I'll be as successful as Junie."

Junie turned to her. "Didn't I tell you? Isn't he just so amazing?"

"How does he do that?" Gia whispered.

"Later."

Knowing pretty much how the rest of the act would go, Jack pulled out a folded pamphlet he'd picked up downstairs. The cover read

THE MENELAUS MANOR
RESTORATION FOUNDATION

over a grainy picture of this old stone house. So that was where the donations went.

He opened the yellow tri-fold brochure and out fell another, smaller pamphlet, almost the size of the three-by-five billet he'd just filled out. The cover showed a crude illustration of a human silhouette falling into a pit next to the title, "The Trap." He flipped it over and almost laughed aloud when he saw the words "Chick Publications." A Born Again mini-comic. The opening pages showed a Christian character debunking a self-described channeler.

Some prankster was slipping Jack Chick's fundamentalist tracts into Ifasen's brochures. How rich.

Jack checked Ifasen, who had a fresh envelope held on high, but this time he skipped the incantation. Maybe he was in a hurry. He shook his head as if trying to clear it, scrinched up his eyes, then shook his head again. Finally he lowered the envelope and cast a disapproving look at Claude.

"The spirits refuse to answer this. They want me to tell you to buy a calculator."

He slit the envelope and unfolded the card—again holding it by the upper left corner. He read: " 'What is the square root of 2,762?' " He frowned at Claude, his disdain palpable. "What did I say about frivolous questions that waste the spirits' time?"

Claude grinned. "It's a question that's plagued me for years."

Junie gave him a fierce look and slapped him on the knee. Jack decided he liked Claude.

He put aside the Chick pamphlet and was starting to read Ifasen's propaganda on this house and its history when Gia nudged him.

"Pay attention. You might be next."

Jack refolded the brochure and trained his attention on Ifasen who had raised another envelope. He gave a couple of shudders, then, "Your sister sends you her love from the Other Side. She says she is well and to get on with your life."

Jack couldn't help feeling a chill. He knew the game, knew Ifasen was winging it here, but this was exactly what Kate would say.

Ifasen was unfolding a card, holding it as usual by the upper left corner. "Does that answer your question, Jack?"

"Completely," Jack said softly.

Gia looked at him with wide eyes and grabbed his arm. "Jack! How could he—?"

He cocked his head toward her and whispered, "An educated guess. He's very good."

"How can you write that off as a guess?"

"Easy. Of course, if he'd said, 'Kate sends her love,' that'd be a whole other ballgame. Big problem writing that off."

Another envelope had been thrust into the light, and now Ifasen was frowning again.

"I'm having trouble with this. I sense a number trying to come through, but the seismic static has increased. I'm not sure, but I believe the number is two." He opened his eyes. "And that's all."

Ifasen wore a puzzled frown as he slit this envelope, but when he read the message, he smiled. "Two." He looked up. "Does that satisfy you, Gia?"

"I . . . I think so," Gia said.

Jack glanced at her and thought she looked a little pale. "What did you ask?"

"Tell you later," she said.

"Now."

"Later. I want to see if he knows where Junie's bracelet is."

"The last envelope," Ifasen said, thrusting it up into the light. He closed his eyes, went through the shuddering deal, then said, "It is not stolen. You will find it in the large blue vase." He looked at Junie who was on her feet. "Do you have a large blue vase?"

"Yes! Yes!" She had her hands pressed against her mouth, muffling her words. "Right next to the door! But that can't be! How could it possibly get in there?"

"The spirits didn't say *how*, Ms. Moon," Ifasen told her. "They simply said *where*."

"I've gotta go! I've so gotta get home and check that vase!" She ran up to the podium and threw her arms around her psychic. "Ifasen, you're the best, the greatest!" She turned to Jack and Gia and Karyn and Claude. "Isn't he fantastic! Isn't he just so incredible!"

Jack joined the applause. Nothing incredible about Ifasen, but he was good. He was very good.

3

"Sweet Jesus!" Lyle Kenton said when their uninvited guests were finally gone. He'd already dropped his Ifasen persona; now he dropped into the recliner in the upstairs sitting room and rubbed his eyes. "What happened here tonight?"

His brother Charlie, no longer the subservient Kehinde, gave him a reproachful look from where he leaned against the couch, taking tiny sips from a Diet Pepsi. That was the way he drank: no gulps, just lots of quick, tiny sips.

"Ay, yo, Lyle. I thought you was eighty-sixin' it with taking the Lord's name in vain."

Lyle waved an apology with one hand and twisted one of his dreads in the other as he reran the past hour through his brain. Not the laid-back Friday night he'd planned. He and Charlie had been sitting in the living room, channel surfing in search of something watchable on the tube when Junie Moon had come a-knockin'.

"I tell you, Charlie, when I saw Moonie standing there on the front porch with that crowd behind her, I thought we were cooked. I mean, I figured she'd tumbled to your little visit and brought down the heat."

Of course, on further reflection, he'd realized that if it really had been the heat, Junie Moon wouldn't have been with them.

"Coulda been worse," Charlie said, pacing back and forth in front of the couch, a deep purple velvet affair that had come with the house. Everything in the room—the furniture, the upright piano, the murky landscapes in gilded frames on the walls—had been here when they'd bought it ten months ago. "Coulda been the banger who done the drive-by."

Lyle nodded, feeling his neck tighten. Just last Tuesday night he'd been standing by the picture window in the waiting room downstairs when a bullet whizzed right by his head. It had punctured the pane without shattering it, leaving a hole surrounded by a small spiderweb of cracks. He'd dug it out of the wall, but since guns weren't his thing, he couldn't tell what caliber it was. All he could be sure of was that it had been meant for him. The incident had left him shaken and more than a little paranoid. He'd kept the curtains pulled ever since.

The reason, he knew, was that a lot of well-heeled clients had started migrating from the Manhattan psychics to Astoria since Lyle had joined the game. None of those players was happy about it. A slew of angry, threatening, anonymous phone calls over the past few weeks had made that clear. But one of them—hell, maybe a group of them—had figured that phone calls wouldn't cut it and decided to play rough.

But Lyle hadn't called the police. They say the only bad publicity is no publicity, but this was an exception. A sensational story about his being shot at could be pure poison. People might stay away for fear of being caught in the middle of a shoot-out between warring psychics. He could imagine the quips: *A trip to this psychic might put you a lot closer to the dearly departed than you intended.*

Oh, yes. That would be a real boon to business.

But worse was the gut-clawing realization that someone wanted him dead.

Maybe not dead, he kept telling himself. Maybe the shot had been a warning, an attempt to scare him off.

He'd find that easier to believe if he'd been in another room at the time.

Nothing else had happened since. Things would settle out. He just had to keep his head down and give it time.

"But it wasn't," Lyle said. "It was just Junie Moonie and friends. So there I was, just starting to relax after finding out she's here because she can't wait till tomorrow for her session. I open the door, and what happens? *Bam!* The world starts to shake. I gotta tell you, bro, I almost lost it."

Charlie's grin had a sour twist. "I know you lost that busta accent."

"Did I?" Lyle had to smile. He'd been affecting a mild East African accent for so long now—used it twenty-four/seven—that he'd thought his Detroit ghetto voice dead and buried. Guess not. "Shows how much I was worried about you, man. You're my blood. I didn't want this whole house comin' down on your head."

"I 'preciate that, Lyle, but Jesus was with me. I wasn't afraid."

"Well, you should have been. An earthquake in New York. Whoever heard of such a thing?"

"Maybe it's a warning, Lyle," Charlie said, still pacing and sipping. "You know, the Lord's way of telling us to get tight."

Lyle closed his eyes. Charlie, Charlie, Charlie. You were so much more fun before you got religion.

My fault, he supposed. My bad.

A few years ago, when they'd been working a low-budget spiritualist storefront in Dearborn, a faith healer came to town and he and Charlie had gone to see how the guy worked his game. Lyle had kept his eye on all the wheelchairs the healer had brought along, and how his assistants would graciously offer them to unsteady looking old folks who tottered in—the same folks who'd "miraculously" be able to walk again after the healer prayed over them. While he was doing that, his younger brother had been listening to the sermon.

Lyle had gone home and written up notes for the future when he opened his own church.

Charlie had bought a Bible at the tent show, brought it home, and started reading it.

Now he was a Born Again. A True Believer. A Big Bore.

They used to make the bars together, pick up women together, do everything together. Now the only things that seemed to interest Charlie were reading his Bible and "witnessing."

Yet no matter what he did or didn't do, Charlie was still his brother and Lyle loved him. But he'd *liked* the old Charlie better.

"If that earthquake was the Lord's work and aimed at us, Charlie, he sure shook up a lot of people besides us."

"Maybe lots of people besides us need shaking up, yo."

"Amen to that. But what was with that scream? You've got to let me know when you're going to pull a new gag. The house shaking and the ground rumbling were bad enough, but then you throw in the scream from hell and everyone was ready to run for the river."

"Didn't have nothing to do with no scream," Charlie said. "That was the fo' *reals*, bro."

"Real?" In his heart Lyle had known that, but he'd been hoping Charlie would tell him different. "Real what?"

"Real as in not something I cooked up. That sound didn't come from no speakers, Lyle. It come from the *house*."

"I know. A bunch of these old beams shifting in the quake, right?"

Charlie stopped his pacing and stared at him. "You connin' me? You really gonna sit there and tell me that sounded like wood creaks to you? Betta recognize that was a scream, man. A human scream."

That was what it had sounded like to Lyle too, but it couldn't have been.

"Not human, Charlie, because the only humans here besides you and me were our uninvited guests, and they didn't do it. So it just *sounded* human, but wasn't."

"Was." Charlie's pacing picked up speed. "Come from the basement."

"How do you know that?"

"I standin' by the door when it went down."

"The basement?" Lyle felt a chill ripple along his spine. He hated the basement. "Why didn't you tell me?"

"Didn't 'xactly have time. We had guests, remember?"

"They've been gone for a while now."

Charlie looked away. "I knew you'd wanna go check it out."

"Damn right, I do." He didn't, not really, but no way he was going to sleep tonight if he didn't. "And would you sit down or something? You're making me nervous."

"Can't. I'm too jumpy. Don't you feel it, Lyle? The house has changed, yo. Noticed it soon as we come back inside after the quake. I can't explain it, but it feels different . . . strange."

Lyle felt it too, but wouldn't say so. That would be akin to buying into the same sort of supernatural mumbo jumbo they sold to the fish. Which he refused to do. But he had to admit that the room lights didn't seem quite as bright as before the quake. Or was it that the shadows in the corners seemed a little deeper?

"We've had a nerve-jangling week and you're feeling the effects."

"No, Lyle. It's like it ain't just us in this house no more. Like something else moved in."

"Who? Beelzebub?"

"Don't you go crackin' on me. You know you feel it, dawg, don't tell me you don't!"

"I don't feel nothin'!"

Lyle stopped and shook his head at the double negative. He'd spent years erasing the street from his vocabulary, but every once in a while, like a weed, it popped through the Third World turf he'd been cultivating. Ifasen's accent said old Third World, his dreads said new Third World; Ifasen was an international man who recognized no barriers—not between races, not between nations, not even between life and death.

But Third World was key. The affluent, white, New Age yo-yos who made up the demographic Lyle was chasing believed that only primitive and ancient civilizations retained access to the eternal truths obscured by the technophilia of western post-industrial civilization. They'd accept just about anything an East African named Ifasen told them, but would brush off the same if it came from Lyle Kenton of Detroit's Westwood Park slums.

Lyle didn't mind the act; kind of liked it, in fact. But Charlie wouldn't make the effort, declining to become what he called an "oreo." So he became the silent partner in the act. At least he agreed to dress the part of Kehinde. Left on his own he'd be baggied out with a dukey rope, floppy fat sneaks, and a backward Tigers cap. A hip-hop Born-Again.

Lyle jumped and spilled some beer on his pants as the phone rang. Man, his nerves were jangled. He looked at the caller ID: Michigan. He picked up.

"Hey, sugar. I thought you'd be on the plane by now."

Kareena Hawkins's velvet voice slunk from the receiver. The sound gave Lyle a rush of lust. "I wish I were. But tonight's promotion ran way over and the last plane out is gone."

He missed Kareena. She ran the PR department of a Dearborn rap station. At twenty-eight she was two years younger than Lyle. They'd been just about inseparable before he moved east, and had been carrying on a long-distance relationship the last ten months, the plan being for Kareena to move east and get a job with a New York station.

"So take a morning flight."

He heard her yawn. "I'm beat, Lyle. I think I'll just sleep in."

Lyle couldn't hide his disappointment. "Come on, Kareena. It's been three weeks."

"Next weekend'll be better. I'll call you tomorrow."

Lyle pressed his case awhile longer but to no avail. Finally they ended the call. He sat there a moment, staring at one of the crummy pictures on the wall and feeling morose.

Charlie said, "Kareena ain't gonna make it, I take it?"

"Nah. Too tired. That job of hers is—"

"Hate to say it, bro, but she playin' on you."

"No way. Don't talk like that."

Charlie shrugged and mimed zipping his lip.

Lyle didn't want to admit it but he'd begun suspecting the same thing. He'd gotten the growing impression that despite all her early enthusiasm for a career move, Kareena had cooled to the idea of leaving her comfy niche in Dearborn and challenging the New York market. And now she was cooling on him.

Only one thing to do: Take some time off next week and head west. Sit her down, talk to her, show her how important she was to him and how he couldn't lose her.

He looked at Charlie and said, "Let's go check the cellar."

Charlie only nodded.

Lyle led the way down to the first level, through the old-fashioned linoleum-floored kitchen, and down the cellar steps. He flipped the light on and stopped, staring.

"Jeees—" Realizing Charlie was right behind him, he stopped himself, then added, "—and crackers."

According to the real estate agent who'd sold them the place, the cellar had been finished by a previous owner, two prior to Lyle. Whoever he was, he'd had no taste. He'd put in a drop ceiling with fluorescent lights, tacky fake wood paneling in some blah shade of pecan on the walls, and painted the concrete floor orange. Orange! It looked like a rec room out of a bad movie from the sixties, or maybe the fifties. Whatever, it did *not* belong in Menelaus Manor.

But now a huge crack split its orange floor.

"Peep this!" Charlie said as he brushed past Lyle and approached it.

The jagged crack ran the entire width of the floor, wall to wall, east to west, widening to a couple of inches near the center. *Crack* was an understatement. The concrete slab of the floor had been broken in half.

His brother was already crouched by the opening when Lyle arrived.

"Looks deep," Charlie said.

Lyle's heart stumbled over a beat as he saw his brother

start to wriggle his fingers into the crack. He grabbed Charlie's wrist and snatched it back.

"What kind of fool are you?" he shouted, angry and frightened. "What if that floor decides to shift back? What are you going to do with a right hand that's got no fingers?"

"Oh, right," Charlie said, cradling his fingers as if they'd been hurt. "Good point."

Lyle shook his head. Charlie was so bright in so many ways, but sometimes, when it came to common sense . . .

Lyle studied the crack, wondering how deep the ground was split beneath it. He leaned over and squinted into the opening. Nothing but featureless darkness beyond.

Wait . . . was that—?

Lyle snapped his head up, momentarily dizzy. For a moment there he thought he'd seen stars . . . as if he'd been looking at a night sky, but someone else's sky, like no night sky ever seen from earth . . . a yawning well of stars that threatened to drag him down through the opening.

He backed away, afraid to look again, and as he moved he thought he felt a puff of air against his face. He placed his hand over the opening. A feather-light breeze wafted against his palm.

Damn! Where was that coming from?

"Charlie, look in there and tell me what you see."

"Why?"

"Make like a Nike and just do it."

Charlie put his eye to the crack. "Nathan. Just black."

Lyle looked again and this time saw no stars, no strange sky. But what about a moment ago?

He straightened. "Bring me the toolbox, will you?"

"What wrong?"

"I'm not sure."

Charlie returned in less than a minute. Lyle opened the toolbox and found some two-inch nails. He pressed his ear to the crack and dropped one through. He listened for the clink of it hitting bottom, but it never came.

Lyle motioned his brother closer. "Get your ear down here and see if you hear anything."

A second try yielded the same nonresult for Lyle. He straightened and looked at Charlie. "Well?"

Charlie shook his head. "Could be soft dirt down there. Like sand."

"Maybe. But you'd think we'd hear *something*."

"Got an idea!"

Charlie jumped up and ran back upstairs. He returned with a pitcher of water.

"This gotta work."

Lyle fitted his ear against the crack; Charlie did the same and then began to pour. The faint trickle of the water through the crack was all Lyle heard. No splash, not even a hint of one, from below.

Lyle straightened to sitting. "Just what we need: a bottomless pit under our house."

"What we do?" Charlie stared at him, obviously expecting an answer from big brother.

Lyle didn't have one. He definitely didn't want the city to know about this. They might condemn the place and boot him out. He hadn't come all the way from Michigan to get kicked out of the first home he'd ever owned.

No, he needed someone discreet who knew his way around construction and could tell him what was wrong and how to fix it. But he'd only been in town ten months and—

"Dear Lord!" Charlie cried, jamming a hand over his nose and mouth. "What *that!*"

Lyle didn't have to ask. He gagged as the odor hit him. It lifted him to his feet and sent him staggering toward the stairs. Charlie was right behind him as he pelted up to the first floor and shut the door.

Lyle stood in the kitchen, gasping as he stared at his brother. "We must be sitting over a sewer line or something."

Charlie stared back. "One that run through a graveyard. You ever smell anything stink so bad? Even close?"

Lyle shook his head. "Never." He'd never imagined anything could smell that foul. "What next? A meteor through the roof?"

"Tellin' you, Lyle, the Lord's puttin' us on notice."

"With a stink bomb? I don't think so."

Although the odor hadn't reached the kitchen, Lyle didn't want to take any chances. He and Charlie stuffed wet paper towels into the spaces between the door and its molding.

When they'd finished, Lyle went to the fridge and pulled out a Heinie keg can. He could have done with a double deuce of Schlitz M-L right now, but that was way too street.

"You not gettin' bent, are you?" Charlie said.

He handed Charlie another Pepsi. "When was the last time I got bent?"

"When was the last time you had an earthquake open a bottomless pit under your house?"

"Good point." He took a long cold gulp from the can and changed the subject. "By the way, one of the guys with Moonie tried to pull a fast one tonight, and I don't mean Mr. Square Root."

"The bama-looking Joe?" Charlie said, resuming his pacing.

"Bama-looking Jack, if we're to believe the name he wrote. I knew he was trouble right from the start. Heard me calling you by your real name when we were evacuating and wanted to know why I yelled 'bomb' when the quake hit. I kept an eye on him after that. He didn't miss a trick. He watched your every move, then mine. Good thing I was onto him, otherwise I might have missed seeing him tear a corner off his billet."

"So that's why you was holding them by the top corner. You always hold them bottom center." Charlie frowned. "You think he here to make trouble?"

Lyle shook his head. "No. I got the impression he didn't even want to be here. I think he was bored and having a little fun with me. He knew exactly what I was doing but he was cool with it. Just sat there and let the show roll."

Lyle wandered into the waiting room; Charlie followed, saying, "Maybe he in the game."

"Not ours. Another game, but don't ask me what." Lyle

had sensed something going on behind that white guy's mild brown eyes; something that said, *Don't mess.* "Some game of his own."

Lyle prided himself on his ability to read people. Nothing psychic about it, no spirits involved, just something he'd been able to do as long as he could remember. A talent he'd honed to a fine edge.

That talent had found the visitor named Jack a hard read. Bland-looking guy: nothing-special clothes, brown hair, mild brown eyes, not handsome, not ugly, just . . . there. But he'd moved with a secret grace inside a damn near impenetrable shield. The only thing Lyle had sensed about him besides the steer-clear warning was a deep melancholy. So when he'd seen his question—"How is my sister?"— Lyle's instincts shouted, *Recently deceased!*

If the reaction of the woman with him was any indicator, Lyle had scored a bull's-eye.

"But we came out okay," Lyle said. "We may have hooked a future fish or two, and after Moonie finds her long lost bracelet right where I told her it would be, she'll be singing my praises to anyone who'll listen."

Charlie sat down at the upright piano that had come with the house, and pounded the keys. "Wish I could play."

"Take lessons," Lyle said as he drifted to the front picture window.

He pulled back the curtain just enough to reveal the bullet hole at the center of its crack web. Before filling it with translucent rubber cement, he'd run a pencil through the hole with ease. So small, and yet so deadly. For the thousandth time he wondered—

Movement to his right caught his eye. What? God *damn!* Someone was out there!

"Hey!" he shouted as a burst of rage drove him toward the front door.

"Whassup?" Charlie said.

"Company!" Lyle yanked open the door and leaped onto

the front porch. *"Hey!"* he shouted again as he spotted a dark figure racing away across the lawn.

Lyle sprinted after him. Somewhere in his brain he heard faint cries of *Danger!* and *Bullets!* but he ignored them. His blood was up. Good chance this was the banger wannabe who'd done the drive-by, but he wasn't driving now, and he wasn't shooting, he was running, and Lyle wanted a piece of him.

The guy was carrying something. Looked like a big can of some sort. He glanced over his shoulder. Lyle caught a flash of pale skin, then the guy was tossing the can Lyle's way. It didn't go far—sailed maybe half a dozen feet then hit the ground with a metallic sound and rolled. Unburdened, the guy picked up speed and beat Lyle to the curb where he hopped into a car that was already moving before the door closed.

Lyle pulled up at the sidewalk, gasping for air. Out of shape. Charlie came up beside him, breathing hard, but not as hard as big brother.

"See his face?"

"Not enough to recognize. But he's white."

"Figured that."

Lyle turned and headed back. "Let's go see what he dropped."

He squatted by the object and turned it over. A gasoline can.

"Shit!"

"What he gonna do? Burn a cross?"

"Doubt it." Whites were in the minority on these streets. Another dark face moving in was a nonevent. "This is business. He was looking to burn us out."

He rose and kicked the can, sending it rolling across the grass. The New York psychic game had only so many players. One of them had done this. He just had to find out who.

But how?

4

"All right," Gia said. "We're finally alone. Tell me how Ifasen did what he did."

She'd been dying to know ever since they'd left the psychic's house, but they'd been stuck driving Junie home. Since Karyn and Claude lived on the Lower East Side as well, they'd tagged along. Jack had dropped all three outside Junie's apartment building and now he was ferrying Gia uptown on First Avenue.

Despite the late hour, progress was slow. Gia didn't mind. Time with Jack was never wasted.

"First let's decide where we're going," Jack said. "Your place or mine?"

Gia glanced at her watch. "Mine, I'm afraid. We're getting to the end of the sitter's time frame."

Vicky, her eight-year-old, still would be up. She rarely failed to cadge extra hours of TV out of her sitters.

Jack sighed dramatically. "Another celibate night."

Gia leaned close and nuzzled his ear. "But it's the last one for the next week. Did you forget that Vicky leaves for camp tomorrow morning?"

Gia had been *trying* to forget it. She'd hated the week Vicky had been gone last summer—the seven loneliest days of the year—and was dreading her departure tomorrow.

"I did. Forgot completely. I realize you'll miss her terribly, as will I, but I know just the thing to ease the pain of separation."

Gia smiled and twirled a lock of Jack's hair. "And whatever would that be?"

"That's my secret until tomorrow night."

"I can't wait. And speaking of secrets, what's Ifasen's?"

"No-no," Jack said. "First you tell me the question you asked. If 'two' was the answer, what was the question?"

She shook her head. She now found herself a little embarrassed by her question. If she could get away without revealing it . . .

"You first. Tell me how that man can give answers when he doesn't know the question."

"You're sure you want to know?" Jack said, turning his head to give her a smile.

A smile from Jack . . . so few of those since Kate's death. She missed them.

"Why wouldn't I?"

"Might spoil the fun."

"I can handle the truth. How does he do it?"

"Pretty much the same way Johnny Carson did when he pulled his Karnak the Magnificent shtick."

"But he was reading off cue cards."

"Exactly. And in effect, so is Ifasen."

Gia shook her head, baffled. "I don't get it. We sealed those envelopes. We heard him give the answer, we watched him open the envelope and read the question."

"Things aren't always as they appear."

"I know that only I knew what was written on my card."

"Not after his brother Kehinde did his work."

"Kehinde? But he just—"

"Appears to be a gofer? That's what you're supposed to think. But Kehinde is key. Ifasen put on the show, but he couldn't have done it without his brother's help. The method is called 'one ahead.' If you remember, right after Kehinde collected the sealed envelopes he took the bowl around to the rear of the podium and made a show of covering it with the cloth. That's the key moment. Because while you think he's fiddling with the cloth, he's really slitting open one of the envelopes and removing its card— or billet as the psychics like to call them. He was also tossing in a marked envelope containing a blank card."

"Why?"

"Think about it. When Ifasen—and by the way, if that's his real name, mine is Richard Nixon—when he removes the white cloth on the bowl, he looks down and reads the question on the card Kehinde opened for him. Then he picks up one of the sealed envelopes and raises it above his head. But he doesn't answer the question in the raised envelope; he answers the question on the card in the bowl."

"I get it!" Gia said, feeling a burst of pleasure as all the pieces fell into place. "After he answers the question in the bowl, he tears open the envelope and pretends to read the question he just answered, but actually he's seeing the *next* question."

"Exactly. And for the rest of the show, he stays one envelope ahead—which is how the method got its name."

"And the blank card in the extra marked envelope is so Ifasen won't wind up one short." She shook her head. "It's so simple."

"The best tricks are."

Gia couldn't hide her chagrin at being so easily fooled. "Am I so gullible?"

"Don't feel bad. You've got plenty of company. Millions, I'll bet. That trick's been conning people since the eighteen hundreds. Probably started as a sideshow mentalist gag, then the spiritualists picked it up and they've been milking it ever since."

"So Ifasen's a fake psychic."

"That's redundant."

"How do you know so much about it?"

Jack shrugged, but didn't look her way. "You pick things up here and there."

"You told me earlier you once helped a psychic. One of your customers?"

"No. I worked for one, as a helper, playing the gofer like Kehinde, plus doing behind-the-scenes stuff."

"No!" She'd never imagined. "When?"

"Long time ago, when I first came to the city."

"You never told me."

"Not necessarily something I'm proud of."

Gia laughed. "Jack, I can't believe this. After all the things you've done. . . ."

She saw him glance at her, then train his eyes back on the traffic again. He said nothing, but that look said it all: *You don't know all the things I've done. Not even close.*

How true. And Gia preferred it that way. The Jack she saw on almost a daily basis was even tempered and good-natured, gentle and considerate in bed, and treated Vicky like his own daughter. But she knew he had another side. She'd seen it only once. That had been when—

Had it been almost a year already? Yes. It was last August when that filthy creature abducted Vicky. She still remembered Jack's face when he heard about it, how it had changed, how he'd bared his teeth, how his normally mild brown eyes had become flat and hard. She'd looked then into the cold harsh face of murder, a face she never wanted to see again.

Kusum Bahkti, the man Jack had gone after that night . . . he disappeared from the face of the earth, as if he'd never been.

Jack killed him. Gia knew that and, God help her, she'd been glad. She was still glad. Anyone who wanted to harm her little girl deserved to die.

Kusum wasn't the only man Jack had killed. Gia knew of one other for sure: the mass murderer he'd stopped in mid-slaughter on a subway car back in June. For a while the mystery "Savior" had been all the media talked about, but the furor had pretty much died down now.

Gia was sure there had been others. She didn't know this for a fact, but it was a reasonable conclusion. After all, Jack made his living fixing situations for people who'd run out of aboveground options. When that happened, some of them went underground in search of a solution. A few of those wound up with Jack.

So Jack's clientele—he insisted on calling them customers instead of clients—was hardly the cream of society. And to solve their problems he sometimes had to mix it up with some abominable lowlifes, people ready to kill to prevent Jack from doing his job. Since Jack was still alive, she had to assume that some of those others were not.

None of these were happy thoughts, and Gia preferred to tuck them out of sight where she didn't have to deal with them. She loved Jack, but hated what he did. When she'd stepped off the bus from Iowa to pursue her dream of being an artist, she'd never known a man like Jack could exist, let alone that she'd wind up with him. She was a tax-paying, law-abiding citizen; he was not.

She'd finally forced herself to face the truth: she loved a criminal. He wasn't on the FBI's Ten Most Wanted list, or on anyone else's wanted list, for that matter—because none of the list makers knew he even existed—but he definitely lived outside the law. She couldn't imagine how many laws he'd broken and continued to break every day.

But strangely he was the most moral man—her father aside—that she'd ever met. He was like an elemental force. She knew he would never break faith with her, never leave her in the lurch, never allow her to come to harm. She knew that if it ever came down to it, he'd give his life for her. She felt safe with Jack, as if surrounded by an impenetrable shield.

No one else could give her that feeling. Last year at this time, they'd been split. Jack had told her when they first met that he was a "security consultant." When Gia had learned how he really made his living, she'd walked out. She'd dated other men during the hiatus, but they all seemed so insubstantial after Jack. Like wraiths.

And then, despite all the hurt and invective she'd heaped on him, when she and Vicky had needed him most, he'd been there.

"I mean," she said, rephrasing, "with all the scams you've pulled through the years—"

"Scamming a scammer is different. The fish these psychics hook don't know any better. I think people should get something real for their money, not just smoke and mirrors."

"Maybe smoke and mirrors is what they're looking for.

Everybody's got to believe in something. And after all, it's their money."

Jack glanced at her. "Am I hearing right? Is this the Gia I know?"

"Seriously, Jack, where's the harm? Probably better than throwing it away at Foxwoods or Atlantic City. At least they can get some comfort out of it."

"You can lose the ranch in a casino and, trust me, you can lose just as much to a psychic. The bitch I worked for . . ." He shook his head. "*Bitch* is not a term I use lightly. It took me a while to realize what a foul, vindictive, *small* person she was, and when I did—"

"Did she cheat you?"

"Not me. I was already disillusioned with her and her crummy little game, but the icing came when she scammed some little old lady into signing over a valuable piece of property to her; convinced her it was what her dead husband wanted her to do."

"Oh, no." The image twisted inside Gia.

"That was when I walked."

"But they're not all like that."

"The open ones are."

"Open?"

"There's two kinds of mediums. The closed mediums really believe in the spirit world and what they're doing; they've bought the whole package. As a rule they limit themselves to readings—tarot cards, palms, tea leaves, that sort of thing. They don't put on a show. Open mediums, on the other hand, are all show. They're con men who know it's a scam, who trade background information on their suckers, and are always looking for bigger and better ways to hoodwink them. They knowingly sell lies. They promise a peek into the afterlife, but they use special effects like ectoplasm and voices and spirit writing to fool people into believing they've delivered."

"But Jack, I'll bet a fair number of people derive some comfort from them. Look at you tonight. If you didn't know what you do, and let's say you maybe half-believed, wouldn't you have found comfort in that message from Kate?"

"Sure. But here's my point: it wasn't from Kate. It was from Ifasen. He told a lie. If I'd come to him as a private client, all I would have got for my money was a lie."

"And peace of mind which, in a way, is priceless."

"Even if it's built on a lie?"

Gia nodded. "If a placebo cures your headache, you're rid of your pain, aren't you?"

Jack sighed. "I suppose so." He shook his head. "The really sad thing about so many of these open psychics is that they're truly talented. They possess amazing insight into people, an instinct for reading body language and picking up on every nuance of speech and dress. They *know* people. They could be ace psychologists. They could make a great living in the straight world—you know, doing well while doing good. But they'd rather stay on the fringe, playing their games."

"Hmmm," Gia said. "Sounds like someone I know but I can't quite place the name. I think it begins with a J . . ."

"Very funny. Except I don't play games. I deliver. And if I don't, it's not for lack of trying." He shot her a rueful smile. "But you know, I do believe old Ifasen did something for me tonight. I know he just rattled off a stock message from the 'Other Side,' but to tell the truth, he happened to hit on exactly what Kate would have said."

"You mean about getting on with your life?"

"Yeah."

"How many times have I told you that Kate wouldn't want you to spend the rest of your life moping around? And when was the last time I mentioned that very thing? How many hours ago? Two? Three maybe?"

He grinned sheepishly. "Yeah, I know. But sometimes you have to hear it from a stranger. Anyway, I think it's time for me to get back in the saddle again. I've got a couple of calls in my voice mail right now. I'll check them out tomorrow, and if one of them is right for me, I'll be back to work."

"That's wonderful."

What am I saying? Gia thought.

She hated Jack's work. It was usually dangerous. Every time he hired on to "fix" a situation, he ran the risk of being hurt. But worse, because the police were as much a threat as any hoodlum he took on, he couldn't count on them for help if he got in over his head. When Jack went off to work, he went alone.

How many times had she pleaded with him to find something less dangerous to do? He'd compromised by promising to restrict his fix-it work to situations he could repair at arm's length, where he didn't have to show his face or get personally involved. Gia believed he tried his best to keep that promise, but too often the jobs didn't go as planned.

But his interest in returning to work meant he was pulling out of his funk. That, at least, was good.

"Maybe you should go back for a private session," she said. "Maybe he'll tell you to get into a safer line of work. And maybe you'll listen when *he* tells you. Heaven knows you don't listen when I do."

"I think we should stay away from Ifasen, but not for that reason."

"Meaning?"

"I think he's got trouble."

"You mean because he yelled 'bomb'?"

"That . . . and other things."

"Like what?"

"A patched bullet hole in his front window, for instance."

"You're sure?"

He nodded. "It could have been there when he bought the house, but he's obviously renovated the place, so . . . someone's giving him a hard time."

"But who—?"

"Other psychics. The lady—I use the term loosely—that I once worked for used to go berserk when she lost a sitter to another psychic. She called herself Madame Ouskaya but her real name was Bertha Cantore. I used to think she'd seen *The Wolfman* too many times and ripped off the name of that old actress Maria Ouspenskaya who played the gypsy, but that was giving her too much credit. I can't imagine her ever sitting though the credits of a movie. Finally one night, when she'd had a few too many gins and was sailing a few too many sheets to the wind, she told me that she'd cadged it off an ancient Russian neighbor who'd died when Bertha was ten. But you know how they talk about a leopard never changing its spots? That was Bertha. She may have called herself Ouskaya, but that didn't hide her true nature. Her father was Sicilian and she had a hitman's temper. She'd send me out to slash tires and break windows and—"

"Did you?"

Jack didn't look at her. "Most of the time I just told her I did, but sometimes . . . sometimes, yeah, I did."

"Jack . . ." She couldn't keep the dismay out of her voice.

"Hey, I was hungry, stupid, and a lot younger. I thought what was bad for her was bad for me. I hadn't figured out yet that *she* was bad for me. Hell, if she knew how to make bombs, she'd probably've wanted me to plant them, or wire ignitions to blow the competition away." He shook his head. "What a nutcase."

"Could she be the one Ifasen's afraid of?"

"Nah. Couple of years ago I heard that she'd, as they say in the trade, migrated to the Other Side." A quick glance Gia's way, embarrassment in his eyes. "Let's not talk about her, okay? Makes my teeth hurt just to think about her."

Gia knew getting off the topic of this Madame Ouskaya would probably turn the conversation to her question to Ifasen. She cast about for a diversion and spotted the pamphlet Jack had brought from the psychic's house. She snatched it up.

" 'The Menelaus Manor Restoration Foundation.' What's this?"

"Sounds like a scam. Take donations to renovate the

house you're living and working in. A win-win proposition for Ifasen if I ever heard one."

"Is all this true?" Gia said, gathering flashes of the house's history of mayhem by the light of street lamps they passed.

"I never got a chance to get into it. What's it say?"

She turned on the console lamp and held the brochure under the glow. "It says the place was built in 1952 by Kastor Menelaus. He died of cancer, and was the last owner to 'pass on to the Other Side' due to natural causes."

Jack grinned. "This sounds like it's gonna be *good!*"

"His son Dmitri, who inherited the house, committed suicide in the early nineties. The next owners, a Doctor Singh and his wife, had the place for a few years, did some renovations, and then someone cut their throats while they were sleeping." She looked up at Jack. "This is awful! I hope it's fiction."

"Read on."

Gia was liking this less and less. "The previous owners, the ones before Ifasen, were Herbert Lom and his wife—"

"Not the actor—the guy who played in the Hammer *Phantom of the Opera?*"

"It doesn't say. He and his wife Sara disappeared after— oh, God." Something about a mutilated child. Her stomach turned and she closed the brochure.

"After what?"

"Never mind. Jack, this is sick! It's like the place is cursed. He has to be making this stuff up."

Jack was shaking his head. "Doubt it. Too easy to get caught. My guess is he's taken a few facts and embellished them to within an inch of their collective lives. Read on."

"I'd rather not."

"Just skip to some part that's not gory."

Reluctantly she reopened the brochure and skipped down a paragraph from where she'd left off. "Ifasen quotes himself here: 'I chose Menelaus Manor because the violent deaths have left behind strong psychic vibrations. The souls of those who died here do not rest easy, and their ongoing presence weakens the divide between our world and the Other Side, making Menelaus Manor the perfect site for the church I will establish here.'" Gia looked at Jack. "Church?"

Jack smiled. "The ultimate scam. Tax-free heaven, and completely legal. Like minting money. How do you think the Scientologists can afford to sue anyone who says a discouraging word about their racket?"

"He says here donations will go toward 'putting the Manor at peace with this world and in harmony with the next.' What does that mean?"

"It means renovations will probably go on forever. Or at least until Ifasen crosses over to the Other Side himself."

"Careful, Jack," she told him. "Keep talking like that and I'll start suspecting you're a cynic."

"Me?"

Jack pulled into Sutton Square and stopped before Gia's door. He pulled her close and kissed her.

"Thanks for dragging me out tonight. Earthquakes and psychics in cursed manors . . . you sure know how to show a guy a good time."

She returned the kiss. "Anytime. And tomorrow night I'll show you an even better time."

"Hot-*cha!*"

Laughing, they got out of the car. Jack put an arm around her shoulders; he started to walk her the short distance to her door, but stopped halfway there.

"Hey. Wait a sec. You never told me your question. What was it?"

"It was nothing. Just some silliness I was playing around with. Don't—"

"Who loves silly more than me? Tell, Gia. I won't go home until you do."

"All right." She could see no way out of it. "I asked, 'How many children will I have?'"

"And he told you two." Jack grinned. "I wish I believed in this stuff. That would mean I'd be the father of number two. At least I assume I'd be."

"He said it with such assurance."

"That's because he's a pro. And because he figured it was a safe number. Consider it from his angle: You look younger than your years; Ifasen figures you've got one child, maybe two. So even if you have no kids, if he answers two or three, he's golden. Three would be the safer number, but I've got a feeling this guy likes to play close to the edge. He took a chance and said two."

"But if I never have another child, he'll be proven wrong."

"By the time you know that for sure, you'll have forgotten about Ifasen. Or he can deny that's what he said. He can't lose. So don't waste brain time thinking about it."

But that wasn't so easy for Gia. She remembered feeling a little queasy this morning. But she couldn't be pregnant. She was on the pill, and she was faithful about taking it every morning . . .

Except back in June when she and Vicky had flown out to Iowa to visit the family. She'd forgotten to pack her pills. Unusual for her because she never forgot her pills. But it hadn't mattered because Jack wasn't with her. And as soon as she returned she'd immediately started back on them.

But right after she returned she and Jack had . . .

Gia felt a twinge of nausea. She could think of worse things that could happen, but she didn't want this, not now . . .

It wasn't possible . . .

Maybe not. But first thing tomorrow, as soon as Vicky was on that bus to camp, she was picking up a home pregnancy test kit.

IN THE
IN-BETWEEN

For a long time it was not. But now it is.

For a long time it was not aware. But now it is.

Barely aware. It does not know what or who it is or was. But it knows that at some time past it existed, and then that existence was ended. But now it exists again.

Why?

It does not know where it is. It reaches out as far as it can and vaguely senses other presences, some like itself, and many, many more unlike it, but can identify none of them.

The disorientation makes it afraid, but another emotion pushes through the fear: rage. It does not know the source of the rage but clings to the feeling. Acceptance makes the rage grow. It nestles in the rage and waits for a direction in which to unleash it . . .

IN THE WEE HOURS

Lyle awoke shivering.

What was wrong with that damn air conditioner? It was barely cooling the room when he'd gone to bed, now it was freezing him out. He opened his eyes. His first-floor bedroom faced the street, so he kept the blinds pulled at night; the light seeping between the slats now was the yellow glow of the street lamps, not the pale gray of dawn. He blinked the glowing clock display into focus: *2:32.*

He groaned softly. He couldn't find the energy to get up, so he pulled his sheet closer around his neck and tried to fall back into sleep. But thoughts of fires and attempts on his life wouldn't allow it.

Someone wanted him dead . . .

That had kept him up for a while. After a few more beers to take the edge off, he'd hit the rack; but sleep had played coy while he lay awake here in the dark listening for any unusual noises. Finally he'd drifted off.

The room grew colder still, its chill seeping through the sheet to wrap him in an icy embrace. He kicked his leg out over the edge of the bed. Damn it all, he'd have to get up and—

Wait. The air conditioner wasn't running. No mistake about that. This old place didn't have central air so he'd had to buy window units, and they were anything but quiet.

Lyle froze. Not from the cold but from another sensation: he was not alone in the room. He could feel a presence somewhere in the darkness at the end of the bed.

"Charlie?"

No response from the shadows, no rustle of clothing, no whisper of breathing, but the stiff hairs on his arms and the tight skin along the back of his neck told him that someone else was here. He knew it wasn't his brother—Charlie would never play with his head like this—but he had to ask again.

"Charlie, damn it, is that you?" He heard a tremor in his voice, in sync with his quivering heart.

As the cold became more intense, Lyle slid back against the headboard. He wormed his hand between the mattress and box spring and came up with the carving knife he'd placed there earlier. With its handle in a sweaty death grip, he fumbled his free hand toward the bedside lamp, and clicked it on.

Nothing happened. He clicked once, twice, half a dozen times more. Still no light. What was going on? It had worked just fine a few hours ago. Was the power out?

No. The clock display was still—

Then the clock blacked out, just for a second, as if a dark shape had passed in front of it.

Lyle's heart was pounding madly now. He sensed whoever it was coming closer, moving toward him around the side of the bed.

"I've got a knife, damn it!" His hoarse, dry voice cracked in the middle. "Stay back!"

But whoever it was moved relentlessly forward until he hovered over Lyle, leaning closer . . .

"Fuck you!" Lyle screamed and rammed the knife straight ahead.

Whatever the blade sliced into, it wasn't clothing or flesh; more like powdery snow, and *cold*—Lyle had never felt such cold. He drew back his hand and tried to drop the knife but his numb fingers wouldn't respond.

And then the lamp came on. Lyle jumped, gasped, and thrust out the knife again—to attack, defend, he didn't know, the blade seemed to move of its own will—but he saw no one.

Gone! But that couldn't be. And the cold—gone too,

leaving cloying, humid air in its wake. He looked at the knife and cried out when he saw the thick red fluid oozing down the blade. He hurled it to the floor . . . and saw what else lay there.

"Charlie!"

Oh God oh Christ it was Charlie on his back, legs and arms splayed, his chest a bloody ruin, and his glazed eyes staring at Lyle in shocked surprise.

Lyle felt as if his bones had dissolved. He slid off the bed and crumpled to his knees beside his dead brother.

"Charlie, Charlie," he mumbled through a sob as he bent over him. "Why'd you do it? Why'd you do something so *stupid!* You knew—"

"Lyle?"

Charlie's voice. Lyle snapped upright.

"Lyle, what do you *want?*"

Behind him. He turned and there, across the room, in the doorway on the far side of the bed, stood Charlie. Lyle opened his mouth but couldn't speak. It couldn't be. It . . .

He turned back to the floor and found it empty except for the knife. No Charlie, no blood on the rug or the blade.

Am I losing it?

"What's going on, man?" Charlie said, yawning. "Why you callin' me this hour?"

Lyle looked at him again. "Charlie, I . . ." His voice choked off.

"Hey, you all right?" Charlie said, his expression concerned instead of annoyed as he stepped forward. "You look bust, bro."

Finally he could speak. "I just had the worst nightmare of my life. It seemed so real and yet . . . it couldn't have been."

"What happened? I mean, what it about?"

"Someone here, in the room, coming for me . . ." He decided not to tell Charlie how the dream had ended.

Charlie nodded. "Well, no mystery where that come from, yo."

Right. No stretch to interpret this dream, but Lyle

couldn't shake its remnants . . . the cold . . . and the presence.

"But I was so sure someone was here." He pointed at the knife on the floor. "I even tried to cut him."

Charlie's eyes widened as they fixed on the blade. "Sweet Lord, I can see I better start locking my door at night case you start sleepwalking."

He grinned to show he was only kidding. Lyle tried to return the smile, and hoped it didn't look as sick as he felt. If Charlie only knew . . .

Lyle picked up the knife and turned it over and back, shuddering at the memory of the blood he'd seen coating it. He examined his worn reflection in the surface of the blade, as pristine as when he'd taken it from the cutlery drawer earlier tonight.

Okay, so he hadn't stabbed Charlie. Thank God for that. But against all reason he couldn't shake the feeling that someone else had been here in this room tonight.

Maybe he should go out and find himself a gun.

IN THE
IN-BETWEEN

It still does not know who or what or where it is, but memory fragments flash like meteorites through its consciousness, frightening glimpses of sharp objects and gushing red liquid.

It must leave here, must get out, OUT!

SATURDAY

1

"I'll be fine, Mom," Vicky said as Gia gave her one last great big hug before releasing her to the camp-bound bus. "You're just having separation anxiety."

Gia had to laugh as she pushed her daughter back to arm's length. "I'm having *what*?"

"Separation anxiety. I read about it in the camp brochure."

"But *you're* supposed to have it, not me."

"I am. I'm worried you're going to cry when I leave."

"I won't. I promise."

Another kiss and a long hug—how she loved this little eight-year-old who sometimes acted forty—and then Gia backed up to stand with the other parents.

No tears, she told herself as she watched Vicky step up into the maw of the idling bus. It will only upset her.

She and Vicky had cabbed down to the pick-up spot by the UN Plaza, with Vicky doing most of the talking. A good thing, because Gia wasn't feeling so hot this morning. Her stomach felt queasy. Nerves because Vicky was leaving her, or something else?

Nerves, she'd told herself. Has to be.

Whatever the cause, the bumpy cab ride hadn't helped matters. She'd been very happy to listen to Vicky rattle on about how she couldn't wait to work with clay on the lathe at art camp this year, because she'd been too young last time.

Gia kept her emotions pretty well in hand until Vicky took a seat by a window and waved to her. Gia saw the dark hair she'd braided into a French twist this morning, saw that big smile and those sparkling blue eyes, and almost lost it. But she gamely forced a tremulous smile and blinked to keep the tears at bay.

What kind of a mother am I? She's only eight and I'm sending her off to stay with strangers for a week. I must be crazy!

But Vicky so loved art camp. She'd tried it for a few days last year and this time pleaded to stay for a week. Gia knew she had talent and wanted to give her every opportunity to nurture it.

But a whole week away in the Catskills . . . that was forever.

The door closed, the engine gunned, and the bus moved off. Gia waved till it was out of sight, then allowed herself the luxury of a few tears and sniffles. She looked around and noticed she wasn't the only one with moist eyes on this sultry summer morning.

She decided to walk back. It wasn't far and the exercise would do her good.

Besides . . . she had a stop to make along the way.

Half an hour later Gia stood at the antique white porcelain sink in the upstairs bathroom and stared at her third pregnancy test in fifteen minutes.

Negative. Just like the other two.

But she *felt* pregnant. That was why she'd stopped and picked up three different brands of home test kits, just to be sure.

They all told her the same thing, but that didn't change how she felt.

The phone rang. Thoughts of a bus accident, Vicky hurt, flashed through her mind and she snatched it up.

"Gia!" said a familiar woman's voice. "It's me, Junie!" She sounded excited, all but burbling.

"Oh, hi. Did you find—?"

"That's why I'm calling! When I got in last night I went

straight to the big blue vase by the door and turned it upside down. Want to guess what dropped out?"

"Don't tell me—your bracelet?"

"Yes!" She laughed. "Right where Ifasen said it would be! I couldn't believe it! I hardly go near that vase. I don't know how it got in there but I was so happy I cried. Isn't he just so amazing?"

Gia didn't respond, thinking about what Jack had said last night, how he'd explained Ifasen's billet-reading trick. All fine and good, but how could he explain this? Gia wouldn't buy that it was an educated guess like when Ifasen told her she'd have . . .

Oh, God! He'd said she'd have two children . . . and here she was, feeling pregnant.

"Hey, Gia," Junie said. "You still there?"

"What? Oh, yes. Still here. I'm just wondering how this can be possible. How could he have known something like that?"

"He didn't. The spirits did. They told him, and then he passed it on to me. Pretty simple, don'tcha think?"

"Hmmm," Gia said. She felt a crawly sensation in her stomach that had nothing to do with morning sickness. "Right. Simple."

She ended the call as quickly as possible without being rude, then wandered to a front window and stared out. Her eyes fixed on the townhouses across the square from hers without really seeing them.

Maybe that was all this was . . . the power of suggestion. She'd screwed up her pills, a psychic said she'll have two children, and then her subconscious went to work, making her feel pregnant.

The tests—three of them, no less—said otherwise.

But home kits weren't all that accurate in the very early stages of a pregnancy. The labels did warn about false negatives.

A blood test . . . that was supposed to be extremely accurate, positive within days of conception.

She found her Daytimer and looked up her gynecologist's number. No way Gia expected Dr. Eagleton to see her on a Saturday, but no reason she couldn't order the test for her, maybe at someplace like Beth Israel, and Gia could run up there, have her blood drawn, and wait for the results.

Yes, she thought, punching in the number. Let's get this settled once and for all.

As much as Gia loved Jack, she did not want to be pregnant.

2

Lyle awoke hot and sweaty. He could hear the air conditioner in the window running like a bandit, yet the room felt like a steam bath. Damn thing was only a month old. Couldn't be going south already.

He opened his eyes and lifted his head. Someone had pulled up the blinds and opened all his bedroom windows.

Lyle rolled out of bed. What was going on here? Had Charlie done this?

He had no intention of cooling the rest of Astoria so he slammed his windows shut and stalked down the hall to the rear bedroom. He barged in and found Charlie sprawled on his sheets, both windows wide open, and *his* AC going full blast.

"Damn it, Charlie, what are you up to?"

Charlie lifted his head and blinked at him. "Whassup, bro?"

"The windows, for one thing! What's with opening the windows? It's gonna be ninety today."

"Didn't open no windows."

"Yeah? Well then who did? Ice-T?"

He slammed them closed, then stepped back into the hall. He was headed for his room when he felt a warm breeze flowing up the stairwell. He ran downstairs and found all the waiting room windows and the front door wide open.

"Charlie!" he shouted. "Charlie get down here!"

When Charlie stumbled in he gaped at the open windows and door. "Dawg, what you doing?"

"Me? I locked that door last night myself, chain lock and all. *I* didn't get up and open it. And since there's only two people in this house, that leaves you."

He shut and relocked the door as he was speaking.

"Don't look at me, yo," Charlie said, closing the windows. "I been racked out."

Lyle stared at his brother. Charlie used to be a def joker who could spin out a line like no one else. But ever since he'd been born again, he told the truth—about everything, even if it hurt.

"Then who . . . ? Shit! Someone got in!"

Lyle raced to the channeling room. If they'd wrecked the equipment . . .

But no, the room looked fine. No obvious damage. A quick survey by Charlie and him revealed it to be just as they'd left it. Except for the windows. During the remodeling he'd painted the panes black and draped them with heavy curtains to block the tiniest ray of light. Now the drapes were pulled back and the windows thrown open, allowing sunlight to flood the room. It changed the look entirely, making all his carefully arranged mystical touches look . . . tacky.

Relieved that nothing had been damaged, Lyle closed the windows, pulled the drapes, and headed back toward the kitchen.

"We're running late, Charlie. We've got a noon sitting, so—"

Lyle almost tripped when he came back through the waiting room: the windows and the front door were open again.

Charlie stumbled to a stop behind him. "What in the name of the Lord—"

"The Lord's got nothing to do with this, Charlie. They're still here!"

Lyle darted into the kitchen—where the windows and back door all stood open—and grabbed two knives. He handed one to his brother.

"All right. We know he's not down here. So you plant yourself by the stairs to make sure no one sneaks down, while I sweep upstairs."

Lyle's heart was already running in high gear as he took the steps up two at a time; it further picked up its tempo as he moved down the hall, knife held before him. He'd grown up in a tough neighborhood, but he'd stayed away from the crazies, the crackheads, and the bangers. He'd had fights along the way, mostly shoving matches, one that got his face cut when someone pulled a boxcutter, but that was it. So he wasn't exactly practiced in knife fighting. He didn't even know if he could stab somebody, but he was mad enough now to find out.

He checked the hall closet—empty. Moved on to his bedroom. Shit! The windows were open again. How the hell? But the screens weren't pushed out so no one had gone out that way. He checked his closet, then closed the windows.

Same with Charlie's room: open windows, empty closet. Who was opening these things? After closing them he moved to their sitting room—actually a converted bedroom; what had been the living room and dining room downstairs was now the Channeling Room.

All clear here.

Downstairs he rechecked the kitchen and pantry, going so far as to look behind and under the sofa in the waiting room.

"Okay. Both floors clear. That leaves the cellar."

First he and Charlie locked up, front and back, then stood in the center hall before the cellar door.

"If he's still in the house, that's where he'll be.

Charlie shook his head. "The paper towels still there, yo."

Right, Lyle thought. To keep the stink in the cellar. Forgot about that.

"We'll look anyway."

He pressed his hand over his nose and mouth as he pulled open the door. He started down the stairs and risked a sniff half way down. No stench, just the typical musty basement odor.

"It's okay," he told Charlie, close behind him. "The stink's gone."

Searching the basement was a snap: no closets, no heavy furniture, nobody hiding. The crack was still there, though, big as ever.

Relieved, Lyle let out a long, slow breath. Whoever had been in the house was gone.

But when they got back up to the main floor, Lyle felt a warm, humid breeze. Uneasy, he approached the waiting room.

Someone had opened the windows again.

"How're they doing this, Charlie? Did they rig our house while we were sleeping?"

Charlie was the mechanic half of their partnership. He made the otherworldly illusions happen. He hadn't done well in school—more for lack of interest than lack of ability—but he knew how things worked. He could break down any piece of machinery and put it back together. If anyone could explain this, it would be Charlie.

"Don't see nathan," Charlie said as he inspected one of the windows. "Even if I did, you know what it take to whip up this sorta rig overnight? Gotta have a whole crew with drills and pry bars and hammers."

"Okay, then maybe they did it some day when we were out for a while."

"Still don't see nothin' gonna open no window. I mean, it gotta be pushed or pulled, and ain't nothing here gonna do that."

"Take the windows apart if you have to. There's got to be some sort of servomechanism in there that's doing it."

He wasn't quite sure what a servomechanism was, but it sounded good.

"Maybe we got ourselfs a demon."

"Not funny, Charlie."

"Ain't kidding, bro. Nothin' in or on this window to make it move."

"Got to be. We both know that the only demons and ghosts in this world are the ones manufactured by the likes of you and me. Someone's trying to gaslight us, Charlie. Scare us off. Only we don't scare, right?"

Before Charlie could answer, Lyle heard the click of the front door latch, the door he'd locked just minutes ago. With his mouth going as dry as leather, he watched it swing open with a soft, high-pitched creak.

Lyle leaped through the opening onto the front porch. No one. Empty. He turned in a quick circle, looking for someone, something, anything to explain this. He stopped when he saw the plants.

"Charlie, come here."

Charlie had been inspecting the front door. He straightened and stepped up beside Lyle. "I can't find no—dear Lord!"

All the foundation plantings—the rhodos, azaleas, and andromedas—were dead. Lyle hadn't noticed anything wrong with them last night, but now they weren't simply wilted, they were brown and dried up as if they'd been dead for a month or more . . . as if something had sucked the juice of life out of them.

"Someone must've sprayed them with weed killer."

"When this gonna stop, Lyle?"

He heard the fear in his brother's voice and laid a reassuring hand on his shoulder.

"We'll be all right, Charlie. Things have never come easy for us, and I guess this is no exception. But we always come through, don't we. Somehow the Kenton brothers always manage to come through. We stick together and we'll be okay, Charlie."

Charlie smiled at him and held out his hand for a low five. Lyle gave him a dap.

But when he turned back to the yard he felt a deep rage begin to bubble through his blood.

Whoever you are, he thought, you go ahead and try whatever you can against me, but don't you hurt or frighten my little brother. You do and I'll hunt you down and squash you like the bug you are.

He stared at the dead plants. The sitters for the first session would be arriving in less than an hour and the place looked like hell. No time to spruce it up.

Shit. He'd hardly expected to be welcomed with open arms by the local competition when he moved here from Dearborn, but he never anticipated anything like this. Someone was using every dirty trick under the moon to run them out.

Well, they weren't budging. Do your damnedest, whoever you are. The Kenton boys are here to stay.

3

"You didn't feel a thing?" Jack said.

Abe shook his head. "Not even a wiggle. Some earthquake. A quakeleh, you should call it."

Abe Grossman, dressed as always in a half-sleeve white shirt and crumb-speckled black pants, sat perched on his stool, legs akimbo, one hand resting on his ample belly while the other guided a large piece of crumb cake into his mouth.

Jack leaned on the customer side of the scarred counter at the rear of Abe's store, the Isher Sports Shop. The morning papers lay scattered between them. It had become an irregular tradition of sorts, now and then during the week, but almost always on Saturday and Sunday mornings: Abe bought the papers, Jack brought breakfast.

Jack ran his finger down a column of type on page three of the *Post* and stopped when he found what he wanted.

"Says here the epicenter was located in Astoria. How about that? Gia and I were at ground zero."

"Ground less than zero, maybe," Abe said with a dismissive shrug. "No fires, no injuries, no *tumel*. This is a quake?"

"They clocked it at two-point-five Richter—about the same as the one that hit the East Eighty-fifth Street area in early '01."

"Another nonevent, as I remember." He pointed to the crumb cake. "You're not having?"

"I, uh, brought something different."

Jack pulled a sausage McMuffin from the sack; his mouth watered as he unwrapped it. He waited for the reaction. Took about two nanoseconds.

"What's this? Meat? Juicy meat for you and for your old friend Abe a fat-free coffee cake?"

"You don't need the meat. I do."

"Says who?"

"I do. And I thought you were trying to lower your cholesterol."

"*You're* trying to lower my cholesterol."

True enough, Jack admitted. But only because the guy was riding the heart attack express, and Jack wanted him around for a lot more years—as many as possible.

"And even if I was," Abe said, "I should get a second-class breakfast on a Saturday morning?" He stuck out a hand. "Give. Just a *bisel*. A *biseleh*."

"Once you get into shape, I'll go out and buy you a whole—"

"What?" He patted his belly. "A sphere is not a shape?"

"Okay then, how about I buy you a sausage McMuffin when you can touch your toes?"

"If God wanted us to touch our toes he'd have put them on our knees."

There was no reasoning with this man. "Forget exercise. Forget cholesterol. I get the sausage because I have a special need."

"And that would be?"

"Last night we went to a party. But before the party we went out to eat, so to speak, at Zen Palate."

Abe made a face. "*Nebach*! Where they serve tofu in the shape of a turkey?"

"I don't remember seeing that."

"Stop by on Thanksgiving. Gia's idea, I assume."

"Yeah, well, she's off meat, you know."

"Still?"

"Yeah, and she wanted to try it."

"*Nu*? What kind of tofu did you have?"

"Fried."

"Fried is best. At least you're sure it's dead."

"Even worse: they don't serve alcohol. Had to pop out to the deli on the corner to get some beer."

"Should have grabbed a pastrami on rye while you were there."

Jack remembered the dirty looks he'd gotten from the couple at the next table when he'd popped the top on a forty of Schlitz. Imagine if he'd unwrapped a pastrami, or a cheesesteak. The horror.

"Tell me about it. I've been obsessing on meat ever since. So when I passed McDonald's this morning I couldn't resist."

"In that case I won't insist on a share. Eat. You deserve it after suffering through Zen Palate."

Jack wolfed down the sandwich without looking at Abe. Out of consideration he should have finished it before stepping through the door. Next time . . .

"Look at this," he said around a mouthful as he tried to move the conversation away from food. "A major fault runs right up the East River."

"So? There are a number of major faults on the local school board."

"No, seriously." Jack traced the fault line with his fingertip. "Says here it's called Cameron's Line. Supposedly it's where the continental plate of Africa bumped the North American plate."

"Nobody tells me anything. When did this happen?"

"About 320 million years ago. You were just a kid then. Says the fault line runs from Staten Island up into Connecticut and Massachusetts. But look here." He angled the page so Abe could see. "It makes a detour from the East River right through the heart of Astoria, then loops back to the river." Wonder filled him. "I'll be damned. That psychic's house sits right atop Cameron's Line."

"Psychic's house?" Abe said. "You're not—"

"Not a chance," Jack sad. "It was a lark of sorts."

He recounted Junie Moon's quest for her lost bracelet.

Abe shook his head. "The dumbing of America: government-accredited schools of astrology, school boards deciding to teach creationism in science, classes people paying hundreds of dollars for vials of water because someone labeled it 'Vitamin O,' the return of homeopathic cures—most of which are no more than Vitamin O—magic crystals, feng shui . . . Oy Jack, I'm losing hope."

"Well, you were never exactly Little Mary Sunshine to begin with."

Abe had been predicting—and was well prepared for—a civil and economic holocaust since Jack had known him.

"But one should be able to hope. I'd always thought that as the breadth and depth of human knowledge increased, people would gradually emerge from the darkness into the light. A lot of us prefer the shadows, it seems."

Jack said, "It's the whole New Age thing. Somehow it got mainstreamed. A bonanza for the bunko artists. But what I want to know is, why now? We were climbing out of all that mystical crap, but ever since the seventies it seems we've been sliding back. What turned us around?"

Abe shrugged. "Maybe science is the cause."

"I'd think science would be the solution."

"Maybe I should say it's a reaction to science. We're all looking for transcendence—"

"Transcendence."

"A life beyond this one. A noncorporeal existence. In other words, we want we should go on. You believe in transcendence, Jack?"

"Wish I could. I mean, I'd love to think that some spark in me was going to go on and on, but . . ."

"What? You don't have enough ego to believe you're eternal?"

"To tell the truth, I don't think about it much. Either way, I can't see how it would change my day-to-day life. I know only one way to live. But what's this got to do with science?"

"Tons. The more science pushes back the unknown, the more uncertain transcendence seems. So people overreact. The rational gives them no comfort, so they toss it out and cling to the irrational, no matter how potty."

Jack looked at Abe. "We both know there are things in this world that don't have an easy explanation."

"You mean like the rakoshi."

"Right. They didn't exactly yield to the scientific method."

"But they were real. Don't forget, I was down there at the Battery when that one came out of the harbor. I saw it with my own eyes, saw it slice up your chest. You go through something like that, who needs belief? And you, you still have the scars. You *know*."

Jack's hand instinctively moved to his chest and fingered the rubbery ridges through the fabric of his T-shirt.

"But a rakosh doesn't fit with what we know of the world."

"True. But the key word there is 'know.' I can't explain it, but maybe someone else can. A maven with special knowledge perhaps. I contend that everything is explicable—everything, that is, except human behavior—if you have sufficient knowledge. The knowledge part is critical. You and I both have some of that knowledge—you more than I because you've seen more of it. We know there's a dark force at work in this world—"

"The Otherness," Jack said, thinking about how it had intruded on his life over the past year. "But that's just a name somebody gave it."

"From what you've told me, it's not a thing; more like

a state of being. The word 'Otherness' doesn't tell us much about it. Whatever it is, at this point it's unknowable. We do know that it can't be warded off by crystals and charms and it won't be summoned by incantations and sacrifices. So all the mumbo-jumbo these New Agers and the End of Days folk and the UFO cultists and all their fellow travelers immerse themselves in is useless. The real darkness in this world doesn't reveal itself; it abides by its own laws and follows its own agenda."

Jack found himself thinking about his sister. He blamed her death on the Otherness.

"I never told you what Kate said to me just before she died. Something about 'the dark' coming. She said the virus in her head was letting her see it. She said the 'dark is waiting but it will be coming soon.' Said it was going to roll over everything."

"With all due respect to your sister—and I should maybe never forgive you for not bringing that fine woman to meet me—she was in extremis. She probably didn't know what she was saying."

"I think she did, Abe. I think she was talking about the Otherness getting the upper hand here. It sort of fits with scraps I've been picking up since the spring. The events after that conspiracy convention, hints from the guy running the freak show, and what that crazy Russian lady said to me at Kate's graveside, they all hint at the same thing: a bad time coming, one that'll make all other bad times look like a picnic. The worst time ever for the human race, worse than all the plagues and world wars rolled into one."

Abe stared at him, his expression grim. This fit in with the civil holocaust he'd been predicting forever. "Did she say what we could do about it?"

"No."

Kate had also told Jack that only a handful of people were going to stand in the way of the darkness, and that he was one of them. But he didn't mention that.

Abe shrugged again. "Well, then?"

"That's not why I brought it up. I'm wondering if maybe

people sense this darkness approaching. Not consciously, but on a primitive, subconscious level. Maybe that explains why so many people are turning to fundamentalist and orthodox religions—ones that offer a clear and simple answer for everything. Maybe that's why conspiracy theories are so popular. These people sense something awful coming but can't put their finger on what it is, so they look for a belief system that will give them an answer and a solution."

"What about us poor schmucks who don't have a belief system to lean on?"

Jack sighed. "We'll probably be the ones stuck in the trenches dealing with the real thing when it comes along."

"You think this earthquake had something to do with it?"

"I can't see how, but that doesn't mean anything. Lately I've seen too many innocent-seeming situations take a sharp turn and head into the can at ninety miles an hour."

He thought about last night ... and how that quake seemed to hit just as he and Gia stepped over the threshold of Menelaus Manor. He wanted to think that was coincidence, but it was not comforting to know that the house sat on a crack in the earth's crust, a direct channel down to a lode of ancient rock that was not resting easy.

He wondered if Ifasen was feeling any aftershocks.

4

"Now, if we will all place our hands on the table, palms flat down ... that's it ... when we're all relaxed, we shall begin."

Lyle looked at his three sitters arrayed around the round oak pawfoot table. The two middle-aged women, Anya Spiegelman and Evelyn Jusko, had been here before, and he knew all about them. Vincent McCarthy was new. A blank. All Lyle had known about him until his arrival a few moments ago was his name.

But now he knew a fair bit about him. And he'd learn much more in the next few minutes. Lyle loved the challenge of a cold reading.

"I want everyone to close their eyes for a moment and breathe deeply . . . just a few breaths to calm you. Turmoil interferes with spirit contact. We must be at peace . . ."

Peace . . . Lyle needed to be relaxed to do this right. At least the house was at peace. The windows and doors had stopped opening shortly before the sitters arrived. Now . . . if only he could be at peace.

Not easy after calling Kareena's apartment this morning and having a man answer, hearing him say Kareena was in the shower and ask if he was from the radio station.

He had to put his anger and his hurt on hold. He'd let Kareena screw with his emotions, he wasn't about to let her screw up his livelihood. Put aside the negative feelings and be positive . . . at least for now. Concentrate on Vincent McCarthy.

Lyle opened his eyes and studied him. He guessed his age in the neighborhood of forty, and knew he had a few bucks. His Brooks Brothers golf shirt and expensive lightweight summer slacks said so; so did the shiny new Lexus SC 430 hardtop convertible he'd parked in the driveway. No tattoos on his tanned forearms; no earring; just a simple gold band on the ring finger. And check out those fingers: clean, no calluses, manicured nails.

So we're dealing with a married, well-heeled white dude in his forties. He's come to Astoria to sit in a darkened room on a perfect Saturday for golf. That can only mean he's big-time worried about something.

Money? Not likely.

Business. Also unlikely. If Vincent is in business he either owns it or he's a high-up executive. He knows his way around a spreadsheet and a boardroom; he's not going to consult the spirit world about a territory where he considers himself an alpha male.

Marriage? Possibly. The skills that make him successful in the money end of his life do not necessarily transfer to the emotional side. He could be a klutz in the relationship arena.

Health? He looks well himself, but he could be worried about someone else's health. Wife, parent, or child.

Lyle closed his eyes and decided to go with health. Nudge around the perimeter with a series of try-ons and see what the man would reveal. If that didn't pan out, he could backtrack to the marriage, but he doubted that would be necessary.

"Since the spirits shun the light, we will make the room more inviting to them."

Back in Charlie's command post, a little room behind the south wall that he'd packed with all his electronic gizmos, his brother would pick up Lyle's words through the tiny microphone hidden in the chandelier directly above, and act accordingly. Sure enough, the overhead bulbs dimmed until only the faint glow of a single red bulb lit the table area.

"I feel it," Lyle said. "I feel the gates opening . . ." Charlie's cue to direct a little cold air at the table. ". . . to allow us contact with the Other Side." He let his head fall back, opened his mouth, and let out a long, soft, "Aaaaaaaaaaaaahhhh."

The sound wasn't all show. A good deal of it was real, a pliant ecstasy easing from his soul, like leisurely sex—

That he wasn't having.

Stop! Don't blow this because of a cheating . . .

Easy . . . easy . . . he reminded himself that this was when he felt most alive, this was when he was in control, when he ruled this, his little corner of the world. The rest of his life might be in chaos right now, but in this time, in this place, he called the shots. He was the master . . .

Master of illusion . . . that was his self-declared moniker in his teens. And he hadn't been stroking himself. That was exactly what he'd become after Momma died. Or rather, was killed. She'd been carrying a sack of groceries through

Westwood Park on her way back from the market, crossing the street with the walking green, when two cars out of nowhere, one chasing the other, trading 9mm slugs, ran the red and knocked her forty feet through the air. The hit-and-run bastards were never found.

To the rest of the city she'd been just another noncombatant fatality in Detroit's crack wars. But to Lyle and Charlie she'd been the world. Their father was a shadow in Lyle's memory and didn't exist at all in Charlie's. Dad's brother, Uncle Bill, used to stop by now and again, but nobody had heard from him since he left for the West Coast.

So there they were, the Kenton brothers, Lyle sixteen, Charlie twelve, all alone, existing on the help of the neighbors, but all too soon the Child Welfare folks came sniffing. He and Charlie could pretend no one was home for only so long before they missed one too many rent payments and wound up on the street or, worse, were split up and placed in foster care.

So Lyle decided to become his Uncle Bill. He'd been tall for his age then, and with the help of a fake beard and some make-up, he fooled the social worker. He still remembered Maria Reyes, MSW, a good woman with a sincere desire to help. She believed that Lyle was Bill Kenton; she believed that Saleem Fredericks—a friend from downstairs in the project he borrowed for the home inspection visits—was Lyle.

And Lyle learned something then: the power of belief, and the even greater power of the desire to believe, the *need* to believe. Ms. Reyes believed because she *wanted* to believe. She didn't want to split up the brothers; she'd wanted a blood relative as legal guardian, and so she'd believed everything Lyle tossed her way.

Or had she? Years later Lyle began to wonder if Ms. Reyes had seen through him all along. Wondered if she'd been taken in not by his performance but by his determination to hold together the remnants of his tattered family, and that was why she'd allowed him to become his own legal guardian. Someday he'd have to track her down and ask.

Whatever the truth, sixteen-year-old Lyle Kenton had found his calling: the scam. If he could scam the city, he could scam anyone. His first paying gig was as a slider for a downtown monte game, watching the street for the heat, ready to make the call that would fold the game. He quickly learned the shaker's verbal codes and moved up to the stick position where he'd stand around the table and shill the marks into the game, but all his off hours he spent practicing the moves so he could become a shaker and start his own game.

But after a particularly close call when he'd barely outrun one of the plainclothes D's who'd broken up their game, he cast about for something equally profitable but a little less risky. He found it: a psychic hotline. An audition with a phony Jamaican accent got him hired. After a few hours of practice with a list of cold-reading questions, he joined the crew of men and women—mostly women—in a loft filled with phones and baffle boxes.

Everything he was taught had been geared to keeping the mark on the line as long as possible. First, get the name and address so the mark can be put on a mailing list as a customer for everything from tarot decks to fortune-telling eight balls. Next, convince them you've got a direct line to the Afterlife and the wells of Ancient Knowledge, tell them what they want to hear, make them beg for more-more-more, say anything you want but *keep them on the fucking line*. After all, they were paying five or six dollars a minute to hear psychic wisdom, and Lyle was getting a piece of the action. In no time he was bringing down a grand or better a week without breaking a sweat.

He—as Uncle Bill—and Charlie moved out of the projects and into a garden apartment in the suburbs. It wasn't much, but after Westwood Park, it was like Beverly Hills.

That was when he'd begun calling himself Ifasen—he'd found it in a list of Yoruba names—and developing a West African accent. Soon hotline callers were asking for Ifasen.

No one else would do. This did not endear him to his bosses, who were in the business of selling a service, not creating star players.

So in his off hours he started looking for something new. On a sunny Sunday morning in Ann Arbor he stumbled across the Eternal Life Spiritualist Church. He sat in on a healing session. The needle on his bullshit meter immediately jumped into the red zone but he stayed for the worship and messages meeting. At the end, as he watched one person after another write "love offering" checks to the church, he knew this was his next step.

He joined the Eternal Life Church, signed up for medium development workshops, and hit it off with the pastor, James Gray. Soon he was serving the church as a student medium, which meant he became privy to and a participant in all the chicanery. After a year or so of this, the Reverend Doctor Gray, a big, burly white guy who thought having a young African-sounding black man as an assistant added to the mystical ambiance of his church, took him aside and gave him some invaluable advice.

"Get yourself educated, son," he told Lyle. "I don't mean a degree, I mean *learning*. You're gonna be dealing with all sorts of people from all walks of life with many different levels of education. You want to be a success in this you've got to have a wide range of knowledge on a lot of subjects. You don't need to be an expert in any of them, but you need a nodding acquaintance."

Lyle took that advice, sneaking into classrooms and auditing courses at U of M, Wayne State, and the University of Detroit Mercy, everything from philosophy to economics to western literature. That was where he began scouring the street from his speech. Didn't earn a single credit, but a whole world had opened up to him, a world he took with him when he and Charlie left Ann Arbor for Dearborn to strike out on their own.

There Lyle set himself up in a storefront as a psychic advisor. They worked their asses off to perfect their techniques. The money was good, but Lyle knew he could do better. So they moved on.

And landed here, in an upper corner of Queens, New York.

Do it before you're thirty, they said. Well, Lyle had turned thirty last month, and he'd done it.

And now, sitting in the first real estate he'd ever owned, Lyle Kenton slipped his hands forward along the polished oak surface of the table, allowing the ends of the metal bars strapped to his forearms within the sleeves of his coat to slip under the edge of the tabletop. He raised those forearms and his end of the table followed.

"There it goes!" Evelyn whispered as the table tipped toward her. "The spirits are here!"

Lyle eased back on his arms and worked one of the levers Charlie had built into the legs of the pawfoot table to raise its far side, right under Vincent McCarthy's hands. Lyle peeked and saw McCarthy's eyebrows arch, but he gave no sign that he was overly impressed.

"Whoops!" Anya giggled as her chair tilted in response to an electronic signal from Charlie's command post. "There it goes again! Happens every time!"

Then Evelyn's tilted, then McCarthy's. This time he looked perplexed. Table tipping he might be able to write off, but his chair . . . ?

Time to make him a believer.

"Something is coming through," Lyle said, squeezing his eyes shut. "I believe it concerns our new guest. Yes, you, Vincent. The spirits detect turmoil within you. They sense you are concerned about something."

"Aren't we all?" McCarthy said.

Lyle kept his eyes closed but he could hear the smirk. Vincent wanted to believe—that was why he was here— but he felt a little silly too. He was nobody's fool and wasn't about to let anyone pull a fast one on him.

"But this is a deep concern, Vincent, and not about anything so crass as money." Lyle opened his eyes. He needed to start picking up on the nonverbal cues. "This wrenches at your heart, doesn't it."

McCarthy blinked but said nothing. He didn't have to; his expression spoke volumes.

"I sense a great deal of confusion along with this concern."

Again, he nodded. But Lyle had expected that. If McCarthy wasn't confused, he wouldn't be here.

Lyle half-closed his eyes and pressed his fingers to his temples, assuming his Deep Concentration pose. "I sense someone from the Other Side trying to contact you. Your mother perhaps? Is she still alive?"

"Yes. She's not well, but she's still with us."

That could be it. But now to salvage the remark about the mother.

"Then why do I have this sense of a definite maternal presence? Very loving. A grandmother, perhaps? Have your grandmothers crossed over?"

"Yes. Both."

"Ah, perhaps that's who it is then. One of your grandmothers . . . although I'm not sure which side yet. But it will come, it will come . . . it's getting clearer . . ."

McCarthy, Lyle thought. Irish. Would Grandma McCarthy have been over here or back in Ireland? Didn't matter that much. Lyle knew a surefire Irish grabber. Never failed.

"I'm sensing a great love for an American president in this person . . . can that be right? Yes, this woman had a special place in her heart for President Kennedy."

Vincent McCarthy's eyes damn near bugged out of his head. "Gram Elizabeth! She *loved* Kennedy! She was never the same after he was shot. This is incredible! How can you know that?"

What Irish grandmother didn't love Kennedy? Lyle wondered.

"Oh, you wouldn't believe what he knows," Anya whispered.

"Ifasen's amazing," Evelyn added. "Knows everything, just everything."

"I know nothing," Lyle intoned. "It's the spirits who know. I am but a channel to and from their wisdom."

Lyle could see the hunger in McCarthy's eyes. He wanted more. He was knee deep in belief and wanted to take the plunge, but his Irish Catholic upbringing was holding him back. He needed a push, wanted a push. And Lyle would give it to him, but not quite yet.

Better to let him dangle for a while.

Lyle turned to Evelyn.

"But something else is coming through, a stronger signal, directed, I believe, at Ms. Jusko."

Evelyn's hands flew to her mouth. "Me? Who is it? Is it Oscar? Is he calling me?"

Yes, it was going to be Oscar, but Lyle intended to draw this out a bit. Oscar was her dear departed dog. Two months ago she'd come to Lyle wanting to know if he could contact her pet on the Other Side. Of course he could. Trouble was, she hadn't told him what breed Oscar was or what he looked like, and Lyle hadn't been about to ask.

He didn't have to.

During the first sitting—private at Lyle's insistence, because animals were so hard to track down on the Other Side—Charlie had sneaked in while the lights were out and borrowed Evelyn's handbag. Back in his control room he'd rifled through it and found a stack of pictures of a mahogany Vizsla. He'd relayed a description to Lyle's ear piece. Before returning the bag he appropriated a dog whistle he'd found lodged in the bottom of the bag.

Lyle had amazed Evelyn by describing Oscar to her, right down to his jeweled collar. The woman had been so grateful to learn that he was happy chasing rabbits through the Elysian Fields of the Afterlife that she'd left a $2,500 love donation on her way out the door.

"Yes," Lyle said now. "I believe it's Oscar. And he seems a little upset."

"Oh, no!" Evelyn said. "What's wrong?"

"I'm not sure. It seems you misplaced something of his and he wonders if you still care about him."

"Misplaced? What could I have misplaced?"

In a few moments, Evelyn was going to receive her first apport—an object magically transported by the spirit world from one place to another. Following Lyle's cues, Charlie—dressed all in black—would approach when the time was right and drop Oscar's old dog whistle onto the table.

"I'm not sure. Oscar's not telling me. No, wait, he's got something with him, holding it in his jaws. I'm not sure what it is or what he intends to do with it. He's coming closer . . . closer . . ."

Charlie too should be coming closer—

"Why is it so cold?" Anya said.

"Yes," Evelyn agreed, rubbing her upper arms. "It's freezing in here."

Lyle felt it too. A blanket of dank, frigid air had settled over the table. He rubbed his hands together. His fingers were going numb. But he sensed more than just a drop in temperature. A change in mood seemed to have moved in with the cold air. Anger . . . no, more than anger . . . a bitter, metallic rage . . .

Lyle jumped as Anya screamed. He saw her and her chair fly backward and crash against the wall. McCarthy's chair tipped back, dumping him onto the floor. Lyle felt himself pushed forward, as if by a hurricane-force wind, jamming his abdomen against the table, and then the table itself tipped, precipitating him onto Evelyn. As they tumbled to the floor, Lyle heard glass breaking all around him. He rolled over and saw the drapes flying back as the blackened window panes shattered, imploding one after the other and littering the floor with glittering shards of glass. Stark yellow sunlight poured in. The statues he'd arranged around the room were tumbling over, some of them cracking on the hardwood floor.

Then, as suddenly as it had begun, the tumult ceased. Dazed, Lyle struggled to his feet and helped Evelyn to hers. McCarthy was helping Anya up. No one looked seriously injured by the incident, but the Channeling Room . . . it was a shambles. Lyle did a slow turn and saw that every piece of glass in sight—the windows, even the two mirrors on the walls—had been smashed.

"It's your fault!" Anya screamed, pointing a trembling finger at Evelyn. "You angered your dog's spirit, and now look what happened!"

Evelyn began to cry. "I don't know what I did! I can't imagine what the poor dear could be upset about!"

"Let's stay calm, everybody," Lyle said. "I don't think Oscar was responsible for this."

He goddamn well knew no fucking dead dog had anything to do with it, but who *was* responsible? And how had they done it?

"This is incredible!" Vincent McCarthy was saying. "I never believed . . . thought this was all bullshit . . . but now . . ."

"I think it was the earthquake last night," Lyle said, trying to salvage the situation. "Seismic waves radiate into the spirit world and cause . . ."

What was the word he was looking for? He shoved his shaking hands into his pockets. His heart was pounding and his brain had been scrambled by this cataclysm. Think, damn it! *Disruption*—that was the word.

". . . and cause disruptions in the transmission of information. Maybe it would be better if we rescheduled this for another time. Next Saturday, perhaps?"

"Oh dear, I don't think I can wait that long!" Evelyn said. "If poor Oscar is upset—"

"Maybe a private session tomorrow night, then," Lyle said. "The seismic disturbances will have faded by then. I believe I can squeeze you in. As a matter of fact, I'll make it a point to squeeze you in."

"Oh thank you, Ifasen! Thank you!"

Got to salvage something from this debacle, he thought.

"I want to come back too," Vincent McCarthy said.

"Me too!" Anya cried.

Lyle held up his hands. "I'll see that you're all taken care of. Let's just move into the waiting room so I can find places where I can schedule you."

5

"Tell me that was you, Charlie," Lyle said after he'd ushered the three sitters out the door. "Tell me that was some new gag that went wrong."

Charlie shook his head. "Nuh-uh. I was crawlin' my way to the table with the dog whistle when the spirits started wrecking things."

"The *spirits*? Charlie, boy, have you lost your mind?"

"Forgive me, Lord, I know it's a sin to believe in such things, but how else you gonna explain what happened here?"

"Last night you said it was God sending us a warning, now it's spirits? Make up your mind, Charlie."

"Making up my mind ain't the point, yo. I don't *know* what's happenin', but you gotta be blind or stupid or both not to know *something's* happenin'!"

"Yeah. We're being gaslighted. You saw that guy running last night. You saw the gas can. You going to tell me now that was a spirit?"

"No. Course not. But that different. That—"

"No different. They couldn't burn us out, so they're trying to scare us out. First the doors and windows, now this. Same people behind everything."

"Yeah?" Charlie said. "Then we up against some real geniuses. Anybody who can open and close windows and doors and mess up a room like they did today should be workin' for the CIA."

"Maybe they once did. CIA's into everything." He gestured at the shattered windows. "Sound shatters glass, right? How about ultra-high frequency sound waves that . . ."

Charlie was shaking his head. "No way. We got company, man. Told you that last night. The earthquake opened a gate and shook somethin' loose. This house possessed, yo."

"And I told you I'm not going there! Some very human assholes tried to scare us and scare off our sitters. That's it, pure and simple. But guess what? It backfired. The fish thought they witnessed a bona fide, super-duper supernatural event and they're totally sold. They think Ifasen's the realest of the real deals and they want more-more-more!"

He started when the phone rang. Without thinking—normally he'd check the ID or let the voice mail pick it up—he snatched it off the cradle.

"Yeah, what?" he snapped.

6

"H-hello?" Gia said. She hadn't been prepared for such a gruff reception. "Is . . . is this Ifasen?"

A brief pause, the sound of a throat being cleared, then a more cultured voice. "Pardon me. Yes, this is he. Who is calling, please?"

Gia almost gave in to an urge to hang up. She had no clear idea why she had called in the first place. This was so unlike her . . .

She'd gone to the Beth Israel outpatient lab this morning where they drew her blood for the pregnancy test. Dr. Eagleton's service had said she'd requested stat results, but when 2 P.M. rolled around and Gia hadn't heard, she called in and learned that Dr. Eagleton was off call. The covering doctor did not return her calls. He left a message via the service that he knew nothing about Gia's lab test and saw no reason why it couldn't wait until Monday.

So she'd called the Beth Israel lab but they'd stonewalled

her, saying they couldn't release results to patients, only the ordering doctor.

Burning with frustration, she'd paced the house. Normally she would have talked it over with Jack, but this was not a normal situation. And she didn't know how Jack would take all this. So out of sheer desperation she'd looked up Ifasen's number in his brochure and called him.

Crazy, she knew, but she could be pregnant . . . with her second child . . . and Ifasen had told her she'd have two. Jack's rational explanations from last night faded into background noise; he hadn't heard about Junie's bracelet then, how Ifasen had known exactly where it would be.

What else did Ifasen know? She had to ask. She could imagine Jack's expression when he learned that she'd called a psychic. But what could it hurt?

Besides, feeling crummy and worrying about being pregnant had thrown her off balance. The medical profession was doing its best to make her psycho, so she figured she'd give this a shot. Call it alternative medicine.

She swallowed and said, "I was there at your place last night. At the billet reading with Junie Moon. I was the one who asked how many children I'd have."

"Yes. I remember. What can I do for you?" His words came quickly, sounding clipped, impatient.

"I was wondering if I could ask you about your answer."

"My answer?"

"Yes. You told me I'd have two children, and I was wondering how you knew that. I don't mean to insult you, but I need to know if you were guessing or—"

"I am sorry Miss, Mrs. . . . ."

"DiLauro. Gia DiLauro."

"Well, Gia DiLauro, I am afraid that now is not exactly a good time to discuss this. Perhaps later in the week, when things have settled down a little."

Settled down? Something in his voice . . .

"Has something happened?"

"Happened?" Abruptly his tone sharpened. "Why do you think something has happened?"

She remembered Jack's impression that Ifasen was afraid of something, and his theory of what and why.

"Did someone make more trouble for you last night after we left?"

"What?" The voice jumped a register. "What are you talking about?"

"One of your competitors, isn't it. Jealous because you're stealing their clients, am I right?"

The silence on the other end was answer enough.

Gia said, "You're probably thinking, 'Hey, *I'm* the psychic here,' right? But it's nothing like that."

"If you have anything to do with—"

"Oh, no. Please don't think that. I never heard of you before last night. But maybe I can help."

"This is not your concern. And even if it were, I do not see how you—"

"Oh, no. Not me." She laughed; it sounded high and nervous just like she felt. "I'd be no help at all. But I know someone who's very good at this sort of thing. I'll have him give you a call."

Ifasen hemmed and hawed, obviously not wanting to admit that someone with his connections to the Other Side needed help, but once he learned that the matter would be handled with the utmost discretion with no connection to the police, he relented. But he wanted to make the call, so Gia gave him Jack's voice mail number.

What did I just do? Gia thought after she hung up. *Me, the one who keeps wanting Jack to find another line of work, I just got him a job. Maybe.*

What on earth had possessed her to do such a thing?

Because as much as she hated Jack's work, she wanted to see him back to his old self. That meant getting off his butt and taking on fix-it jobs again. And this one sounded kind of safe. A couple of competing psychics duking it out over clients. Jack could handle them with his eyes closed.

But then, Ifasen had been worried about a bomb last night, hadn't he. She'd forgot about that. How could she be so stupid?

Call him back. Right. Tell him to forget the number she'd given him. Lose it. But why would he listen to her? If he was going to call, he'd call. But maybe he wouldn't call. Maybe he'd figure he could handle this on his own.

She could only hope.

7

Wondering at the damn funky turns life can take, Jack strolled through the dusk up the front walk of Menelaus Manor for the second time in twenty-four hours.

The first shock was hearing a message from Ifasen on his voice mail. The second was learning that Gia had given him the number. She'd explained the how and why of it between bouts of lovemaking late this afternoon and into the evening. He still didn't quite understand it. She seemed fixated on the two-children bit. Why? He sensed she wasn't telling him everything, but that was unlike her. Usually he was the one with the secrets.

Like the bullet hole in Ifasen's picture window, for instance. He'd spotted it on their way out last night. If he'd seen it going in he'd have turned her around and headed home immediately. Didn't want Gia anywhere near a house someone was using for target practice.

Ifasen's voice mail message had played it coy, saying he was being harassed but giving no specifics. When Jack had called him back the man had said he wanted to try to handle the matter without the police because of the risk of adverse publicity. Did Jack think he could help?

The idea of doing a fix-it job for Ifasen appealed to Jack. Psychics operated in the sort of quasi-legal demimonde he was comfortable in. Plus it offered the possibility of running a con on some scammers, and that was always fun.

So now he was back. A lot more lights on tonight—the front porch and most of the windows were aglow. As Jack stepped up on the porch he noticed that the windows running off to his right were covered in heavy black cloth. The "channeling room," if he remembered, and they hadn't been like that last night. Something must have happened since then. Something bad enough to prompt a call for help.

Jack reached for the bell, but the door opened before he rang.

Ifasen—or the guy who called himself Ifasen—stood in the doorway, staring at him. "You?"

"Hello, Lyle."

The dark eyes widened in the dark face. "Lyle? I don't know who—?"

"You're Lyle Kenton, and I'm the one you called."

"But . . . you were here . . ."

"Last night. I know. Can I come in?"

Lyle stepped aside and Jack slipped past him into the waiting room. His brother stood inside, a few feet behind.

Jack extended his hand. "I'm Jack. You must be Charles."

Charles shook his hand, but his eyes were on his older brother. "How . . . ?"

"Simple, really. All you need is a computer. It's a matter of public record that Lyle and Charles Kenton own this house."

Jack made it sound as if he'd done the search. But Abe had been the one. He was better at that sort of thing.

Jack wandered over to the picture window and examined the bullet hole, noticed how it had been plugged with some sort of glue.

"Looks like a .32." He turned to Lyle. "You have the slug?"

Lyle nodded. "Want to see it?"

"Maybe later."

"Did some checking up on you too," Lyle said. "Or tried to."

"Really." Jack would have been surprised if he hadn't. "Find my website?"

Another nod. "Charlie did."

"Repairmanjack.com," Charlie said with a hint of disdain. "Pretty beat site. Nothin' but a box to send you email."

"Serves my purposes."

Lyle fingered the end of one of his dreadlocks, twisting it back and forth. "I asked around some. Found someone who's heard of you, but he didn't think you were real. He heard you mentioned by someone who knows somebody whose sister's uncle hired you once. Something along those lines. Like you're some kind of urban legend."

"That's me. Urban legend." Jack hoped to keep it that way. He jerked a thumb over his shoulder at the pierced window. "Just one shot?"

"One's enough, don't you think? Tried to burn us out last night but I chased them off before they could get the fire started."

"Guns, fire . . . heavy stuff. You've really pissed someone off."

"I guess so."

"Makes the Chick pamphlets look like a joke."

Lyle frowned. "Chick? What're you . . . ?"

Jack picked up one of the Menelaus Manor brochures and shook out another of the Christian fundamentalist tracts he'd found last night.

He saw Charlie grimace and gaze at the ceiling, so he handed it to Lyle, saying, "Got to be careful who you let into your waiting room."

Lyle frowned as he flipped through the pamphlet. "Yeah, I do." Then he flung it against his brother's chest. "How many times have I—?" He cut himself off and glared. "Later, bro."

Jack took a mental step back and watched the pair, trying to get an angle on what was going on. A little tension between the Kenton brothers. Then he noticed the WWJD pin on Charlie's shirt.

A Born Again? Part of a spiritualist con? Crazy. It explained the Chick pamphlets, but nothing else.

He wondered how or if that played into why he was here.

Jack cleared his throat. "Any idea which of your competitors might be behind your troubles?"

Lyle shook his head, setting his dreads in motion. "I don't recall saying it was a competitor."

Is this the way we're going to play it? Jack thought as he glanced around. He needed to break through the My-name-is-Ifasen-and-I-am-a-true-psychic façade if this was going to work.

"Okay, then . . . what else have these mysterious bad guys hit you with?"

"Tried to spook us out this morning by playing games with the doors and windows, then they wrecked the Channeling Room."

"That's why the windows are draped outside?"

Lyle nodded. "They're trying to scare off my clients."

"Clients?" Here was a chance to see if he could get a rise out of Ifasen. "That's probably how they think of themselves. But let's call them what you call them: sitters . . . marks . . . fish." As Lyle stared at him, Jack smiled and shrugged. "I used to be in the game."

"Game?" Lyle said, his expression going stony. "This is no game. This is my life."

"And your livelihood—a good one, most likely. But you probably already knew I was onto you. I figure you saw me notch my billet last night."

No reaction. The Kenton brothers might as well have been statues.

Time to push a little harder.

"By the way, which one of you sneaked into Junie Moon's apartment and hid her bracelet?" Jack pointed to the younger brother. "I'm betting it was Charlie here. Am I right?"

Charlie's gaze flicked to his brother and back, telling Jack he'd scored a bull's-eye.

"You're accusing us of a crime," Lyle said. His lips had thinned, eyes had narrowed to slits.

"One I've committed myself. The medium I worked for used to send me on errands like that." It was SOP: rifle the sitter's purse while the lights are out, cut a duplicate house key, then pay a visit when nobody's home. "When it works, it's a beaut, isn't it."

"I wouldn't know," Lyle said, still not giving an inch.

Jack tried again. He stepped back and checked out the overhead light fixture.

"That where you stashed the bug? Lady I worked for bugged her waiting room and listened to the sitters as they hung out. Pulled all sorts of inside info from their chatter."

The brothers went into statue mode again.

"Look, guys," Jack said, "if we're going to be working together, we've got to be straight with each other."

"We're not working together yet."

"Fair enough. How about I take a look at what they did to your Channeling Room?"

Lyle stared at him, obviously wary.

"Maybe this is a bad idea," Jack said, only partially faking annoyance as he turned toward the door. "You've already wasted some of my time. Don't see much point in letting you waste more."

"Wait," Lyle said. He hesitated again, then sighed. "Okay, but nothing you see here goes past these walls, agreed?"

"Consider me a priest. With Alzheimer's."

This pulled a grin from Charlie, which he hid behind a cough. Even Lyle's lips twisted a little.

"All right." He moved toward the door to the Channeling Room. "Take a look."

Jack stepped through ahead of the brothers and strode to the middle of the room. He could see that some of the statues had been damaged, and spotted a couple of gaps where mirrors had hung, but on the whole the room didn't look so bad.

"You have to understand that we spent the whole afternoon cleaning up," Lyle said. "Every piece of glass in this room was shattered."

"A bazillion pieces," Charlie said.

"How? Shotgun?"

Lyle shook his head. "We haven't figured that out yet."

"Mind if I take a look around?"

"Be our guest. You get any ideas, we'd love to hear them."

Jack wandered to the oak seance table. He bent and examined the thick legs and paw feet.

"That area fine," Charlie said. "You wanna check out the windows and mirrors that—"

"I'll get to them."

He found the levers in one of the legs. He seated himself and worked them with his feet, tilting the table this way and that. He nodded his appreciation.

"Smooth."

He checked the chairs and found the tip of a steel rod in one leg of each.

"How's this work? A little motor in the seat that pushes the rod down, right? Activate it with a remote and it tilts the sitter's chair. Sweet. You guys design this stuff yourself?"

Charlie glanced at Lyle, who sighed again. "Charlie's the mechanical guru."

Well, well, well, Jack thought. They've finally opened up. Let's hope it's smoother going from here on in.

"How do you handle vibrations from the motor?" he asked Charlie.

"Padding," he said. "Loads of it."

"Nice work," he said, giving him a sincere thumbs up. "Very nice."

Charlie's grin told Jack he'd made a friend.

He moved to the windows, pulled the drapes aside. Every pane was broken, blown into the room, not out. But the old-fashioned wooden mullions that had held them in place remained untouched.

He went from one window to the next; whether facing front, side or rear, the story was the same.

How the hell . . . ?

He turned to the brothers and shrugged. "I've got no answer for you."

"You can't help us?" Charlie said.

"Didn't say that. Can't tell you how this was done, but I can help see it doesn't happen again."

"How?" Lyle said.

"Keep an eye on the place. I'm a one-man operation. I'll put in some personal watch time outside when I can, and set up some motion-triggered cameras for when I can't."

"Why not motion-triggered alarms?" Charlie said.

Lyle grunted. "How about motion-triggered machine guns?"

"Scaring them off isn't as important as finding out who they are. Once we know that, I track them down, and then you tell them to lay off."

"Oh, that'll work," Charlie said with a derisive snort. "Suppose they don't wanna lay off?"

"Then I convince them."

"How?" Lyle asked.

"That's my department. That's why you'll be paying me the big bucks. I can make life miserable for them. When I'm through they'll wish they'd never messed with, or even *heard* of the Kenton brothers."

Charlie grinned. "I'm down with that."

Lyle frowned, then turned to Jack. "Let's talk about these 'big bucks' you mentioned."

8

After they'd adjourned to the kitchen, where Lyle and Jack drank beers and Charlie sipped a Pepsi, Lyle tried to angle for a low-ball price, pleading financial straits after the major renovations to the old place, and now the repairs they'd need. Jack wasn't buying, but he did allow for three payments instead of the usual two: he'd take half down, a quarter when he identified the culprits, and the final quarter when he got them to stop.

Lyle still held out, saying he and Charlie would have to discuss it, go over the books, blah-blah-blah before making a final decision. But Jack sensed the decision had been made. He was on.

Damn, it felt good to be working again.

"Let's talk about possible bad guys," Jack said as Lyle handed him a fresh Heineken. "Could anyone local be behind this?"

Lyle shook his head. "There's an old gypsy on Steinway who reads palms and such, and that's about it. Astoria's got a lot of Muslims, you know, and if you believe in Islam, you can't believe in spiritualism."

Jack was thinking things must have been pretty tense around here after the World Trade disaster, but all that had gone down before the Kentons' arrival.

Which brought Jack to a question that had been niggling him since last night. "Then why Astoria?"

"Manhattan's too expensive. All the real estate agents told me rents had dropped after the Trade Center attack, but even so, they were still too high for the amount of space we need."

"For your eventual church."

From Charlie's uneasy expression and the way he started fingering his WWJD pin, Jack figured he'd hit a sore spot.

"When do you figure you'll get yours going?"

"Never, I hope," Charlie said, glaring at Lyle. "Because that's the day I walk out."

"Let's not get into that now, okay?"

Jack tried to break the sudden tension by gesturing at this house around them. "So you went out and found this place in the wilds of Queens."

"Yes. I wanted it because of its history. And because of its history, the price was right."

"All those murders in your brochure are for real?"

Charlie nodded. "Absolutely. This place got some evil history."

"Fine. But the real money's either in Manhattan or in Nassau County, and you're in the great nowhere between. How do you get the money people to make the trip?"

Jack sensed a combination of pride and pleasure in Lyle's grin.

"First off, it's not such a trip. We're handy to the Triboro Bridge, the Queens-Midtown Tunnel, the 59th Street Bridge, the BQE, and the LIE. But the main spur to get them coming here was by having someone tell them to stay away."

"Enlighten me," Jack said.

"My previous mediumship," Lyle said, leaning back, "was in a town—don't ask which because I won't say— that was also home to a fair-size population of Seventh Day Adventists."

"Who've got to believe that spiritualism is a sin."

"Worse. It's the work of Satan, a direct link to the Horned One. They'd post signs around town warning people away, even went so far as to picket my storefront one Sunday. I was pretty scared and worried at first—"

"For about ten minutes," Charlie said.

"Right. Until I realized this could be the best thing that ever happened to me. I called the local papers and TV stations—at the time I wished they'd chosen a Saturday for their protest, but Saturday is their Sabbath—but the media showed up anyway and the result was amazing publicity. People started asking, 'What is it about this Ifasen that has the Adventists so worked up? He must really be onto something.' Let me tell you: business *boomed*."

Jack nodded. "So, in a sense, you were banned in Boston. Works almost every time."

"Not Boston," Charlie said. "Dearborn." He looked at Lyle and found his brother glaring at him. "What?"

Jack leaned back, hiding a smile. So the Kenton brothers were from Michigan. In the psychic trade you tried to hide as much of your past as possible, especially if you were operating under a phony name. But also because lots of mediums had an arrest history—usually for other bunko scams—and a fair number had had careers as magicians and mentalists before discovering that, unless you were a superstar like Copperfield or Henning, conjuring tricks paid off far better in the seance room than in cocktail lounges and at kids' birthday parties.

He wondered what the Kentons' histories might be.

"Okay that's all fine for Dearborn," Jack said, "but I don't remember any stories about Astoria Adventists acting up."

"Because there aren't any," Lyle said, turning away from his brother, "or at least no group big enough to suit my needs. But I'd planned for that. Before leaving Dearborn"— another scathing look at Charlie—"I laid some groundwork by taking out an ad in the *News-Herald* to announce my departure. I said I was leaving because the local Adventists had turned so many people against me that I could no longer continue my mediumship in such an atmosphere. I was beaten. They'd won. They wouldn't have Ifasen to kick around anymore. Or words to that effect."

"But I thought you said business was booming."

"It was. Especially 1999. Man, the six months leading up to the millennium had been incredibly good. Best ever." Lyle's voice softened to a reminiscing tone. "I wish '99 could've gone on forever."

Jack knew a couple of grifters who'd told him the same thing. From palm reading to tarot to astrology and beyond, the millennium had proved an across-the-board bonanza for the hocus-pocus trade.

"But it was time to move on," Lyle said.

He rose and leaned against the counter. The more he talked, the more his detached Ifasen pose melted away. The guy probably had no one but Charlie to open up to, and he plainly longed to talk about this stuff. It came spilling out in a rush. Jack doubted he could have stopped him if he wanted to.

"So Charlie and I packed up our show and took it on the road. We bought this place ten months ago and spent most of our savings renovating it. Once we had things set up the way we wanted, I called up the Adventists who'd harassed me before. I told them—using another name, of course— that I was a fellow Adventist who wanted to let them know that the devil Ifasen they'd driven out of Dearborn had resettled in my neighborhood and was starting up his evil schemes to threaten the unwary souls of Astoria. They'd closed him down before. Couldn't they do it again?"

"Don't tell me they bussed in a crew of protesters?"

"That would have been okay, but I had a better idea. I'd already started advertising in the *Village Voice* and the *Observer*. I sent the Adventists copies of my ads and suggested they take out space on the same pages to tell folks God's truth."

"You didn't need the Adventists for that," Jack said. "You could have run your own counter ads."

"I could have. But I wanted them to be legit if the papers ever checked them out. Plus, those big display ads aren't cheap. I figured if I could get someone else to foot most of the bill, why not?"

"And did they go for it?"

"All the way. I sent them a hundred-dollar money order to get the ball rolling and they took off from there. Big weekly ads for a month."

Jack laughed. "I love it!"

Lyle grinned, the first real break in his studied cool, and it made him look like a kid. Jack found he liked the guy behind the mask.

"Serves them right," Lyle said, his smile fading. "Tried to ruin my game because it interfered with theirs."

"Difference is," Charlie said, frowning, "that they believe in what they're doing. You don't."

"Still a game,' Lyle said, his mouth twisting as if tasting something bitter. "Just because we know it's a game and they don't doesn't change things. A game's a game. End of the day we both deliver the same bill of goods."

Tight, tense silence descended as neither of the brothers would look at each other.

"Speaking of delivering," Jack said, "I gather the ads served their purpose?"

"Oh, yeah," Lyle said. "The phone rang off the hook. The ones who made that first trip out here have mostly all come back. And they've been bringing others with them when they do."

"Mostly from the city?"

A nod. "Like ninety percent."

"I'm sure I don't have to tell you that most of these people were going to other mediums before you came along. And if they're your regulars now, that means they've left somebody else. I'll be very disappointed if you don't have a list somewhere of who they were seeing before you."

"I do."

"Good. I'll be equally disappointed if you haven't run financials on every sitter who's walked through that door as well."

Lyle's expression calcified; he said nothing.

Come *on*, Jack thought. This guy was an overwound clock. Jack didn't know a player in the spiritualist trade who didn't use names, licenses, credit cards, bank accounts, and Social Security numbers if they could get them, to peek at their sitters' financials.

Finally Lyle's lips twisted into a tight approximation of

a reluctant smile. "I can predict no disappointment on that score."

"Excellent. Then here's what you do. Divide your sitters up by their previous gurus; then list them in order of their net worth and/or generosity. Identify the psychics who've lost the most high rollers to you and we'll make that our short list of suspects."

Lyle and Charlie glanced at each other as if to say, Why didn't we think of that?

Jack tossed off the rest of his beer and rose. "Getting late, guys. One of you call me tomorrow about whether or not we're in business."

"Will do," Lyle said. "If we decide yes, when will you want the down payment?"

"Since tomorrow's Sunday, I can pick it up Monday. Cash only, remember. That's when I'll start."

On the way out, even though it was dark and he wasn't officially hired, Jack had Lyle give him a tour of the yard. As he stepped off the front porch he noticed that all the foundation plantings were dead.

"Hey, if you're into this look, I know a bar in the city you'll just love."

"Forgot to mention that. Happened overnight. They must have been poisoned."

"Nasty," Jack said, fingering a stiff, brown rhodo leaf. Felt as if it had died last month and spent the time since in the Mojave Desert. "And petty. I don't like petty people."

Something about the dead plants bothered him. He'd done some landscaping work as a teen. Remembered using defoliants now and again. Didn't remember anything that killed so quickly and thoroughly. Almost as if they'd had all their juices sucked out overnight.

The dead foundation plants aside, the rest of the shrubbery scattered about Menelaus Manor's double lot offered a number of good surveillance points at ground level, but he'd need a high perch. The pitch of the house roof was too steep; the garage roof looked better but was only one story high.

"That garage looks like an afterthought."

Worse than an afterthought. More like a one-car tumor off the right flank of the original structure, destroying its symmetry.

"According to the real estate agent," Lyle said, "that's exactly what it was. Built in the eighties by the original owner's son after he inherited the place—"

"And before he offed himself."

"Obviously. If I ever find a reason to buy a car, I'm sure it'll come in very handy after I've been shopping. Opens right into the kitchen area. Great for when it's raining."

"Or when you don't want anyone to see what you're unloading."

Lyle frowned at him. "Yeah, I guess so. Why'd you say that?"

"I don't know," Jack said. "It just came to me." And that was true. The idea had leaped into his head. He shook it off. "Let's check out that big maple," he said, pointing toward the street.

"Maple," Lyle said as they walked through the dark toward the street. "I'll have to remember that."

"Didn't have many trees where you grew up, I take it."

He sensed Lyle stiffen. "What makes you say that?"

"Your accent's good, but Charlie . . ."

"Yeah, Charlie," Lyle said through a sigh. "I couldn't do this without him, but I can't let him speak when a sitter's around. He just doesn't get it."

They arrived at the maple that hugged the curb and spread over the sidewalk and the street. It looked good and sturdy but the branches had been trimmed far up the trunk. The lowest hung about ten feet off the ground.

"Give me a boost," Jack said.

Lyle gave him a dubious look.

"Come on," Jack said, laughing. "I know how it's a matter of pride with you scammers about getting your hands dirty, but a little alley oop is all I need and I'll take it from there."

Shaking his head, Lyle laced his fingers together and boosted Jack up to where he could grab the limb. As Jack clambered onto the branch, he noticed Lyle stepping back between two parked cars and into the street.

"Where you going?"

"No offense, but I figured I'd get out of the way in case you and/or that branch come down."

"Aw, and I was counting on you catching me if—"

Jack heard an engine rev. He looked down the street and saw a car with its lights out racing Lyle's way.

"Incoming!"

Lyle looked around but didn't react immediately. Maybe he didn't see the car right away because its lights were out. When he finally did move, jumping back toward the curb, the car swerved toward him, missing him by a thin breeze as it creased the fender of the parked car to his right.

"That them?" Jack shouted as he swung down from the tree.

The car didn't stop, didn't even slow. Jack glanced at Lyle, who looked shaken but otherwise unscathed.

"I-I don't know."

Jack took off. I'm not even hired yet, he thought as he sprinted along the sidewalk.

He'd started running by reflex but didn't stop. Starting a job without a down payment was against Jack's rules, but after this, Lyle was a pretty sure bet to come across. And a look at the mystery car's license plate tonight might save Jack days of surveillance next week.

He kept to the sidewalk, hoping the driver wouldn't spot him. As the car passed under a street light he saw that it was either yellow or white, but he couldn't identify the make or model. Couldn't be something distinctive like a PT Cruiser, could it; no, had to be one of those generic-looking mid-size sedans that could be a Camry, a Corolla, a Sentra, or any of half a dozen other models. With its lights still off, the Camrollentra's license plate remained hidden in the shadow of the bumper.

Ditmars Boulevard lay maybe a hundred yards ahead. The traffic light showed red. Would the car stop?

Fat chance. Jack saw its brake lights glow as it slowed, but that was it. The Camrollentra cruised the red and turned right.

Jack kept moving, putting a little more juice into his stride. Probably a waste of energy, but who knew? Might get lucky and find that the mystery car had plowed into a cab and locked bumpers. Stranger things had happened.

He rounded the corner and skidded to a stop . . . just like the traffic. People out on the town for Saturday night had done what the red light hadn't.

Jack started moving again, at a more relaxed pace this time, sorting through the cars in the jam as he strolled past the brightly lit store fronts. Within the first twenty-five yards he found two Camrollentras, one white, one pale yellow. Swell.

But the yellow one had a dented front fender and its headlights were out. The woman in the passenger seat kept looking over her shoulder. Her gaze swept right past him. Looking for someone with lots darker skin, no doubt.

Gotcha.

She faced front again, banging on the dashboard and pointing ahead, obviously telling her driver to get moving. But cars were lined up ahead and behind, and the opposite lane was no better. They'd move when everyone else moved.

Coming almost parallel, Jack ducked out of her line of sight and squatted, pretending to tie his shoe. After checking to make sure no one was paying attention, he crab-walked between two parked cars. This placed him two feet from the target car's right rear tire. He was close enough now to see that he was dealing with an aging Corolla. He wormed the black-handled Spyderco Endura Lightweight out of his back pocket, did a one-hand flick-out of the four-inch serrated blade, and jabbed it through the sidewall of

the tire. Then he slunk back to the sidewalk, made a show
of tying his other shoe, and rose again to his feet.

Without a glance back, he checked out the store signs
and found a Duane Reade. He'd go with that. Hoped it had
what he wanted.

It did. Gotta love these Duane Reades. Called themselves
pharmacies but carried so much more. Just about everything
anyone could need.

Like duct tape.

And pantyhose.

Jack walked along, noting that traffic had thinned. He
paused by a trash receptacle to open the pantyhose package;
he cut off one of the legs and threw the rest away. Then
he moved on, searching for the yellow Corolla. He went
three blocks without seeing it. Had they decided to keep
driving, flat tire or no? He hadn't figured on that because
it was sure to draw attention, maybe even a police stop,
and they'd want to avoid something like that.

As he was crossing a side street, heading into block four,
he heard a clank of metal off to his right. Stopped, listened,
heard a man's voice cursing in English. Peered up the block
and saw a man and a woman by the curb just past a street-
light. The man knelt by the wheel of a pale Corolla that
had pulled in next to a fire hydrant, the woman stood, as
if on guard.

"Come on, come on!" said the woman. "Can't you do
this any faster?"

"Fucking lugs are rusted. I—" Another clank. "Shit!"

Jack stepped off Ditmars and crept up the other side of
the street, keeping low behind the parked cars. When he
came even with the Corolla he found a pool of shadow and
watched from there.

The man was average height, maybe forty, with receding
hair and a medium-size gut; she was pint-size, five-one,
tops, and built like a fire plug. The mouth on her would
make Eminem blush.

Obviously the guy hadn't changed too many tires, and
his companion's constant bitching didn't help, but finally

he got the spare onto the wheel. When the car was off the jack, the woman got back into the front seat.

As the man gathered up his tools, Jack pulled the pantyhose leg over his head; slipped his left wrist through the roll of duct tape and ripped off a six-inch length; stuck this to his left forearm and waited for the man to lift the flat tire.

When he did, Jack dashed across the street, straight at him. He didn't see Jack until he was in his face. Guy's mouth dropped open into a terrified *O* as he looked up but both his hands were burdened with tire, making him a sitting duck for the fist that rammed into his nose. Dropped the tire as his head snapped back. Jack grabbed his shirt, hauled him forward, and flung him into the trunk. Guy was dazed, didn't struggle as Jack pushed his legs over the rim and slammed the lid closed.

Without slowing Jack slipped around to the passenger side, pulling his knife and flicking out the blade as he moved. The raised trunk lid had hidden him from the passenger. Now he yanked open the door and slapped a hand over her unsuspecting yap.

He wiggled the knife blade before her terrified eyes and spoke, raising his pitch in a bad German accent, one that wouldn't have made the cut even on *Hogan's Heroes*.

"Vun peep unt you ah dead!"

She glanced at his stocking-distorted face, made a soft noise that sounded like, *"Gak,"* then shut her mouth.

"Dat's da spirit."

Jack replaced the hand over her mouth with the length of duct tape. Then he pulled her out of the front and pushed her face down on the back seat where he taped her hands behind her back and wrapped up her ankles.

Final touch: flipped her face up and taped over her eyes—a vertical strip on each, then twice around the head. Rolled her onto the floor, then got her buddy out of the trunk and went through the same procedure on him.

All told, a two-minute process. Maybe less.

Jumped into the driver's seat, hit the ignition, and they

were rolling. Pulled off the stocking and rubbed his itching face. Then he addressed his whimpering, struggling audience of two.

"You ah probably vondering vhy I haff brought us togezzer like zis. It iss a mattah of money. I need, you gots. So vee ah all going zumplace nize unt private vhere vee can make zee exchange. Nuzzing perzonal. Opportunity has knocked unt I haf anzzered. Do not giff me troubles unt you vill valk avay in vun piece. Zat iss clear, yah?"

He didn't care if they bought the accent; he simply didn't want them to recognize his normal speaking voice when they heard it. Because if his plans worked out, they'd be hearing it fairly soon.

9

After driving aimlessly for twenty minutes, making a succession of unnecessary lefts and rights, bogus three-point turns, Jack was fairly lost. He figured if he was confused, his passengers had to be completely disoriented.

He found Ditmars Boulevard again, reoriented himself, then meandered back to the Kentons' house. When he pulled into the driveway, Lyle and Charlie hurried out onto the front lawn. Jack jumped out and motioned them to be quiet. He led them to the car and pointed through the rear window. The brothers started when they saw the two bound forms on the back seat and turned to him with wide eyes. Jack motioned them to open the garage door.

When the car had been moved inside and the door closed behind it, Jack motioned them into the house.

"They're the ones?" Lyle said, his voice barely above a whisper even though the car was far out of earshot.

Jack nodded.

"The ones who tried to run me down?"

"The same."

"But how did they wind up . . . ?"

"Part of the service."

"Who are they?"

"We'll find that out in a couple of minutes. By the way, I hope I'm hired. Otherwise I'll have to throw them back."

"Don't worry," Lyle said. "You're hired. You're so very hired. Do we sign a contract or something?"

"Yeah," Jack said, and stuck out his hand. "Here it is." Lyle shook it, then Charlie.

"That's it?" Lyle said.

"That's it."

"Ay, yo, you kidnapped them!" Charlie said.

"Technically, yes. Does that bother you?"

"No, but the cops, the FBI—"

"Won't ever hear about this. Those people never saw me, and they don't know their car is parked in your garage." Jack rubbed his hands together. Time to learn a little about the Kenton brothers. "So, the question now is, what do you want to do to them? We can break their arms, break their legs, break their heads . . ."

He watched their expressions, was glad for the revulsion reflected there.

"Oh, man," Lyle said. "This afternoon I wanted blood. I wanted to kill them. Now . . ."

"Yeah," Jack said. "They are kind of pathetic looking. Personally I prefer messing with heads to breaking them."

"Mess with their heads," Charlie said, looking relieved. "Yeah, I'm down with that. Sound like the way to go."

Lyle nodded. "Fine with me. How?"

"First off, some rules. Only I speak in their presence, and I'll sound like Colonel Klink. Not a word out of you two because they might know your voices. We don't want them connecting you with this, right?"

They both nodded.

"Good. That settled, the first thing we'll do is take them out of the car, lay them on the floor, strip search them—"

"Yo. Rewind there. Strip 'em?"

"Right. I think a little humiliation will be good for the souls of a couple of attempted murderers, don't you? Plus, it'll keep them cowed; nothing makes you feel more vulnerable and helpless than being without your clothes. On top of all that, it'll scare the hell out of them, wondering if we've got some twisted sexual plans for them."

"But we don't, right?" Charlie said with a pleading look.

"You kidding?" Jack said. "You got a look at them. Having them lying around naked will be lots tougher on us than them."

"And after that?" Lyle said.

"We comb through their clothes, their wallets and pocketbooks, the glove compartment, learn everything we can about them, then decide how you guys get even."

Jack noticed their reluctant expressions. Like true scam artists, they didn't like getting physical.

"If it makes you too uncomfortable, I can do it alone. But things'll move much faster if I have some help."

Lyle glanced at Charlie, then sighed. "Lead the way."

10

Twenty minutes later they were back in the kitchen.

Jack dumped the man's wallet, the woman's pocketbook, and the contents of the glove compartment onto the table, then began sorting through them.

Lyle had this dazed expression. He'd looked that way since they found a .32 caliber pistol in the trunk's now-empty spare tire well.

"Those two people," he muttered. "They want me dead."

"What gives you that idea?" Jack said. "Just because they

shot at you, tried to burn down your house, and run you down with their car?"

"This isn't funny."

Jack looked up from the car registration and driver licenses he'd collected. He had to lighten this guy up.

"Damn right it's not funny. Especially cutting their clothes off." He cringed at the memory of the woman's pale, squat, flabby body. "I had to keep mentally dressing her."

Finally a smile from Lyle. This was one major stiff.

"Okay," Jack said. "From what I can gather here, we're dealing with a married couple, Carl and Elizabeth Foster."

Lyle pulled a stack of business cards from the purse and shuffled through them. "I'll be damned!"

"Not if I can help it," Charlie said.

If Lyle heard, he didn't acknowledge the remark. "She's Madame Pomerol! I've heard of her. She was on Letterman."

Jack rarely watched talk shows. "She's big time?"

"Pretty much. Upper East Side. I hear she's been hot the past few years. Her name's popped up quite a bit from my sitters—a *lot* of them used to be Pomerol regulars."

"There you go," Jack said. "You know who, and now you know why."

"They Upper East Side?" Charlie said. "How come they got such a hooptie ride?"

Jack was about to explain that it was a city thing, but Lyle cut him off.

"The bitch!" he muttered, still staring at Madame Pomerol's business card. "She tried to kill me!"

"The husband was driving the car that just missed you, don't forget," Jack told him. "Looks like a joint effort to me."

"Yeah, but I bet she's been running the show."

Charlie said, "Yeah, well, don't really matter who was the shot calla. The right-now real is that our garage is holdin' two butt-naked honkies tied up like calves ready for slaughter. What we gonna do with them?"

"Not sure yet," Jack said. He was winging it here; usually he went into a job with at least half a plan, but events tonight had moved too swiftly. "The more immediate question is, What are we gonna do *to* them?"

Charlie was watching Jack. "What you mean, 'to'? I know they tried to hurt us—"

"They tried to *kill* us, Charlie," Lyle said. "Not hurt us, *kill* us! Don't you forget that!"

"A'ight. So they tried to off us. But that don't give us no right to off them." He was fingering his WWJD button again. "We gotta turn the other cheek and hand them over to the police."

Jack didn't like the way this was going. "Do that and you leave yourself open for charges like assault and battery, kidnapping, unlawful confinement, and who knows what else," he said. "You want that?"

"No way," Charlie said.

"And who said anything about killing them?"

"Well, the way Lyle talkin'—"

Lyle said, "I didn't mean we should kill them, Charlie. For Christ sake, you know me better than that! It's just that I don't know what we've accomplished here besides figuring out who they are. We let them go and they're right back on our asses tomorrow, trying to off us or run us out of town. I don't want to keep looking over my shoulder, man. I want this done with!"

"That's where I come in," Jack said. He felt the adrenaline start to flow, singing along his nerves as the beginnings of a plan took shape. He took one of the Madame Pomerol business cards from Lyle and waved it in the air. "We've got their address. We've got a set of their keys. Let's see if we can rig some surprises for them."

Charlie nodded. "I'm down with that. What you got in mind?"

"Still working on it, but I think I can find a few ways to keep Madame Pomerol too distracted to worry about bothering you. At least in the short run. We can worry about the long run later. But if I'm gonna make a move it's got to be tonight, and that means I'll need some help." He turned to Charlie. "Where's your key cutter?"

Charlie blinked and looked at Lyle. "Key cutter?"

"I know you've got one. Take me to it. We're wasting time."

"Do it," Lyle said.

Charlie shrugged. "Okay. We doin' copies of their crib keys?"

"You got it. And while we're at it, what do you keep in the way of spare parts for your magic tricks?"

Charlie grinned. "Got boxes and boxes."

"Swell. Show me your stock and let's see if you've got anything we can put to use."

Jack didn't know how the night would turn out, but he knew he'd be a lot later getting to Gia's than he'd planned. Had to give her a call soon. But not now. His blood was tingling and he felt more alive than he had in months.

11

Lyle ground his teeth as he wandered into the garage for another check on Madame Pomerol and her husband. Jack and Charlie had raced off to the city almost two hours ago, leaving him in charge of the . . . what? Prisoners? Hostages? Human garbage?

Whatever they were they were back in their car—the husband on the rear floor, Madame Pomerol on the back seat, both face down. Lyle had taken the tattered remnants of the clothes they'd cut off them earlier and tossed them over their naked bodies. But that hadn't been enough, so he'd found an old blanket to cover them. He didn't want to have to see their puckered, hairy asses every time he checked on them.

His fury frightened him.

Mainly because the windows and doors had started opening themselves again. Taking a shot at him, trying to run him down, he could handle that. Where he came from, you understood that. But sneaking into his house, changing it, wiring it to do strange things . . .

His house, goddammit! The first home he'd ever truly been able to call his own, and these pathetic lowlifes had invaded it, defiled it, made parts of it theirs instead of his.

It made him crazy, made him look long and hard at the carving knives in the kitchen, made him open their car trunk and stare at the nickel-plated pistol they'd fired at him.

But as much as he could think of murder, he knew he couldn't do it. No killer in his heart.

Yet God, how he'd love to scare the shit out of these two. Grab them by their scrawny necks and drag them through the rooms, holding their own piece to their heads, threatening to start busting caps on them if they didn't tell him what they'd done to his house, then stand over them and make them undo it, jab and poke them with the barrel when they didn't move as fast as he wanted.

But Jack had said the Fosters mustn't know where they were, mustn't connect their abduction to Lyle and Charlie Kenton. Lyle had never been one to take orders blindly, but this Jack guy . . . Lyle had to make an exception for him. You pay a man that kind of bread, you'd better listen to him. Besides, the man got things *done*.

The phone rang. Lyle checked the caller ID and picked up when he recognized Charlie's cell number.

"We through, bro," Charlie said. "We done our business and we headin' home."

"What'd you do?"

"Tell you when I get there, but lemme tell you, dawg, it *fine*! This Jack is righteous! Now, we took care of our end, you take care of yours. See ya."

Lyle hung up and took a deep breath. *My end* . . .

Jack had laid it out before leaving with Charlie. Sounded easy then, but seemed risky now.

He took a deep breath and headed for the garage.

12

Lyle stopped the Fosters' car in the shadow of a construction Dumpster. With all the rebuilding still going on in the financial district, these things were on every other block; this one seemed particularly large and isolated. He killed the lights and checked the street: nothing moving. This part of Manhattan was just about the quietest spot in town on a Saturday night.

He checked his watch. He'd made good time. The BQE had been light so he'd followed it all the way down to the Brooklyn Bridge and across into lower Manhattan. He'd driven like a timid Sunday school teacher, sticking to the speed limit all the way, signaling every lane change, spending as much time looking in his rearview mirror as through the windshield. The last thing he needed was to get stopped for some minor violation and have to explain what was under the blanket in the rear.

Lyle picked up the carving knife from the seat beside him and thumbed the edge. He noticed the blade quivering in the faint light.

I've got the shakes, he thought. He cast an angry glance over his shoulder. *They* should have the shakes.

But he'd never done anything like this before.

Let's get this over with.

He pulled the blanket off Madame Pomerol's flabby body, turned her over, gripped her under the arms, and started dragging her from the car. She struggled and he could hear whimpers of fear through her gag, her breath whistling in and out her nose. She'd just spent hours stripped naked, bound, gagged, and blindfolded. Both of them had to be terrified beyond anything they ever could have imagined.

Too bad, Lyle thought as he laid her out on the pavement. Just too goddamn bad.

Next he dragged her husband from the car and rolled him over, face down like his wife. As soon as the man's belly flattened out on the asphalt, a puddle began to form around his mid-section.

What's the matter? Lyle wanted to shout. Think you're gonna die? Think what you planned for me is coming down on you?

He lowered the knife toward the woman and cut three quarters of the way through the tape binding her wrists, then did the same with the man. They'd be able to rip the rest of the way through without too much difficulty.

He hopped back into their car and roared away, looking around, looking over his shoulder, wondering if anyone had spotted him. Lyle was beginning to believe they might get away with this.

He drove to Chambers Street and parked by a fire hydrant. He left the windows down, the doors unlocked, and the trunk open; he left their cut-up clothes on the front seat but folded the blanket and took that along. He dropped the keys through a sewer grate on his way to the subway station on the corner. He'd chosen this spot because the W train stopped here. It also stopped in Astoria, six blocks from his house.

While he was waiting for the train, as per Jack's instructions, he found a pay phone and dialed 911. He noticed his fingers trembling as they dropped the coins into the slot.

Damn! He was still juiced.

He told the operator he'd heard something that sounded like gunshots up on Chambers Street . . . said he thought it had something to do with a yellow Corolla parked by a hydrant.

The first thing the cops would do would be to check the glove compartment where they'd find the car registration. Next they'd check the trunk and find the .32. Jack had said he'd give high odds that the gun was unregistered.

When the Fosters reported the car stolen, they'd have to explain the unregistered pistol found in their trunk, most likely with their prints on it. If it could be linked to a crime, so much the better. If not, Jack said he had further plans for Madame Pomerol.

Lyle was dying to know what he'd cook up next.

13

Jack let himself into Gia's house through the front door. He punched a code twice into the alarm keypad—first to disarm, then to rearm it. He glided upstairs and spoke a soft hello into the dark bedroom. Receiving a muffled mumble in reply, he ducked into the bathroom for a quick shower, then slipped under the covers and snuggled against Gia.

"You awake?" he said, nuzzling her neck.

She was wearing a short T-shirt and panties, and he was in the mood. He was definitely in the mood.

"How was your night?" she muttered through barely mobile lips.

"Great. How was yours?"

"Lonely."

Jack slipped a hand under her shirt and cupped a breast. It fit perfectly in his hand.

"Just hold me, Jack, okay? Just hold me."

"Not in the mood?"

"Sometimes a girl just likes to be held."

Concerned, he released her breast and folded his arms around her. Couldn't remember the last time Gia had referred to herself as a "girl."

"Anything wrong?"

"Just lying here thinking."

"About what?"

"Possibilities."

"Oh? Got to be about a million of them out there for you. All good."

"I wish I were so sure."

"You're worried about something," he said, pulling her closer. "I sensed it this afternoon. What's up?"

"Like I said, just thinking about possibilities . . . and the big changes they might bring."

"Good changes or bad?"

"Depends on how you look at them."

"You're losing me here."

Gia sighed. "I know. I'm not trying to be mysterious. It's just . . . sometimes you worry."

"About what?"

She turned and kissed him. "Nothing. Everything."

"If something's bothering you, shouldn't I know?"

"You should. And when there's—when it's something real—you'll be the first to know."

She slid her hand down his abdomen and gripped him.

"What about just being held?" he said, instantly responding.

"Sometimes that's plenty . . . and other times it's not quite enough."

IN THE
IN-BETWEEN

Other less frightening memories have filtered back to the nameless and placeless one . . . glimpses of tall buildings and sunlit yards, all so tantalizingly familiar, and yet so resolutely out of reach.

But as comforting as these memories are, they do not lessen the ambient rage. What they represent is gone, and the sense of loss intensifies the rage. The only thing that tempers the fury, keeps it from consuming the nameless one in a blinding explosion is confusion . . . and loneliness . . . and loss.

If it had eyes, it would cry.

Still unable to fathom its identity and location, it senses a vague purpose behind its awakening. Like the source of the flitting memory fragments, the nature of the purpose remains elusive. Yet it is there, ripening. Soon, nurtured by the rage, it will blossom.

And then someone, something must die . . .

IN THE WEE HOURS

Lyle awoke to the sound of music . . . a piano . . . something classical. The delicate melody sounded vaguely familiar, but he couldn't identify it. He'd bought some classical CDs for background music in the waiting room, but he'd picked them at random and never listened to them himself. Never understood why people liked classical; but then, he couldn't understand why people liked to drink Scotch either.

Charlie? Not a chance. Not Charlie's taste at all. And Charlie was in the sack. He'd come back from his night ride with Jack babbling about how bustin' he was, how they'd set it up to give Madame Pomerol a taste of her own medicine, and how he wished he could be there when it went down. But then he'd faded fast and said goodnight.

Lyle threw off the sheet and swung his feet to the floor. He didn't want to know the time. Whatever it was, it was too late. He'd given up on trying to keep the windows closed so he'd turned off the AC and gone to bed with them open. The temperature at the moment wasn't too bad, though.

But what's with the music? The same song over and over.

Had Madame Pomerol and her husband screwed with his music system as well? After last night he'd hoped he'd heard the last of them.

As Lyle pounded down the stairs toward the waiting room, he noticed something about the music . . . thin . . . just a piano. Where were the strings and the rest of the orchestra? And then he realized it wasn't a CD . . . it was live . . . someone was playing the piano in the waiting room.

He burst into the room and stopped dead on the threshold. The lights were out. The only illumination came from the faint glow of the street lights through the open front door. A dark figure sat at the piano, tinkling away on the keys.

Lyle's shakes from earlier in the evening returned, now more from dread than adrenaline, as he reached for the light switch. He found it, hesitated then flipped it.

He groaned with relief when he saw Charlie seated on the piano bench, his back to him. Charlie's head was turned, his eyes closed, a small smile playing about his lips as his fingers danced over the keys. He seemed to be enjoying himself.

The look on his face sent a trickle of ice water down Lyle's spine.

"Charlie?" Lyle said, closing the front door and moving closer. "Charlie, what are you doing?"

He opened his eyes; they were glassy. "I'm playing 'Für Elise.' It's my favorite." Charlie's voice . . . but not his diction. He looked like he used to get back in his pre-born again days when he was doing a couple of blunts a night.

The cold spine trickle became a torrent. Charlie didn't play piano. And even if he did, he wouldn't be diddling this light-fingered tune with the funny name.

Lyle's tongue felt thick, sticky. "When did you learn to play piano, Charlie?"

"I had my first lesson when I was six."

"No, you didn't." He put his hand on his brother's shoulder and gave it a gentle shake. "You know you didn't. What are you pulling here?"

"Just practicing." He picked up the tempo. "I've got to play this note perfect for my recital."

"Stop it, Charlie."

He played faster, his fingers flying over the keys. "No. I've got to play it twenty times a day to make sure—"

Lyle reached over and grabbed his brother's wrists. He tried to pull them away from the keyboard but his brother fought him. Finally Lyle threw all his weight into it.

"Charlie, *please!*"

They both came away from the piano together, Charlie tipping over backward on the piano seat and landing on the floor, Lyle staggering but keeping his feet.

For an instant Charlie glared at him from the floor, his eyes blazing with rage, then his face cleared.

"Lyle?"

"Charlie, what on—?" Then Lyle saw the blood on the front of his shirt. "Oh, Christ! What happened?"

Charlie stared up at him with a bewildered look. "What goin' on, bro?"

He started to rise but Lyle pushed him back. "Don't move! You've been hurt!"

Charlie looked down at the glistening red stain on the front of his shirt, then looked up again.

"Lyle?" His eyes were afraid. "Lyle, what—?"

Lyle tried not to lose it. His brother, something awful had happened to his baby brother. They'd been through so much and now . . . and now . . .

He wanted to run for the phone to call Emergency Services, but was afraid to leave Charlie's side. There might be something he could do, *needed* to do right now to make sure he survived until help arrived.

"Take your shirt off and let's see. Maybe it's not so bad."

"Lyle, what *wrong* with you?"

Lyle didn't want to see this. If it was only half as bad as it looked it was still terrible. He yanked up Charlie's shirt—

And gaped.

The skin of his chest was unbroken, without a trace of blood. Lyle dropped to his knees before him and touched his skin.

"What on earth?"

Where had all that blood come from? He yanked the shirt back down and gasped when he found it clean and dry and pristine white, as if fresh from the dryer.

"Lyle?" Charlie said, a different kind of fear in his eyes

now. "What happenin' here? Is this a dream? I went to bed, next thing I know, I'm here on the floor."

"You were playing the piano." He struggled to his feet and helped Charlie up. "Don't you remember?"

"No way. You know I can't—"

"But you were. And playing pretty well."

"But how?"

"I wish to hell I knew."

Charlie grabbed his arm. "Maybe that it. Maybe that crack in the cellar let a little bit of hell into this house. Or maybe there always been a bit of hell in this place, considerin' what happened here over the years. Whatever it is, it's gettin' to you."

Lyle was about to tell his brother to cool it with that shit when the front door unlocked itself and swung open.

SUNDAY

1

Gia cleaned up the breakfast dishes. Not a task she minded as a rule, but today . . . scraping leftover scrambled eggs from the bottom of a frying pan roiled her already queasy stomach. The eggs had been for Jack; she'd whipped them up and mixed in crumbled soy bacon strips for a don't-ask, don't-tell breakfast. He hadn't asked if he was eating real bacon and she hadn't told. Not that he would have minded. Jack ate just about everything. Sometimes, when he was in his Where's-the-beef? mode, he'd complain about too many vegetables, but he rarely failed to clean his plate. A good boy. She never had to tell him about the starving children in China.

He'd said he had an appointment with a new customer this morning—someone who claimed he couldn't wait until Monday—and had wandered off to the townhouse's little library to kill some time before he had to leave.

"How about a shnackie?" he said as he wandered back.

She looked up and smiled at him. "You just ate breakfast an hour ago."

He rubbed his stomach. "I know, but I need a little shomething."

"How about a leftover bagel?"

"Shuper."

"You've been reading one of Vicky's *Mutts* books, haven't you?"

"Yesh."

"Well, get yourself out of Mooch mode and I'll toast you one."

He sat down. "After a week of this you'll never get me

to leave." He looked at her. "Wouldn't be so bad if I stayed, would it?"

Oh, no. Their recurrent topic of contention: whether or not to live together.

Jack voted yes, and had been pushing for it—gently, but persistently—since late last year. He wanted to be a bigger part of Vicky's life, be the kind of father her real father had never been.

"It would be great," Gia said. "As soon as we're married."

Jack sighed. "You know I'd marry you in a heartbeat if I could, but . . ."

"But you can't. Because a man with no official existence can't apply for a marriage license."

"Is a piece of paper so important?"

"We've been over this before, Jack. Marriage wouldn't matter if I weren't Vicky's mother. But I am. And Vicky's mom does not have a live-in boyfriend, or manfriend, or significant other, or whatever the latest accepted term is."

An archaic mindset. Gia freely admitted that, and had no problem with it. The values by which she guided her life were not weather vanes, changing direction with every shift of the social climes; they were the bedrock on which she'd grown up, and they still felt solid underfoot. They formed her comfort zone. She didn't care to impose them on anyone else, and conversely, didn't want anyone else telling her how to raise her child.

She believed in raising a child by example. Definitely hands-on, setting rules and limits, but being bound by her own rules as well. None of this do-as-I-say-not-as-I-do nonsense. If Gia wanted Vicky to tell the truth, then Gia must never lie; if Gia wanted Vicky to be honest, then Gia must never cheat.

The perfect example had presented itself last week when she and Vicky had gone to the liquor store. Knowing Jack would be around a lot during Vicky's absence, Gia had picked up a case of beer, plus a couple of bottles of wine. On the way out of the store Vicky whispered that the cashier hadn't scanned one of the wines. Gia had checked her receipt and, sure enough, Little Miss Never-Miss-a-Trick was right. She'd turned around, pointed out the error, and paid for the extra bottle. The clerk was astounded, the manager had wanted to give her the bottle for free, and two other customers waiting on line had looked at her as if to say, What planet are you from?

"Why didn't you just keep the bottle, Mom?" Vicky had asked.

"Because it wasn't mine."

"But no one knew."

"You knew. And once you told me, I knew. And then keeping it would have made me a thief. I don't want to be a thief."

Vicky had nodded at the obvious truth of that and then started talking about the dead bird she'd seen yesterday.

But living the life she wanted Vicky to live meant sacrifices. It meant no moving in with Jack, no Jack moving in with her. Because if sixteen-year-old Vicky one day asked if her boyfriend could move into her bedroom, Gia wanted to be able to look her daughter straight in the eye when she said no.

How in the world could Gia ever explain to Vicky her love for Jack? She couldn't explain it to herself. Jack flouted all the rules, thumbed his nose at society's most basic conventions, and yet . . . he was the most decent, most moral, *truest* man she'd met since leaving Iowa.

But as much as she loved him, she wasn't sure she wanted to live with him. Or with anyone else, for that matter. She liked her space, and she and Vicky had plenty of that here on Sutton Square. This high-priced, oak-paneled, antique-studded piece of East Side real estate belonged to the Westphalen family, of which Vicky was the last surviving member. Her aunts had left the townhouse and most of their considerable fortunes to her in their wills, but they were listed as missing instead of dead. It would be years before the place and the fortunes were officially Vicky's, but until then the executor let them live here to keep up the property.

So . . . if Gia and Jack ever came to a living arrangement, she and Vicky would not be moving to Jack's little two-bedroom apartment. He'd come here. After they were married.

"What do we do, then?" he said.

She buttered the bagel and placed it before him. "We go on as we are. I'm happy. Aren't you?"

"Sure." He smiled at her. "But I could be happier waking up with you every morning."

That part she'd love. But the rest . . . she wasn't sure she could handle living with Jack. He kept bizarre hours, sometimes out all night if one of his jobs called for it. She became aware of these incidents only after the fact; she'd sleep through the night thinking he was safe in his apartment watching one of his strange old movies. Living with Jack would change all that. She'd be wide awake wondering where he was, if he was in danger, praying he'd come back in one piece, or come back at all.

She'd be a wreck. She didn't know if she could live like that.

Better this way. At least for now. But what if . . . ?

Gia suppressed a groan of frustration. If only she knew the results of that pregnancy test. She'd sneaked a call to Dr. Eagleton's service while Jack was in the library and was told she was off until Monday. The same uncooperative doctor was covering for her, so Gia didn't bother calling him. She'd have to wait till tomorrow.

She watched Jack wolf down his bagel. If that test comes out positive tomorrow, she thought, what will you say?

2

"This is wack, dawg!" Charlie said angrily, slapping the newspaper against the kitchen table and rattling the breakfast dishes. "Totally wack!"

Lyle looked up at his brother over the edge of the *Times* sports section. "You okay?"

He'd been worried about Charlie since that strange episode last night, but Charlie seemed unconcerned; maybe because he didn't believe he'd been playing the piano. He thought Lyle had had another nightmare.

And who could blame him? Especially after Lyle wailing about blood all over his chest and then finding no wound. But this was the second time he'd seen Charlie with a hole in his chest. He didn't believe in premonitions, and considering what he'd been seeing, he didn't want to.

As he sat here with the sun and a summer breeze pouring through the open—what else?—windows, worrying about portents of future calamities seemed silly.

"Trip to this," Charlie said, a mixture of anger and disgust twisting his features as he shoved a section of the *News* across the table. "Top right column."

When Lyle saw the headline he had a premonition—oh, yes—as to what it was about. The first sentence confirmed it.

SHE SHOULD'VE SEEN IT COMING

Elizabeth Foster, known to certain wealthy Manhattanites as psychic advisor Madame Pomerol, was picked up in the financial district last night wearing nothing but a large piece of cardboard. Her husband Carl was similarly attired. The couple explained that

they had been driving near their home on the Upper
East Side when suddenly they were "aported" out of
their car—and their clothes as well!—by mischievous
spirits who were angry at them. The spirits whisked
them through the night and dumped them naked in
Lower Manhattan. Madame Pomerol claims that certain spirits are angry at her for forcing them to return
many items that they have previously stolen from her
clients.

"I don't believe this!" Lyle said, looking up at Charlie.
"She's turning the whole thing into a commercial for her-
self!"
He read on . . .

Two years ago, Madame Pomerol was just another
among the scores of spiritualist mediums working the
city's psychic beat until she appeared on *The Late
Show with David Letterman.* Although Letterman gen-
erally made light of her psychic claims during her appearance, the exposure made her a celebrity and she
has become one of the most prominent and prosperous
mediums in the five boroughs.

Despite her claims of psychic abilities, however,
Madame Pomerol didn't know where her car was. Police had to tell her that they'd located it shortly after
they found her, not on the Upper East Side where she
claimed to have been snatched from it, but on Chambers Street, a short distance from where the couple was
found.

"The spirits must have aported the car after they
aported us," Madame Pomerol said.

The psychic couldn't explain how this was done.
Nor could she explain the .32 caliber pistol found in
the trunk of the car, other than to say that, "The malicious spirits must have placed it there. They want to
get me into trouble because they're furious at my ability to undo their mischief."

The Fosters were not charged at this time, but might be in the future, pending investigation of the weapon.

"They damn well better be charged!" Lyle said. "They tried to kill me with that gun!"

"She pretty quick on her feet, ain't she," Charlie said.

"Yeah. Too quick, maybe."

That harpy had turned what should have been humiliation into a publicity stunt. Lyle wondered if he would have been quick enough to do the same.

Charlie said, "Ay, yo, leastways now she got something else to think about besides us."

"Yeah. She and the mister have got to be worried about that gun. But even if they skate on that, maybe all this publicity'll help her pick up enough new business so she'll stop caring about the clients we siphoned off."

Charlie grinned. "She ain't gonna be so crazy about one new client comin' in today, know'm sayin'?"

"You mean Jack."

"Yeah, my whodi, Jack."

"You really like him, don't you."

Charlie nodded. "I first saw him I'm thinkin', this the guy gonna pull our butts outta the fire? Nuh-uh. But was I off. My bad. He rag out like some kinda bama, but he the furilla gorilla, bro."

Lyle felt a twinge of jealousy at the admiration in his little brother's voice.

"Think he's up to putting Madame Pomerol in her place?"

Charlie shrugged. "Sure had her in her place last night, yo. We checked her appointments when we was over her 'temple.' She got four flush fish set for a group sitting this afternoon. Jack gonna try to wheedle his way in." He grinned. "And that's when the fun'll begin, know'm sayin'?"

"We should be doing our own Sunday sittings," Lyle said. They'd been over this countless times before, but he couldn't help bringing it up again. "It would be a big day for us. People are home, it's a spiritual day, and if they're not going to church, maybe they'd come here."

Charlie's grin vanished. "I told you, Lyle, you do a sittin' on a Sunday, you do it without me. I hope someday I be forgiven for what I help you do the other six days of the week, but I know I'll burn in hell sure for luring God-fearing folks away from praising the Lord on a Sunday. If I ever—"

Lyle started as a voice spoke from the adjoining room. He gripped the edge of the table and was halfway to his feet when he recognized Bugs Bunny.

"The TV," he said, feeling his muscles start to uncoil. For some reason it had suddenly blared to life. He glanced at Charlie. "You got the remote in your pocket or something?"

Charlie shook his head. "No way. Never touched it."

They both jumped at the sound of gunfire, then Lyle realized that too came from the TV. He might have laughed then, but it wasn't funny. The TV room was what remained of the old dining room, which used to connect to what was now the waiting room, but they'd closed off the opening during the remodeling. No way in or out of the TV room now except through here, the kitchen.

Lyle stared at his brother for an uneasy moment, then he picked up a knife and straightened to his feet. No way anyone could be in there, but it never hurt to be ready.

"Let's go see what's up."

Knife held low against his thigh, Lyle stepped into the next room, but found it empty. On the screen the early, long-snouted Bugs was taunting a shotgun-toting Elmer Fudd. Lyle spotted the Cartoon Network logo nestled in the lower right corner.

"You been watching cartoons?" he asked Charlie.

"Not lately."

He glanced around, found the remote on the recliner, and hit the number of the Weather Channel. "Might as well see what the weather's going to be."

The Weather Channel came on, but the set immediately

flipped back to the Cartoon Network. Lyle tried again, with
the same result. Annoyed now, he punched random numbers, but the set always returned to the Cartoon Network.

"What is this shit?"

He went to the window and peered outside.

"What you looking for?" Charlie said.

"Oh, I've heard stories of pranking kids using a universal
remote on a neighbor's set."

The yard was empty.

"Yo, maybe it the Fosters, you know, messing with our
heads again."

"This seems too petty, even for them. Besides, I'm pretty
sure they've got other things on their minds this morning."

Hell with it, he thought, and hit the power button.

The screen went dark. But a second later it buzzed to
life again. He hit POWER half a dozen times in a row but
the damn set kept turning itself back on.

Charlie said, "Lemme deal with this."

He reached behind the set and pulled the power plug,
killing the picture.

Lyle held out a hand for a five. "Now why didn't I think
of—"

They both jumped as the screen lit again, this time with
Jerry the mouse flattening the head of Tom the cat with a
frying pan. Lyle pointed to the plug in Charlie's hand.

"You must have pulled the wrong one."

"The other's the VCR. Look at it. The display still lit."

"Pull it anyway."

Charlie reached back and yanked out the other cord, but
Tom and Jerry kept up their nonstop mayhem.

Charlie threw down the cords as if they were live snakes.
"I'm geese, man."

"Hey, don't bail on me. You're the electronics guru here.
Figure this out." But Charlie kept moving, disappearing
into the kitchen. "Where you going?"

"Where I go every Sunday at ten: church. You should
give it a shot, bro, because there ain't nothin' electronic

wrong with that TV. It's haunted, yo, know'm sayin'? *Haunted*!"

Lyle turned and watched the cartoon characters race about on the screen of the unplugged TV. After the last couple of night's crazy visions of Charlie with a hole in his chest, Lyle had begun to wonder if he might be cracking up. But he wasn't imagining this TV thing. They'd both seen it.

No way he was buying into a haunted TV set, though. There had to be an explanation, a rational one—like some kind of battery inside—and he was going to find it.

Lyle headed for the garage and his toolbox . . .

3

Jack sat in the rear of Julio's and sized up his latest potential customer. The man had introduced himself simply as Edward, without offering his last name, a precaution Jack could appreciate.

A few of the regulars were already at the bar getting their first dose of the day. Morning sun filtered through the funeral procession of dead ferns, Wandering Jews, and spider plants lining the front window, then moved on to light up the cloud of tobacco smoke hovering over the bar. Jack's was the only table without the burden of upended chairs. The relatively cool air back here in the shadows wouldn't last; the day was promising to be a scorcher. Julio had opened the rear door for cross ventilation, to waft out the smell of stale beer before he had to close up and turn on the AC.

He approached now with a coffee pot.

"You want anything in the java, meng?" he said as he refilled Jack's cup. "Little hair o' the dog?"

Julio had his name on the front window. He was short and muscular, with a pencil-line mustache. And he stank.

"Had a canine-free night," Jack said, and tried to ignore the odor. He'd got his first cup up front, which Julio had poured from the far side of the bar. He hadn't noticed the smell then.

Julio shrugged and turned to the customer. "Top you off?"

"That would be lovely," Edward said with a Barry Fitzgerald brogue.

Come to think of it, he sort of looked a little like Barry Fitzgerald too: sixty-five, maybe even seventy from the look of his gnarled hands, white hair, compact frame, twinkling blue eyes. He was oddly dressed: on top he wore a graying T-shirt that might have been white once but had spent too many cycles in with the dark wash; below the waist he was dressed for a funeral with black suit pants—shiny in the seat from wear—and black socks and shoes. He'd brought a large manila envelope that lay between them on the table.

Edward frowned and sniffed. He rubbed his nose and looked around for the source of the odor. Jack felt he had to say something.

"Okay, Julio, what's the new aftershave?"

Julio grinned. "It's called Chiquita. Great, huh?"

"Only if you're trying to attract radical chicks who happen to be nostalgic for the smell of tear gas."

"You don't like it?" He got a hurt expression. He turned to Edward. "What you think, meng?"

Edward rubbed his nose again. "Well, I, um—"

"You ever been Maced, Edward?" Jack said.

"Well, no, I can't say that I have."

"Well, I have, and it's pretty close to Chiquita."

Just then the old Wurlitzer 1080 against the front wall roared to life with "Paradise by the Dashboard Light."

Jack groaned. "Meatloaf? Before noon? Julio, you've got to be kidding!"

"Yo, Lou!" Julio called, turning toward the bar. "You play that, meng?"

A rhetorical question. Everyone in the place—except Edward, of course—knew Lou had a jones for Meatloaf songs. If he had the money, and if the other regulars didn't strangle him along the way, he'd play them all day and all night. One night a couple of years ago he overdid it. Played "Bat Out of Hell" one too many times. Some writer from LA—a friend of Tommy's, this jolly-looking guy Jack never would have guessed had it in him—pulled out a .357 and killed the machine. Julio had picked up this classic Wurlitzer as a replacement and didn't want it shot up like its predecessor.

Lou shrugged, grinning and showing sixty-year-old teeth stained with fifty-nine years of nicotine. "Could be."

"What I tell you 'bout Meatloaf when the sun out, eh? What I tell you?" He strode over to the jukebox and pulled the plug.

"Hey!" Lou cried. "I got money in there!"

"You jus' lost it."

The other regulars laughed as Lou harrumphed and returned to his shot and beer.

"Thank you, Julio," Jack muttered.

Meatloaf's opuses were hard to take on any day—twenty-minute songs with the same two or three lines repeated over and over for the last third—but on a Sunday morning . . . Sunday morning required something mellow along the lines of Cowboy Junkies.

"So, Edward," Jack said after a sip of his coffee, "how did you get my name?"

"Someone mentioned to me once that he'd enlisted your services. He said you did good work and weren't one for telling tales."

"Did he? Mind telling me who that someone might be?"

"Oh, I don't think he'll be wanting me to talk about him, but he had only good things to say about you. Except for your fee, that is. He wasn't too keen on that."

"Do you happen to know what I did for him?"

"I don't think he'll be wanting me to talk about that either." He leaned forward and lowered his voice. "Especially since it wasn't exactly legal."

"Can't believe everything you hear," Jack said.

"Are you telling me then," Edward said, flashing a leprechaun's grin, "that you're as gossipy as the village spinster and you work for free out of the goodness of your Christian heart?"

Jack had to smile. "No, but I like to know how my customers find me. And I like to know which ones are shooting their mouths off."

"Oh, don't worry about this lad. He's a very careful sort. Told me in the strictest confidence. I might be the only one he's ever told."

Jack figured he'd let the referral origin go for now and find out what this little man wanted from him.

"Your call mentioned something about your brother."

"Yes. My brother Eli. I'm very concerned about him."

"In what way?"

"I fear he's . . . well, I'm not quite sure how to be putting this." He seemed almost guilty. "I fear he'll be after getting himself into terrible trouble soon."

"What kind of trouble and how soon?"

"The next couple of days, I'm afraid."

"And the trouble?"

"He'll be getting violent, he will."

"You mean, going out and beating people up?"

Edward shrugged. "Perhaps worse. I can't say."

"Worse? Are we talking about some sort of homicidal maniac here?"

"I can be assuring you that he's a rather proper sort most of the time. He owns a business, right here in the city, but at certain times he . . . well . . . I think he goes off his head."

"And you think one of those times is soon. That's why this couldn't wait till tomorrow."

"Exactly." He wrapped his fingers around his coffee cup as if to warm them. But this wasn't January, it was August. "I'm afraid it's going to be very soon."

"What makes you think so?"

"The moon."

Jack leaned back. Oh, no. He's not going to tell me his brother's a werewolf. Please say he's not.

"Why, is it full?"

"Quite the opposite. Tomorrow is the new moon."

New moon . . . that sent a ripple through Jack's gut, tossing him back a few months to when the drawing of some very special blood from a very special vein had to be timed to the new moon.

But this didn't sound anything like that.

"Lunatic . . . the origin of the word is *luna* . . . moon."

"Yes, I know," Edward said. "And it's not as if this happens every new moon. It's just that it's going to happen this one."

"How do you know?"

"Eli told me."

"He told you he's going to go wilding or something tomorrow night and—"

"It could be tonight. Or Tuesday night. The new moon phase lasts more than one day, don't you know."

"Why would he tell you?"

"He just . . . wanted me to know, I guess."

Jack knew the answer to the next question but felt obliged to ask. "Just where do you think I fit in?"

"Well, it's not something I can be going to the police with, is it now. And I'm too old to be doing it meself. So I was hoping you'd be watching over him."

Jack had been afraid of that. Guardian angel to some lunatic. Make that new lunatic.

"Afraid not, Ed. I'm not in the bodyguard business."

"Wait, now. It's not like a real bodyguarding job. You wouldn't be after protecting him from someone else. You'd only be protecting him from himself. And it's only for three days, lad. Three days!"

Jack shook his head. "That's the problem. No way I can spend three days baby-sitting some wacko."

"It wouldn't be three whole days. Just at night, after he closes his shop."

"Why do you need me at all? Why not just hire a professional bodyguard? I can get you a couple of numbers."

"Oh, no," Edward said, vigorously shaking his head. "It's imperative that he not know he's being watched over."

"Let me get this straight: you want me to bodyguard your brother without him knowing his body's being guarded?"

"Exactly. And the beauty part is, you might not be having to do a thing. He might not go off at all. But if he does, you can be there to restrain him, and perhaps be preventing him from hurting himself or anyone else in the process."

Jack shook his head. Too weird.

"Please!" Edward said, his voice rising. He reached into his back pocket and wriggled out a thick legal-size envelope. His trembling hands unfolded it and pushed it across the table. "I scraped together every spare cent I have. Please, take it all and—"

"It's not a matter of money," Jack said. "It's time. I can't spend all night watching this guy."

"Then don't! Just watch him from the time he closes his shop till, say, midnight. We're talking about a few hours a night for three nights, lad. Surely you can do that."

Edward's intense concern, almost anguish, for his brother wormed under Jack's skin. Three nights . . . not forever. The only other fix-it he had running was the Kenton brothers, and he didn't think watchdogging their place would be necessary after last night.

"All right," Jack sighed. "For three nights, I suppose I can give you something."

Edward reached across and grasped both Jack's hands. "Oh, bless you, lad, that's wonderful! Wonderful!"

"I said 'something.' No guarantees."

"I know you'll be doing your best. I know you won't let me down."

Jack pushed the envelope back toward Edward. "Give me half of that. I'll keep an eye on him for three nights. If nothing happens—that is, if I don't have to step in and restrain him—we'll call it even. If there's any rough stuff, any at all, you owe me the other half."

"Fair enough," Edward said as he lowered the envelope into his lap and began counting the bills. "More than fair, actually."

"And speaking of rough stuff, it may come down to putting the hurt on him if he decides not to listen to reason."

"Hurt? How?"

"Disable him. Put him down hard enough so that he won't be able to get back up."

Edward sighed. "Do what you must. I'll trust in your judgment."

"Right," Jack said, leaning forward. "Now that that's settled, where is he and what does he look like?"

Edward jutted his chin at the manila envelope on the table. "You'll be finding it all in there."

Jack opened the flap and pulled out a slip of paper plus a candid photo of a balding man who appeared to be about sixty years old. Jack stared at the upper-body shot; the man's face was partially turned away.

"Doesn't look much like you."

"We had different mothers."

"So he's really your half-brother."

Edward shrugged and kept counting bills.

Jack said, "Don't you have a better photo?"

"I'm afraid not. Eli doesn't like to be photographed. He'd be upset if he knew I took that one. I wish I could be telling you more about him, but we weren't raised together, so I hardly know him."

"But he came to you and told you he was going to do something crazy?"

"Yes. It's the weirdest thing now, isn't it?"

"I don't know about the 'weirdest,' but it earns a spot in the 'odd' category."

Jack glanced at the sheet of paper. "Eli Bellitto" was printed in large letters.

"Bellitto?" Jack said. "That's not an Irish name."

"Who said it was?"

"Nobody, but, I mean, you've got this Irish accent and that's an Italian name."

"And because the 'O' is on the wrong end you're after saying that Eli can't be Irish? Would you believe that where I grew up in Dublin we had a Schwartz on our block? God's truth. His accent was thicker than mine, don't you know. My American uncle came to visit and couldn't understand a word he said. And then there was—"

Jack held up his hands surrender style. "Point made, point taken." He tapped his finger on the downtown address below the name. "What's this 'Shurio Coppe' mean?"

"That's the name of his shop. He sells—"

"Don't tell me. Curios, right?"

Edward nodded. "Antiques, odd stuff, rare books, and all sorts of grotesque thingies."

"Where's his home?"

"Right over the store."

Well now, Jack thought. Isn't that convenient. It meant he wouldn't have to trail this bozo all the way out to someplace like Massapequa for the next three nights.

"When's close-up time?"

"The store? Usually at nine, but he'll close early tonight because it's Sunday. You'll be wanting to get there before six."

He handed Jack the thinned envelope and stuffed the remaining bills into his pants pocket. Then he leaned back, closed his eyes, and placed a hand over his heart.

"You all right?" Jack said, thinking he might be having a heart attack.

Edward opened his eyes and smiled. "I am now. I've been worried sick about this since he told me. I felt I had to be doing something, and now I have. I'd never be forgiving meself if he hurt some poor innocent..." He stopped, glanced at his watch, then slapped his hands on the table. "Well, I've taken up enough of your time, Mister Repairman. I'll be letting you get on with your day."

Jack waved and watched him thread his way through the

tables and disappear out the door. He thumbed through the bills in the envelope and stared at the photo of Eli Bellitto. Two days, two fix-it jobs. Not bad. Although this Bellitto deal wasn't exactly a fix-it. More like preventive maintenance.

He glanced at the clock over the bar's FREE BEER TO-MORROW . . . sign. Time to get rolling. Had to get home and fix himself up for his date with Madame Pomerol.

4

"Your dad gave a def sermon this morning," Charlie Kenton said

He stood next to Sharleen Sparks at the sink in the basement of the New Apostles Church. After the morning service he'd come down here with her and a few other volunteers to pitch in on the church's weekly Sunday dinner for the poor and homeless. The sink was old and rusted, the big gas oven battered and scarred, but both did their jobs. The linoleum floor curled up in the corners, the old tin ceiling flaked here and there, but a spirit of love and giving that Charlie sensed around him made it all feel new. He'd just peeled his way through the first half of a bushel bag of potatoes; his fingers ached but he didn't mind at all. It was for a good cause.

"Yes, praise God," she said. "He was in rare form today."

Charlie glanced up from the potato he was peeling to steal a peek at her, wondering what to say next. Had to say *something*. He'd been waiting for a chance to talk to her alone, now he had it and his mind was flatlined. Maybe it was her beauty, inside and out, or the fact that she didn't seem to know she was beautiful.

She had corn-rowed hair, huge brown eyes, and a smile

that made his knees go gumby. She was wearing a white T-shirt under her loose denim overalls, the bib front doing a poor job of hiding her full breasts. He tried not to look at them.

He'd never been this tongue-tied before his conversion. Back in those days he'd been some kinda playa, ragged out in chains and silk, always stocking a little powder and some boo-yaa weed. The women he called bitches and bizzos back then painted on their clothes and faces, wore wigs and big jingly zirconium earrings. Not one thing real about them, but they was easy. He'd sidle up to one, offer a taste of this or that to get her loose, mack her up and down with a few sweet lines, and soon they'd be heading to his place or hers.

He shook his head. A life of sin. But he had the rest of his life to make up for it.

"Sharleen," said a deep voice, "do you mind if Charles and I have a few private words?"

Charlie Kenton looked up to see Reverend Josiah Sparks, a big man whose black face was made all the blacker by the mane of white hair and beard that wreathed it. He'd just arrived after trading the clerical suit and collar he'd worn at the service for a work shirt and bib-front overalls like his daughter's.

Sharleen gave Charlie a concerned look. "Oh, um, sure Daddy."

After she'd moved away to one of the stoves, the rev peered at him through the thick lenses of his rimless glasses. "Have you given more thought to the matter we've been discussing?"

"Yes, Rev. Every day."

The Reverend Sparks took up a knife and began quartering the peeled potatoes, then throwing the pieces into a pot. Eventually they'd be boiled and mashed.

"And what have you decided?"

Charlie hesitated. "Nothing definite yet."

"It's your soul that's at stake, son. Your immortal soul. How can there be even an instant of indecision?" ·

"There wouldn't be ... if Lyle weren't my brother, know'm sayin'?"

"It matters not that he's your brother. He's leading you into sin, making you an accomplice in his evil. You must break off from him. Remember, 'If thine eye offend thee, pluck it out, for it is better to enter into the kingdom of God with one eye, than have two eyes and be cast into hell fire.' "

"Word," Charlie replied.

"Yes, it is. The Word of God, spoken through Matthew and Mark."

Charlie glanced around. Sharleen was out of earshot and no one else was nearby at the moment. The rev was keeping his voice low. Good. Charlie didn't want the whole congregation to know his problems. Especially Sharleen.

Sometimes he wondered if he'd made a mistake in opening up to the rev about Lyle's spiritualist act. The man now saw Charlie as a member of his flock in danger of losing his salvation, and he was determined to save him.

"But what about *Lyle's* soul, Reverend? I don't want him in the everlasting fire."

"You told me you've witnessed to him, is that correct?"

"Yes, many times. Many, many times. But he just ain't hearin'."

The reverend nodded. "Your words are seed falling on rocky ground. Well, you must not give up on him—never give up on a soul in need—but you must not neglect your own salvation. You must make sure your own soul is safe before you try to save your brother's. And to do that you must renounce his evil activities."

Charlie looked away, bristling. Reverend or not, no one should talk about his brother like that.

"Lyle's not evil."

"He may not appear so, but he's doing the devil's work. Jesus warned us against his sort: 'Beware of the false prophets, who come to you in sheep's clothing, but inwardly are ravenous wolves.' "

Charlie felt a hot stab of anger. "He's *not* a wolf, Rev."

"Son, you must face the fact that he's leading souls along a path away from Jesus, he is doing Satan's work. And as long as you're with him, you are an accomplice. You must first remove yourself from his influence, then you must strive to counter his evildoing. The best way to do that is to lead him to salvation."

Charlie stifled a laugh. Lead Lyle? Ain't nobody never led Lyle nowhere.

"That last part won't be easy."

"Do you want me to go speak to him? Perhaps I—"

"No!" The knife jumped and Charlie almost cut himself. "I mean, it's better if he don't know I been jawin' 'bout him. He won't like no outsider mixin' in, know'm sayin'?"

So far Charlie had kept Lyle's location from the rev. Didn't want anyone in the church connecting him to Ifasen the spirit medium. That was why he'd joined a church in Brooklyn instead of Queens. The weekly ride on the subway was long, but worth it.

"Then it's up to you, son. I'll be praying for you."

"Thank you, Rev. I'll need those prayers, because leaving's gonna be so hard. First off, he's blood, my only brother. I'll be breaking up all that's left of the family."

What Charlie couldn't explain, because he was sure Reverend Sparks wouldn't understand, was that he and Lyle were a team. They'd been a team since Momma died. Lyle had scammed the Man to keep them from being split up, got them onto the government cheese to keep them from starving, and they'd been scammin' the world ever since. After Lyle had gone to such lengths to see that they stayed together, how could Charlie look him in the eye and say he was splitting?

And something else Charlie couldn't tell the rev, something dark and guilty: he *liked* running the game. Loved it, in fact. He loved piecing together new gags to wow the marks. When a sitting went according to script, when all the bells and whistles were working, it was so def. Lyle would have those people in the palm of his hand, and Charlie would know he had a big part in putting them there.

Times like that he felt stoned, better than stoned, better than he'd ever felt back in the days when he was doing coke and weed.

But for the sake of his soul he was going to have to put all that behind him.

And do what?

That was the question. What else was he good for? Maybe work in the theater doing special effects? He couldn't list any experience so he'd have to start off as an apprentice at the bottom of the pay scale and work his way up . . . to what?

Nothing he could do in the straight world would ever touch the high he got from working with Lyle.

With Lyle . . . that was the real kicker, that was what made it real. The rev said he and Lyle had to part. And they'd never been apart.

But Reverend Sparks was right. For the sake of his soul, and to deserve Sharleen, he was going to have to make the break. And soon.

5

Jack stared at his reflection in the mirrored wall of the elevator as it made its way to the fourteenth floor. He blew a pink bubble with the big wad of gum he was chewing, then checked out his appearance. He'd wanted somewhat of an eccentric look today, so he'd chosen a reddish mullet-style wig, banged in the front and long and thick in the back; a thick, dark brown mustache draped his upper lip. He wore a light green, western-style shirt, buttoned all the way to the top, dark green twill pants, and Doc Martens. He'd strapped some padding around his waist to give him a medium-size gut. Too bad he didn't have a pierced earlobe; a rhinestone stud would have made a nice finishing touch.

He checked to make sure enough of the wig's long back was draped over his left ear to hide the earpiece. One of the tasks he and Charlie had completed last night was planting a bug in Carl Foster's command center. The receiver was taped to the small of Jack's back; its slim, almost invisible wire ran up to his collar and around the back of his ear.

He'd cabbed over from his place on the Upper West Side and arrived unannounced in the lobby of Madame Pomerol's building half an hour before the high-roller sitting she'd scheduled for this afternoon. He'd found a doorman waiting. Thankfully the building didn't keep one on duty around the clock, or he and Charlie would have had to abort their mission last night. As it was, all they'd had to do was use their copies of the Fosters' keys to unlock the glass front door and stroll in.

This afternoon the doorman, a dark Hispanic named Silvio, had allowed him to call upstairs from the lobby. Jack had told the man who answered—presumably Carl Foster—that he wanted to schedule a private reading in the very near future.

Come right up.

Carl Foster—looking so much better clothed—answered Jack's knock on the door of suite 14-B. He wore all black—black turtleneck jersey, black shoes, black socks—and Jack knew why. His skin appeared reddened around the eyes and mouth—irritated by, say, duct tape adhesive, Carl?—but otherwise he didn't look too much the worse for last night's wear.

Carl Foster's forehead seemed permanently furrowed, perhaps as a result of keeping his eyebrows raised, as if he existed in a state of perpetual surprise. Jack hadn't noticed it last night, but then, Foster had had good reason to be surprised then.

He ushered Jack into a small waiting room furnished with an antique desk and half a dozen upholstered chairs.

The muted colors on the walls and the thick Oriental rug lent an atmosphere of quiet comfort and tasteful opulence. Business appeared to be good for Madame Pomerol.

Foster extended his hand. "Welcome to Madame Pomerol's Temple of Eternal Wisdom. I am Carl Foster. And you are . . . ?"

"Butler," Jack said, adding a hint of the South to his accent as he gave the hand a hearty shake. "Bob Butler. Pleased to meetcha." Jack chewed his gum with an open mouth as he looked around. "Where's the lady?"

"Madame? She's preparing for a reading."

"I wanna talk to her."

"I thought you wanted to schedule a private reading."

"I do, but I'd like to speak to the head honcho first."

"I'm afraid that's quite impossible. Madame Pomerol's time is very valuable. However, you should know that I have her complete trust. I screen all her clients and make her appointments."

Jack had figured that, but he wanted to seem like a rube.

"Screen? Why would I have to be screened? You mean to tell me I might not be good enough for this Madame Pomerol?"

"Oh, no, of course not. It's just that there are certain religious groups and even some atheist groups who do not approve of Madame's work. They've been known to try to waste her time and even disrupt her readings."

"I'd think she'd be able to sniff them out in advance herself. I mean, being a psychic and all."

Foster offered him a wan smile. "The word 'psychic' is so often misused. Madame is a spirit medium."

"There's a difference?

"Of course. So many so-called psychics are charlatans, little better than sideshow performers. Madame has a special gift from God that allows her to speak to the souls of the departed."

"So she can't like, predict the future?"

"At times, yes. But we must remember that any special

knowledge she might have comes from the spirits, and they do not tell her everything."

"Well, I ain't connected with no religious group. No worry there. I'm here because I got some important questions for my uncle. I can't ask him myself—him being dead and all—so I figured I need a psychic type."

This was Jack's cover story. He'd make an appointment for tomorrow but wouldn't keep it.

"What sort of questions?" Foster asked nonchalantly as he moved behind the desk.

There's a good helper, Jack thought. Finding out as much as he can in advance.

He smiled but let an edge creep into his tone. "If I thought you could answer them, I wouldn't need Madame Pomerol, would I?"

Foster forced a good-natured laugh. "No, I suppose not. Who referred you to Madame Pomerol, by the way?"

"Referred? No one. I read about her in the paper this morning. I figured if she was tight enough with the spirits that they're playing tricks on her, then she's the lady for me."

Foster nodded as he pulled a sheet of paper from the desk's top drawer. He indicated the chair on the other side.

"Please have a seat and fill out this questionnaire."

"What for?"

"Just a formality. It's a nuisance, I know, but as I explained, circumstances have forced us into screening our clients." He handed Jack a pen. "Please fill that out completely while I go get the appointment book and see about setting up your private reading."

"By the way," Jack said, "what's a private session cost?"

"Five hundred dollars for a half hour; one thousand for an hour."

Jack parked his gum in his cheek and gave a low whistle. "Pretty damn steep."

"She *is* the best," Foster said.

"I'll be counting on that."

Jack watched Foster leave, then turned his attention to

the form, pretending to study it. He knew he was on camera. The overhead smoke detector housed a wide-angle mini-cam; he'd seen the monitor in one of the back rooms last night. He figured Foster was watching him now, waiting to see if he rifled through any of the desk drawers. But Jack already had been through them and knew they held nothing but pens, paper clips, and questionnaires.

The camera was a good way to check out a potential sitter who was an unknown quantity, but it also came in handy when using the three microphones that had been installed here and there about the room. Sitters tend to yak it up before a group session, allowing an eavesdropping medium to pick up invaluable information; but it wasn't really useful if you didn't know who was talking.

"What's going on out there?" he heard Madame Pomerol say through the tiny speaker in his ear piece. *"Who's the dork?"*

"New fish."

"Well, reel the fucker in, baby. Reel him in."

Yeah, Jack thought. Reel me in.

The questionnaire contained a run of standard intake questions—name, address, phone numbers, and so on—but tucked into the middle was a box for the client's Social Security Number.

Jack suppressed a smile. Yeah, right. He had a collection of SSNs, none of them legitimately his, but he wasn't about to use one of them here. He wondered how many people, in zipping through the form, unthinkingly filled in that blank along with all the others, unaware of the wealth of information, financial and otherwise, it laid open to the medium.

Jack had used the Bob Butler name because he'd once met a Robert Butler who lived in the Millennium Towers, a high-rent high-rise in the West Sixties. He wrote in that address and put down one of his own voice mail numbers for home phone.

Foster returned with the appointment book. Jack watched his eyes as he scanned the almost completed questionnaire, and saw an instant of disappointed narrowing—the blank SSN box, no doubt. But Foster said nothing. Wise. Better not to make an issue of the omission and risk showing too much interest in a client's worldly status.

"Now," Foster said, seating himself behind the desk, "I believe we can squeeze you in for half an hour on Tuesday. Would three o'clock be convenient?"

"How about now?"

"Oh, I'm afraid that's impossible. Madame has a group reading at three."

"Well, why don't I sit in on that?"

"That would not do. These four clients always book readings together. An outsider at the table would upset the spiritual dynamics Madame has worked so hard to establish. Quite impossible, I'm afraid."

This guy loved the word impossible. But Jack had something he was sure he'd like more.

"Oh, I don't want to take part in the session," Jack said, unbuttoning his shirt's left breast pocket. "I just want to watch. Won't say a word. I just want to be a, you know, fly on the wall. And I'm willing to pay for the privilege."

Before Foster could say impossible again, Jack slapped a coin onto the desktop. It landed with a weighty thunk. He saw instant recognition in Foster's eyes and watched his raised eyebrows stretch even further into his forehead when he saw the galloping antelope stamped into its gleaming gold surface. A one-ounce Krugerrand. He didn't have to know the spot price of gold to realize that this newcomer was offering a hefty price to be a mere observer.

"That's gold, Carl. And gold is what my uncle told me is the best way of dealing with the spirit world."

"That's very generous, Mr. Butler," Foster said, licking his lips—the sight of gold did that to some people. "Tell me: Did your uncle have many dealings with the spirit world?"

"All the time. Never met a medium he didn't like, is what my aunt used to say."

"And how about you?"

"Me? This'll be the first time I've been within a mile of a seance."

"Do you have any idea what to expect?"

"My uncle once mentioned seeing ectoplasm and stuff like that, but I was never sure what that was all about."

Foster reached out a finger and touched the coin. "I hope you realize it's a most unusual request."

He'd taken the bait. Now Jack had to set the hook.

"I wouldn't know about that. Way I figure, it's gonna take me a while to work out these issues with my uncle. A half-hour session won't hack it. I'm going to need hours of sessions, a bunch of them. But before I invest that kind of dough, I want to know what I'm getting into. I want a look at what the lady's offering. If I'm convinced she's the real deal, then I'll make an appointment for the next available slot she's got free so we can get to work tracking down my uncle in the Great Hereafter. That sound fair to you, Carl?"

"What I think doesn't matter," Foster said. "It's all up to Madame. I'll go ask her."

As Foster disappeared again, Jack leaned back and listened.

"*You heard?*" he said to his wife.

"*Yeah, I heard. And he wants to pay with gold?*"

"*The real thing. Take a look.*"

"*Lotta money just to sit and watch and get nothing out of it. You think this fucker's on the up and up?*"

"*Well, he's put hard currency where his mouth is. And maybe a Krugerrand's no big deal to him. Maybe he's got a closet full of them.*"

"*All right. Let's do it. But keep him away from the table, in case he's some kinda nut case.*"

"*Will do.*"

When I'm finished, Jack thought, you'll *wish* I'd been a nut case.

Foster returned and told Jack, yes, he could observe the group reading as long as he agreed to remain in his seat and speak not a word. Jack agreed and the Krugerrand went into Carl Foster's pocket.

He cooled his heels awhile till the sitters showed up for the group reading. The four middle-aged women, two blondes—one heavy, one a bulimia poster girl—a brunette, and a redhead arrived as a group, all oozing Prada, Versace, and other overpriced designer wear he didn't recognize. On Jack's visit here last night he'd found dollar signs drawn next to their names in one of the Fosters' notebooks. Not only did these four book regular sessions, but they were very generous with their "love donations."

Their names slipped past him but Jack did his best to be pleasant and charming when introduced to the four. They could queer his whole plan if they objected to his presence. At first they were cool to him—probably put off by his mullet head and odd attire—but once they learned he was a psychic virgin they warmed up, apparently delighted for the chance to make a believer out of him. They gushed about Madame Pomerol's powers, but not one of them mentioned her mishap last night. Apparently they didn't read the *Daily News*.

Soon enough the big moment came and they were ushered into the reading room. Jack hadn't fully appreciated the room last night because he and Charlie had used flashlights. Now that it was fully illuminated, he was struck by the sheer *weight* of the decor. Velvet drapes in heavy folds, thick carpeting, satin-flocked wallpaper—all in various shades of red. Suffocating, like the inside of a coffin.

So this is what it's like to be buried alive.

He watched as Foster seated the four ladies around an ornate round table under a huge chandelier suspended over the center of the room.

Four sitters at five hundred a pop, Jack thought. Beats my hourly rate by a parsec or two.

Foster then indicated a lone chair set against a side wall, maybe a dozen feet from the table, for Jack.

"Remember," he said in a low voice. "You are here to

observe. If you speak or leave your chair you'll disrupt the spirit presences."

Jack knew the only presence he'd disturb would be Carl Foster, slinking around after the lights went out. But he simply nodded and looked serious.

"Gotcha."

Foster exited and a moment later he heard him say, *"Okay, the fish are in the barrel. Get out there and start shooting."*

Finally Madame Pomerol herself appeared, her short, dumpy frame swathed in a flowing, pale blue, gownlike get up, beaded to within an inch of its life; some sort of white turbanlike thing sat on her head. Jack barely recognized her. But then, he hadn't seen her at her best.

Madame greeted the four sitters warmly, smiling and chattering in a French accent that had not been in evidence last night when she was cursing at Carl and their car.

Finally she came over to Jack and extended a ring-laden hand, dangling at the wrist as if awaiting a kiss. Jack rose and gave it a quick shake as unbidden visions of the woman naked and bound with duct tape swam through his head. He shuddered and chased them away.

Clothes make the woman too.

"You are chilled, Monsieur Butler?"

Her ice blue eyes glittered at him. If she had any facial irritation from the duct tape, she'd hidden it with make-up. Her thin, lipsticked lips were curved into a smile.

"No, ma'am. I just never been to one of these things before."

"Nothing to be afraid of, I assure you. You are observing, yes? So just hold your seat and your tongue and I will show you wonders that are, quite simply, *incroyable.*"

Jack smiled and nodded as he reseated himself, knowing nothing she could conjure here would come within light-years of the reality he'd experienced since last summer.

She hit a light switch on her way back to the table. This turned off the spotlights recessed in the ceiling, but the chandelier remained lit.

Madame Pomerol made some introductory remarks, explaining—"for the benefit of our guest"—how she would go into a trance that would release ectoplasm from her body and open a gateway to the Other Side. Her spirit guide, an ancient Mayan priest named Xultulan, would then speak to the living through her.

"One more thing before we proceed," she said in a grave tone. "I know my four dear friends at the table are well aware of this, but I must repeat it for the sake of our newcomer. Should ectoplasm manifest itself, please, please, *please* do not touch it. It exudes from my body and soul, and contact with anyone else will cause it to flee back into my body. The sudden return of so much ectoplasm can harm a medium. Some of us have actually been killed by recoiling ectoplasm that was touched by heedless clients. So remember: gaze upon it in wonder, but do not touch."

Jack tuned her out. The rap was standard stuff; only the names changed from medium to medium. He was waiting for the lights to go out and the show to begin. That was when he'd make his move.

Finally the four sitters and the medium had laid their hands flat on the table. The clear bulbs on the low-hanging chandelier faded, but the few dim red ones among them remained lit. Darkness swallowed the rest of the room, but the table and its occupants were bathed in a faint red glow.

Madame Pomerol began a tuneless hum, then let her head loll. Soon the table began to tip to the accompaniment of giggles and gasps of wonder from the sitters. Their chairs, however, stayed flat on the floor. Charlie had given his brother's operation a leg up, so to speak, over Madame's.

And then the lady let loose a long, low moan that echoed throughout the room. Jack realized then that she had a wireless microphone hidden on her—in that turban thing, he'd bet—and her husband had just turned it on. Impressive reverb effect. No doubt she had an earpiece just like Jack's so Carl could cue her when a sitter asked a tough question.

Another moan, and then something happened. Jack heard

one of the sitters gasp as a pale glow appeared atop Madame Pomerol's head.

Hello, Mr. Ectoplasm, Jack thought.

The glow expanded to a rough circle behind her, framing her head like a halo. It hovered there a moment, then began to flow upward, streaming from her head in a ghostly plume, six, eight, ten feet into the air, and then it pulled free of the medium and began to undulate back and forth above her.

"Xultulan, hear my call," Madame Pomerol intoned, her voice echoing again. "Lend us your otherworldly wisdom as you lead us to the souls of the departed. I have with me four seekers after the dear departed . . ."

Yeah-yeah-yeah, Jack thought, reaching inside his shirt. No sense in waiting any longer. Besides, her phony accent was wearing on him.

He found the lipstick-size remote stashed inside his belly padding and located the business end. He fixed a shocked expression on his face, then pressed the button with his thumb.

The overhead spotlights blazed to life to reveal a shocking tableau.

The four sitters and Madame Pomerol sat in their places, but behind the medium stood a man dressed from head to toe in black—his turtleneck and slacks were remarkably similar to Carl Foster's, but he'd added black gloves and a black ski mask with narrow slits for eyeholes. He held two long black manipulating rods from which a billowy length of chiffon dangled. The sudden illumination revealed him swinging it in undulating arcs through the air above his wife. A scream from one of the women—she apparently thought the room had been invaded by some weird terrorist—froze him in mid-wave.

Jack caught a brief, sudden glare from Madame Pomerol as her eyes bored into his, and was glad he'd prepared his expression beforehand.

Suddenly she laughed. "You should see your expressions!" Another laugh. "Carl, our little demonstration really took them by surprise!" She began to applaud. *"Magnifique! Magnifique!"*

"I . . . I don't understand," one of the blondes said.

Madame Pomerol looked over her shoulder and laughed again. "Take off that mask, Carl, and put down those silly sticks."

"I demand an explanation," said the redhead.

"And you shall have one, Rose," Madame said, fully composed now. "If you read the papers, I'm sure you know that fake spirit mediums are popping up all the time, making fantastic claims to prey on the needs of gullible believers, trying to entice them away from those, such as myself, with the true gift. Carl and I arranged this little show to demonstrate how easily one can be fooled. I control all the lights here, of course, and when I deemed the time ripe, I turned them on so that you might witness charlatanry and fakery *in media res.*"

Whoa! The lady throws in a little Latin.

Jack wished he had a way to work the remote again. Nothing he'd love more now than to start turning the lights off and on while she was spinning out her line of crap. But he couldn't allow himself to be seen reaching into his shirt.

It was such a weak line, though, straining toward the breaking point under the transparent weight of its own bullshit, that he didn't see any need to help it along. He had to strain to keep from laughing out loud.

Had to hand it to the lady, she was glib. Delivered her lines with utter conviction. But any minute now these four sitters would begin to scatter, fleeing this Temple of Eternal Wisdom to tell all their rich friends and everyone else they knew that Madame Pomerol was a class-A fake. Word would spread like a virus. If she was bent out of shape before about losing a few suckers, just wait till these four got through talking. She'll qualify as a *Cirque du Soleil* contortionist.

"Really?" said the other blonde. "You staged this all for us?"

"Of course, Elaine." She pointed to Jack. "And that was

why I broke with my usual procedure and allowed a newcomer to observe a reading. I wanted Mr. Butler to witness firsthand the cheap tricks of the conscienceless swindlers who sully the reputations of all the truly gifted spirit mediums."

As the sitters stared at Jack he saw something in their eyes, something he didn't want to see.

No. This can't be. They're buying into her lame-o story. I don't believe this. How can they be so gullible?

An unmasked Carl approached the table with the material he'd been waving in the air.

"See?" he said, grinning as he held it out for the ladies to feel. "Nothing more than cheap chiffon."

"But it looked so real," the brunette said. "Exactly like when ectoplasm comes out of Madame during—"

Madame Pomerol cleared her throat and rose to her feet. "I think it is time for a little break. Please wait in the outer room while Carl removes these tools of chicanery. In a few minutes we will reconvene and make true contact with the Other Side."

Jack followed the women into the waiting room. As soon as the door closed behind them, he heard Madame Pomerol say, *"What the fuck just happened?"*

"I wish I knew," her husband replied. *"I can't imagine how—"*

"Fuck imagine! Find out! I want the real story, not your fucking imagination! The electronics of this operation are your responsibility and obviously you fucked up!"

"I didn't fuck up! I haven't changed anything!"

"Well, something's changed. Find out what!"

"I'm going to check that switch."

"Shit! I've never been so embarrassed in my whole fucking life!"

"But you handled it beautifully."

"Yeah, I did, didn't I. And those four bimbos swallowed it. Do you believe that? Sometimes I'm ashamed of the caliber of people we have to deal with. I mean, how fucking stupid can you get?"

Jack wished he had the ability to play this conversation through a speaker in the waiting room. If only he'd thought of that. He'd heard Madame Pomerol's salty tongue last night and should have seen this as a golden opportunity to let her clients know what she really thought of them.

The Fosters lapsed into silence while Jack wondered how to play Madame Pomerol's sitters. He decided to listen first. Maybe he could find a way to salvage the day. He sidled up to the redhead whose name he remembered was Rose.

"Well," he asked in a low voice, remembering the hidden mikes, "what do you make of this?"

"I think it's stunning," she said. "What courage!"

"I feel so honored," said the dumpy blonde. "To think, she chose us—us!—for this demonstration! I can't wait to get into my psychic chat room and tell everyone how wonderful she is!"

The will to believe, Jack thought, fighting a wave of leaden chagrin. Never underestimate the will to believe.

And that was just what he'd done.

He remembered an experiment James Randi once ran on psychics and their marks. He set up a pair of sitters with a psychic, and after the reading they emerged very impressed with how the psychic had been able to see right into their minds. When Randi showed them a videotape of the session and pointed out that the psychic averaged fourteen or fifteen erroneous statements for every correct one, the sitters were unfazed. Even with the evidence of a poorly done cold reading staring them in the face, they remained impressed by the handful of correct guesses and disregarded all the wrong ones.

The will to believe . . .

Jack saw two options. He could show the women his remote and tell them he'd rigged the lights to expose Madame Pomerol as a fake. But he doubted very much that he'd sway them.

The will to believe . . .

The other was to play it cool and return for another go at the Fosters.

He decided on number two.

"*Shit!*" Jack heard Foster say. "*Look what I found in the light box!*"

"*What's that?*"

"*A remote control on-off switch!*"

"*Fuck me! You've gotta be kidding!*"

"*Believe me, I know these switches.*"

"*You think it's that new guy?*"

"*Could be, but how would he have got in here to install the switch? And don't forget, he paid us in gold.*"

"*Gotta be those niggers then! Fuck!*" She then began stringing together innovative combinations of every four-, ten-, and twelve-letter expletive known to humankind.

"*You think so?*" Foster said when she ran out of breath.

"*Fuck, yes! They're the ones who tied us up last night and—*"

"*That was a white guy.*"

"*Did you see him!*"

"*No, but—*"

"*Then what the fuck do you know?*"

"*It was a white guy's voice.*"

"*It was them, I'm telling you! They must've taken our keys and come here and fucked us up. Who knows what else they've done! They're gonna pay for this. Oh, are they gonna fucking pay!*"

This wasn't going the way Jack wanted. The whole idea of coming here had been to distract them from the Kentons.

"*All right,*" Foster said. "*Let's just say it was them. After what happened, do you really want to risk going back to Astoria? Our car's impounded, all our credit cards are gone, not to mention the humiliation of having to walk around Lower Manhattan dressed in cardboard.*"

"*They're gonna pay! Maybe not this week, and maybe not next, but first chance we get, we're gonna fuck those niggers over good!*"

Conversation between the two Fosters stopped, and Jack assumed that the Mrs. had stomped off while Carl reassembled the light switch.

Jack and the four women hung out for another ten minutes or so, then Foster reappeared to welcome them back into the reading room.

Jack hung back.

"Is something wrong, Mr. Butler?"

"Yeah. I think I've seen enough."

"I hope there's no misunderstanding here. You see—"

Foster thought Jack was bailing out. He cut him off to put him straight.

"I think that was real gutsy of her to pull that stunt. That shows me she's got real confidence in her powers. I'm totally impressed."

Foster switched gears like a Formula One driver. "Well, I took you from the start as a man of intelligence and discrimination."

"So when's the soonest I can book my own private session with the lady? You told me you had half an hour open Tuesday afternoon. Nothing at all tomorrow?"

Foster pulled the appointment book from the desk drawer and thumbed through the pages. He frowned.

"I'm afraid not. Tuesday is the soonest. Is three o'clock good for you?"

This lady was doing gold-rush business.

"I guess it'll hafta be. I'd really prefer an hour but, maybe a half-hour session for starters is best. You know, to see if she can make the right contact."

"Oh, she can, I assure you."

"Okay, see you then."

Jack let himself out and made for the elevator. Once inside and headed down, he slammed a hand against the wall of the car. Damn. He'd read this one all wrong. He saw what his mistake had been: He'd tried to strike at the Fosters indirectly, through their clientele. Wrong angle. He knew now he'd have to take the battle directly to them.

He had a half-formed plan of how to do that. He'd need the Kenton brothers' help to fill in the rest. He just hoped Madame Pomerol wouldn't be able to wriggle free next time.

6

Jack stood outside the screen door and watched Lyle's cautious approach.

"Can I help you?"

"Lyle, it's me. Jack."

Lyle stepped closer, his expression saying, Who is this fool kidding? Then he grinned.

"Well, I'll be damned. It *is* you. Come on in."

Jack stepped inside. "Didn't have time to change my clothes." He started to peel off his wig. "Man, this thing is hot."

"And beat ugly too."

He turned to see Charlie popping in through the front door behind him.

"So you're back," Lyle said to his brother. He glanced at his watch, thinking. "Finished your good works for the day?"

Good works? Had he been to church?

"Yowzah." Charlie turned to Jack. "Yo, G. How'd it go down?"

He hated reporting less than complete success, but they had a right to know.

"Well, the good news is the remote light switch worked perfectly . . ."

They all had a good laugh as he described exposing Carl in the act of waving fake ectoplasm through the air, then . . .

"But the rest didn't pan out. The lady cooked up some lame story about setting all this up in advance to demonstrate how other fake mediums will try to fool them."

"And they bought it?" Lyle said.

Jack nodded. "She's pretty glib."

"Aw, maaaan," Charlie said.

Lyle's voice took on a bitter edge. "So last night was all for nothing then?"

"Not quite. I've got an afternoon appointment Tuesday, and there's a lot I need to do between now and then if I'm going to bring them down."

"More electronics?" Charlie said, his eyes lighting.

"Not this time. This is going to be all manual—sleight of hand stuff. But I need your help with the setup. Do you subscribe to the Blue Directory?"

Lyle's expression was blank. "Blue . . . ?"

"The medium I worked for used to subscribe to a book that had all sorts of information on hundreds of sitters."

"Oh, right. I saw a copy years ago, but I don't get it. We use a website—"

Should have figured, Jack thought. It was the computer age.

"You mean the directory's online now?"

"What we use isn't run by the Blue Directory people, but it's the same sort of thing. All you do is pay an annual fee for a password and—"

"Let's check it out," Jack said. "I need to find a dead guy to fit a certain profile."

Lyle looked at his brother. "Charlie's the computer guy. Want to take care of this?"

"Sure." He started toward the kitchen. "This way, my man."

Lyle grabbed his arm. "Use the one in the command center."

"But this one's closer."

"We've got a little problem in there."

Charlie gave him a look. "The TV's still . . . ?"

Lyle nodded. "Simpler if we all just head for the Channeling Room."

Jack felt as if he were missing every other word. "What's wrong?"

"Electrical problems in the TV room," Lyle said. "That's all."

Jack was sure that wasn't all, but obviously they wanted to keep it between themselves.

Charlie led the way to his command center off the Channeling Room. Jack knew this was where he controlled the sound, the lighting, and all the mechanical effects during the sittings. The computer's monitor was just one of many screens among the wires, the key cutter, the cameras, the scanner, the photocopier, and mysterious black boxes racked around the room. The swimming fish of the screen saver showed that the computer was already up and running.

Charlie seated himself before it and tapped the keyboard. Half a minute later the screen filled with the welcome page of a website with the innocuous name of www.sitters-net.com. The page contained boxes for user name and password set against wallpaper of a blue sky with fluffy white clouds.

"Kind of obvious, isn't it," Jack said.

Lyle shrugged. "Probably gets hits from baby-sitters now and again, but 'sitter' is pretty much an inside term."

Jack knew the practice of listing the vital stats of sitters went back half a century at least. It started with mediums keeping private data on card files; then they started sharing cards with other mediums. Finally someone began collecting stats from all over the country and publishing them in a blue-covered directory sold only to mediums. His old boss, Madame Ouskaya, had been a subscriber. The Internet was the inevitable next step.

Charlie hit some keys and "d-town" appeared after USER ID, followed by a string of asterisks in the PASSWORD box. He hit ENTER and a few seconds later a search page appeared.

Jack said, "I remember the old Blue Directory used to hang onto the names of sitters even after they were dead— just in case some relative decided later to try and contact them."

"This one does the same thing."

Charlie clicked the mouse pointer on an icon near the

top of the screen. "This take us to the O-S section."

"O-S?"

"Other Side."

"Got it." Jack rested a hand on Charlie's shoulder. "Okay, do a search for 'coin collector' and see what comes up."

" 'Coin collect' might get us more hits, yo."

He typed in "coin+collect." A few seconds later a list of half a dozen names appeared.

Only half a dozen? Jack was disappointed. He leaned closer to the screen searching for dates.

"I need a guy who's died in the past year or so."

"Ay, yo, trip this," Charlie said, tapping a finger on the screen over the fourth name down. "Matthew Thomas West. Died January twenty-seventh."

Jack looked and saw the typical documentation: name, address, date of birth—and, in this case, date of "crossing over"—along with Social Security number, the names of his wife—deceased sixteen years before him—and his brother and parents, even his dog, but no kids. Plus a list of his interests. Matthew West's big passion, besides his wife, with whom he'd been communicating through mediums for many years, was rare coins.

This guy looked perfect except for the address. Minnesota . . .

He shook his head. "I was hoping for something closer. Let's check out the others." He stared at the screen awhile, then shook his head again. "Nope. Looks like I'll have to make do with Uncle Matt from St. Paul."

"*Uncle* Matt?" Lyle said.

"I talked up a fictional uncle to Foster that I wanted Pomerol to contact for me. Fortunately I never gave his name. Well, now we have a name. Uncle Matt the Minnesotan. Can you print him out for me?"

"Done deal," Charlie said. "But what you got going?"

"A sting. If things go right, I hope to tempt Madame Pomerol into pulling the old Spanish handkerchief switch on me."

Charlie frowned. "Spanish handkerchief? Whuddat?"

"An old Gypsy con," Lyle said. "And I do mean *old*. Probably been running a couple hundred years now, and grifters are still working updated versions on the street." He looked at Jack. "But how's that—?"

"Once she sets up the switch on me, I'm going to work a double switch right back at her—one with a nasty barb at the end."

"Okay, but I still don't see what that's gonna do for us— me and Charlie."

Jack held his hands high like a preacher. "Have faith, my sons, have faith. I can't tell you all the details because I haven't figured them out yet. But trust me, if this works, it will be a sting of beauty."

Charlie handed Jack the printout. "You a natural at this. Why ain't you still in?"

Jack hesitated. "You really want to know?"

"Yeah."

You're not going to like this, he thought.

"I got out because I found it an empty enterprise. I wanted to be doing something where I gave value for value."

"We give value," Lyle said, a bit too quickly.

Charlie shook his head. "No we don't, bro. You know we don't."

Lyle appeared to be at a loss for words, a new experience for him, perhaps.

Finally he shrugged and said, "I could use a beer. Anyone else?"

Jack had a sense this was mere courtesy—did Lyle want him to leave?—but took him up on it anyway. A beer would be good right now, and maybe he could find out why he was so on edge.

Instead of drinking in the kitchen as they had last night, Lyle sat him down in the waiting room. And like last night, Charlie had a Pepsi.

"So," Jack said after they'd popped their tops and toasted

the coming downfall of Madame Pomerol, "what kind of electrical problem you having?"

Lyle shrugged it off. "Nothing serious."

"Yeah right," Charlie said. "Like a haunted TV ain't serious."

Lyle glared at his brother. "No such thing as haunted *anything*, bro."

"Then what—?"

Lyle held up a hand. "We'll talk about it later."

Haunted TV? Sounded interesting. Then again, maybe not if that meant it played nothing but "Casper the Friendly Ghost" cartoons.

"Anything I can do?"

"I'll straighten it out," Lyle said, but he didn't look convincing.

"Sure?"

"If I may quote: 'Philosophy will clip an angel's wings, Conquer all mysteries by rule and line, Empty the haunted air, the gnomed mine.' "

"The gnomed mine . . . gnomed with a *G*?"

Lyle nodded. "With a *G*."

"I like that."

"It's Keats."

"You're quoting Keats?" Jack laughed. "Lyle, you've got to be the whitest black guy I've ever met."

Jack had expected a laugh, but Lyle's expression darkened instead.

"What? You mean I'm not a real black man because I know Keats? Because I'm well spoken? Only white men are well spoken? Only white men quote Keats? Real black men only quote Ice-T, is that it? I'm not a real black man because I don't dress like a pimp and drive with a gangsta lean, or drape myself in dukey ropes and sit on my front porch swiggin' forties?"

"Hey, easy. I was just—"

"I know what you were just, Jack. You were just acting like somebody who's got this MTV image of what's black, and if a guy doesn't fit that he's some kind of oreo. You're not alone. Plenty of black guys look at me that way too. Even my own brother. Better get over it—you and him and them. It's a white man's world, but just because I'm making it in that world doesn't mean I'm trying to become white. I may not have a degree, but I've audited enough courses to qualify for one. I'm educated. Just because I didn't major in Black Studies doesn't make me a whitey wannabe; and just because I refuse to let the lowest black common denominators define me doesn't make me an Uncle Tom."

"Whoa!" Jack held up his hands. He felt as if he'd stepped on a mine. "Sorry. Wasn't looking to offend."

Lyle closed his eyes and took a breath. When he let it out he looked at Jack. "I know you weren't. You didn't deserve that. I apologize."

"I'm sorry. You're sorry." Jack rose and extended his hand. "I guess that makes us even then?"

"Even." Lyle's smile was tinged with embarrassment as they shook. "See you tomorrow. I'll have the first half of your fee ready."

Jack tossed off the rest of his beer and headed out, making a mental note: Lyle Kenton = short fuse.

7

As soon as Jack was out the door Lyle grabbed Charlie's arm and dragged him toward the TV room.

"You've got to see this."

Charlie snatched his arm free. "Yo, what up with you, bro? Whatchu go and gaffle Jack like that for?"

Lyle felt bad about that. Jack had said white and he'd seen red.

"I'm a little on edge, okay? A lot on edge. I apologized, didn't I?"

"You mad at him for what he say 'bout value for value?"

"No. Of course not."

Not mad . . . but it had stung. Maybe that was why he'd gone off about the "whitest black guy" remark.

Lyle didn't kid himself. He was a flimflam man, but he wasn't a cad. He didn't go after people who couldn't afford it—no poor widows and the like. His fish were bored heiresses, nouveau riche artists, yuppies looking for a New-Age thrill, and dowagers seeking to contact their dead poodles in the great boneyard of the Afterlife. They'd probably spend the money on a trip to Vegas or another fur coat or a diamond or the latest status toy—like so many of his clients who never eat at home but simply *must* have a Sub-Zero refrigerator in their kitchen.

"And why keep this licked TV a CIA secret?"

"Our business. Not his."

More than that, he didn't want to distract Jack with any of their side problems. Keep him focused on getting Madame Pomerol out of their lives, that was the most important thing.

"Take a look."

He led Charlie to the entryway of the room and stopped. He let him see the basketball game that was running on the set.

"Yo, it stopped playing the Cartoon Network. What you do?"

"Nothing. It switched on its own." He watched his brother's face. "Okay. You spotted that. What else do you see?"

His gaze lowered to the floor. "All kinda circuit boards and junk." He glanced at Lyle. "You been messin' with my stuff?"

Lyle shook his head. "That's all from inside the set."

"Inside?"

"Uh-huh. I took it apart after you left. Damn near cleaned out the box. Practically nothing but the tube left in there, but it keeps on running. Still unplugged, by the way."

He saw Charlie's Adam's apple bob as he swallowed. "You messin' wit' me now, ain't you."

"Wish I were."

Lyle had had most of the day to adjust to the craziness of their TV, but watching it still gave him a crawly sensation in his gut.

"Hey," Charlie said slowly, staring at the screen. "Who that playing?" He stepped closer. "That look like . . . it is—Magic Johnson with the Lakers."

"You finally noticed."

"What you got on—Sports Classics?"

Lyle handed him the remote. "Flip around the channels. See what you get."

Charlie did just that, and wound up on CNN where a couple of talking heads were discussing Irangate.

"Irangate? Whuzzat?"

"Something that happened when you were too young to care." Lyle barely remembered it himself. "Keep surfing."

Next stop was a close-up of a big-haired blonde crying so hard her make-up was running down her cheeks.

Charlie's eyes widened. "Ain't that . . . ? What's her name?"

"Tammy Faye Baker," Lyle said. He'd known what to expect, but even so, his mouth was growing drier by the minute. "Keep going."

Then came a football game. "Hey, the Giants. But that look like snow on the sidelines."

"It is," Lyle said. "And check out the quarterback."

"Simms? Simms ain't played for . . ."

"A long time. Keep going."

He picked up speed, flashing through a news show where the Bork nomination was being discussed, then to a review of *Rain Man*, a Dukakis-for-President ad, and then two dreadlocked guys prancing around on MTV.

"Milli Vanilli?" Charlie cried. "Milli *Vanilli*? This is like *Trek*, man. We in some kinda timewarp or somethin'?"

"No, but the TV seems to be. Everything showing on that tube comes from the late eighties."

Lyle stood with his brother and watched Milli Vanilli swing their plaits and lip-synch "Girl, You Know It's True," but he heard next to nothing. His mind was too busy rooting through everything he had learned or experienced in his thirty years to find an explanation.

Finally Charlie said, "Now do you believe me? We haunted."

Lyle refused to board that train. Had to quell this queasy, uneasy buzz in his gut and stay calm, stay rational.

"No. Crazy as all this seems, there's got to be a rational explanation."

"Will you give it up! You always laughing at the sitters who believe any fool thing we throw at them. You call them compulsive believers, but you just like them."

"Don't talk like a fool."

"It's true. Listen yo'self! You a compulsive *non*believer! if it don't fit with how you want things, you deny it, even when it smacks you upside the head!"

"I don't deny that this TV is running without power or cable and showing stuff from the eighties. I'm just not jumping right off the bat to some supernatural explanation, is all."

"Then why don't we haul it to some scientists and have them look at it and see what they can come up with?"

Some scientists . . . what did that mean? Where do you find "scientists"?

"I'll look into it in the morning."

"You do that," Charlie said. "I don't wanna squab. I'm steppin' off. Gonna do some reading."

"On ghosts?"

"No. The Good Book."

As Lyle watched Charlie head for the upstairs, he almost wished he had something like that to comfort him.

But all he had was an impossible TV.

8

Jack made good time driving downtown. He wanted the car along in case Bellitto took off in a cab. He found Eli Bellitto's antique store in the western reaches of SoHo. His Shurio Coppe occupied the ground floor corner of an old triple-decker ironclad that had seen better days. A couple of the cast-iron columns on the facade looked as if they were coming loose from the underlying bricks. Odd to see an ironclad here; most of them were further east.

Still in his Bob Butler outfit and mullet wig, Jack wandered up to the store's main front window. Under the elaborate gold-leaf script of "Shurio Coppe" was the phrase, "Curious Items for the Serious Collector." Holding center court in this window was a large stuffed fish, a four-foot sturgeon with hooded brown eyes, suspended on two slim wires so that it looked as if it were floating in midair. The thick down of dust on its scales said that it had been swimming in that window for a good long time.

Jack moved on to the front door and checked the hours card. Eli's brother had been right. Sunday hours were noon to six. Jack checked his watch. Five-thirty now. Why not kill the remaining half hour till closing by browsing the shop? Might find something interesting.

He stepped up to the front door and pushed it open. A bell jangled. A man in the aisle directly ahead looked up.

Here was the brother himself. Jack recognized him from the photo Edward had given him: Eli Bellitto. At six feet he looked sturdier in person, and the photo had missed his cold dark eyes. He wore a perfectly tailored three-piece charcoal gray business suit with a white shirt and a striped tie. With his sallow skin, high cheekbones, dark brown

hair—dyed?—and receding hairline he reminded Jack of
Angus Scrimm. Sure as hell looked nothing like his brother.
Edward had said they had different mothers, but Jack wondered if they might have different fathers as well. Maybe
somebody's mother had fooled around with the local peat
cutter, or whoever straying Dublin wives might have fooled
around with sixty years ago.

"Good evening," Eli Bellitto said. "Can I help you?"

His voice surprised Jack. A trace of an accent, but not
Irish. He remembered that Edward had said they were
raised apart. Maybe in different countries?

"Just browsing," Jack said.

"Go right ahead. But please be aware we close promptly
at six and—" As if on cue, a number of clocks began to
chime. The man pulled a pocket watch from a vest pocket
and popped open the cover. He glanced at it and gave Jack
a thin-lipped smile. "Exactly half an hour from now."

"I'll watch the clocks," Jack said.

On the other side of the store he saw a heavyset older
woman with a loud voice and a tragic resemblance to Richard Belzer giving instructions to a younger red-haired man
as she guided him through the store, pointing out price tags.

New help, Jack guessed.

He turned away and meandered among books, plaques,
mirrors, dressers, desks, lamps, vases, sculptures of stone
and wood, ceramic bowls, china cups, stuffed birds, fish,
and animals, clocks of all shapes and vintages, and more,
curios ranging from the splendid to the squalid, from Old
World to New, Far East to Near, patrician to plebeian, ancient to merely old, exorbitant to bargain priced, Ming Dy-
nasty to Depression Era.

He fell in love with the place. How long had this store
been here and why hadn't anyone told him about it? Hundreds of square feet crammed with a vast and eclectic array
of truly neat stuff.

He wandered the aisles, opening book covers, angling
mirrors, running his fingers over intricately carved surfaces.
He stopped in a corner as he came upon an antique oak

display case, oval, maybe five feet high, with beveled glass
on all sides. The case itself carried no price tag, and the
items within were untagged as well. These were of much
more recent vintage than the rest of the stock and seemed
jarringly out of place. Arrayed on the three glass shelves
within were what might best be described as trinkets, knickknacks, baubles, and gewgaws, none of which were more
than ten or fifteen years old and could have been picked up
at any garage sale.

He looked closer and saw a stack of Pog disks, a Rubik's
cube, a Koosh ball with purple and green spikes, a bearish
looking Beanie Baby, a red Matchbox Corvette, a gray Fur-
bie with pink ears, a red-sneakered Sonic the Hedgehog
doll, a tiny Bart Simpson balancing on an even tinier skate-
board, and a few other less identifiable tchotchkes.

But the item that grabbed Jack's attention was a Roger
Rabbit key ring. For an instant, as his eyes drifted past it,
he thought he saw it shimmer. Nothing obvious, just the
slightest waver along its edges. As he snapped to it, he saw
nothing unusual. Probably just a defect in the window. Old
glass was like that, full of ripples and other defects.

He stared more closely at the little plastic figure and noticed that some of the red had rubbed off its overalls, and
off the yellow gloves at the ends of his outstretched arms.
But what struck him and grabbed him was the intense pale
blue of Roger's eyes. Supine in his somewhat cruciform
pose, he seemed to be staring at Jack, imploringly. Real
pathos there, which was way out of character since Roger
was pretty much a moron.

The little key ring made him think of Vicky, who'd taken
to the *Roger Rabbit* video lately. Watched it a minimum of
three times a week and could do a fair mimic of Roger's
saliva-laden, "Pppppleeeeease, Eddie!" Vicky would love
this key ring.

Jack looked for the knob on the door and found instead
a sturdy padlock. Odd. Every other piece in the store, no
matter how small, had to be more valuable than all of these
put together. Why the lock?

"We're getting ready to close now," said a voice behind him.

Jack turned to face the proprietor himself. The older man's expression was neutral.

"So soon?"

"Six o'clock is closing time today," Bellitto said. "Is there anything I can help you with before we lock the door?"

"Yes," Jack said, turning back to the display case. "I'm interested in one of these doo-dads."

"I can't imagine why. They are beyond question the least interesting items in the shop. Remnants of recent fads. Detritus of pop culture."

"Exactly why I want one."

"Which, may I ask?"

"The Roger Rabbit key ring."

"Oh, yes." His thin lips curved into a small, tight smile. "That one's special. Very special."

"Not so special. I'm sure half a zillion were sold, but no one's making them any more, and I know someone who'd really—"

"I'm so very sorry. It's not for sale."

"You're kidding."

"I assure you that I do not . . . kid."

"Then why put them on display?"

The anemic smile returned. "Because it pleases me."

"Oh, I get it. Kind of like a joke. Lock up the junk and leave the valuables lying around. You didn't strike me a postmodern dude."

"I should hope not. Let's just say that these tiny treasures carry a certain sentimental value for me and I like to leave them out where people can see them."

"Does the sentimental value of that Roger Rabbit Key ring exceed ten bucks?"

"I'm afraid it does."

"How about fifteen?"

He shook his head. "No."

"Twenty-five, then?"

"No."

"Fifty?"

"Sorry."

"A hundred?"

A head shake. Bellitto's smile had broadened. He was enjoying himself.

This was crazy. The guy couldn't mean it. Turn down a hundred bucks for that little piece of junk?

Jack took a quick look at Bellitto's ears. Nope, no hearing aids.

Okay, time to call his bluff.

"How about five hundred?"

Another head shake.

Smug son of a bitch, Jack thought. How can he say no? All right, one more try. This one *has* to get him.

"Mister, I will give you one thousand dollars—are you listening?—*one thousand* US dollars for that key ring. And that's my final offer. Take it or leave it."

"I prefer to leave it, thank you."

Jack's shock was tinged with relief. He'd allowed himself to get carried away here. A thousand bucks for a worthless little tchotchke like that? Who was crazier here?

He looked back at Roger Rabbit, whose eyes still held that imploring look.

"Sorry, guy. Maybe next time."

"No next time," Bellitto said. "When I said, 'Not for sale,' it was not a sales ploy. I meant it."

"I guess you did. Still, can't blame a guy for trying."

He glanced at his watch. "Past closing time, I'm afraid."

Jack said, "Yeah," and started for the door.

"Tell me, Mr. . . . ?"

"Butler," Jack said.

"Tell me, Mr. Butler. Would you really have paid me a thousand dollars for that key ring?"

"That's what I offered."

"Talk is cheap, Mr. Butler."

"So it is. And this is just more talk. So I guess we'll never really know, will we."

Jack gave him a wave and stepped through the door into the twilight.

Eli Bellitto . . . the man seemed a model of cool control. Jack sensed no seething cauldron of violence readying to erupt. Sensed no passion at all, in fact. Admittedly it had been a brief meeting, and in his experience he'd found that people were rarely what they seemed, but Eli Bellitto seemed a long way from a new-moon lunatic.

He hoped he was right. He'd play watchdog for three nights and that would be that.

He made a show of casual window shopping, doing a slow sidestep to the end of the building, then crossing the street to a furniture store, already closed. At six sharp Jack saw the redheaded trainee clerk step out and head up toward Houston, followed by the older woman. With a clattering chorus, metal shutters began unrolling from their cylindrical bins over the windows. Bellitto came out a moment later and locked them down. Then he rolled down a similar shutter over the door by hand. After that was locked, he strolled right, turning the corner and moving a dozen paces down the side street to where he entered a doorway.

Home sweet home, Jack thought. Now be a good boy, Eli Bellitto, and stay in for the night. Catch up on all those *Sopranos* episodes you missed during the season.

He crossed back over to Bellitto's side, to check the street number, and he heard something crunch beneath his feet. He looked down and found a scatter of broken glass, some pieces frosted, some clear. As he moved on he glanced up and found the source: the lens of the street light had come loose and fallen. No . . . the bulb was missing, or broken off. He thought he could make out a couple of deep dings in the metal casing. Yeah. No question. Someone had shot out the street light. With a pellet gun, most likely.

Jack looked around. Didn't like this. The dead light would leave Bellitto's end of the street in darkness. Who'd done it? Bellitto himself? Or someone out to get him?

Jack continued to move down the block until he came to a small bistro across the street. A few couples sat around the white resin tables on the sidewalk. Jack positioned himself at one that gave him a view of Bellitto's door, and ordered a Corona, no lime. He'd nurse a few, eventually have dinner, killing the hours till darkness. Then he'd find a shadowed spot with a view of the doorway—not too hard with the street light out—and camp there till midnight.

Jack kicked himself for taking this nothing job. Instead of sitting alone at this rickety table, he could be hanging at Gia's, having a drink with her and playing sous chef as she fixed dinner.

But Edward had been so frightened that his brother might hurt somebody, and Jack had responded to that. Still, he could have let this one go by. He'd promised Gia he'd stay away from the rough jobs. At worst, this one might involve a little roll and tumble, but he didn't think he'd have too much trouble controlling Eli Bellitto.

He wished all his fix-its were like the Kentons'. He was looking forward to Tuesday's encounter with Madame Pomerol. That had all the makings of a fun fix.

IN THE IN-BETWEEN

She realizes she is female, but nothing beyond that. She knows she once had a name but she can't remember it.

She also knows that she did not live in this place, this old cold house. She had a warm home somewhere but cannot remember where it lies. And even if she did, she could not go there.

She cannot leave. She has tried, but she is tied to this awful house. She wishes she knew why. It might explain this terrible sourceless rage that envelops her.

If only she could remember her name!

She is lonely, but not alone. There are others in this place. She has reached out but cannot make contact. Yet she keeps trying . . .

IN THE WEE HOURS

Lyle awoke to the sound of running water. His room was dark, the windows open to the night, and somewhere . . .

The shower.

"Now what?" he muttered as he pulled the sheet aside and hung his legs over the edge of the bed.

He blinked and brought the display of his clock radio into focus: *1:21*. He stared dully at the red LED digits. He felt drugged. He'd been way down in deep, deep sleep and his brain and body were still fumbling back to alertness. As he watched the display, the last digit changed to a zero.

1:20?

But just a few seconds ago it had been . . . or at least he'd thought it had been . . .

Never mind. The shower was running. He jumped off the bed and hurried to the adjoining bathroom.

Lyle felt the steam before he saw it. He fumbled along the wall, found the light switch, and flipped it on. Billows of moisture filled the bathroom, so thick he could barely find his way. He made it to the shower and reached out toward the curtain . . .

And hesitated. Something told him not to pull it open. Maybe one of those premonitions he didn't believe in, maybe the result of seeing too many horror movies, but he sensed something besides running water behind the curtain.

Feeling suddenly cold despite the enveloping hot mist, Lyle backed away, one step . . . two . . .

No. He wasn't giving in to this. With a strangled cry that anticipated the terror of what he might see, Lyle leaped forward and slashed the curtain aside.

He stood there in the steam, gasping, heart pounding,

staring at a shower running full blast at max heat. But the spray wasn't running straight into the tub. It was bouncing against something . . . something that wasn't there and yet was. And after the spray struck whatever it was, the water turned red and ran down into the tub to swirled away into the drain.

Lyle closed his eyes, shook his head, then looked again.

The shower continued to run and billow up steam, but the spray now flowed uninterrupted into the tub, and remained clear all the way down to the drain.

What's happening to me? he thought as he reached in and turned the knob.

And then he sensed someone behind him in the steam.

"Wha—?"

He spun and found no one. But movement to his left caught Lyle's eye. Something on the big mirror over the sink . . . dripping lines forming on the moisture-laden glass . . . connecting into letters . . . then . . .

Words.

Who are you?

Lyle could only stare, could only think that this wasn't happening, he was dreaming again, and pretty soon—

Three more question marks, each bigger than the last, added themselves to the end of the question.

Who are you? ? ? ?

"I . . . I'm Lyle," he croaked, thinking, It's a dream, so play along. "Who are you?"

I dont know

"Why are you here?"

The same words were rewritten below.

I dont know. Im scared. I want to go home

"Where's home?"

I DONT KNOW

Then something slammed against the mirror with wall-rattling force to create a spider-web shatter the size of a basketball. The lights went out and a blast of cold tore through the bathroom, plunging the climate from rain forest to arctic circle. Lyle leaped for the light switch but his bare foot hit a puddle; he slipped and went down just as he heard another booming impact break more of the mirror. Glass confetti peppered him with the third impact. He crouched on his knees with his forehead against the floor, hands clasped over the back of his head as whatever was in the room with him pounded the mirror again and again in a fit of mindless rage.

And then as suddenly as it began, it stopped.

Slowly, cautiously, Lyle raised his head in the echoing darkness. Somewhere in the house—down the hall—he heard running footsteps, and then his brother's voice.

"Lyle! Lyle, you all right?" The bedroom light came on. "Dear God, Lyle, where are you?"

"In here."

He rose to his knees but could find neither the strength nor the will to regain his feet. Not yet.

He heard Charlie's approach and called out, "Don't come in. There's glass on the floor. Just reach in and hit the light."

Lyle was facing away from the doorway. When the light came on he looked over his shoulder and saw a wide-eyed and slack-jawed Charlie staring at him.

"What the fuck—" Charlie began, then caught himself. "Dear Lord, Lyle, what you done?"

Charlie's use of a word he had expunged from his vocabulary since he'd been born again told Lyle the true depth of his brother's shock. Looking around, he couldn't blame him. Glittering slivers and pebbles of glass littered the floor; the big mirror looked as if Shaq had been bouncing a granite basketball against it.

"Wasn't me."

"Then who?"

"Don't know. See if you can find a blanket and throw it on the floor so I can get out of here without making hamburger of my feet."

While Charlie went looking, Lyle pushed himself to his

feet and turned, careful to stay in the glass-free circle of floor under him.

Charlie reappeared with a blanket. "This one pretty thin but—"

He stopped and stared, a look of abject horror stretching his features.

"What?"

Charlie pointed a wavering finger at Lyle's chest. "Oh, God, Lyle, you—you cut yourself!"

Lyle looked down and felt his knees soften when he saw his T-shirt front soaked in crimson. He pulled up the shirt and this time his knees wouldn't hold him. They buckled and he crumbled to the floor when he saw the deep gash in his chest, so deep he could see his convulsively beating heart through the opening.

He looked up at Charlie, met his terrified eyes, tried to mouth a word or two but failed. He looked down again at his chest . . .

And it was whole. Intact. Clean. No hole, no blood, not a drop on his skin or his shirt.

Just like what had happened to Charlie last night.

He looked up at his brother again. "You saw that, right? Tell me you saw it this time."

Charlie was nodding like a bobble-head doll. "I saw it, I saw it! I thought you was buggin' last night, but now . . . I mean, what—?"

"Throw that blanket down. I want to get out of here."

Charlie held onto one end and tossed the rest toward Lyle. They spread it out atop the glass-littered tile and Lyle crawled—he didn't trust his legs to support him so he *crawled*—to the door.

When he reached the carpet Lyle stayed down, huddling, shaking. He wanted to sob, wanted to vomit. Things he'd always disbelieved were proving true. The pillars of his world were crumbling.

"What just happened in there, Lyle?" Charlie said, kneeling beside him and laying an arm across his shaking shoulders. "What this all about?"

Lyle gathered himself, swallowed the bile at the back of his throat, and straightened his spine.

"You know what you said about this house being haunted? I'm beginning to think you're right." He looked up at the clock radio, which now read *1:11*. Who knew how long it had been running backwards. It could be three in the morning for all he knew. "Fuckit, I *know* you're right."

"What we do about it, man?"

Something strange and angry had invaded their house. Was that anger directed at him? At Charlie? He hoped not, because he sensed it ran wide and frighteningly deep. Charlie wanted to know what they were going to do. How could he answer that without even knowing what they were facing?

He grabbed Charlie's arm and got to his feet.

"I don't know, Charlie. But I know one thing we're *not* doing, and that's leaving. This is *our* place now and nobody, living or dead, is chasing us out."

MONDAY

1

Gia was staring at the clock when the phone rang.

She sat at the kitchen table, a mug of green tea cooling next to her elbow. An hour, almost to the minute, since she'd called Dr. Eagleton's office about her pregnancy test. The receptionist had said her results weren't in yet, but she'd call the Beth Israel lab and have them fax it over.

Jack was gone. After making a few cryptic calls earlier this morning, he'd gone out to run a few errands, and since then Gia had barely moved.

But she moved now, rising, stepping to the phone, checking the caller ID, seeing the name *A. Eagleton MD* on the display. Her breath caught a moment, she hesitated, then snatched up the receiver.

"Yes?"

"Ms. DiLauro?" A girl's voice. She sounded like a teenager.

"Speaking." Her hand felt slick on the plastic.

"This is Dr. Eagleton's office returning your call. Doctor says to tell you that your pregnancy test is positive."

Gia felt her body go rigid. She brought up her second hand to help grip the receiver, to keep it from falling.

"You're . . . you're sure?"

"Positive." She giggled. "I mean, yes. Doctor wants you to arrange an appointment for some routine preliminary blood work. When do you think you can—?"

Gia hung up on her and sat down.

I'm pregnant. With Jack's baby . . . Jack's and mine.

She should be bursting with joy, she knew, but she wasn't. Instead she felt uncertain, and maybe a little afraid.

Gia closed her eyes. I'm not ready for this . . . the timing's all wrong.

She picked up the mug of tea, looking to warm her chilled hands, but the cup was nearly room temperature. She took a sip of the pale yellow liquid but it tasted sour on her tongue.

Of course this wasn't just about her. There was Jack. Telling him wasn't a matter of if—because he had every right to know—but a matter of when. It was so very early in the pregnancy, a time when too many things could go wrong and end in miscarriage. She'd had two of those before Vicky was born.

Then the question of how he'd react. She knew Jack, probably better than anyone else in the world. Even better than Abe. But she still wasn't sure how he'd deal with it in the long run.

She knew his first reaction would be joy. He'd be happy for her, for himself. A baby. She wanted to see him grin, see his eyes glow. And she knew it might be enough to drag him out of his funk over losing Kate. One life ends, then a new one begins.

But telling this early carried risks. What if, say, next week, she miscarried?

Jack, you're a father-to-be! You're first child is on the way!

No, wait. Never mind. Your child is gone. Sorry.

Considering how down he'd been, was it right to risk putting him on that sort of emotional roller coaster? Wouldn't it be better, kinder after what he'd just gone through to wait until she was sure her pregnancy was firmly established?

Or was she just buying herself more time before she had to face up to the task of telling him?

So those were the short-term issues. But what about long term? When it sank into Jack what raising a child, what true fatherhood would mean to his independence, his treasured autonomy . . . what then? Would he think the cost too high?

2

The yellow plastic sandwich board sign stood in the middle of the sidewalk, its red letters reflecting the morning sun.

ERNIE'S PHOTO I-D
ALL KINDS
PASSPORT
DRIVERS LICENSE
TAXI

Jack cut around it and stepped through the open doorway into a tiny store packed to the ceiling with miniature Statues of Liberty, New York City postcards, customizable T-shirts, sports caps, and anything else Ernie could cram into a rack or onto a shelf. Ernie's shop made Abe's seem like the wide open range.

"Hey, Ern."

The skinny, droopy-faced man behind the counter wore an ugly orange Hawaiian shirt and had a Pall Mall dangling from the corner of his mouth, J-P Belmondo style. He looked up and winked.

"Witcha in a minute, sir," he said and went right back into his spiel to an old Korean tourist about a pair of Ray·Ban Predators.

"We're talkin' big savings here. Real money." He pronounced it *monnay*—like "Monday" without the *d*. "I'm tellin' you, these list for ninety bucks. I can let you have 'em for fifty."

"No-no," the old man said. "I see down street for ten. Ten dollah."

"But they're knock-offs. They ain't the real thing. You

buy 'em today and tomorrow morning the lenses'll fall out and the temples'll break off. But these, my friend, these are the real deal."

Jack turned away and pretended to browse through a rack of bootleg videos. Nothing Ernie sold was the real deal.

His mind wandered back to Gia. He'd slept over again last night. Nice. He loved waking up next to her. But she'd seemed so jumpy this morning. She'd looked impatient when he'd been making calls, and he'd gotten the impression she'd been waiting for him to leave. He didn't consider himself the easiest person to live with, but was he getting on her nerves already?

The old guy had haggled Ernie down to thirty-five and left wearing his cool shades.

"Hey, Jack," Ernie said, folding the money into his pocket. Too many years of unfiltered cigarettes had given him a frog's vocal cords. "How y'doin'. How y'doin'." He shook his head. "Tough t'make a buck these days, y'know? Real tough."

"Yeah," Jack said, easing up to Ernie's combination display case and counter. Half a dozen faux Rolexes glittered through the crisscrossed scratches in the glass. "Things are tight all around."

"These street guys are killin' me. I mean, what overhead they got? They roll out a blanket or set up a cardboard box and they're in business. They're sellin' the same stuff as me for a fin over cost. Me, you wouldn't believe the rent I gotta pay for this here closet."

"Sorry to hear that." Ernie had been crying poverty since a number of his fake ID sources dried up after the World Trade Center catastrophe. He'd been Jack's main source of driver's licenses and photo IDs for many years. "You get the queer we talked about?"

"Sure did." He pointed to the door. "Make us look closed, will ya?"

Jack locked the door and flipped the OPEN sign to CLOSED. When he returned to the counter, Ernie had a stack of currency on the glass.

"Here she be. Five K of it."

Jack picked up one of the hundred-dollar bills. He snapped it, held it up to the light. Not too crisp, not too limp. "Looks pretty good to me."

"Yeah, it's good work but they're cold as bin Laden's ass. Every clerk from Bloomie's to the lowliest bodega's got that serial number tacked up next to the cash register."

"Perfect," Jack said. Just what he wanted. "What do I owe you?"

"Gimme twenty and we'll call it even." He grinned as he started stuffing the bills into a brown paper bag. "I'll knock the price down to fifteen if you take more off my hands."

Jack laughed. "You're really looking to dump this junk, aren't you."

"Tell me about it. Stuff was golden for a while, but 'bout all it's good for now is lightin' cigars and stuffin' cracks in a drafty room. Can't even use it for toilet paper. Liability having it around."

"Why don't you just burn it?"

"Easier said than done, my man. Especially in the summer. First off, I ain't got no fireplace in my apartment, and even if I did, I wouldn't want to burn it there. And the bums ain't lightin' up their trashcans in this heat, so I can't just walk by and dump a few stacks into the fire. I'm gonna hafta wait till winter. Till then, I'm glad to have someone take even a little off my hands."

"What are friends for?" Jack said, handing him a twenty and taking the paper bag.

Ernie looked at him. "I don't get it. Why you want bad queer when I can get you good? Whatta you gonna do with it?"

Jack smiled. "Buy myself a stairway to heaven."

3

"You're sure you want to go in?" Jack said as he pulled his car into an empty parking spot about half a block from Ifasen's house.

Gia thought about that a second. "Of course. I wouldn't have come otherwise."

He shook his head. "You've never, ever done anything like this before."

She smiled at him. "First time for everything, right?"

Like being a father, she thought.

She was such a coward. Jack had said he was going to pay a call on Ifasen—although he was calling him Lyle now—to pick up a fee, and she'd told him she wanted to come along. She'd explained it as some sort of proprietary interest—after all, she'd found him the job—and had kidded him about collecting a finder's fee.

But she had a more serious reason for going with him. Two of them, in fact.

First, she'd decided to tell him about the pregnancy now rather than later. She wasn't good at hiding things or keeping secrets. It wasn't her nature. Best to put it out in the open where they both could deal with it.

But she hadn't found an opening. Or so she'd told herself during the trip from Midtown to Astoria. Truth was, she simply hadn't been able to admit that she'd been so careless.

She'd tell him on the way home for sure.

The second reason was that she wanted to ask Ifasen—Lyle—about his two-child prediction. The rational part of her brain knew it had been a trick or a lucky guess, or whatever, but another part kept asking, Did he know? And if so, was there any more he could tell her? She knew the questions would keep bouncing around her mind until she had some answers.

Yes, she knew it didn't make sense, and that this wasn't like her, but . . .

Hey, I'm pregnant. I've got hormones surging every which way. I don't have to make sense.

Jack had his arm around her waist as they walked along the uneven sidewalk toward Lyle's yard.

Lyle . . . it carried nowhere near the spiritualistic ring, the psychic vibrations of Ifasen.

"You have returned?"

Gia jumped at the sound of a lilting woman's voice behind her. She and Jack turned as one.

"Pardon me?" Gia said.

An Indian woman in a red sari. Gia thought she looked familiar, and then remembered she'd seen her Friday night. Right here in fact. She'd worn a blue sari then, but she had the same big German shepherd on a leash.

"You must not go in there," the woman said. "Very bad for you."

"You told us that the other night," Jack said, "but nothing happened. So why are you—?"

"Something did happen!" Her black eyes flashed. "Earth tremble!"

"So what are you telling us?" Jack said. "If we go in there again there'll be another earthquake?"

"I am telling you it is a bad place, dangerous for both of you."

The woman seemed so sincere, and that struck an uneasy chord within Gia. When her dog looked up at her with his big brown shepherd's eyes and whimpered, it only added to her disquiet.

"Thank you for the warning," Jack said. He took Gia's arm and guided her away, toward the house. "Let's go."

Gia complied, but as they moved away she glanced back over her shoulder to see the woman and her dog staring after them.

She leaned against Jack. "What was she talking about?"

"She could be talking about the house's history, or she might think we're heading in to attend a seance and because of that our salvation is in jeopardy. Who knows?"

Gia glanced back again but the woman and her dog were gone. Moved on, she guessed.

As they headed up the walk toward the house Gia tried to put her unease behind her. To lighten up she pointed to the dead brown leaves on all the foundation plantings.

"Who's his gardener? Julio?"

Jack laughed. "No. Just one phase of the harassment he's been suffering. If all goes well, that will come to an end real soon."

"But no rough stuff, right?"

"Pure subterfuge, my dear, and nothing more."

Good, she could have said. *I don't want your child growing up without a father.*

But she didn't want to lay that on him just as they walked through Lyle Kenton's door.

The man who had been Ifasen answered Jack's knock. He wore a cutoff Spartans sweatshirt, blue running shorts, and was barefoot.

"Jack," he said, but his smile was weak, distracted. "Right on time. Come on in."

"I don't know if you remember Gia," Jack said. "She was here Friday night with Junie and the rest of us."

"Yes, of course." He gave Gia a fleeting smile and a quick little bow. "Nice to see you again." He seemed tense.

Jack must have noticed it too. As he guided Gia ahead of him through the door he said, "Something wrong?"

Lyle shook his head. "Some strange stuff going on with the house last night."

"You think it's the Fosters?" Jack looked surprised. "They should be—"

Lyle shook his head. "Definitely not them."

"That's good. Anything I can do?"

His eyes took on a strange look. Not fear, not anger.

More like dismay. "Not in your field. I'll go get your money."

Whatever was going on, he didn't seem to want to talk about it. But maybe he'd talk about Friday night.

"Before you go," Gia said as Lyle started to turn away, "can I ask just one question?"

He stopped and looked at her. "Certainly."

"It's about Friday night . . . when you were answering those questions we'd written on those cards."

"The billet reading. What about it?"

"Well . . ." She glanced at Jack who was watching her with a puzzled expression. She felt foolish. He'd already answered the question for her, but she had to hear it again, in the flesh. "I don't know if you remember my question . . . I asked—"

" 'How many children will I have?' Correct? And I told you it would be two, I believe." Another quick half-smile. "Did you want a different answer?"

"I . . . I want to know why you said that number. Was it just a guess, or was it, I mean, do you know something?"

"Gia," Jack said, "didn't I—"

"I know, Jack, but just let me hear it from him."

Lyle was looking at Jack.

"Go ahead," Jack said. "Tell her." He paused, then added, "The truth."

Lyle hesitated, then shrugged. "Just a guess. Nothing more."

"You're sure? No little voice, no psychic emanations?"

"Just a guess. Anything else?"

"No. That's all. Thanks for your honesty."

Lyle gave another of his little bows and opened a door behind him. As he receded down a hallway, Gia saw what looked like a kitchen and windows opening onto the rear of the house.

"Told you," Jack said when they were alone. He looked a little annoyed that his explanation hadn't been enough.

"I'm sorry, Jack."

"Nothing to be sorry for." He was staring at her. "But is

that why you wanted to come along today? To ask him that?"

She nodded. "Dumb, huh."

Maybe it wasn't so dumb, considering her present condition, but she sure felt dumb.

He smiled at her. "Nothing you do is dumb. It's just that I don't understand this sudden fixation on something a complete stranger said."

"I'll explain later . . . on the way home." I hope.

Jack was still staring at her. "I don't get it. What—?"

Just then Lyle returned with a white, legal-size envelope. He handed it to Jack.

"Here you go. First half. When do you think the second payment will be due?"

"Assuming all goes well," Jack said, "in a few days."

"Phase two is still on for tomorrow afternoon?"

Lyle obviously was trying to be cryptic. He probably didn't know that Jack had told her about the Kentons' problems with Madame Pomerol on the drive out. Gia decided to leave it that way.

She didn't catch Jack's reply because movement in the hallway behind Lyle caught her attention. She rose on tiptoe and craned her neck for a better look.

A pale-skinned girl with long blond hair was walking down the hall toward the kitchen. She was dressed in what looked like riding clothes—breeches and boots. Was there a stable nearby? She looked to be about Vicky's age— couldn't have been more than eight or nine. Gia wondered where she'd come from and what she was doing here.

As the girl turned the corner into the kitchen, she glanced over her shoulder and her blue eyes locked with Gia's. And Gia saw in them a depth of need, of longing that pierced her heart.

Lyle's glance flicked toward her. He must have seen something in her face. "Something wrong?"

"Who's the little girl?"

Lyle whirled as if he'd heard a shot behind him. "Little girl? Where?"

"Right there, in the hall." He was blocking her view now. Gia leaned left to see and found the hall empty. "She was there a second ago."

"There's no girl in this house, big or little."

"I saw her. A little blonde." Gia pointed down the hall. "She was right there, walking toward the kitchen."

Lyle turned and hurried down the hall.

"Charlie!" he called. "Come down here a sec, will you."

Gia followed Lyle, noting the stairway to the second floor on her left. It struck her as an odd design until she realized that the house had been remodeled to accommodate the Channeling Room. She heard Jack behind her.

Lyle angled through the kitchen and leaned into an adjoining room for a quick look. Apparently satisfied no one was there, he went to the open back door. He pushed on the screen door and stood on the small stoop to survey the backyard. The midday sun gleamed off his dreadlocks. After a moment he stepped back inside and stared at Gia as the screen door slammed closed behind him.

"You're sure you saw a little girl?"

"Very."

He turned toward the rear door again. "Then she must have run out through the backyard."

"I doubt that," Jack said.

Gia turned to see him standing next to a door that opened onto a down staircase.

"Why?" said Lyle.

"Because we didn't hear the screen door slam. Unless she took the time to ease it closed before running away, she's still here." He jerked a thumb toward the cellar stairs. "And I bet I know where."

Lyle's brother arrived from the second floor. He wore a tank top and sweat pants with the legs bunched up under the knees; his black-and-white Lugs, with the tongues lolling over their untied laces, looked like thirsty dogs.

Lyle quickly introduced Gia as "Jack's friend" and she was struck by the warmth in Charlie's smile when he bumped knuckles with Jack. The smile faded as Lyle told him about the little girl Gia had seen.

Jack and Gia waited in the kitchen while Lyle and Charlie searched their basement. Jack stepped to the back door and peered through the screen at the small backyard.

Without looking at her, he said, "Did you ever sneak into a stranger's house when you were a little girl?"

"Are you kidding?"

"Did you ever even *think* about doing such a thing?"

"Never. I'd be scared to death."

"You mean, sort of like Lyle and Charlie are right now?" He turned toward her and lowered his voice. "I'm not saying they're scared to death, but they're sure as hell frightened by something. I don't know about you, but I don't find little girls particularly frightening. So what's really—?"

She heard footsteps on the stairs and turned to see the Kenton brothers emerge from the cellar.

"Empty," Lyle said. "She must have run out the back door."

"Without making a sound?" Jack said.

Lyle shrugged. "There's no place else she could go." He gave Charlie an uneasy look. "Is there?" Then he turned to Gia. "Are you—?"

"Yes, I'm sure," she said, more sharply than she intended. "I'm not in the habit of hallucinating."

Gia described her fully, leaving out only the longing in the child's eyes.

"A blond kid," Charlie said, rubbing his jaw. "Not many blondes around here, know'm sayin'?"

"Maybe you should keep your doors locked when you're upstairs," Gia said.

Lyle's expression was bleak. "I wish we could."

"I hate to break this up," Jack said, pointing to his watch, "but I've got to pick up some props for my date with Madame Pomerol."

The good-byes seemed strained and strange, with Gia feeling that the Kenton brothers wanted them to go and yet somehow didn't want to be left alone in the house.

"Something going on with those two," Jack said as they walked toward his car. "They're jumpy as mice."

"I wonder why," Gia said. "And I know I saw that little girl, Jack. I can't explain how she got in or how she got out, but I know what I saw."

"I believe you. And the strange thing is, I think the brothers Kenton believe you too, although it seems they'd rather not."

She looked around for the Indian woman. She wanted to say, See? We went in and here we are out again, and nothing happened. But she was nowhere in sight.

Jack opened the car door for her and she slipped into the passenger seat. When he'd seated himself behind the wheel, he turned to her.

"And speaking of belief, now do you believe that his guess about two kids was just that: a guess?"

"I do," she said, thinking, here it is, this is the moment. "But you've got to understand where I'm coming from and why I was obsessing on it."

Jack started the car. "Tell me."

Gia hesitated, then blurted, "I'm pregnant."

4

Jack started to laugh—for a second there he thought Gia had said she was pregnant—and then he saw the look in her eyes.

"Did you say . . . pregnant?"

She nodded and he saw a glimmer of tears. Joy? Dismay? Both?

Some tiny corner of Jack's brain realized that this was a fragile moment, and it was laboring to find the right thing to say, but the remainder of his brain had gone to mush as he struggled to grasp, to comprehend the meaning of those words . . .

I'm pregnant.

"M-mi—" He caught himself. He'd been about to say, *Mine?* A reflex. Of course it was his. "We're having a baby?"

Gia nodded again and now her lower lip was trembling as the tears started to slip down her cheeks.

Jack slipped across the seat and folded her into his arms. She sobbed as she pressed against him and buried her face against his neck.

"Oh, Jack, I didn't mean for this to happen. Don't be mad. It was an accident."

"Mad? Jeez, Gia, why would I be mad? Shocked, yes, baffled too, but mad is the last thing. It's not even on the map."

"Thank God! I—"

"How long have you known about this?"

"Since this morning."

"And we rode all the way out here together and you didn't say a word? How come?"

"I meant to, but . . ."

"But what?"

"I didn't know how you'd react."

This was a new shock. "What did you think I'd do? Walk out? Why on earth—?"

"Because of all the changes you'll have to make if you stay on."

"Hey." He held her tighter. "I'm not going anywhere. And I can handle any changes. But let's just say I did stomp out, what would you do? Would you . . . end the pregnancy?"

She jerked back to stare at him with red-rimmed eyes. "Have an abortion? Never! That's my baby!"

"Mine too." He couldn't bear the thought of anyone killing their baby. He hugged her again. "I'm gonna be a daddy. Me. I can't believe it. You're sure you're pregnant?"

She nodded. "Beth-Israel sure."

"Wow." The word popped out of his mouth. He laughed. "Hey, am I articulate, or what? But really . . . *wow!* A little somebody made with part of me, walking and talking and growing up."

A piece of him moving beyond him, heading toward infinity. Wonder filled him, buoyed him.

The beep of a horn brought him back to earth. He looked around.

A big guy in a little Kia pointed to Jack's parking space and called, "You stayin' or goin'?"

Jack waved, started the Crown Vic, and pulled away.

"What do you think little Jack will be like?" he said.

" 'Little Jack'? What makes you think it will be a boy?"

"If it's a girl it'll mean you've been fooling around with somebody else."

"Oh, really? How's that work, pray tell?"

Jack puffed out his chest. "Well, I'm so manly I produce only Y sperm."

She smiled. "No kidding?"

"Yep. Never told you before because I didn't think it mattered. But now I feel you deserve to know the truth."

"I've got news for you, buddy. It's a girl. My Amazon ova castrate Y sperms."

Jack laughed. "Ouch!"

With Gia snuggled against him they drove and talked about when it could have happened and what sex it might be and began throwing out girls' names and boys' names and Jack cruised through a changed world, brighter and more full of hope and promise and possibility than he'd ever imagined.

5

Lyle was standing in the kitchen, tossing out the aluminum foil that had wrapped the leftover pizza slices he and Charlie had finished for dinner, when he heard the voice.

He froze and listened. Definitely not Charlie's voice. No . . . a child's. A little girl's. And it sounded as if she was singing.

A little girl . . . Gia had seen a little girl this afternoon. Was she back?

Lyle eased toward the center hall, where the sound seemed to be coming from. No doubt about it. A little girl was singing. The melody was tantalizingly familiar.

As he moved into the hall her voice became clearer, echoing from beyond the closed door at the end of the hall, from the waiting room.

And the words . . .

"I think we're alone now . . ."

Wasn't that from the sixties? Tommy somebody?

He slowed his pace. Something odd about the voice, its timbre, the way it echoed. It sounded far away, as if it were coming from the bottom of a well. A very deep well.

At the door, Lyle hesitated, then grabbed the knob and yanked it open. The voice was loud now, almost as if the child were shouting. The words bounced off the walls, seeming to come from all directions. But where was the child?

Lyle stood in an empty room.

He stepped over to the couch and looked behind it, but found nothing but a couple of dust bunnies.

And now the sound was moving away . . . down the hall he'd just passed through. Lyle moved back to the door but saw no one in the hall. And still the sound kept moving away. He followed it.

"Charlie!" he called as he passed the stairs. He told himself he wanted a witness, but deeper down he knew he didn't want to be alone with this. "Charlie, get down here. Quick!"

But Charlie didn't respond—no voice asking, Whussup? No footsteps in the upper hallway. Probably holed up in his room with his head stuck in a pair of headphones listening to Gospel music while he read the Bible. How many times was he going to read that book?

Lyle followed the voice, still singing the same song, into the kitchen. But once he reached there, the voice seemed to be coming from the cellar.

Lyle paused at the top of the stairs, staring into the well of blackness below. He didn't want to go down there, not alone. Not even with someone else, if the truth be known. Not after last night.

He wondered if this delicate little voice was part of whatever had written on the bathroom mirror before smashing it. Or was the house haunted by multiple entities?

"Charlie!"

But again, no response.

Lyle and Charlie had spent most of the morning talking about whether or not they were really haunted. In the warm light of day, with the shock and the fear of the night before dissipated, Lyle had found it hard to believe in such a possibility. But one look in the bathroom at the maniacally shattered mirror was enough to make him a convert.

The big question was, what could they do about it? They couldn't exactly call Ghostbusters. And even if such a group existed, think of the publicity: *Psychic afraid of ghosts! Calls for help!* A PR nightmare.

The voice was fading now. Where could it go from the basement?

Lyle took a deep breath. He had to go down there. Curiosity, a need to know, pushed him for an answer. Because knowing was better than not knowing. At least he hoped so.

Flicking the light switch he took the stairs down in a rush—no sense dragging this out—and found himself in the familiar but empty basement with its orange-painted floor, pecan paneling, and too-bright fluorescents. He could still hear the singing, though. Very faintly. Coming from the center of the room . . . from the crack that ran the width of the floor.

No . . . couldn't be.

Lyle edged closer and gingerly crouched near the opening. No question about it. The voice was echoing from down there, in the earthquake crevasse under his house.

He bent his head and rubbed his eyes. Why? This house was fifty-some years old. Why couldn't this have happened to the last owner?

Wait, the last owner was dead.

All right, the next owner, then. Why me? Why now?

The voice faded further. Lyle leaned closer. It was still singing "I Think We're Alone Now." Why that tune? Why a bubblegum song from the sixties?

And then the lights went out and the strange little voice boomed from an anemic whisper to a floor-rattling scream of rage that knocked Lyle onto his back. A noxious cloud plumed around him in the dark, the same graveyard odor as the night the crack first appeared, sending him scrambling across the floor and up the steps toward light and air.

Sweating, panting, he slammed the cellar door and backed away until his back hit the kitchen counter. This was getting way out of hand. He needed help, and fast, but he hadn't the faintest idea where to turn.

Sure as hell couldn't call on a psychic. He'd never met one who wasn't a lying son of a bitch.

He had to shake his head. Just like me.

Okay, there were some who really believed in all the crap they fed their sitters, but they were deluded. And he'd found that people who lied to themselves were far more unreliable than those who simply lied to others. He'd take a con man over a fool any time.

Lyle stared at the door and calmed himself. Time to get a grip and face this situation head on. Because what he'd said this morning was true. He was not leaving his home.

He took a deep breath. So. Look at what he had: Assuming that some sort of spirit world was real—and he was being backed into accepting that now—it still had to follow some rules, didn't it? Every action had an effect. Every incident had a cause.

Maybe not. But that was the only way he knew how to approach this. If other rules applied, he'd have to learn them. But for now, he'd go with cause and effect.

That said, what had caused all this? What had awakened this demon or ghost or entity, or attracted it to his home? Was it something he or Charlie had done? Or was someone else behind it?

Those were the first questions. Once he had those answers, the next step would be finding out what, if anything, he could do about them.

6

"More kashi?" Gia said.

Jack held up his plate and said in his best Oliver Twist voice, "Please, ma'am, could I have some more?"

Gia had whipped up one of her vegetarian dinners. She was on a kashi kick these days, so tonight she'd fixed kashi and beans with sides of sautéed spinach and sliced Jersey beefsteaks with mozzarella. All delicious, all nutritious, all as good for a body as food could possibly be; and though he'd push away from the table with a full belly, these meals always left Jack feeling like he'd missed a course.

Jack watched Gia as she scooped more kashi from the pot. The old townhouse had a small kitchen with cabinets and hardwood floor all stained unfashionably dark. Jack remembered when he'd first seen the place last year. Vicky's two old spinster aunts had been living here with their maid, Nellie. The interior looked pretty much the same then, the furnishings hadn't changed, but the place had a real lived-in look now. A child will do that.

Jack let his eyes wander down Gia's trim frame, wondering when she'd start to show, to swell, marveling at the stresses women put their bodies through to bring a child into the world.

He shook his head. If men had to go through that the world would be damn near unpopulated.

Still looking at Gia, he noticed an uncharacteristic tautness in her posture. Her uncertainty over the weekend as to whether or not she was pregnant would explain the mood swings he noticed, but he'd have thought finding out and telling him would have broken her tension. Something else was bothering her.

Jack got up and pulled another Killian's from the fridge. "You don't mind that I'm drinking, do you?"

This was his third Killian's while Gia was still working on her first club soda. The bottle of wine he'd picked up on the way over sat unopened on the counter. Gia had told him that, as much as she loved her Chardonnay, she wouldn't be drinking for the next nine months.

"Not if it's beer. Wine might tempt me, but if the world suddenly forgot how to make beer, I'd never miss it."

"A world without beer . . . what an awful thought."

He wondered how hard it would be for him to give up beer for nine months. One of life's great pleasures was wrapping his hand around a cold one toward the end of the day. He could swear off, but he sure as hell wouldn't like it.

He decided to float the idea past Gia, praying she'd shoot it down.

"If you're abstaining, maybe I should too."

She gave him half a smile. "What would that accomplish? My drinking could affect the baby; yours won't."

He raised his fist. "But how about solidarity, sharing the sacrifices of parenthood and all that?"

"If you intend to be a real parent to this child, you're going to have to make a lot more sacrifices than I will, so drink your beer."

That had an ominous ring. Jack took a grateful gulp of his Killian's. "I already am a real parent. One of them, at least."

"No, you're the father. That's the easy part. You haven't begun being a parent yet. That's a whole other matter."

Gia seemed edgy. What was she getting at? "I'm aware of the difference between fathering a child and raising a child."

"Are you?" She reached across the table and clasped his hand. "I know you could be a great parent, Jack, a wonderful father figure. But I wonder if you see what lies ahead for you if you make that commitment."

Now he knew where this was going.

"You're talking about the Repairman Jack thing. No problem. Look, I've already cut out certain kinds of fix-its, and I can make other changes. I can—"

She sat there shaking her head. "You're not seeing the big picture. Usually you're way ahead of me on things like this."

"What am I missing?"

She glanced away, then back at him. "I wish I didn't have to say this because it makes me feel like I'm forcing you into something you won't want to do, and maybe even can't do."

"Telling me something isn't forcing me. Just tell me: What am I missing?"

"Jack, if you're going to be a real parent, you'll have to really exist."

Jack's first reaction was to say that he did exist, but he knew what she meant.

"Become a citizen?"

She nodded. "Exactly."

A citizen. Christ, he'd spent his whole adult life avoiding that. He didn't want to change now. Join the masses . . . he didn't know if he could.

"That sounds pretty radical. There must be some way . . ."

She was shaking her head. "Think about it. If this baby was born tomorrow, who could I put down as the father?"

"Me."

"And who are you? Where do you live? What's your Social Security number?"

"Numbers," he grumbled. "I don't think you need the father's numbers on a birth certificate."

"Maybe not. But don't you think the baby would prefer a father who doesn't change his last name every week? Who doesn't fade away when he sees a cop car?"

"Gia . . ."

"All right, I'm exaggerating, I know, but my point is, even though no one knows you exist, you live like a hunted man, Jack. Like a fugitive. That's fine when you're single and are responsible only for yourself, but it doesn't work for a parent."

"We've been over this before."

"Yes, we have. In the context of our future together. But it was all conjectural, with no set timetable." She patted her abdomen. "Now we've got a timetable. Nine months, and the clock is ticking."

"Nine months," Jack whispered. That seemed like no time at all.

"Maybe less. We'll have a more precise idea once I have a sonogram. But let's go past nine months. Let's jump ahead five years. And let's just say that you leave your situation the way it is. We don't get married but we're living together here—you, me, Vicky, and the baby. One big happy family."

"Sounds nice."

"But what if I get breast cancer, or fall off a subway platform in front of a train, or—?"

"Gia, come on." What a thought.

"Don't say it couldn't happen, because we both know it could. And right now, if something happens to me, Vicky goes to my parents."

Jack nodded. "I know."

It was logical, and probably the right thing. Her grandparents would be Vicky's only living blood relatives. But it would burn a hole in his life to watch that little girl be taken off to Iowa.

"But what if my folks aren't around when something happens to me? If they're dead, then it's not just Vicky who's at risk, but our baby as well. What happens to those two children?"

"I take them."

"No. You won't be able to. They'll be orphans and they'll become wards of the court."

"Like hell."

"What are you going to do? Abduct them? Take off with them and hide out? Change their names and have them live like fugitives? Is that the kind of life you want for them?"

Jack leaned back and sipped from his beer. It tasted sour on his tongue. Because he was seeing it now, all of it, the knotty immensity of the problem. How could he have missed it? Maybe because the quotidian rituals of having no official existence, of pursuing an under-the-radar lifestyle had become to him as natural and reflexive as breathing.

Was he going to have to change the way he breathed?

He stared at Gia. "You've obviously given this a lot of thought."

She nodded. "It has consumed me for three days." Tears welled in her eyes. "I'm not pushing you, Jack. It's just that if anything happens to me I want to know my babies are safe."

Jack rose and moved around the table. He lifted Gia from her seat, slid beneath, then settled her onto his lap. She clung to him.

He put his arms around her and said, "*Our* babies. I

couldn't love Vicky more if she were my own. And I don't feel pushed, okay? Fatherhood wasn't in my immediate plans, but that's okay. I'm flexible. I've learned to adjust quickly to unexpected situations in my work, and I can do it here. It's a responsibility and I'm not about to walk away from it."

"How will you do it?"

"Become a citizen? I don't know. I'm sure my father has my birth certificate squirreled away somewhere, so I'm pretty sure I can show I'm native-born. But I can't exactly show up at the local Social Security office and ask for a number. Folks down there will want to know where I've been these last thirty-six years. And why I've never filed a 1040. I can't just say I've been living abroad. Where's my passport? Records will show I was never issued one. At worst they'll think I'm some sort of terrorist. At best, a wide array of city, state, and federal agencies will be lining up to file tax evasion charges and investigate me for drug or arms trafficking. I don't know how well my past will hold up under that sort of scrutiny. Some law firm will get rich defending me. And in the end I could wind up either broke or in jail or both. Most likely both."

"I won't let you do that. I'd rather take my chances with you as you are than see you risk your freedom. You can't be a parent from behind bars. There's got to be another way. How about false documents?"

"They'll have to be awfully damn good if I'm going to rest my whole future on them. But I'll start looking into it."

Gia tightened her arms around him. "What a spot I've put you in."

"You? You haven't put me anywhere I haven't chosen to be. This is a situation I was going to have to face sooner or later. When I opted out I was, what, twenty-one? I wasn't looking ahead then. I never thought about how I'd get myself back in because I didn't care. Tell the truth, I didn't think I'd be around long enough to have to worry about it."

"Were you trying to get yourself killed?"

"No, but to someone watching me it might have seemed that way. I was reckless. No, that doesn't even touch it. I was nuts. I look back at some of the risks I took and wonder how I ever survived. I had this feeling of immortality then that gave me the confidence to try anything. *Anything*. A few nasty close calls eventually woke me up, but for a while there . . ." He shook his head at the memory. "Anyway, I'm still kicking, and now that it looks like I might actually survive this lifestyle, I can't see myself wanting to go on living in the cracks when I'm seventy."

Gia let go a little laugh. "A semi-senile Repairman Jack. Not a pretty picture."

"Can you see me stopping in at Julio's for my afternoon warm milk, then hustling around, dodging the IRS and AARP in my walker? What a sight."

They laughed, but not for long.

"Is there a way out of this?" Gia said.

"Has to be. It needs a fix. I earn my living fixing things. I'll figure something out."

Jack hoped he sounded a lot more confident than he felt. This could be his biggest fix-it job—his own life.

He stared out the back door at the fading light in the reddening sky, then glanced at the old oak clock on the wall above the sink.

"Oops. Speaking of fix-its, gotta go."

He felt Gia stiffen. "That bodyguard job you told me about?"

"More like baby-sitting than bodyguarding."

She leaned back and looked at him. "You be careful."

He kissed her. "I will."

"Remember, you're Daddy-To-Be Jack, not Wildman Jack."

At the moment, Jack wasn't quite sure who he was.

7

Ensconced in his sidewalk seat at the bistro down the block from Eli Bellitto's Shurio Coppe, Jack was nearing the bottom of his first Corona—no lime, please—with his eye on Bellitto's door. He'd ditched the mullet wig and odd clothes he'd worn in the store last night. He wore a baseball cap to hide his hair and keep his eyes in shadow, but otherwise he was pretty much himself tonight.

He'd watched the older woman and new clerk leave, seen Bellitto lock up and make the around-the-corner trip home. Twilight had faded into night, clouds had curdled in the formerly clear sky and then fused into a lumpy, low-hanging lid. Bellitto's door floated in a deeper pool of darkness due to the broken street lamp at that end of the block.

More traffic tonight than last. A battle-scarred delivery truck rolled by, retching a tubular cloud that lingered in the air behind it, slowly drifting Jack's way, obliterating the delicious odor of sautéed garlic that had been wafting from the kitchen. Jack coughed. The joys of dining al fresco.

More people too, so he engaged in his favorite pastime: watching them. He saw a couple of pale-faced, black-lipped goth chicks swish by in ankle-length black dresses. Then an odd interracial couple wheeling a baby carriage: he very dark in a button-down shirt, tie, and khakis with his hair processed as straight as Fifth Avenue, she porcelain white in bib overalls and long, puffy, light brown dreadlocks trailing down her back. A trio of teenage girls bounced by in off-the-shoulder blouses, bellbottoms, and cork platform soles—the seventies were back.

Jack checked the placement of the slapper resting inside his loose plaid shirt. The eight-ounce lead weight in its head pulled the fabric out and down, giving him a bit of a gut. He'd worn his black twelve-inch Fryes with the classic harness and ring tonight, and his .38 AMT Backup sat strapped inside the right one. He hoped he wouldn't have to use either. All quiet on the block. Everything pointed toward another nothing night, which was not, except for the boredom, such a bad thing.

His mind turned to his conversation with Gia, and the spot he was in: How did he legitimize his existence without risking his freedom? The obvious way was to become somebody else—take over the identity of a legitimate, law-abiding, Social Security numbered, tax-withholding, 401(k)-contributing, 1040-filing citizen. Obvious, but not very feasible. Impossible if said citizen were still alive.

But what if he were dead?

That might work. But how? As soon as this good citizen's death certificate was registered, his Social Security number would be added to the Social Security Death Index; anything Jack tried to do with the dead man's SSN after that would ring alarms throughout the credit industry, and eventually in the Department of the Treasury.

No thank you.

The ideal candidate would be a nutso recluse with no wife, no kids, no living relatives of any sort. He had to be within ten years either side of Jack's age and had to die unnoticed in his newspaper-crammed apartment—

No, wait. Better yet, he dies alone in his remote, Ted Kaczynski–style cabin deep in the woods. Jack would come upon his corpse, give him a decent burial, and walk away with the deceased's identity.

Yep, had a bit of a mental breakdown and hid myself away for a while, but now I'm back and ready to rejoin the rat race.

Jack snorted. Yeah, right . . . that'll happen. And who'll lead me to the cabin? The Easter Bunny?

Had to be a way, damn it.

He heard a distant rumble. The air smelled of rain and he remembered hearing on the radio that some was expected. He wished he'd paid more attention. Now tonight held the prospect of being wet as well as bored.

Swell.

He was about to order a second Corona, and maybe some steamed shrimp to wolf down before the rains came, when he saw a car pull into the curb by the fire hydrant near Bellitto's door. He couldn't scope out the make and model because of the headlights and the broken street lamp.

Jack dropped a five on the table and started up the street. He had a feeling about this car. He might be wrong, and if he was, no big deal. But if right, he'd be left flatfooted if he stayed put here.

As he approached the end of the block he made the car as a maroon Buick Park Avenue. Bellitto stepped out of his doorway and the driver—big guy with a shaved head, putty-colored skin, and no neck—unfolded himself from the front seat. Wore a tight black T-shirt with the sleeves rolled up a couple of turns, which only emphasized the length of his arms—the knuckles practically brushed the ground, like a gorilla's. He obviously worked out and God forbid someone might not notice those biceps and triceps.

Jack had parked his car in a lot on the corner of West Houston, a block further up. To avoid attracting attention, he waited until he'd passed the Buick before breaking into a run. His boots weren't designed for running but he was doing all right. Chanced a backward glance to memorize the Buick's plate number but couldn't make it out because of the mud smeared across it. Accidental, or on purpose? Also noticed Bellitto getting into the driver seat while the big guy headed for the passenger side.

Seemed to Jack that Eli Bellitto was not likely to get hurt if he hung around with a guy that size. Unless of course he started picking on Mr. Gorilla Arms himself.

But Eli's brother Edward had been more concerned that he might hurt someone else. And if these two here were to gang up on someone, a heap of hurt could go down.

At the lot, Jack waved to the attendant, jumped into his Crown Vic, and hit the ignition. He'd paid in advance so he could get moving fast if needed. Right now he needed.

He kicked up gravel leaving the lot and caught up to Eli Bellitto and company as they waited at a red light three blocks down. The mud-smeared plate bothered him. The splatters did too good a job of hiding the numbers.

Jack followed them downtown. The rain started as they crossed Canal Street into Chinatown. He thought they might be heading for Brooklyn but they passed the turn for the Manhattan Bridge. Crossed the Bowery and merged onto Catherine Street. With the hulking lit-up forms of the Al Smith Houses looming ahead on the right, the Buick slowed to a crawl, hugging the curb as if looking for something or someone. Finally it stopped dead.

Were they going to add a third rider? This was getting complicated.

Jack looked around for options. Eli and his buddy Gorilla Arms would pick him up if he stayed right behind them. Not many people out on a drizzly Monday night. He wished it weren't raining. Maybe then he could get some clarity on what they were looking for.

He had an impression that Gorilla Arms had turned in his seat and looked his way, so Jack flashed his high beams, as if impatient for them to move on. Bellitto's hand snaked out the window and waved him around.

With an angry blare of his horn, Jack swung around the Buick and glided up the block.

Now what?

Jack spotted a tiny store, lights still on, newspapers racked out front under an awning. As good an excuse as any to stop and keep Bellitto in sight.

Double-parked and left the engine running while he hopped out and trotted across the wet sidewalk. Approached the narrow storefront and noticed not a word in sight was English, not even the newspaper headlines. Couldn't tell if the ideograms were Chinese, Korean, or Vietnamese. Not that it mattered. He was only going to pretend to shop, maybe buy a pack of gum at most.

At the open door, Jack stepped aside to let a little Asian

boy scoot past; a white plastic shopping bag dangled from his wrist. He watched the kid stop under the awning and open a small red umbrella, then hurry off into the rain.

Kind of young to be out alone at this hour, Jack thought.

Stepped inside, smiled and nodded to the wizened old Asian woman inside, and said, "I'm just going to look around."

She gave him a little bow, waved her hand, and babbled something he hadn't a prayer of understanding.

Jack turned back to the window. Through the grime and the rain he noticed the Buick starting to move again.

Damn!

He threw a buck on the counter and grabbed a newspaper on the way out. Holding it over his head as a makeshift umbrella—and to shield his features from Bellitto and his passenger—Jack dashed back across the sidewalk. As he moved he glanced left and right along the deserted sidewalk.

Where was the kid?

He saw something on the curb, protruding from between two cars, right near where Bellitto had been idling. The Buick was pulling away, but the alarms ringing through Jack's instincts forced him to make a quick detour. He ran over to the spot and saw what it was: a little red umbrella, upside down in the gutter, collecting rain in its bowl. But no kid.

Had Bellitto and Gorilla Arms grabbed him? Jack knelt and checked under the cars, found nothing but water and oil spots, then rose and stared after the retreating Buick's red rear lights.

Shit! That had to be it. Those two fuckers had snatched that little kid.

Grinding his teeth, Jack ran for his car.

Now he saw why Edward had said he wanted to hire Jack to protect his brother not so much from other people as from himself. His fear had been for the harm that might befall an innocent victim. He must have known his brother was a creep. And known he was getting ready to strike.

Damn him! Why hadn't Edward just called the cops? But obviously he'd wanted to keep it secret. After all, who wanted to go public that his brother was a pedophile? So Edward was trying to have it both ways—prevent another crime but do it under the table. Fine. Jack could appreciate that. But if he'd had the facts in advance, he would have handled this differently. He sure as hell wouldn't have let that little boy walk past Bellitto's car alone.

Shit! Shit! Shit!

He jumped into his car and spun his tires getting back into the traffic flow.

"Where are they?" he muttered, anger welling as he strained to see through the rain-smeared windshield. He pounded on the steering wheel. "Where the fuck are they?"

He wound further downtown and ran parallel to the on-ramp to the Brooklyn Bridge, but couldn't find them. Gambling that they'd be returning to Bellitto's place, he raced back uptown.

He let his high, tight shoulders drop and allowed himself an instant of relief when he spotted the Buick turning onto Bellitto's block. But only an instant. Who knew what condition that kid was in, or what they'd done to him already.

Again, the flare of anger. If only I'd known.

Jack killed his headlights and double-parked. Used the same newspaper to cover his head as he traveled the last block on foot.

Watched Bellitto pull into the curb before his door. Crossed the street in time to see Bellitto step out and open the rear door. Gorilla Arms emerged carrying a blanket-wrapped bundle in both arms. A child-size bundle. He kicked the door shut as Bellitto led the way across the shadowed sidewalk. Now Jack knew the reason for the shot-out street light.

Closer now, he searched for some sign of movement within the blanket but saw none. His gut gave a lurch as an ankle and a little sneaker fell free of one of the folds and dangled in the rain.

Shit, he might be too late.

A dark place within him cracked open, leaking boiling fury into his bloodstream. Wanted to pull his .38 and charge in and start capping faces, but it was two to one and a kid in the middle who might be salvageable. So instead of charging he slowed his pace and put a weaving stagger into his step. He reached inside his shirt, slipped his hand through the slapper's wrist loop, and gripped the hard leather handle.

The two men froze on the one-step front stoop when they noticed Jack's approach. Bellitto's hand hovered before the lock as he stared Jack's way. Jack kept shuffling by, head down under the paper, ostensibly lost in an alcohol or drug-induced fog, but watching them from the corner of his eye.

"C'mon!" Gorilla Arms hissed to Bellitto. "I'm getting soaked."

As soon as he passed them, Jack peeked over his shoulder, saw their backs turned, and made his move. Spun, pulled out the slapper, and darted toward the stoop. Door just starting to swing open. Had to take out Gorilla Arms first.

Jack slipped in close and put everything he had into a kick behind Gorilla Arms's left knee. Felt the square toe of his boot sink deep into the nerve-, vessel-, and tendon-loaded concavity.

Gorilla Arms let out a loud sharp cry, something like, "Ahhh!" as his knee buckled under him. He went down on that knee, still cradling the blanket bundle, and that lowered his skull to perfect home-run height. Jack took aim at the bald head hovering before him and put shoulder, arm, and a snap of the wrist behind the slapper. Like swatting a T-ball. The leather-clad lead weight landed with a meaty *thwak!* and Gorilla Arms keeled over sideways with a groan. The blanket bundle landed atop him.

Heard Bellitto's keys drop and turned to find him fumbling in the side pocket of his suit coat. Jack gave a quick, backhanded swing of the slapper that grazed the side of his head. Bellitto lurched away, stumbled, and landed on his back.

Jack turned back to Gorilla Arms, saw him shake his head and push himself up on one elbow. Tough. Or maybe he had a two-inch-thick skull. Gave him another shot behind the ear and that crumpled him. Down for the count.

Jack suppressed the boiling urge to work the two of them over, mess them up royally, but even with the dead street lamp overhead, enough light leaked up and down the block from the live ones to make him feel exposed out here. Someone might have seen this little tussle and be calling 911 right now. Plus the kid was limp as a sack of grain inside that blanket. No time for fun. Had to find some help, the medical kind.

Stuffed the slapper back into his shirt and bent to lift the kid, caught a blur of movement behind and to his right, twisted away and felt a sharp pain score his right flank.

Bellitto—rearing back to stab at him again with a knife that would have been sticking out of the center of Jack's back now if he hadn't moved.

Jack rolled to his feet and took it to Bellitto, headbutting him as he grabbed his knife hand and slammed him back against the door. He pressed against Bellitto, chest to chest, belly to belly, trapping him. He had Bellitto's left wrist locked in his right hand, low, against their thighs. His left fingers were wrapped around the knife hand, higher, at shoulder level.

He spoke through his teeth. "Care to dance?"

Bellitto shook his head. Blood trickled from his nostrils. "You hurt me." He seemed surprised . . . shocked.

"That's only the beginning."

Jack had been cut and though the pain was minimal, it only stoked his fury. He wanted—needed—to hurt back.

He glanced at the long slim blade. Looked like a stiletto, a seven-incher. Dark streaks on the blade. Blood. Jack's.

"But I'm invincible . . . invulnerable."

"Really."

"Yes!"

He tried to knee Jack in the groin, but Jack had his own knees locked against him. He tried to angle the blade toward Jack, grunting with the effort, his breath rasping in Jack's face.

Jack was stronger, turned the angle back toward Bellitto as he forced the knife downward. Between them.

Bellitto struggled more violently but sagged back when Jack headbutted him again. Goddamn that felt good. Wished he had a steel plate in his head so he could keep that up. Smash his face to creep jelly.

The knife was now between their chests but Jack kept forcing the blade lower. Bellitto's half-dazed eyes grew large as he realized where the point was headed.

"No!"

" 'Fraid so," Jack said.

. . . lower . . .

"No, please! You can't!"

"Watch me."

"This isn't happening!"

"Not like dealing with little boys, is it. That's what you prefer, right. Little boys . . . someone you can have total control over?"

"No, you don't understand."

. . . lower . . .

Bellitto tried to release the knife but Jack squeezed his fingers, keeping them wrapped around the handle.

"Oh, but I do," Jack cooed. "I do, I do, I do. And now the control's on the other side. And how does that feel, you piece of shit?"

"It's not like that! Not like that at all!"

. . . lower . . .

"Then call for help. Go ahead. Scream at the top of your lungs."

Bellitto shook his head. The rain had plastered strands of his thin hair over his forehead.

"Right," Jack said. "Because the cops would want to know about the kid, how he got here, what you did to him."

Jack knew the cops could already be on their way. Had to wrap this up and move.

Tightened his grip on Bellitto's knife hand. "I just hope you didn't do something like *this*."

Drove the blade downward into Bellitto's groin, deep, felt it slice through fabric and flesh, then broke free, taking the knife with him.

Bellitto's eyes bulged as his jaw dropped open. With a long, high-pitched gasp of agony he doubled over, knees knocked, hands clutching his crotch.

"Next time you look at a kid—*every* time you look at a kid—remember that."

Jack folded the bloody knife and stuck it in his pocket. Some of that blood was his and he didn't want his DNA profile ticking like a time bomb in some computer criminal database for all eternity. His right flank stung as he turned. Looked and saw a dark stain spreading through his rain-soaked shirt.

Damn. How had he let that happen?

Moved to the blanket bundle draped across the still un-conscious Gorilla Arms. Loosened some of the folds and exposed the kid's round face. His eyes were closed. Looked like he was sleeping. Touched the forehead. Still warm. Placed his cheek over the slack little mouth. Warm breath flowed. Caught a sweet chemical smell. Chloroform?

Relief flooded through Jack. Still alive. Drugged up until Bellitto and Gorilla Arms could get him inside for whatever sick games they had planned.

No games tonight.

But now what? Instincts screamed to take off and call 911 as soon as he reached his car. But that meant leaving the kid alone with these two oxygen wasters. One of them might decide that dead kids tell no tales. Gorilla Arms was out cold and a whimpering Bellitto lay doubled over in the fetal position on the stoop; neither seemed in much con-dition to harm anyone at the moment, but Jack didn't want to risk it.

He picked up the kid. The movement caused a jab of pain in his flank. Checked the street for cars. One coming. Waited for that to pass, then dashed through the rain around the corner; keeping low behind the parked cars, he carried him one block east, then up toward Houston. When he got within half a block of the lights and traffic there, he found a sheltered doorway and gently placed his burden on the dry steps. The kid stirred, then went limp again.

Jack ran the three blocks back to his car. As soon as he got it rolling he picked his cell phone off the front seat and dialed 911.

"Listen," he told the woman who answered. "I just found an unconscious kid. I don't know what's wrong with him. You better get here fast." He rattled off the address, then hung up.

He drove to a spot around the corner from the kid's street where he double-parked again. He left the engine running and hurried back to the corner where he found another doorway that offered a view of the kid. Exactly twelve long minutes before he heard the sirens. As soon as the howling EMS rig flashed into view, Jack scooted back to his car.

Just as he was turning the ignition, he heard another siren and saw an ambulance flash by, heading in the direction of the Shurio Coppe. Bellitto must have called for help on his own cell phone. Should have thought of confiscating that as well as his knife. Let him lie there and bleed a little longer.

Speaking of bleeding . . .

Jack pressed his hand against his side and it came away red. He didn't have to take off his shirt to know a few butterflies weren't going to do the job. He needed stitches. That meant a visit to Doc Hargus.

Jack reached for the phone and hoped Hargus was on the wagon this week. Doc could probably sew up a cut like this in his sleep, but still . . .

Jack didn't insist that his doctor have a license. Hargus's had been revoked, and that was fine; it meant that the rules about reporting certain kinds of wounds would be ignored. But he also preferred that the person passing needle and thread through his flesh be reasonably sober.

After Doc did his work, Jack intended to go straight home, find Bellitto's brother's phone number, and give him a call. He had a bone to pick with Edward Bellitto.

IN THE
IN-BETWEEN

Finally, she knows her name. Stray bits and pieces of her life are floating back, but not enough. Not nearly enough.

She yearned for these memories in the hope they would tell her why she is here, and why this boundless rage suffuses her. But these bits of flotsam on the featureless sea of her existence yield no answers.

And no comfort. The flashes from her past life and memories of the joy she took in day-to-day existence only emphasize the enormity of what she has lost.

But her abilities have grown. She can manifest herself in the physical world that surrounds her. She did it earlier today. And she can make herself heard, but not in the way she wishes. She cannot speak, but for some strange reason she can sing. Why is that? And why that song? She seems to remember that it was her favorite once, but she cannot understand why. She hates that song now.

She hates everything. Everything, and everyone.

But even more she hates being here, being a shadow among the living. She realizes that she was once alive and is now dead. And she hates that. Hates all the living for having what she does not. For having a past, a present, a future!

That is the worst part. She has no future. At least none that she can see. She is here, she is now, she has a vague, undetermined purpose, but after that is completed, what happens to her? Will she be cast back into the darkness, or must she remain here, forgotten, alone?

She drifts on . . . waiting . . .

IN THE WEE HOURS

Charlie awoke in the dark and listened.

Was that . . . ? Yes. Someone was crying. The sound was echoing down the hall. High-pitched, like a child.

Charlie couldn't be sure if it was a boy or a girl. He sat up and listened more closely. Not so much a sound of sadness as a whimper of terror, and so devoid of hope it tore his heart.

Not a real child, he thought. It's a spirit, a demon sent here to lead us astray.

He pulled the covers over his head and shivered in the warm darkness.

TUESDAY

1

Gia wiped a tear from her eye as she hung up the bedside phone.

After hearing from Jack last night about the child he'd saved, Gia had called Vicky's camp first thing this morning, just to make sure everything was okay there. She trusted the camp and its security, trusted the counselors, but she'd had this steamrolling urge to hear her daughter's voice.

The director had told her that Vicky and the other kids were at breakfast. Was it an emergency? No, just ask her to give her mother a ring when she was through.

Gia had spent the next ten minutes thinking about child molesters and how the horrors they subjected their little victims to should be visited upon them a hundred—no, a thousandfold.

The call came while she'd been making the bed. Vicky was fine, great, wonderful, having the time of her life, and wanted to tell her about the hippo she'd made in her clay modeling class, rattling on about how she'd started out making a pony but the legs wouldn't hold up because she couldn't get the body right so she'd made the legs thicker and thicker and shorter and shorter until the horse could stand without collapsing or tipping over but by then it looked like the fattest horse in the world so instead of calling it a horse she told everyone she'd made a hippo. Wasn't that the funniest, Mom?

It was. So funny it had been all Gia could do to keep from breaking down and sobbing.

God, she missed her little girl.

Gia couldn't remember the last time she'd felt lonely, but with Jack out running an errand, and Vicky off in the

Catskills, the house seemed more than empty. It was barren, a wasteland, an echoing shell with no heart, no life.

Get a grip, she told herself. It's not that bad. Vicky will be back soon. In just four days and three hours, to be exact. It seemed like forever.

And when Vicky returned, should she tell her about the baby?

No. Too soon.

All right, but if not now, when? And how? How to tell her daughter that Mommy screwed up big time and got pregnant when she hadn't wanted to.

Who's the daddy? Why, Jack of course.

Which meant that the new baby would have a daddy while Vicky didn't. Vicky's father, Richard Westphalen, was missing and officially presumed dead. Gia knew, unofficially, that Vicky would never see her father again.

No big loss. While alive, Richard had been a nonparticipant in his inconvenient daughter's life. Over the past year and a half, Jack had become Vicky's father figure. He doted on her and she loved him fiercely. Partly, Gia was sure, because Jack was in many ways a big kid himself. But he took time with her, talked *to* her instead of *at* her, played catch with her, came along and sat with all the other kids' parents to watch her T-ball games.

He was everything a good father should be, but his real child was now growing inside Gia. Would Vicky see the new baby as a threat, someone who'd come between her and Jack and usurp his love? Gia knew that would never happen, but at eight years of age, could Vicky grasp that? She'd already had one father abandon her. Why not two?

All excellent reasons for Vicky to hate the new baby.

Gia couldn't bear the thought of that. One possible solution was marrying Jack. A hopelessly mundane, pedestrian, bourgeois solution, she knew, cooked up by a terminally mundane, pedestrian, bourgeois person, but as her husband, Jack could officially adopt Vicky as his daughter. That symbolic cementing would give Vicky the security she needed to accept the new baby as a sister or brother rather than a rival.

The marriage was a problem, though. Not a matter of would Jack marry her, but could he? He'd said he'd find a way. She had to trust that he would . . . if he lived long enough.

Some godawful mess I've made.

She yawned as she finished tucking in the sheets and straightening the spread. Little wonder she wasn't sleeping.

Bad enough to be worrying about Vicky and the new baby, but then Jack comes in last night with a thick bandage on his side. Told her he'd been stabbed by the very man he'd been hired to protect, who'd turned out to be some sort of pedophile.

She'd changed his dressing this morning and gasped at the four-inch gash in his flank. Not deep, just long, he'd told her. Doc Hargus had sewn him up. Gia inspected the neat running suture that had closed the wound. She'd never liked the idea of Jack going to an old defrocked physician, but last summer she'd come to trust Hargus after he guided Jack's recovery from other, worse wounds.

She was angry with Jack for getting hurt. Would he ever learn?

But then, if he did learn, did change, would he still be the same Jack? Or would some fire within him go out and leave her with a hollow man, a wraithlike remnant of the Jack she loved?

Add that to the list of things to keep her awake at night.

And then, last night, when she'd finally fallen asleep . . . visions of the mysterious little girl she'd seen in the Kenton house drifted through her dreams. Her eyes . . . Gia had caught only the briefest glimpse of them as the child had glanced back over her shoulder, but their deep blue need haunted Gia, in her dreams, and even here and now in her waking hours.

Who was she? And why such longing in those eyes? It seemed a need Gia might fill if she only knew how.

No question about it, she had to go back to that house.

2

"Got it," Jack said, tapping his finger on a story in the newspaper.

He'd grabbed the *Daily News* from Abe's counter as soon as he'd walked in and thumbed through it, looking for stories about the little Asian kid and the wounded Bellitto.

He'd found a two-inch column reporting that a Mr. Eli Bellitto of SoHo had been stabbed and a companion, Adrian Minkin—so that was Gorilla Arms's name—had been bludgeoned by an unknown assailant last night. Both were admitted to St. Vincent's.

Predators playing victims, Jack thought. Smart.

But the story about the recovery of a kidnapped Vietnamese boy got big play, with a picture of little Duc Ngo and another of his mother.

"*Nu*?" Abe said as he arranged—with surprising delicacy for his pudgy fingers—strips of lox across the inner surface of a sliced bagel. "Got what?"

"A story about the kid those pervs snatched last night. He's okay."

"What kid?"

Abe didn't look up. He was busily smearing the other half of the bagel with cream cheese—the lowfat kind. Although, considering the amount he was slathering on, he wasn't sparing himself any calories or fat.

"Hey, leave some for me," Jack told him.

He'd brought breakfast, as usual, splurging on lox—not Nova, because Abe liked the saltier kind—but trying to help Abe in the calorie department with the lowfat Philly.

"What kid?" Abe repeated, ignoring him. "What pervs?"

Jack gave him a quick rundown of last night's events, then ended by quoting from the *News* story.

"Listen to his mother: ' "I was so worried," said Ms. Ngo. "Little Duc insists on going out every night to buy ice cream. He has gone a hundred times and never had trouble. It is so terrible that children are not safe in this city." ' " Furious, Jack slammed his hand on the paper—and winced as he felt a tug on his wound. "Can you believe that? What a load of crap!"

"What's not to believe?"

"He's seven years old! It was ten o'clock and pouring! Like hell he wanted to go out. The real deal is she and her boyfriend send that little kid out every night so they can get it on while he's down on the street. But she's not going to tell that to the *News*, is she!"

He hit the paper again, harder this time—resulting in another painful yank on his wound—his fist landing on the picture of the kid's mother. He hoped she felt it, wherever she was.

"You saved him from death, maybe worse." Abe chomped into his freshly constructed bagel-and-lox sandwich and spoke around the bite. "You performed a *mitzvah*. You should be happy instead of angry."

Jack knew Abe was right but as he stared at the grainy black-and-white photo of little Duc—taken at school, most likely—all he could see was his limp body wrapped in a soggy blanket.

"She calls herself a parent? She should be protecting her kid instead of putting him in harm's way. Oughta be an exam you have to take before they let you become a parent. Guy shoots a couple million sperm and one of them hits an egg and *bam!*—a baby. But are either of the two adults capable of bringing up a child? Who knows? Children are a big responsibility. They should only be entrusted to people who can be responsible parents."

Listen to yourself, he thought. You're ranting. Stop.

He looked up and found Abe staring at him.

"*Nu*? Is there some part of this story I'm missing? What's all this *tumel* about parents?"

Jack wondered if he should tell Abe, then instantly decided he had to. How could he not? He knew it would go no further. Abe was as tightlipped as a clam.

"I'm going to be one."

"You? A father?" Abe grinned and wiped his right hand on his shirt before thrusting it across the counter. "*Mazel tov*! When did you find out?"

Jack gripped the hand, still slightly slick with salmon oil. "Yesterday afternoon."

"And Gia, she's comfortable with the prospect of saddling the world with a child who has half your genes?"

"She's fine with the child part. It's what kind of a father I can be that's causing problems for us."

"You as a good father? There's a question about this? Look at the training you're getting already with Vicky. Like a daughter she is."

"Yeah, but there are, you know, legal issues I'm going to have to deal with."

He explained those while Abe finished his bagel and began preparing another.

"She makes sense, that Gia," Abe said when Jack finished. "I have to give her that. But what I think I'm hearing here is the end of Repairman Jack."

Jack winced inwardly at hearing it so starkly put, but . . .

"I guess that pretty well sums it up."

"Citizen Jack," Abe said, shaking his head. "Doesn't have quite the same ring as Repairman Jack."

Jack shrugged. "The name wasn't my idea anyway. You're the one who started calling me that."

"And now I'll have to stop. So when do you become Citizen Jack?"

"First I have to figure out *how*. Any ideas?"

Abe shook his head. "A tough one, that. To make you a newborn citizen with no illegal baggage . . . this will take some thought."

He cut the second lox-and-bagel combo in half and gave part to Jack.

Jack took a bite, relishing the mixture of flavors and textures. He relaxed a little. Knowing that someone else was working with him on this eased some of the weight from his shoulders.

"While you're thinking," he said, "I'm going to call Eli Bellitto's brother and give him some hell."

Jack had gone straight to Gia's last night after Doc Hargus had finished stitching him up. He'd stopped by his apartment this morning and picked up Edward Bellitto's number on the way to Abe's. He wormed his Tracfone and the slip of paper out of his jeans, started to dial, then . . .

"What the . . . ?"

"What now?"

"He only wrote down nine digits."

Jack stared at the paper. Edward hadn't used hyphens, putting all the numbers in a straight string. Jack hadn't noticed till now that he'd been shortchanged one digit.

Abe leaned forward and looked at the paper. "A two-one-two area code—that means he's here in the city. Maybe he was in such a hurry or maybe he was a little *farblondzhet* from worrying about his brother so he left off the last digit. If that's the case, you can try all the possibilities. Only ten."

"But what if he left off a number in the middle? How many calls will that take?"

"Millions, you're talking."

"Swell."

Jack wondered if the missing digit was an accident at all. Maybe Edward didn't want Jack contacting him. Maybe he'd planned a vanishing act all along. If so, there went the second half of Jack's fee.

Very few of his customers ever tried to stiff him, and none of those had succeeded. Edward might be the first.

Abe pointed to Jack's cell phone. "Your new Tracfone, it's working out?"

"So far, so good. They should call it the Untraceable-fone."

Jack had picked up his at a Radio Shack along with a prepaid airtime card. He'd activated his phone online from a computer terminal in the Public Library without giving his name, address, or any credit information. Per-minute charges were higher than calling plans from Verizon and the like, but you had to sign contracts and go through credit checks for those. For Jack, the Tracfone's anonymity was priceless.

"I should maybe get one. For when I call you. You gave me that number, right?"

"You, Julio, and Gia have it, and that's it."

An idea struck Jack as he finished his bagel. He picked up his phone.

"You know, maybe I don't have to make a million calls to track down Edward Bellitto. Maybe I can simply ask his brother Eli."

"You think he'll tell you?"

"Can't hurt to try."

After information gave him St. Vincent's main number, Jack called and asked for Eli Bellitto's room.

A hoarse voice answered. "Hello?"

"Mr. Bellitto? This is Lorenzo Fullerton from the St. Vincent's accounting office. How are you this morning?"

Abe raised his eyebrows, rippling the bare expanse of his scalp, and mouthed the name: *Lorenzo Fullerton?*

Jack shrugged. It was a name he'd come up with years ago and used whenever he was pretending to represent officialdom.

"What do you want?" The voice sounded weak as well as hoarse.

Good. In pain too, Jack hoped.

"Well, your intake form isn't clear. We can't make out the name and address of your brother Edward. We'd all be terribly grateful if you could please clarify this little matter for us."

"Brother? I don't have a brother named Edward or anything else. I'm an only child."

3

Eli Bellitto slammed the receiver back onto its cradle. The abrupt movement evoked a jab of pain from his heavily bandaged groin. He groaned and looked at his doctor.

"You have idiots in your administration."

Dr. Najam Sadiq smiled. "You will hear no argument from me," he said in decent English.

Dr. Sadiq had been making late rounds in St. Vincent's when Eli arrived in the emergency department; as the most immediately available urologist, he'd been assigned to Eli's case.

Eli tried to shift his position in the bed and that ignited another bonfire of pain. He glanced at the morphine pump attached to the pole next to his bed. A PCA pump, the nurse had called it. Patient Controlled Analgesia. A button clipped to the bed rail allowed him to self-medicate— within limits—but he'd been holding off because the drug made him foggy and he feared saying the wrong thing. He didn't think he could hold off much longer though.

At least he'd had the presence of mind last night to demand a private room. He didn't care how much it cost. The last thing in the world he needed now was a nosy roommate.

"As I was saying," Dr. Sadiq said, "you are a lucky man, Mr. Bellitto. Very lucky. If that knife had sliced but a quarter of an inch further to the left, we would have had a much bigger problem."

Eli thought, I've got oxygen running into my nose, morphine hooked into my left arm, an IV running into my right, and a tube in my bladder draining bloody urine into a bag hanging near the floor. This is not lucky.

Dr. Sadiq went on. "The knife sliced into the base of your penis, just missing your urethra. We saved your penis without much trouble, but we could not save the right testicle, I'm afraid. It was too badly lacerated. I had to remove it."

The room seemed to darken around Eli as he listened. Not so much the details—that he had been sexually maimed and mutilated, that a piece of him had been amputated— but that it had occurred at all. What had happened to his invulnerability? Why had it failed him?

More importantly, who was that man last night? Had it been a chance encounter, or could he have been following him and Adrian? Could he know about the Circle?

Eli forced a smile. "I'm not thinking about starting a family. Not at my age."

"But you do not have to worry too much about sexual function. There will be scarring, of course, and that may interfere with erections, but with proper care and therapy, you should be able to resume normal sexual function within a couple of months."

Eli didn't care about sexual function. Last night had not been about sex, although the man who had attacked them seemed to think so. Not that Eli could blame him. Two men in the dark with an unconscious boy . . . the prosaic, untutored mind would naturally leap to such a conclusion. But the Circle was devoted to concerns far more profound than mere sex.

Eli wanted no more talk about his wounds or his chances for full recovery. He changed the subject.

"My friend, Mr. Minkin, the one with the head injuries . . . how is he doing?"

Adrian was an ox, yet their attacker had felled him in an instant and left him senseless.

Dr. Sadiq shook his head. "That I do not know. He was admitted to the neurology service. Is he your . . . partner?"

"Partner?"

Now why on earth would Dr. Sadiq think Adrian had anything to do with the shop? Unless . . . could he be even considering that he and Adrian were *lovers*? Yes, that had to be it.

Anger flared in Eli. What's wrong with this world? Everything is *not* about sex!

"Oh, no," Eli said. "He's just an old friend."

A tiny shift of his hips was rewarded by a disproportionate shock of pain. He was suddenly very tired.

"I think I'd like to rest now, doctor."

"Of course," Dr. Sadiq said. "I'll look in on you again during my evening rounds."

As soon as the door closed Eli grabbed the morphine delivery button and began jabbing at it like a telegraph operator. Soon a delicious lethargy suffused him, pushing away the pain and worries about strange men who lunged out of the darkness.

4

Jack stopped in front of Municipal Coins on West Fifty-fourth. He'd planned to come by yesterday but Gia's revelation had blown that plan clear out of the water.

Midday sun gleamed off the polished gold and silver coins in the window display, but Jack's attention was more focused on Eli Bellitto's last words than on precious metals.

I don't have a brother named Edward or anything else. I'm an only child.

Somebody was lying.

Eli Bellitto was a child molester, most likely a child killer—you go to the trouble of abducting a child as Bellitto and his buddy had, you're not likely to let him go—so lying was hardly a stretch. But why lie about having a brother to someone you thought was a hospital administrator? Unless you didn't want to acknowledge that brother.

But Eli Bellitto hadn't sounded like he was lying. Edward, on the other hand . . .

The phone number he'd given Jack was bogus, as was no doubt much of the story he'd laid on him. Edward had a Irish accent, Eli didn't. The two supposed brothers looked nothing alike.

No question . . . Edward had lied.

What particularly rankled Jack was that he'd made Edward—if that was his real first name; his last sure as hell wasn't Bellitto—for a straight shooter. Every so often a customer tried to pull a fast one, but Jack usually found out before any damage was done. Since many of his jobs involved getting even, with maybe inflicting a little hurt on someone if necessary, Jack made sure to do a fair amount of backgrounding before he took any action. But Edward had wanted Jack to keep people *from* being hurt, so he'd taken the man at his word.

But if he wasn't Eli Bellitto's brother, who the hell was he? Had he hired Jack to be there when Bellitto snatched that child? Seemed so. But how had he known?

Jack figured chances were slim to none he'd ever find out.

Still, he wasn't quite ready to write this off as a bad deal. Not yet. The phone number Edward had given him wouldn't allow that. If you're going to leave a phony number, you simply write down an area code and seven random digits. Why leave one out? It didn't make sense.

Jack's brain held a closetful of things that didn't make sense. He'd pitch this in with the rest.

He pushed through the door and entered the cool interior of Municipal Coins.

"Mr. Blake!" said a man who had been rearranging a tray in a long row of display cases. He bustled forward and shook Jack's hand. "So good to see you again!"

"Hello, Monte. Call me Jack, okay?"

He'd been telling Monte for years to call him Jack but the man must have been born with an extra formality gene that made it impossible for him to address a customer by his first name.

"I'll do that," he said. "Yes, I'll do that."

Monte was half owner of Municipal Coins. Every time Jack looked at him, the word *thick* sprang to mind: thick body, thick lips, even his curly black hair. But he moved like a ferret. Had a numismatic database for a brain and an MBA from Yale, but the only business he had any desire to administrate was rare coins.

"Just bought a big collection," he said, motioning Jack toward the rear of the store where he kept the cream of his inventory. "Some incredible pieces came in last week. You've got to see them. Absolutely gem."

Jack was one of Monte's regular customers. Probably saw him as a well-heeled collector of rare coins, but Jack's stash of coins was more than a collection. They were his life savings.

Without a Social Security number—a real one—he couldn't invest in CDs or stocks; he wouldn't have wanted to under any circumstances because that would mean paying taxes, a burden Jack had managed to avoid thus far in his life. So whenever he accumulated a lump of cash, he put it into gold coins, some of them bullion type, like Krugerrands, but mostly the rare and collectible. Not an exciting investment, but other facets of his life provided enough adrenaline and he saw no need to look for more in the investment realm. He'd missed the rocketing stocks of the nineties, but he'd also missed the crash of the aughts.

"Not looking for coins today, Monte," Jack said.

And I won't be buying many more if I keep allowing myself to get stiffed by customers who lie to me.

"Just a social call then?" Monte said, doing a fair job of hiding his disappointment. "Always good to see you, Mr. Blake, no matter what the occasion."

"But I *am* in the market for something to display my coins. Where are those clamshell cases you've been telling me about?"

Monte had been pushing a new line of pocket-sized display cases on Jack for months, telling him they were the latest and greatest thing for the collector who wanted to safeguard his coins when he showed them off. Jack had repeatedly turned him down.

"What're you planning?" Monte said, grinning as he reached up and pulled a cardboard box from a wall rack. "Taking them to a show? Or maybe give the relatives a peek?"

The last thing Jack wanted to do with his collection was display it, but he was going to have to bite the bullet and bring some of them out for the Madame Pomerol sting.

"Relatives," Jack told him. "Gonna give my Uncle Matt a peek."

"Lucky him."

From the box Monte removed a pair of keys and an oblong metal case that ran eight inches long and was just shy of five inches wide; its tapered brushed chrome surface gleamed under the lights.

"See?" Monte said, pointing. "Recessed hinges at this end and a lock at the other."

He stuck one of the keys into the keyhole and turned it. The lid popped open revealing a clear plastic shield. Under that, gray felt molded into angled slots that would display coins of varying sizes

"But the real beauty of it is this shield here: Tough clear plastic that keeps people's hands off. Remember that old song, 'You can look but you'd better not touch'?"

" 'Poison Ivy,' " Jack said. "The Coasters. Atco label. Nineteen-fifty-nine."

"Oh. Right. Yeah, well, that's what this case is all about. And if anyone, God forbid, knocks the case over, the shield will keep your coins from rolling all over creation."

Jack turned the case over in his hands. Perfect.

"How do I open the shield?"

"Another beauty feature. See that little lever recessed into the side? You turn your key over and use the edge to pull it up to where you can grab it. No one 'accidentally' popping open the lid."

"Beautiful," Jack said. "I'll take two."

5

Jack stepped out of the Sports Authority on Sixth Avenue in Chelsea with his purchases tucked into the same bag as the coin cases. He now had the raw materials for his encounter with Madame Pomerol this afternoon; all he had to do was assemble them. That would take half an hour, tops, which meant he still had a couple of hours to kill.

A trip down to the Shurio Coppe might be in order. Chat up the staff. See how the boss was doing. Maybe even cop a shurio.

He decided to walk. He liked to stroll the city, especially on warm days like this when the sidewalks were crowded. It fed his people-watching jones and kept him in tune with what the average New Yorker was wearing.

Average New Yorker . . . right. If such a creature existed, it was a chimerical beast. Take a simple item like men's headwear, for instance. In the first few blocks heading downtown Jack passed a gray-suited Sikh wearing a red turban, a three-hundred-pound black guy in a tiny French beret, a skinny little white guy in a Special Forces beret, a rabbi type wearing—despite the heat—a long frock coat and a wide-brimmed black sealskin hat, and then the usual run of doo-wraps, Kangols, kufis, and yarmulkes.

But Jack was gratified to see that the most common headwear by far was what he was wearing: the baseball cap. Yankee caps outnumbered Mets, but not by much. Jack's sported the orange Mets insignia. Although ninety percent of the caps he saw were worn backwards or sideways, and although Jack tended to avoid nonconformist looks, he wore his beak first. Backwards, the adjustable strap irritated his forehead; beak first it shadowed his face.

He figured in his Mets cap, aviator mirror shades, white Nike T-shirt, jeans, and tan work boots he was as good as invisible.

Jack walked through the door of the Shurio Coppe at around 1 P.M. He didn't see any customers. He found the red-haired assistant behind the marble sales counter unpacking a box. Jack noticed the return address: *N. Van Rijn—Import/Export.*

"Is Eli in?"

"Are you a friend of his?"

"I ran into him last night."

The clerk blinked. "You did? When?"

"Last night. Why? Is something wrong?"

"Yes! He's in the hospital!"

"Really? Oh, I'm so sorry to hear that. This is shocking! Did he have a heart attack or something?"

"No! He was stabbed! It happened right around the corner. Right on his own doorstep!"

Jack slapped his hands against his cheeks. "Get out! Is he all right?"

A nod. "I think so. He called earlier and said he should be home in a few days, but he won't be back to work for a while. It's terrible, just terrible."

"Isn't it, though," Jack replied, shaking his head sadly. "What kind of a world is it when an innocent man gets stabbed for no reason at all?"

"I know. Terrible."

"Which hospital?"

"St. Vincent's."

"I'll have to stop by and see how he's doing."

"I'm sure he'd like that." The assistant shook his head again, then took a deep breath and looked at Jack. "In the meantime, is there something in particular I can help you with?"

"No," Jack said. "I think I'll just browse." He looked around. "You're here alone? Where's . . . ?"

"Gert? She's off and I can't reach her. She'll be back

tomorrow." He looked around uncertainly at the laden shelves. "I wish she were here now."

I don't, Jack thought. This is perfect.

He placed the bag with his purchases on the counter. "Would you watch this if I leave it here?"

"I'd be happy to."

Of course he would. Shops like this paid extra attention to browsers with shopping bags. All it took was the flick of a finger to push an expensive little item off a shelf and into a bag. Giving up the bag would make the clerk less watchful and free up both of Jack's hands.

The object of Jack's desire lay in the locked display case rightward and rearward, so he headed left front. He found an old, wooden, owl-shaped clock whose eyes moved counter to the pendulum. Or at least they were supposed to. It appeared to have been overwound. The price wasn't bad. He already had a black plastic cat clock with moving eyes at home; this would make a good partner. An owl and a pussy cat.

Jack carried the clock to the counter.

"If you can get this working, I'll buy it."

The clerk smiled. "I'll see what I can do."

That should keep him occupied, Jack thought as he sidled away to the right, toward the old oak display case.

Had his shim picks ready by the time he reached it. Checked the second shelf and, yes, the Roger Rabbit key ring still lay among the other tchotchkes. And the padlock still locked the door.

He'd noted Sunday that the lock was a British brand, a B&G pin tumbler model. Good, solid lock, but hardly foolproof. Opening it was a five-second procedure: two to find the shim with the right diameter for the shackle, one to slide the little winged piece of steel into the shackle hole of the lock housing, one to give it a twist, and another to pop the lock.

Jack pocketed the shims. A quick glance around—the clerk was bent over the clock and no one else in sight— then another five seconds to slip off the lock, open the door, grab Roger Rabbit, close and relock the door.

Success.

He stared at the cheap little key ring. It felt strange in his hand . . . just a bit too cool against the flesh of his palm, as if he'd pulled it from a refrigerator. And still that imploring look in Roger's wide blue eyes.

Originally he'd wanted it for Vicky. But Vicky wasn't involved anymore; he didn't want her near anything Eli Bellitto had owned, touched, or had even looked at. Jack wasn't sure why he wanted it now. Bellitto had turned down a ridiculous amount of money for the silly thing. That meant it was important to him. And what was important to Bellitto might be important to Jack. Or maybe Jack wanted the key ring to harass Eli Bellitto, just for the sheer hell of it.

Before turning away he let his gaze roam once more over the shelves of the display case and the junk they carried . . . the Pogs and Matchbox car and Koosh ball and . . .

A notion struck Jack, a possibility so sick and cold he felt a layer of frost form on his skin.

These were all toys . . . kids' stuff . . . all belonging to a guy who'd snatched a kid last night.

Jack stood before the cabinets and swayed with the vertiginous certainty that these were trophies, mementos emptied from the pockets of other missing kids. And Eli Bellitto was flaunting them. How many hundreds, even thousands of people had walked by this case and stared at its contents, never guessing that each one represented a dead child?

Jack couldn't bring himself to count the items. Instead he looked down at the key ring in his hand.

Who did you belong to? Where is your little owner buried? How did he die? *Why* did he die?

Roger's eyes had lost their imploring look. They were a flat dead blue now. Maybe Jack had simply imagined that look, but it had served its purpose: He wasn't through with Eli Bellitto.

He wondered what his own face looked like. He had to compose his expression, look calm, casual.

He took a deep breath, let it out. Tossing the key ring casually in his hand, he headed for the counter.

"Sorry," the clerk said as he approached. He tapped the owl clock before him on the counter. "I can't get it working."

Jack shrugged. "I'll take it anyway." He knew a clock-smith who'd have it ticking in half a minute. "What's your name, by the way?"

"Kevin."

"I'm Jack, Kevin." They shook hands. "You're new here, aren't you."

"Fairly."

Chalk one up for me, he thought. He'd got the impression on Sunday that this fellow was new.

"Well, good luck here. It's a great store. Oh, yeah," he said, as if suddenly remembering. He tossed the key ring onto the counter. "I'll take this as well."

Kevin picked it up and turned it over, examining it. "Never seen this before."

Jack let out a breath. He'd been counting on that. Even if Kevin had been working here awhile, he might not have paid attention to the contents of a cabinet he couldn't open.

"I found it on a shelf back there."

"Where?"

Jack jerked a thumb to the right. "Back there."

"Hmmm. Trouble is, there's no price on it. I don't even think we carry anything like this."

"I'll give you, oh, say, ten bucks for it."

Kevin reached for the phone. "I'd better just check with Mr. Bellitto first."

Jack stiffened. "Hey, don't bother Eli. I'm sure he needs his rest."

"No, it's okay. He told me to call if I have any questions."

Jack suppressed a groan as Kevin tapped in the numbers. He'd wanted to slip away with the key ring—no fuss, no hassle. That might not be possible now. But if he had to grab it and walk out over Kevin's objections, that was what he'd do. One way or another, Jack and Roger were leaving together.

Apparently Kevin called Bellitto's room directly because seconds later he said, "Hello, Mr. Bellitto, it's Kevin. Sorry to bother you, but I've got an item here with no price tag and I was wondering—"

Even from his spot across the counter Jack could hear the angry squawking from the ear piece.

"Yes, sir, but you see—"

More squawks.

"I understand. Yes, sir, I will." He hung up. "I'm afraid this is going to take a while. I'm going to have to go through the inventory and find similar items and price this accordingly." He shook his head as he gazed at the key ring. "Trouble is, I'm pretty sure we don't—"

"Let me make it easy for both of us," Jack said. "I'll pay for the clock and give you ten bucks for the key ring. If it comes to more, I'll settle up. If it's less, I get a refund. Sound fair?"

"I guess so . . ."

Jack picked up the key ring and dangled it between them. "Hey, let's face it, Kev, we're not talking about a Ming vase here. Just find some paper and write down, 'Roger Rabbit key ring—ten bucks—Jack.'"

"I'll put it in the sale book," he said, opening a black ledger. Kevin dutifully wrote it all down, then looked up. "Just Jack?"

"Sure. Eli will know."

Maybe not right away, Jack thought as he pulled out his wallet. But soon. Very soon.

Jack wanted Bellitto to know the key ring was gone. Because that was when he would begin wondering and worrying.

Jack planned to give him lots to worry about.

6

Morphine might help pain, Eli Bellitto thought as he pressed the PCA pump's button for another dose, but it does nothing for anger.

Imagine Kevin calling him in the hospital with a question like that. Why couldn't you get good help?

He wondered if it might have been unwise to castigate Kevin as severely as he had. With Gert off today and not answering her phone, he was minding the store on his own. No telling what untold damage a disgruntled clerk might do.

Eli was reaching for the phone to call him back when Detective Fred Strauss made his second visit of the day. Strauss managed to be lean and yet paunchy. He wore a green golf shirt under his wrinkled tan suit. As he closed the door behind him, he removed his straw fedora, revealing thinning brown hair.

"It's safe to talk?" Strauss said in a low voice as he pulled a chair closer to the bed.

Eli nodded. "Did you learn anything?"

Strauss worked Vice in Midtown South. He, like Adrian, was a member of Eli's Circle.

"I checked with every emergency room from the Battery into the Bronx. No guy with the kind of stab wound you describe. Are you sure you nailed him?"

"Of course, I'm sure." Eli knew what it felt like to drive a steel blade into human flesh. "He may think he can take care of the wound himself, but he'll need professional care."

"Yeah, but if he knows the right people, he won't need an ER."

How different things would be, Eli thought, if the stranger hadn't rolled aside at that last instant. The knife would have sliced into his lungs once, twice, many times. Eli would now be sitting comfortably at home, and Strauss's only concern would be how to dispose of the stranger's body.

"Nothing else?"

"Well, they found a witness who says she saw a guy running with a child-size bundle in the area, but with the dark and the rain she couldn't even give the color of his hair."

Eli tried to dredge up some distinguishing feature about his attacker but came up empty. What little light had been available had come from behind, leaving his face in darkness. His hair had been drenched with rain. Dry, it could have been brown or black.

But he remembered the voice, that cold, flat voice after he'd driven Eli's own knife into his groin . . .

Next time you look at a kid—every *time you look at a kid*—*remember that.*

Eli ground his teeth. He thought I was a child molester! A common pervert! The idea infuriated him. It was so wrong, so unjust.

"All I can tell you," he said, "is that he wasn't blond."

Strauss leaned close and lowered his voice even further. "That's not what you told the local guys. You said he *was* blond."

Eli leaned back from the onions on Strauss's breath. Everything he'd told the local detectives had been false. He'd sent them looking for a six-foot-three, two-hundred-and-fifty-pound bruiser with long, bleached-blond hair. He hadn't mentioned a word about wounding him.

"Exactly. Because we don't want him caught, do we. At least not by anyone outside the Circle. He might start babbling about the lamb. Fibers from the blanket might be linked to me or Adrian or the car."

"Speaking of cars, the witness said she saw him dump the bundle in a doorway and run back to a car."

Eli stiffened. The movement stabbed a spike of pain through his morphine curtain. "Tell me she didn't see the plates."

"She thought she did. Wrote down the number, but when we traced them we found they belonged to Vinny the Donut."

"Who's he?"

"Vincent Donato. A Brooklyn wise guy."

"You mean mafia?" The thought terrified Eli.

"Don't worry. It wasn't him."

"How can you be so sure?"

"Because Vinny doesn't leave witnesses. Our lady must've missed a number or two in the dark. I'm checking other possible combinations but it's not looking good."

"What about his phone? Someone called EMS about the lamb. It had to be him. Don't those switchboards have caller ID?"

"They do. And they got the number, which looked like a pretty good lead until we found out he used a Tracfone."

"What's that?"

"A pay-as-you-go cell phone. The only personal information you have to give when you sign up is the zip code you'll be calling from most frequently. The one he gave was for Times Square."

"Damn!"

"It's like the guy is some kind of ghost."

"I assure you he's not a ghost," Eli said. "Can you get his phone number from EMS?"

Strauss shrugged. "Sure. Why?"

"I don't know yet. I just want it. It's our only link to him." Eli shifted—very carefully—in the bed. "What about Adrian? What did he see?"

"Adrian's useless. He gets dizzy every time he makes a quick move and won't believe it's August. The last things he remembers were in July."

"Just as well, I suppose," Eli said. "That way he can't contradict my story."

"Never mind your story," Strauss said, rising and pacing

at the foot of the bed. "Who *is* this guy? *That*'s what I want to know! From what you tell me, he knows how to handle himself. Took out Adrian one-two-three. And it sounds like he came prepared, which means he must have been following you two."

"If he was following anyone, it must have been Adrian," Eli said. "He must have spotted Adrian while he was researching the lamb."

All that work, Eli thought. All wasted.

Adrian was such an excellent scout, always keeping an eye out for the next lamb. When the time for a new Ceremony neared, everyone in the Circle began watching the sidewalks. But Adrian was always on alert, even when a new Ceremony wouldn't be necessary for almost a full year, he kept watch. He'd been so excited with this latest find: the right age, adhering to a predictable schedule. The perfect lamb.

They'd watched and waited, and last night they knew the time had come: a rainy night near the new moon. The pickup had gone off perfectly, they'd been almost through Eli's door, and then . . .

"Doesn't matter who he was following," Strauss said. "He knows about you and Adrian now. Who else does he know about?"

Eli didn't want Strauss feeling too comfortable, so he said, "And if he's been watching this room, he probably knows about you as well."

Strauss stopped his pacing. "Shit! I thought it was safer than the phone."

"It is. You did the right thing. Let's face it, for all we know, he may already know about all twelve members of the Circle. But I have a bigger concern: Why didn't he turn us in? We know he had a phone. Adrian and I were helpless. All he had to do was simply step back and call 911."

"But he didn't," Strauss said, rubbing his neck with his jittery, skinny fingers. "He carried the kid away and then called. Could've been a hero, but he just faded away."

"Taking the knife with him," Eli added. "Why? It was covered with my prints, not his."

"But his blood was on it, along with yours."

A wave of cold rippled up Eli's spine. My blood . . . did he want a sample of my blood . . . for some ceremony of his own, perhaps?

Strauss tapped his fist on the footboard of Eli's bed. "None of this makes any sense. Unless . . ."

"Unless what?"

"Unless the guy knows about the Circle, and how connected we all are. I, for one, would not want to get on the wrong side of us."

True. The twelve men—Eli rather liked the idea of having twelve disciples—who made up the Circle were a diverse lot, with their hands on strings that ran to and from very high places—media, judicial, legislative, even the police. Only Eli lacked civic influence. But Eli had started the Circle, and he controlled the Ceremony.

"What about the lamb?" Eli said. "Will he be a problem?"

Strauss shook his head. "Remembers being grabbed, a smelly cloth pushed against his face, and that's it." He glanced toward the closed door and lowered his voice. "And speaking of lambs, do we have a backup?"

"Gregson has one under watch but he didn't think it was ready for pickup."

"Maybe he can accelerate things. If we miss this window—"

"I know. Only one more new moon before the equinox." The Ceremony had to be completed each year during the phase of a new moon between the summer solstice and the autumnal equinox. "But we still have time."

What a catastrophic shame to lose the little Vietnamese lamb. He'd been ripe for picking, everyone in the Circle had been on standby; the Ceremony could have been completed last night, and they'd all have been set for another year.

"But you know what bothers me the most?" Strauss said.

"You, here, in a hospital bed. Because of the Ceremony you're supposed to be protected, immune to harm. At least that's what you've been telling us." He waved his hand in the direction of Eli's IVs. "How do you explain all this?"

The same question had tortured Eli since the blade of his own stiletto had cut into his flesh.

"I can't," Eli said. "In the two hundred and six years that I have been performing the Ceremony, nothing like this has ever happened. I have come through wars and floods and earthquakes unscathed. Yet last night . . ."

"Yeah. Last night you were anything but protected. Care to explain?"

Eli didn't like Strauss's tone. A note of hostility, perhaps? Or fear?

"I believe the problem is not with me but with the man who attacked me. After personally experiencing his superior strength, and after what you've told me about his elusiveness, I'm beginning to believe that we were not attacked by an ordinary man. I—"

Eli stopped as he experienced an epiphany. Suddenly it was all clear.

"What's wrong?" Strauss said, leaning forward, his expression tight.

"The only way to explain last night's events is to assume that we are dealing with someone who is using the Ceremony himself."

Yes, of course. That had to be it. It explained why the attacker had moved the child away, why he didn't turn in Eli and Adrian to the police; it might even explain his taking the knife. He didn't want to expose the Circle—he wanted to control it. He wanted to usurp Eli's position, and he probably thought some of the leader's blood would aid him in accomplishing that.

"Oh, that's great!" Strauss said, his voice rising. "Just fucking great! How are we supposed to handle something like that?"

Eli kept his tone low and even. This was no time for panic. "The way you would handle anyone else. You have at your disposal the resources of one of the greatest police departments in the world. Use them to find this man. And when you do, bring him to me."

"But I thought you were the only one who knew the Ceremony."

"What I can discover, so can others. You are not to worry about that. Your task is clear: Find him, Freddy. Find him and bring him to me. I will deal with him."

7

Gia stepped out of Macy's with a loaded shopping bag in each hand and headed for the curb to look for a cab. She'd picked up some good bargains that Vicky could wear back to school next month.

She wondered if the driver on the way home would give her the same strange look as the one who'd brought her down here. Probably. She couldn't blame them: Women who lived on Sutton Square did not go to Macy's for a Red Tag sale.

Probably thinks I'm a live-in nanny, she thought.

My address may be one of the best in the city, guys, but I'm living on the income of a freelance commercial artist. I have an active little girl who wears out what she doesn't outgrow. So when Macy's advertises a sale, I go.

As she moved toward the curb she noticed a black woman with a microphone; a burly fellow stood beside her, peering through the lens of the camera on his shoulder. The woman looked familiar but she was oddly dressed—the blouse and jacket on her upper half did not go with the denim shorts on her lower half. Herald Square was jammed and the crowd seemed even thicker around this woman.

Then Gia recognized her as one of the on-the-scene reporters from a local TV station—channel two or four, she couldn't remember which. The woman spotted Gia and angled her way with the cameraman in tow.

"Excuse me," she said, thrusting the microphone ahead of her. "I'm Philippa Villa, News Center Four. Care to answer the Question of the Day?"

"Depends on what it is," Gia said, still edging toward the curb.

"You heard about the kidnapping and return of little Duc Ngo?"

"Of course."

"Okay." Ms. Villa pushed the microphone closer. "The Question of the Day is: Should child molesters get the death penalty?"

Gia remembered how she'd felt this morning, imagining what it would have been like if Vicky had been abducted. Or if someone ever molested the baby growing inside her . . .

"You mean after they've been castrated?" she said.

The woman blinked as a couple of onlookers laughed. "We're just talking about the death penalty. Yes or no?"

"No," Gia said through her rising anger and revulsion. "Death's too good for anyone who'd hurt a child. The guy who snatched that little boy should be castrated. And after that he should have his hands cut off so he can never touch another child, and then his legs cut off so he can never stalk another child, and then his tongue ripped out so he can never coax another kid into his car, and his eyes put out so that he can never even look at a child again. I'd leave him his nose so he can breathe in the stink of his rotten body."

The surrounding gaggle cheered.

Did I just say that? Gia thought. I've been hanging around Jack too long.

"You seem to have a lot of support," Ms. Villa said, glancing around at the crowd. "We might want to air your comments on the news tonight." She smiled. "The *late* news. We'll need you to sign a release to—"

Gia shook her head. "No thanks."

She didn't want to be on TV. She just wanted to get home. She turned as a cab nosed in toward the curb to drop off a passenger.

"Can I at least have your name?" Ms. Villa said as she and the cameraman followed Gia to the cab.

"No," Gia said over her shoulder.

She slid into the rear of the cab as soon as it was empty. She closed the door and told him to head uptown. She didn't look back as the cab pulled away.

What had possessed her to say something like that? On camera, no less. She'd been telling the truth—those had been her exact feelings at the moment—but they were nobody else's business. She certainly didn't want her face on the tube. If she had fifteen minutes of fame coming, she wanted it through her paintings, not from flapping her gums on local TV.

8

Can I handle fatherhood? Jack thought as he knocked on the door to Madame Pomerol's Temple of Eternal Knowledge.

He'd dodged bullets and been punched, stabbed, sliced, and gouged during the years since he'd moved to the city. He should be able to handle fatherhood. At least he hoped he could.

The prospect of being responsible for raising a child to be a decent human being without screwing up along the way filled his mind, made dodging knives and bullets seem an easier task. At least then the choices were clear.

Thank God he'd be only partly responsible and could defer to Gia's hands-on experience.

But what if something happened to her?

Jack shuddered at the possibility and wondered why he was borrowing trouble. This wasn't like him. Was that what parenthood did to you?

Leave all that for later, he told himself. Focus on the now.

He checked the wig so that the long rear strands of its mullet were again draped over his ears, especially the left with its ear piece.

The door opened and Carl Foster stood there. "Ah, Mr. Butler. Right on time."

Mr. Butler? Jack thought. He almost looked around, then remembered that *he* was Butler.

Focus, damn it!

He half wished Gia had waited till tonight to tell him. This was going to be a delicate fix, with pinpoint timing. He had to keep his mind off the future and concentrate on the moment.

"Time and tide don't wait for nobody," Jack said, snapping into character. "That's what I always say."

"Well put," Foster replied, ushering him in.

Today Jack wore jeans, cowboy boots, a white Walking Man collarless shirt, and a plaid sport coat with two deep inner pockets, each heavy with their cargo. He followed Foster to the desk.

"Let's attend to mundane matters first," Foster said. "You have Madame's fee?"

"What? Oh, sure." Jack drew an envelope from a side pocket and handed it to Foster. "Here you go."

Foster opened it and quickly fanned through the five counterfeit one-hundred-dollar bills inside. He looked disappointed.

"I thought you said gold was the best way to deal with the spirit world."

"Yeah well, that's what my Uncle Matt used to tell me, but you know how hard it is to put together a bunch of gold coins that total an exact amount? Too much trouble, if you ask me."

"I could have given you change."

"Never thought of that. Okay, next time it's gold."

"Excellent!" Foster said, brightening as he pocketed the envelope. "You mentioned wanting to contact an uncle? Was he the one you mentioned who used to frequent spiritualist mediums?"

"Yep. Uncle Matt."

"Certainly not Matt Cunningham?"

Oh, you're good, Jack thought. Slick way to draw out some details.

But Jack wanted to be drawn out. He was primed to babble.

"Naw. His last name was West. Matthew West. Great guy. Shame he had to go."

"When was that?"

Jack wondered if Foster was taking mental notes or if Madame herself was seated at their computer, listening to the bugs and typing Matthew Thomas West's name into www.sitters-net.com even as they spoke.

"Early in the year—not sure if it was late January or early February. I just know I never been so cold in my life as at that funeral. Standing outside in that wind at the graveside—boy!" Jack rubbed his hands and hunched his shoulders as if remembering the chill. "I tell you, I thought I'd never feel warm again."

"Really," Foster said. "I recall this past winter being rather mild."

"Here, maybe, but we were freezing our butts off in St. Paul."

"Minnesota? Yes, they certainly do get cold winters out there. Is that where you're from?"

"Me? Nah. Born and raised in Virginia."

"How do you like Manhattan?"

"Love it. Never seen so many restaurants in my life. And they're all crowded." He laughed. "Don't anybody ever eat in around here?"

Foster smiled. "Yes, the Upper West Side offers every cuisine known to man."

Jack narrowed his eyes in a display of suspicion. "How do you know where I live?"

"Why, from the questionnaire you filled out yesterday."

"Oh, yeah." He gave a sheepish grin. "Forgot about that."

Jack had expected the Fosters to check up on him. He'd been the only new face yesterday when the lights had come on, so he had to be a prime suspect. That was why he'd used the name of a real person . . . just in case he had to come back.

But he'd given himself plausible deniability: the remote rig in the light switch could be activated from outside the seance room.

He was sure they'd checked up on him. Foster no doubt took a trip to the Millennium Towers and found that a Robert Butler did indeed live there. If he'd seen the real Robert Butler, the jig would have been up. But obviously he hadn't. If he'd called the number Jack had written on the questionnaire—someone had done just that last night and hung up—he heard an outgoing message from "Bob Butler" confirming the number and instructing him to leave a message after the beep.

The Krugerrand yesterday and today's envelope full of cash should have laid any residual suspicions to rest. At least that was what Jack hoped. These two were the type who tried to kill the competition. What would they do to someone they thought was trying to pull a sting on them?

Jack took comfort in the little .38 automatic nestled in his right boot.

Foster said, "You were close to your uncle?"

"Oh, yeah. Great guy. Split his estate between me and my brother when he died. *Great* guy."

"Is that why you wish to contact him? To thank him?"

"Well, yeah. And to ask him . . ." Jack reached into the left inner breast pocket of his jacket and pulled out one of Monte's clamshell cases. ". . . about this."

Foster's eyes fixed on its chrome finish.

"Interesting." He reached for it. "May I?"

Jack handed it to him and watched his hand drop as it

took the full weight of the box. But Foster made no mention of how heavy it was. The fingers of his free hand glided over the tapered surface, caressing the seam, running across the inset hinges, and coming to rest on the keyhole at the opposite end.

"Do you have the key?"

"Um, no."

"Really. I'll bet there's an interesting story behind this case."

Jack put on a guilty expression as he held out his hand for the case. "You might say that. But that's between me, my uncle, and the lady."

"Yes, of course," Foster said, handing it back to him. He glanced at his watch. "I'll see if Madame is ready."

He stepped away from the desk and entered the seance room, closing the door behind him. Jack listened in on a hurried strategy meeting between Mr. and Mrs. Foster beyond that door.

"He's telling the truth," Madame Pomerol's voice said in his left ear. *"I found the uncle on sitters-net. And get this: He was a coin collector."*

"You should feel the weight of that case he's got. I'm betting it's stuffed with gold coins. Trouble is it's locked."

"That shouldn't be a problem for you. Get a look inside that case. I'll handle the rest."

A moment later Foster reappeared and motioned Jack toward the door.

"Come. Madame is ready."

He ushered Jack into the room. Again that claustrophobic feeling from all the heavy drapes. This time only two chairs huddled against the table.

Foster pointed to the case. "Did that belong to your uncle?"

"I'm pretty sure it did. That's one of the things I want to find out."

"Then I'll have to ask you to place it on that settee over there until later in the session."

Jack looked at the little red velvet upholstered couch

against the wall about a dozen feet away. Jack knew what lay on the other side of that wall: Foster's command center, much like Charlie's but not as sophisticated. He'd found it Saturday night when he'd searched the place.

"Why?"

"Madame finds her gift works better if she is not in proximity to objects that once belonged to the departed she is trying to contact."

Good line, Jack thought as he clutched the case against his chest.

"No kidding? I'd think they'd be a big help."

"Oh, they are, they are, but later. Once she is one with the Other Side, they are invaluable. But early on, when Madame is making the transition, the auras from these objects interfere with her connection."

"I don't know," Jack said, drawing out the words.

Foster pointed to the little couch. "Please. Place it on the settee for now. When Madame has the ear of the spirits, she will ask you to bring it to the table. Have no fear. It will be quite safe there."

Jack made a show of indecision, then shrugged. "All right. If it's gonna help make this work, what the hey."

He walked to the settee and settled the case on the cushions, but his eyes were searching the wall behind it, looking for seams in the wallpaper. He found none, but noticed that the molding here ran in a box pattern just above the level of the settee. He knew one of those rectangles hid a little trapdoor; he'd seen its other side Saturday night.

Empty-handed, he returned to the table and seated himself in the chair the smiling Carl Foster was holding for him.

"Madame will be with you shortly."

And then Jack was alone. He knew he was on camera so he looked nervous, drumming on the table, fiddling with his jacket. While doing that he checked the stack of counterfeit bills inside his left sleeve, and the second metal case in his left inner breast pocket.

All set.

A moment later the overhead spots went out and Madame Pomerol made her entrance in another flowing beaded gown, pink this time. She wore the same turbanlike hat as on Sunday.

"Monsieur Butler," she said in her faux French accent as she extended her bejeweled hand, "how good to see you again."

"Nice to be up close and personal, as it were."

"I understand you wish to contact your late uncle, yes?"

"That I do."

"Then let us begin."

No preliminaries this time, no speech about not touching the ectoplasm. Madame Pomerol seated herself opposite Jack and said, "Please lay your hands flat on the table." When Jack complied she said, "I will now contact my spirit guide, the ancient Mayan priest known to me as Xultulan."

As they had Sunday, the clear bulbs on the chandelier faded, leaving the dull red ones lit. Once again shadows crowded around the table, held off only by the faint red glow from above. Jack glanced toward the settee and his case but could make out no details in the darkness.

Madame Pomerol began her tonal hum, then did her head-loll thing.

Jack guessed the reason for the hum: to help mask any sound of the trapdoor opening in the wall by the settee. Foster was probably reaching for the metal case right now.

This was SOP in the spook trade: snatch the purse, rifle through it for whatever information it contained: driver license, SSN, bank account number, address book, pictures of family members. Foster's command center had a photocopier and a key cutter, just like Charlie's; he could copy documents and keys in minutes.

If the remote switch were still in place it might have been fun to turn on the lights and catch Foster with his hand in the till, but Jack had already played that scene. He was going for a bigger sting today.

The table tipped under his hands and so he felt obliged to let out a startled, "Whoa!"

And then the low, echoey moan from the lady. The amp had been turned on.

"O Xultulan! We have a seeker after one who has crossed over, one with whom he shares a blood tie. Help us, O Xultulan!"

Jack tuned her out and concentrated on time. Foster should have snatched the case by now. He'd have had his pick set open and ready and would be working on the lock. Jack had a key but he'd done a couple of test runs picking the lock himself—and had purposely left a few crude scratches around it. As expected, the little lock turned out to be an easy pick, complicated only by its small size. If Foster had any talent, he should be turning those tumblers just . . . about . . . now.

And now he's lifting the top . . . and freezing at the sight of rows of gleaming gold coins. Not bullion coins like yesterday's Krugerrand, but numismatic beauties from Jack's own collection, worth far more than their weight in gold.

He wants to touch them but the plastic dome stops him. He tries to lift it but it won't budge. It's locked down. But there has to be a catch somewhere, a release . . .

"My case," Jack said, straightening and running jittery hands over his jacket like a man who'd just discovered that his wallet is missing. "I want my case!"

"Please be calm, Monsieur Butler," Madame Pomerol said, suddenly alert and aware and free of her trance. "Your case is fine."

Jack rose from his chair. He put a tremor in his voice. "I-I-I want it. I've got to find it!"

"Monsieur Butler, you must sit down." That was a warning to her husband to put his ass in gear and get this turkey's precious case back on the settee. "I am in touch with Xultulan and he has located your uncle. You can retrieve the case in a few minutes when—"

"I want it now!"

Jack feigned disorientation and wandered in the wrong direction first—he wanted to give Foster enough time to close the case and return it—then lurched around and stumbled toward the settee.

"We're okay," Foster's voice said in his ear. *"It's back on your side."*

Jack couldn't see the settee in the darkness so he traveled by memory, and made sure he banged into it when he reached it. He felt around on the cushion and found the case.

"Here it is!" he cried. "Thank God!"

As he was speaking he slipped that case into his left breast pocket and removed its identical twin from the right. He'd filled the mounts within the first with gleaming pristine beauties that anyone would recognize as valuable for their bullion weight alone. But when Foster saw the dates he'd know they were old. And since they'd looked up Matthew West on sitters-net.com, he'd assume they were rare.

The second case, however, he'd filled with lead sinkers.

"Shit, that was close!" said Foster's voice. *"But worth it. You should see what's in that case. Gold coins. Not more Krugerrands, but old collectibles. They must be worth a fucking fortune. Think of something. We have got to get our hands on those coins!"*

As Jack waded back toward the faintly glowing pool of red around the table, he noticed a look of concentration and distraction on Madame Pomerol's face as she listened to her husband.

She'd probably been ready to scold her sitter, but now she gave Jack a warm, motherly smile.

"See, Monsieur Butler? There was nothing for you to get upset about. You feel better now, yes?"

"Much." He took his seat and used the moment to pull the stack of thirty bogus hundreds from within his sleeve and lay it on his lap. Then he put both hands on the table and clutched the case between them. "I'm real sorry about that. Don't know what came over me. I just got scared, I guess. You know, the darkness and all."

"That is perfectly understandable, especially on your first

visit." She covered her eyes with a hand. "I have made contact with your uncle."

Jack jerked upright in his seat. "Really? Can I talk to him?"

"The connection was broken when you left the table."

"Oh, no!"

"But that is not a terrible thing. I can reestablish it. But it was not a good connection, so I must ask you a few questions first."

"Shoot."

"Your uncle, his middle name was Thomas, yes?"

"You know, I believe it was. Yes, Matthew Thomas West. How'd you know that?"

She smiled. "Your uncle told me."

"Damn! That's scary."

"He seemed upset about something. Do you know what it could be?"

Jack averted his eyes, hoping he looked guilty. "I don't think so."

"Something about an inheritance, perhaps?"

Jack looked awestruck. "You know about that?"

He was perfectly aware that he'd told Foster about sharing the estate with his brother, but it was common for sitters to forget that their own loose lips were the source of most of what a medium told them.

"Of course, but communication was garbled. Something about you and your brother . . ."

Jack started with his story. It jibed with all the available information on sitters-net.com; he'd looked at it from different angles and couldn't see any holes. He hoped Madame Pomerol wouldn't either.

"Yeah. We were his only living relatives. Our folks were gone, and he had no kids."

No kids, Jack thought. Must've died a lonely old man, going to mediums in a vain attempt to contact his dead wife. But that's not going to happen to me. Not now . . .

The realization lit a warm glow in his chest.

"Monsieur Butler?"

Jack snapped to. He'd drifted away. Jeez. Not like him. Couldn't afford to do that or he'd blow the sting.

"Sorry. I was just thinking about Uncle Matt. After he died, his will divided his estate between me and my brother Bill."

"Yes, he told me his wife Alice had died many years before him. They are reunited now."

"You know about Aunt Alice? This is amazing. And they're together again? That's great."

"They are very happy. The inheritance?"

"Oh yeah. Well, I got the house and everything in it." Jack frowned and pushed out his lower lip, just shy of a pout. "Bill got the coin collection. Uncle Matt always did like him better."

"These two things, they were not equal?"

He sighed. "Yeah, they were about equal in dollar value. But all Bill had to do was find a coin dealer to unload the collection. Know what he walked away with? A quarter of a million dollars." Jack snapped his fingers. "Just like that."

"And you had to sell the house. Not so easy."

"Damn right. Had to sell off all the furniture as well. I wound up with the same amount of cash, but I had to keep flying back and forth to Minnesota and it took me until just last week to get it. That's almost six damn months!"

Madame Pomerol gave a Gallic shrug. "But still you have much money now, yes? You should be happy. But none of this tells me why your uncle is so upset."

"Well . . ." Jack looked away again. "I guess it has to do with this little case."

"Yes?"

He took a deep breath and sighed again. "Last week, as I was cleaning out the last of Uncle Matt's stuff before the closing, I came upon the case. It was locked and I couldn't find the key, so I brought it back with me. I was planning on finding a locksmith to open it for me, but . . ."

"But what, Monsieur Butler?"

"I don't think Uncle Matt wants me to have this."

"Why do you say that?

"You won't believe this." He gave a nervous laugh. "But then again, maybe you will, seeing as how you're a medium and all." Another deep breath, a show of hesitation, then, "It's the case." He tapped its shiny surface. "Someone or something keeps moving it on me."

"Moving it?"

Jack nodded. "I keep finding it in places where I never put it. I mean that: *never* put it."

"Perhaps your wife or—"

"I live alone. Don't even have a cleaning lady. But I'm looking for one. You know of anybody? Because I—"

"Please go on."

"Oh, yeah. Well, it kept moving and I kept making excuses, blaming my memory. But Saturday . . . Saturday really got to me. You see, I'd planned to take it down to a locksmith that day, but when I was ready to leave, I couldn't find the case. I looked everywhere in that apartment. And finally, when the locksmith was closed and it was too late to do anything, I found the damn thing under my bed. Under my bed! Just as if someone had hidden it from me. In fact I know it was hidden from me, and I have a pretty good idea who did it."

"It was your Uncle Matt."

"I think so too."

"No. It *was* your uncle. He told me."

"You mean to tell me you knew about this all along? Why'd you let me go on so?"

"I needed to know if you were telling me the truth. Now I do. What you say agrees with what your uncle told me."

Yeah, right.

Foster said, *"There were a bunch of scratches on the case lock. Looked like this jerk tried to pick it himself. Hit him with that."*

Madame Pomerol cleared her throat. "But you left out a few things."

Jack wished he knew how to blush on cue. Probably wouldn't be noticed in this light anyway.

"Such as?"

"How you tried to open the case yourself and failed."

He covered his eyes. "Oh, man. Well, yeah. Tell Uncle Matt I'm sorry about that."

"Also, you believe the case holds valuable coins, and if so, they belong to your brother, yes?"

"Now wait just a minute, there. Uncle Matt left the coin collection to Bill and the house and its contents to me. This here case was part of the contents. So it's rightfully mine."

"Your uncle disagrees. He tells me they are silver coins of little monetary worth."

Jack could feel her eyes on him, looking for some sign that he already knew what the case held. He avoided a quick, negative reaction, but he didn't want to appear too accepting.

"Yeah?" he said, frowning as he hefted the case. "Seems kinda heavy for just silver."

The lady brushed past his doubt. "I know nothing of such things. All I know is that your uncle told me they were of great sentimental value to him. They are the very first coins he collected as a boy."

"No kidding?" Jack was getting an idea of where she might be heading with this.

"Yes, your uncle was hoping to take them along with him when he crossed over, but he could not manage it. That was why they remained in the house."

"Take them into the afterlife? Is that possible?"

She shook her head. "Sadly, no. No money in the afterlife. At least not permanently."

"Can't take it with you, eh? Well, I guess that settles it. I'll just have to give this to Bill."

"Don't let him get away!" Foster cried. *"I'm telling you there's a small fortune in that case!"*

Jack slapped his hands on the table, picked up the case, and made as if to stand. Wasn't she going to say anything? Was she going to let him walk out with all those rare gold coins? A mook like her? He couldn't believe it.

"One moment, Monsieur Butler. Your uncle wishes me

to apport the case to the other side so that he can see them one last time."

"I thought you said that was impossible."

"*I* can do it, but only for a very short while, then they return."

"All right. Let's get to it."

"I am afraid that is impossible right now. It is a grueling procedure that takes many hours, and for which I must be alone."

"You mean I just give you this case and walk away? I don't think so. Not in this lifetime."

"You do not trust me?"

"Lady, I just met you two days ago."

"I have promised your uncle this favor. I cannot break a promise to the dead."

"Sorry."

Madame Pomerol closed her eyes and let her head fall forward. As they sat in silence on opposite sides of the table, Jack debated whether to ask for some security. He decided against it. Better to let her come up with the idea.

Finally Madame Pomerol raised her head and opened her eyes.

She released a heavy sigh. "This is most unusual. Embarrassing almost. But your uncle thinks—"

"Wait. You were just talking to him?" He didn't ask how she'd managed to do that without all the amplified moaning and groaning.

"Yes, and he says I should provide you with a show of good faith."

Even better! Let the idea come from Uncle Matt.

"I don't think I understand."

"As a show of good faith I will put one thousand dollars in an envelope for you to keep while I apport the case to the other side. When I return the case, you will return the envelope."

"A thousand dollars . . . I don't think that's enough. What if the case doesn't come back from the other side? Then

I'm out everything." He tapped the case. "I'll bet the coins in here are worth a couple-three thousand."

"Twenty-five hundred then, but ask no more, for I do not have it."

Jack made a show of considering this, then nodded. "I guess that'll do."

She rose with an air of wounded pride. "I shall get it."

"I hope you're not mad or anything."

"Your uncle is annoyed with you. And so, I must say, am I."

"Hey, it's not like it's for me, you know. I just feel I've got to look out for my brother's interests. I mean, seeing as how the coins in this thing are his and all."

She walked off into the darkness without another word.

She's good, he thought. Just the right mix of arrogance and hurt. And smooth.

He heard a door shut, then the lady's voice started in his ear.

"*Do you believe this shit?*" she said. "*A thousand ain't enough for that dickhead bastard! Twenty-five hundred fucking dollars! Have we got that much in cash?*"

"*Let's see,*" Foster said. "*With the cash donations from this morning and his own five hundred, we just make it.*"

Damn, Jack thought. They were going to give him back his own queer. Oh, well, that had been a risk all along.

"*All right, stick it in an envelope for me. I'll make up the dummy.*" Jack heard rustling paper, then, "*I tell you, I'd love to shove this twenty-five hundred right up that geek's ass!*"

Carl Foster laughed. "*What difference does it make how much he wants? He's not going to walk away with a cent of it.*"

Madame added her own laugh. "*You've got that right!*"

That's what you think, my friends.

While apparently adjusting his position in the chair, Jack counted five bills off his pile of queer and shoved them back into his sleeve, leaving twenty-five in his lap.

"*It's the principle, Carl. He should have trusted me for*

a thousand. It's the fucking principle!" More rustling paper, then, *"All right. I'm set. Showtime."*

With that, the overheads and chandelier came on, flooding the room with light.

What the hell?

Jack glanced down at the pile of bills in his lap. He'd been counting on the semi-darkness of the seance; now he'd have to do his work in full light. This complicated matters—big time.

He leaned forward to cover the bills as Madame Pomerol returned. She carried a white legal-size envelope and a small wooden box. With a great show of noblesse oblige, she tossed the envelope onto the table.

"Here is your good faith. Please count it."

"Hey, no, that's—"

"Please. I insist."

Shrugging, Jack took the envelope and opened it. He noticed it was the security kind with a crisscross pattern printed on the inner surface to keep anyone from scoping out the contents through the paper.

Now the hard part . . . made harder by all this damn light . . . had to play this just right . . . be cool and casual . . .

He removed the wad of bills from the envelope and lowered it beneath the level of the table top. As he pretended to count them he felt the muscles along the back of his neck and shoulders tighten. He knew the Fosters had a camera in the chandelier, but he couldn't remember if it was a simple, wide-angle stationary, or a remote-controlled directional. If Carl Foster spotted Jack's switch, he might do something rash. Like shoot him in the back.

Jack decided to risk it. He'd come too far to back down now. And his ear piece would give him a heads-up if Foster got wise.

Keeping close to the table, Jack switched Madame Pomerol's bills with the counterfeits waiting in his lap.

"It's all here," he said as he brought the stack of queer onto the tabletop and shoved it into the envelope.

He listened for comment from Foster, but the husband remained silent. Had he got away with it?

The lady picked up the envelope, took a quick look inside, then ran her tongue over the glued flap.

"Please check to make sure the lock on your case is secure," she said. "For I wish to return it to you in the exact condition that you gave it to me."

Jack bent over the case, pretending to examine the lock, but kept watch on the lady's hands. There! As soon as his head dipped, he saw her switch the cash envelope with another from her billowy sleeve.

One good switch deserves another. But I'm still one ahead.

"Yep," he said, looking up. "Still locked up tight."

"Now," she said as she opened her little wooden box, "I am going to seal the envelope."

She withdrew a purple candle from the box, followed by a book of matches and something that looked like a ring. She struck a match and lit the candle. She dribbled some of the wax onto the back of the envelope, then pressed the ring thing into it.

"There. I have affixed a spirit seal to the envelope. You are not to open it. Only if the case does not return from the other side may you open it. If you break the spirit seal before then, your uncle will punish you."

Jack swallowed hard. "Punish me? How?"

"Most likely he will make the money disappear. But he may do worse." She wagged a finger at him as she pushed the envelope across the table. "So do not open it before you return."

Very clever, Jack thought. *She's covering all exits.*

"Don't worry. I won't." He put the envelope in his lap, then quickly transferred that plus her twenty-five-hundred dollars to his side coat pocket. "Oh, hey, I got a little business trip tomorrow—overnight to Chicago—so I can't come back till Thursday. Will you have ap-whatevered it by then?"

"Apported. Yes, and I believe it will have returned by then."

You mean, he thought, that you believe you will have been able to replace the gold coins with junk silver by then.

He pushed the case toward her. "Then fire away. And good luck, Uncle Matt, wherever you are."

Jack rose, waved to Madame Pomerol, and headed for the door. "See you Thursday."

He felt laughter bubbling in his throat as he strode through the waiting room and hurried down the hall, but he suppressed it. He didn't want to arouse their suspicions. He took the stairs instead of waiting for the elevator because a load of shit was poised over a windtunnel fan and he wanted to be out of range when it dropped.

"Lock the front door," Madame Pomerol said through Jack's earpiece, *"and let's take a look at those coins."*

Jack had made it to the lobby when he heard Foster say, *"Shit! Something's up with this lock!"*

"What's wrong?"

"Like it's jammed."

Good diagnosis, Carl, Jack thought as he waved to the doorman and stepped out onto the street. He'd broken off a pin tip in the lock of the second case.

Instead of hurrying away, Jack loitered on the sidewalk outside. He wanted to hear this.

"Look at that," Foster said. *"Wonder how that got in there. No matter, it's out now. Only take me a few seconds to . . . there. Now, feast your eyes on—oh, shit! Oh, no!"*

"Let me—" Madame Pomerol cut herself off with a gasp. *"What the fuck? You told me this was packed with gold coins! Are you fucking blind?"*

"It was! I swear it was! I don't know what—"

"I do! The shit pulled a switch! He was conning us from the get-go! And you let him in!"

"Me?"

"Yes, you, you needle-dick jerk! You're supposed to screen these assholes!"

"I did! I checked out his address, I called the phone number he gave me."

"Yeah, well, you can bet your sorry ass the Robert Butler at that address ain't the guy we had here today, and the phone you called is not at that address. Fuck! Fuck! Fuck!"

"Hey, let's look on the bright side. He thinks he walked out of here with two-and-a-half large, but all he's got is sliced-up newspaper. And we've still got his five hundred. I wish I could see his face when he opens that envelope. He may have pulled one over on us, but we're the ones that come out ahead."

"You think I give a shit about that? I don't give a rat's ass about five hundred bucks. What I care about is he scammed us. He's out some cash, but as far as I'm concerned, he came out on top. He walked into our place and fucking scammed us—in our own place! Like we were punk amateurs. If word of this gets out we'll never be able to hold our heads up. We look like big fucking jerks."

That's right, Jack thought, plucking out his ear piece as he moved on. But soon you're going to look like even bigger jerks.

He hoped they stayed good and mad, too mad to see the barb still waiting at the end of Jack's sting.

He pumped his fist as he danced across the street. This was sweet, and going to get sweeter.

9

Gia awoke from a dream about blue eyes.

She yawned and stretched in the big leather recliner where she and Jack would often snuggle together and watch one of his weird movies.

She yawned again. She never napped. She'd sat down

and closed her eyes, just for a minute, and suddenly it was forty minutes later. Maybe it was the pregnancy, combined with being up late with Jack last night. She remembered being very tired carrying Vicky.

Whatever the reason, the nap hadn't refreshed her. Images of the blond child from yesterday had filled her sleep, her sad, lonely blue eyes calling to Gia, beseeching her . . .

For what? Why couldn't she get that little girl out of her head?

The pregnancy again. Sure, blame everything on the hormonal shifts. Being alone in the house on a summer day with no prospect of seeing Vicky till the end of the week didn't help either.

Gia pushed herself up from the chair and grabbed her purse. She didn't want to stay in the house. As soon as she stepped out into the warm humid afternoon she knew where she wanted to go.

She'd never liked the subway—the closed-in feeling of the dark tunnels made her edgy—but today it seemed to be the way to go. A quick walk over to Lexington took her to the Fifty-ninth Street station which she knew to be a stop for the N and R trains, known citywide as the "Never" and the "Rarely." She wasn't familiar with the Brooklyn and Queens lines, but the map by the token booth showed her that the N would take her right to the heart of Astoria.

She was just ahead of rush hour and her car was nearly full; the rocking made her queasy until the tracks broke free of the tunnel and into the air. She sighed with relief as sunlight filtered through the spiderweb-fine graffiti scratches on the windows.

The elevated tracks ended at her stop, Ditmars Boulevard. She stepped out of the car and headed for the stairs down to street level. She had a pretty good idea of Menelaus Manor's location in relation to Ditmars. She'd have to orient herself once she reached—

"Gia?"

She jumped at the sound of her name. When she turned she saw a man with long red hair and a mustache approaching her. For an instant she didn't recognize him, then—

"Jack?"

"Gia, what are you doing here?"

His heels beat a staccato rhythm as he strode toward her along the platform. Were those cowboy boots?

He leaned in to kiss her but she held up a hand. "Without the mustache, please?"

He smiled. "Oh, yeah."

He peeled it off and they kissed.

He kept his hands on her waist and looked into her eyes. "You're the last person I expected to see here. What's up?"

"I'm not sure," she said.

She felt off balance. What had she been thinking, anyway? That she'd just knock on the Kentons' door and ask if they had any little blond girls wandering around their house today? She hadn't thought this through. She'd been operating on impulse and that wasn't like her.

"It's that little girl you saw, isn't it?"

She stared at him. "How on earth did you know?"

"You've mentioned her a number of times since yesterday. She seems to be stuck in your head."

"She is. I don't know why, but I can't stop thinking about her. Maybe if she hadn't disappeared and we'd spoken to her, it would be different. But now, the way it is . . . she's a mystery."

"Not one we're likely to solve. And maybe not something you should be worrying about and traveling to Astoria for. I mean, you being pregnant and all."

"Jack, it's just half a dozen stops from home."

"Yeah, but subways are full of people, some of them sick. I don't want you catching anything."

"You never seemed to worry about that before I was pregnant."

"I did, but now I'm twice as worried, if you know what I mean."

She was touched by his concern for her and the baby, but he was going a bit overboard.

She sighed. "I just wanted to have another look, I guess."

"Well, since I'm on my way to see Lyle and Charlie myself"—he offered her his arm with exaggerated courtliness—"I shall be delighted to escort you there."

Gia batted her eyes and got into the game. "That's very kind of you, sir, but I sorely fear for my reputation if I'm seen walking with a man with that sort of haircut. I might never again be able to hold up my head in polite society."

"A new haircut? Say the word, madam, and it is done."

With a flourish Jack pulled off that hideous wig and shoved it into the pocket of his equally hideous sport coat. She combed her fingers through his tousled hair to straighten it.

"By the way, who picked out your clothes today?"

"Stevie Wonder."

"I suspected." She took his arm and they continued toward the stairway. "You seem to be in a good mood."

"So far it's been a pretty good day."

As they walked he told her about how he'd reversed a scam on an Upper East Side psychic. This was the liveliest she'd seen him in months. The old Jack was back, and Gia was glad.

At Menelaus Manor they found a pair of workmen just leaving; apparently they'd been replacing the broken windows.

Charlie welcomed them in. He didn't ask why Gia had come along, and Jack didn't offer an explanation. Anyway, Charlie seemed too taken with Jack's outfit to care.

"Ain't you ragged out!" he said, pointing to the plaid jacket and grinning. "Oh, you some ragged-out mack today!"

When he finally stopped laughing he said Lyle would meet Jack upstairs instead of in the Channeling Room, which was under repair.

Jack turned to Gia. "Do you mind waiting here while I go upstairs? Got to talk some business. Only take me a minute."

"Talk away," she said. "I'll just hang here and . . . look around."

Jack winked at her and followed Charlie into the hall and up the stairs. When they were gone, Gia casually wandered down the hall and into the kitchen. She poked her head into an adjoining room that held a dismantled TV. The screen was lit, though, showing a Dukakis-for-President ad. Probably the History Channel or a documentary. She went to the rear door and looked out into the backyard: a plot of dry, scrubby grass bordered by a privet hedge. No little girl.

Disappointed, Gia wandered back to the waiting room.

Well, what did she expect, anyway? Still she felt better for coming. She'd made the pilgrimage, now maybe she could stop thinking about that child.

Gia idly picked up one of the Menelaus manor pamphlets to read up on the house again, and a little booklet fell out. The cover read, *WHO, ME?* with "By J. T. C." in the corner. She flipped it over and saw a drawing of a church and the words, "Fisherman's Club" and "A Ministry for Laymen." Published by Chick Publications.

Gia flipped through it and realized immediately that it was a born-again tract exhorting its Christian readers to start "personal ministries" and become "soul winners" by bringing nonbelievers to Jesus.

What was it about fundamentalist sects, she wondered, that made them feel they had to get others to believe what they believed? The drive to convert other people to their way of thinking . . . where did it come from?

A more immediate question: Who was leaving these things here? And what did he or she hope to accomplish? People seeking out spirit mediums like Ifasen had most likely tried out the major religions and rejected them.

She searched through the Menelaus brochures and found another Chick pamphlet called "This Was Your Life!" As she opened it she heard a child's voice begin to sing.

"I think we're alone now . . ."

Gia turned and her heart tripped over a beat. There she was—the little blond girl. She stood in the doorway to the hall, her blue eyes bright as she stared at Gia. She wore the same red and white checkered blouse, the same brown riding breeches and boots as yesterday.

"Hello," Gia said. "What's your name?"

The girl didn't smile, didn't respond. She kept her hands clasped in front of her as she sang and stared at Gia.

"Do you live around here?"

The song went on. She had a good voice, a sweet tone that stayed on key. But the single-mindedness of the singing was making Gia uncomfortable. As the child went into the verse her hands fluttered to her neckline and began unbuttoning her blouse.

The nape of Gia's neck tightened. "What are you doing?"

The relentless singing and the blank look in the child's eyes were all disturbing enough. But now this . . . opening her top . . .

Was she demented?

"Please don't do that," Gia said.

The air in the room thickened as the last button popped free of its hole and the child gripped the two edges of the blouse and spread them, revealing a bare flat chest with a wide, ragged red gash down its center—

No-no-no, not a gash, a gaping bloody hole, a gaping bloody *empty* hole with nothing where her heart should be—

10

Jack was in the middle of describing his doubling back on Madame Pomerol's variation of the Spanish handkerchief scam when he heard Gia's scream. Before he knew he was moving he found himself up and racing for the stairs, leaving behind his rapt audience.

He pounded down to the first floor, his feet barely

touching the stairs, and found her in the middle of the waiting room, doubled over, face buried in her hands, sobbing.

Jack spun, saw no one else about, then grabbed her wrists
and pulled her to him.

"Gia! What's wrong? What happened?"

Her tear-stained face was the color of a freshly shucked
oyster when she looked up at him. "She had no heart! She
opened her blouse and her heart was gone!"

"Who?"

"The little girl!"

"The one you saw yesterday?"

Gia nodded. "She . . . she—" Her eyes widened and she
pointed toward the hall. "Look! There's her blood!"

Jack turned just as Lyle and Charlie piled down the
stairs. He saw a glistening red trail on the hardwood floor
of the hall, saw Charlie's sneaker land in it and slip. Charlie
went down but bounced back up again, staring in horror at
his bloody hands.

"Blood! Dear Lord, where—?" He looked at Jack.
"Who?"

Lyle, poised on the bottom step, pointed toward the
kitchen. "It runs that way!"

He and Charlie moved down the hall, gingerly sidestepping the red splatters. Instinctively Jack started to follow,
but Gia clutched his arm.

"Don't leave me!"

Jack wrapped an arm around her back and held her
closer, trying to absorb her Parkinsonian shakes.

"I won't. Don't worry."

But within him every angry cell was pulling toward the
hall to follow that wet red trail. He wanted—needed—to
find whoever had frightened Gia like this. He didn't know
how they'd done it—faking up a little girl so it looked like
she had no heart—and he didn't care. Anyone who terrified
Gia like this was going to answer to him.

He watched Lyle and Charlie enter the kitchen and follow the trail to the left, heard Lyle say, "It goes down the

steps." Jack heard their feet on the cellar stairs, their voices crying out in shock.

"Jack!" Lyle called. "Jack, you've got to see this! It's ... it's ..." Words seemed to fail him.

Jack glanced at Gia but she shook her head. "Don't you leave me alone here! Please!"

He had to see what they were talking about. He turned and called out, "How about Gia? Is it all right for her?"

"No ... yeah ... I don't know if it's all right for anyone, but I guess so. Just come quick! I don't know how long it will last!"

He looked at Gia again. "Come on. I'll be right at your side, holding on to you."

"Damn right you will," she muttered. She shuddered, then straightened. "All right, let's go. But if it's awful, we get out of here, promise? We head home and we never come back."

"Promise."

They moved like Siamese twins, edging down the hall hip to hip, avoiding the blood on the floor. Stepped into the kitchen, then made the turn and stopped at the top of the cellar steps. A single bulb lit the narrow stairwell. A two-inch railing ran along the right wall. Below, near the bottom steps, he could see Lyle and Charlie, their postures tense, hunched, as they stared into the basement. The steps made a turn where they stood, putting the basement out of Jack's line of sight.

"I'll go first," he said, and started down. He felt Gia close enough behind him to be riding piggyback, a hand on each of his shoulders, squeezing. He steadied himself by gripping the wobbly railing.

Below, the Kenton brothers looked up at him. Lyle's face was tight with strain, Charlie's was slack and beaded with sweat. They looked like frightened kids. Jack wondered what could put these two grown men in such a state.

A few more steps and he found out.

"Holy ..."

"Oh, dear God!" Gia said into his ear and she leaned against him and peered over his shoulder.

The basement floor was awash in bright red liquid. It rose to the level of the bottom stair tread and lapped at the one above it. And it moved, circulating in a slow, counter-clockwise rotation.

Jack said, "That's not . . ."

"Damn right it is," Lyle said. "Can't you smell it?"

Gia's fingers suddenly turned into talons, digging into Jack's shoulders.

"There's someone in there!" she cried.

Jack leaned forward, squinting at the surface of the red lake. "Where?"

"There!" An arm speared over his right shoulder, finger pointing. "Dear God, don't you see it? Right there! A hand, reaching up from the surface! It's a child! That little girl! She's in there!"

"What you talking 'bout?" Charlie said. "Ain't nobody in there."

Jack had to agree. Barely a ripple on the surface from wall to wall.

"I don't see anything either, Gi."

"Are you all blind?" Her voice was taking on a panicky tone. "That little girl is drowning! There's her arm, reaching up for help! Can't you see it? For God's sake, somebody grab it! *Please!*"

Lyle turned to her. "I don't see a thing. I'm not saying you're not, okay, but even if somebody were in here, it's only a foot deep, tops."

Her eyes wild, Gia began trying to squeeze past Jack. "I can't stand this, Jack! I've got to do something!"

Jack wouldn't let her pass. "Gia, no. We don't know what's going down here, and you're too close already." He didn't know what effect whatever was happening might have on the baby.

"Jack—"

"You know what I'm talking about. You shouldn't—"

"The level's rising!" Charlie cried.

Jack turned and saw that the blood had reached the tread of the next to last step.

"Let's all back up a little," Lyle said.

But as he stepped up, his foot slipped. He let out a startled cry as he fell back, arms out, one hand clawing for purchase on the wall, the other reaching for his brother. But Charlie had turned his back and by the time he responded it was too late.

With pinwheeling arms, Lyle hit the pool and sank from sight. Charlie shouted and crouched to jump in after him, but Jack reached out and grabbed his shoulder.

"Wait!"

Jack stared in mute shock at the crimson froth where Lyle had disappeared.

What the hell? Even though the level continued its rise, faster than ever now, the pool couldn't be more than two feet deep. And was it his imagination or was the blood circulating faster too?

Seconds later Lyle broke the surface, splashing and gasping, his head and face coated with blood.

"Praise God!" Charlie cried. He gripped the rickety railing with one hand and leaned out over the pool, reaching with his other. "Get up here!"

But Lyle continued to splash about, trying to shake the blood out of his eyes as the flow pulled him away from the stairs.

"Lyle!" Jack called. "Stand up!"

"Can't! Floor's gone! No bottom!"

"Jack!" Gia said. "The little girl—I don't see her arm anymore! She's gone!"

The blood was lapping at the fourth step now. The flow had rotated Lyle to the far side of the cellar, and as Jack watched he saw an eddying depression begin to form in the center of the blood. The velocity of the rotation accelerated.

"A whirlpool!" Charlie shouted. He leaned further out over the blood, stretching his arms, reaching toward his brother. "Lyle! Grab hold when you come 'round!"

A bottomless whirlpool of blood, Jack thought. Turning

counterclockwise. With the level rising instead of falling. In a cellar in Queens.

Not the weirdest sight he'd ever seen, not by a long shot, but he knew of only one thing that could be behind something like this.

He'd deal with that later. Right now he had to get Lyle out of that pool and Gia out of this house.

He gripped Charlie's arm as Lyle started to float toward them. "I've got you. Grab him as he comes by."

But as Lyle rotated their way, the sucking center of the whirlpool pulled him closer to it and further from the walls. He tried to swim toward Charlie's outstretched hand; Jack could see the desperation in his blood-soaked features as he reached for it, heard his cry of dismay as his fingers fell short by inches and he swirled away.

"Swim!" Charlie shouted. "Swim toward the walls!"

Jack could see Lyle struggling in the thick fluid, doing a crude dog-paddle. He was a lousy swimmer.

"Can't!" he gasped. "Current's too strong!"

"We need rope!" Jack told Charlie. "Got any?"

"Rope?" Charlie's panic seemed to ease as he concentrated on the question. "No . . . we've got string but—"

"Never mind," Jack said. The solution had been right in his hand. He turned to Gia. "I need you to go back up to the kitchen for a minute."

"I'm not leaving—"

"Just stand in the doorway. Please. I need you out of the stairwell to do this. Hurry. We may not get another shot."

She turned and padded back to the top step and turned, watching him with frightened eyes. Jack followed her a few steps, then grabbed the railing with both hands.

"Charlie—help me rip this out of the wall."

Charlie frowned, then brightened. "Right!"

Ten seconds later Jack was easing toward the red pool with the ten-foot railing in his hands. The blood had risen past the halfway mark on the walls and was moving faster. Lyle had rounded the far side of the whirlpool and was coming their way again, but now he was even closer to the black-hole center.

"Quick!" Jack said to Charlie as he stepped onto a blood-covered step. His stomach clenched—it was *warm.* "Grab my belt so I don't go in too."

"Oh, Jack, *please* be careful!" Gia called from above.

With Charlie steadying him from behind, Jack gripped one end of the railing and thrust the other toward Lyle as he swirled by. The far end struck the surface, splashing blood into Lyle's face. He whipped his arms about blindly, slapping his hands on the surface, grasping only air. Jack leaned farther out and felt a tearing pain in his right flank but kept trying to steady the railing against the current and push it closer to Lyle. He hoped he hadn't popped his stitches.

And then one of Lyle's flailing arms made contact. His fingers clutched the wood, then wrapped around it.

"You've got it!" Jack said, feeling himself tilting toward the pool by the extra pull on the railing. Over his shoulder he said to Charlie, "And I hope you've got *me.*"

"Don't worry," Charlie said, then raised his voice. "Get both hands on it, Lyle!"

Lyle did just that, and then Jack and Charlie began hauling him in.

But the pool didn't seem to want to give him up. The maelstrom turned faster and the level began to drop as a loud sucking sound echoed from the center. It took all of Jack and Charlie's combined strength to hold onto the railing, but they were losing this tug of war. Jack tried to put more of his back into it but the pain in his side worsened. He shifted and that caused his feet to slip on the blood.

No! With the speed of that whirlpool now, if he went in too they'd both be lost.

Gia cried, "Jack!"

He heard a thumping behind him and then a slim arm wrapped around his neck, pulling him back.

With Gia hanging on as ballast, Jack and Charlie were able to pull Lyle close enough so he could grab Charlie's hand. Jack tossed the railing into the pool and helped Charlie drag Lyle out. As his brother lay gasping and retching on the steps, Charlie placed his hands on him and bent his head. He seemed to be praying.

Jack slumped back against Gia. "Thanks."

She kissed him on the ear and whispered, "You saved him."

"And you saved me."

As Jack watched the level of the blood fall, he noticed something.

"Look at the walls," he said. "They're dry . . . and no stains."

"Not quite," Gia said, pointing over Jack's shoulder. "What about those?"

Jack saw them too. Halfway up the pecan paneling . . . oddly shaped blotches, evenly spaced around the room. They reminded him of—

"Crosses!" Charlie cried. "Praise God, my prayers have been answered! He's driven the evil from this house!"

Jack wasn't so sure about that.

He watched the current slow and stop as the sucking center of the maelstrom stretched and lengthened into a line. An orange concrete floor slowly appeared as the blood rushed down through the large crack in its center.

"I'll be damned," Jack said. "It split the floor wide open."

"No," Charlie said. "That already there. It cracked in the Friday night quake."

Jack saw Lyle uncoil his blood-soaked body from its exhausted slump into a sitting position.

"The floor wasn't there a couple of minutes ago. I swear, the floor was *gone* when I was in there."

"We believe you," Jack said.

The remaining blood seemed to evaporate, leaving the concrete dry and unstained.

Lyle moved down a couple of steps and poked the toe of his shoe against the orange floor. Apparently satisfied with its solidity, he stepped onto the concrete and walked around in a tight circle that did not cross the large crack.

"What happened here?" he said to no one in particular. "Why? What does it *mean*?"

Jack thought he had an answer, one he didn't like. If he was right, he wanted Gia far, far away from here.

"We'll try to figure it out later, Lyle," he said, then turned to Gia. "Let's get out of here."

"No, wait," Gia said, rising and moving past him down the stairs. "I want to see those crosses."

"Gia, please. This isn't a healthy place, if you know what I mean."

She gave him one of her smiles. "I know what you mean, but this involves me."

"No, it doesn't. It—"

"Yes, it does," Lyle said.

Jack gave him a hard look. "Would you mind staying out of this, Lyle?"

"I can't. I'm in it up to my neck. And Gia's in it too. She's the only one who's seen the little girl. Doesn't that say something?"

"It says she should get the hell out of here."

Gia stepped out onto the floor. "I just want to look at these crosses, okay?"

"No," Jack muttered, rising and following her. "Not okay. But I don't seem to have much say in the matter."

Jack joined her where she'd stopped before one of the glistening red cross-shaped stains on the cheap paneling. The upright part ran about two inches wide and maybe ten inches high; the eight-inch crosspiece flared upward at each end and was set high, almost at the top of the upright. Jack counted eleven of them ringing the cellar wall, maybe six feet apart and about five feet off the floor.

"What a strange kind of cross," Gia said. "And they're the only things in the room still wet."

"Not the only thing," Lyle said. His clothes and dreads were still drenched in thick red blood. "I've got to go change and take a shower." He started to turn away, then swiveled back to them. "That's known as a *tau* cross, by the way. Named because it looks like the *T* in the Greek alphabet; it's also the last letter in the Hebrew alphabet."

Jack stared at him. How did he know all this stuff?

"Tau . . ." Charlie said. "I remember reading in the prophet Ezekiel how the faithful of God would all be signed on the forehead with the letter *tau*." He looked around, nodding. "Yes, this definitely shows that we were saved by the hand of the Lord."

Jack took a closer look. "But the cross piece doesn't quite make it all the way up." Each showed a little nubbin of the upright on top. "Not quite a capital *T*."

As if on cue, all the bloody crosses faded away.

"Look!" Lyle cried, holding out his arms. His clothes were clean and dry, and not a trace of red on his skin or hair. "The blood! It's gone! As if it never happened!"

"Oh, it happened," Jack said, pointing to the banister railing on the floor. "And now it's time to go."

"No, you can't," Lyle said. "We need to talk about this. Everything that's been happening here since the earthquake—"

" 'Everything'?" Jack said. "You mean there's more?"

"Yes. Lots more. And I believe it's all connected to Gia. Maybe even the earthquake."

Jack glanced at Gia and saw her startled look. He turned back to Lyle. "Look, I know you just had a bad experience, so—"

"Listen to me. It's all starting to fall into place. We've been living here almost a year now and in all that time we've experienced not one strange thing." He looked at his brother. "Am I right, Charlie?"

Charlie nodded. "True that. But since Friday night it been one thing top another."

"Right. All the weirdness started Friday night when Gia stepped into this house. The instant she crossed the threshold we had an earthquake, for Christ sake!"

"I crossed with her. We entered together, if you remember. Maybe it's me."

Jack *knew* it was him, but didn't want to go into that now. He wanted Gia out of here.

"But you're not the one who's seen the little girl. On any other day in my life I'd say Gia's arrival with the earthquake was pure coincidence, but not today. Not after what I just went through. And she's the *only* one who's seen this little girl. I'm telling you, I feel it in my gut: that child is connected to what's been going on, and Gia's connected to the child. I want to know how."

"So do I," Gia said. "I mean, that is, if it's true. Because I saw a hand sticking out of that pool. It was right in front of you three but none of you could see it. So either I'm crazy or I'm connected. Either way, I want some answers too."

"Okay, fine," Jack said. He knew Lyle was wrong, but could see from the way this conversation was going that he wasn't going to get Gia home any time soon. "We'll discuss it. But not here. I don't think this house is a healthy place for Gia. There's got to be a restaurant or someplace where we can get a booth and hash this out."

Charlie turned to Lyle. "How about Hasan's up on Ditmars?"

Lyle nodded. "That'll do. On a Tuesday night we can have our pick of the tables. But first I want to take a shower."

"Why?" Jack said. "You look perfectly clean."

"Maybe, but I don't *feel* clean. You three go ahead. It's a easy walk. I'll catch up with you."

Jack nodded absently. Lyle's theory was beginning to bother him. *Could* Gia have been the trigger? The possibility, remote as it was, shot a gout of acid from his gut into his chest.

11

Hasan's turned out to be a small Middle Eastern café and restaurant. The orange awning over the natural wooden front sported English and Arabic. The walls inside were white stucco, trimmed with red and green stripes. A widescreen TV was tuned to some Arab CNN-wannabe channel.

The owners, a smiling middle-aged couple with thick accents, greeted Charlie with the deference earned by a regular customer. The place was only a quarter full and, as Lyle had said, they had the pick of the tables. At Jack's nudging—he didn't want anyone eavesdropping—Charlie chose one in a rear corner. It had a marble top and chairs with woven straw backs.

Jack went into the men's room and took off his shirt. He checked his bandage and found blood starting to seep through. The wound ached but didn't seem too much worse, given how he'd mistreated it. He slipped back into his shirt and packed a couple of paper towels over the bandage.

Lyle arrived a few minutes later, his dreads still wet from his shower. The waitress had brought a Diet Pepsi for Charlie, a Sprite for Gia, and a couple of Killian's for Jack and Lyle.

"I suppose I should tell you about the Otherness," Jack said.

Gia frowned. "Do you think you should go into that?"

"Well, it should explain why I think if anyone triggered the strangeness in that house, it was me instead of you."

Somewhere in the back of his head he heard a voice mutter, *It's always about you, isn't it*. Not true. Most times he didn't want it to be about him, but this time he did. Because he refused to accept Lyle's alternative that Gia had triggered the manifestations. Or maybe he was afraid to accept it. He didn't want Gia involved.

"I know, but it sounds so . . ." She rubbed a hand over her face. "What am I thinking? I was going to say it sounds so far out. But after today . . ."

"Right," Lyle said. "After today you're going to have to go some to be too far out for us. I think we left 'far out' in the dust. Or rather, the blood."

Jack found Charlie staring at him. "You said 'Otherness'? What that mean?"

Jack noticed that the events in the cellar seemed to have scared some of the hip-hop out of the younger Kenton.

The waitress came with the menus.

"Why don't we order, then talk," Jack said.

Gia looked at him. "You can't be hungry after that."

"I'm always hungry."

The menu was bilingual—English on the left, Arabic on the right. Throughout the word vegetable was spelled "vegitible." Hasan's offered salad, falafel, hummus, tahini, baba ganoush, fatoush, lebneh, fried calamari, tajin eggplant, and tajin calamari.

Tajin . . . was that like Cajun?

Lots of kababs—lamb, veal, chicken, and kofta, whatever that was.

Jack nudged Gia. "What are you going to have?"

"I'll have a little hummus and a pita. That's about all I can stomach right now. How about you?"

"I'm thinking about the special."

Gia looked and gasped. "Tongue with testicles? Jack, don't you dare!"

"You know I always like to try new—"

"Don't. You. Dare."

"Okay. Just for you, my dear, I will forego that epicurean delight." He'd had no intention of dining on a dish that sounded like a sex act anyway. "I guess I'll just settle for a lamb kabab."

Once their orders were in, Jack leaned over the table.

"Let me start at the beginning. It may take a minute or two, but a little patience will pay off. It began last summer when a crazy Hindu sailed a boatload of creatures called rakoshi to the West Side docks. They were big and vicious and they threatened someone I care very much about." He glanced at Gia and their eyes met. They'd come so close to losing Vicky, and Jack himself had barely survived. "But they could be killed, and I killed them."

Not all of them. One still survived, but Jack decided not to go into that.

"I thought that was that. It was the strangest occurrence of my life until then, but I put it behind me and moved on. But then, last spring, I learned that the origin of those creatures was not exactly earthly."

Lyle said, "We're not heading for UFOville, are we?"

"No. This is weirder. While looking for a missing wife I fell in with some strange people who told me that the rakoshi had been 'fashioned'—that was the word—of everything bad in humans. Something took human lust and greed and hate and viciousness and distilled it into these creatures without any leavening factors. They were human evil to the Nth."

"You talkin' demons," Charlie said.

"They'd fit the description, I guess."

"And the 'something' you said did this. You talkin' Satan?"

"No. I was told it's called the Otherness."

"Could be just another name for Satan."

"I don't think so. Satan's a pretty easy concept to grasp. He was thrown out of heaven because of his pride and now he spends his time luring souls away from God and stashing them in hell where they suffer for eternity. That about right?"

"Well, yeah," Charlie said. "But—"

"Fine, then." Jack didn't want to get sidetracked here. "But I've had the Otherness explained to me a couple of times and I still don't have a handle on it. Apparently two vast, unimaginably complex cosmic forces have been at war forever. The prize in this war is all existence—this world, other realities, other dimensions, *everything* is at stake. Before you start feeling important, I was told that our corner of reality is just a tiny piece of that whole, and of no special importance. But if one side's going to be the winner, it's got to take all the marbles. Even our little backwater."

"Don't tell me," Lyle said, his tone bordering on disdain. "One of these forces is *Good* and one is *Eeeevil.*"

"Not quite. That would make it easy. The way I understand it, the side that has our reality in its pocket is not good or evil, it's just there. The most we can expect from it is benign neglect."

" 'Thou shalt not have false gods before me,' " Charlie intoned.

"It's not a god. It's a force, a state of being, a ... ." Jack spread his hands in frustration. "I don't know if we can grasp anything that vast and alien."

"Does it have a name?" Lyle said.

Jack shook his head. "No. I've heard someone refer to it as the Ally, but that's not quite right. It will only act on our behalf to keep us in its possession. Other than that it doesn't give a damn about us."

"And the Otherness is ... what?" Lyle said. "The other side?"

"Right. And it doesn't have a name either, but people who seem to know about these things call it the Otherness because it represents everything not us. Its rules are different than ours. It wants to convert our form of reality to its own, one that'll be toxic for us—physically and spiritually."

"That Satan, I tell you!" Charlie cried. Lyle rolled his eyes. Charlie caught it and pointed to Jack. "He just nailed Satan dead on, bro, and you know it. Why don't you stop frontin' and cop to it?"

To head off a looming argument, Jack said, "Well, the Otherness could have been the inspiration for the idea of Satan. I've heard it described as vampiric, and it sounds to me as if its idea of reality would create a hell on earth. So maybe . . ."

"But what does all this have to do with this afternoon?" Lyle said.

"I'm getting to that. This past spring I learned the hard way that the elements in the Otherness responsible for creating the rakoshi wanted my head for killing them. They missed me but a few people and a good-size house vanished from the face of the earth."

"Ay, yo, I remember readin' 'bout that," Charlie said. "Someplace out on Long Island, right?"

Jack nodded. "A little town called Monroe."

"Right!" Lyle said. "I remember trying to think up a way to take credit for it, or at least come up with a way-out explanation that would buy me some PR. But about half a dozen mediums in the city beat me to it." He looked at Jack. "You're telling me that was you?"

"I didn't *cause* it," Jack said. "I just happened to be on the scene. And I wasn't the only one there. Both sides were represented. On the Otherness team was a guy calling himself Sal Roma. Not his real name—he'd stolen it. He seemed pretty tuned in to the Otherness, like he was its main agent here. His name has popped up a couple of times since then, once I think as an anagram."

"An anagram?" Lyle said. "That's interesting. Means there's a good chance his real name is hidden in those letters. I've read that ancient wizards used to operate under aliases for fear that someone who knew their True Name could have power over them."

"I think this guy's just playing games. But if I ever learn his True Name, I'm going to find him and . . ." Jack stopped himself. "Never mind."

Charlie said, "You gotta personal beef with this Roma?"

The thought of Kate made the old pain new. "You could say that."

Jack glanced at Gia. She smiled her sympathy and took his hand under the table. They'd talked a lot about this in the past month or so. Gia believed. She'd seen the rakoshi, so she'd been well down the road to acceptance when he'd explained all this to her. But even after what they'd seen today, the Kenton brothers probably thought he was nuts.

He took a breath. "But back to the big hole in Monroe: Sal Roma and some nasty sort of pet of his were there for the Otherness; the anti-Otherness side was represented by a couple of guys who looked like twins. I was caught in the middle, and the twins were ready to sacrifice me for their purposes—which showed me firsthand how unbenign this so-called Ally power is. Things got kind of complicated, but the upshot is, I walked away and the twins didn't."

"You know," Lyle said, "this is all really fascinating, but what's it got to do with our house?"

"I'm getting to that. I've since learned—or at least I was told—that I've been drafted into the service of the anti-Otherness."

"Drafted?" Lyle said. "You mean you don't have any say about that?"

"Not a thing, apparently. My guess is that because I'm somewhat responsible for the demise of the twins, I'm supposed to replace them. But if the Great Whatever that drafted me thinks I'm going to go trotting about putting out Otherness-started fires, it better think again. I don't know about my predecessors, but I've got a life."

"What you mean, 'Otherness-started fires'?" Charlie said.

"Not sure, but I've got an idea that most of the strange things that happen in this world—what people like to call paranormal or supernatural—are really manifestations of the Otherness. Anything that terrifies, confounds, and confuses us, anything that brings out the worst in us makes it stronger."

Charlie banged his fist on the table. "You talking 'bout Satan, dawg! The Father of Lies, the Sower of Discord!"

"Maybe I am," Jack said, wanting to avoid a theological argument. "And maybe I'm not quite so sure of as many things as I used to be. But I'm pretty sure that I'm tagged as anti-Otherness, and because of that, *I'm* the one who triggered everything that's been going on in your house."

Jack looked around the table and found Lyle staring at him. "You're telling me *you* triggered that earthquake?"

"Either that, or it's all pure coincidence. And I've been told no more coincidences in my life."

Lyle's eyes widened. "No more coincidences . . . that means your life's being manipulated. Now *that's* scary."

"Tell me about it." Jack's gut crawled every time he thought about it. He looked at Gia. "So can you see now why I don't want Gia near that house?"

"Oh, yes," Lyle said, nodding. "Assuming what you've told us is true—and so far you haven't struck me as schizo—then yes, definitely. And as much as I hate to say it—because I've always thought they were such a lame joke—we seem to be dealing with a bona fide ghost. Would something like that be related to this Otherness of yours?"

Jack felt himself bristling. "First off, the Otherness isn't *mine*. I did not come up with the idea, it was pushed on me, and I'd be a much happier man if I'd never heard of it. Second, no one's handed me a book or a manual and said, 'Here, read this and you'll know what you're dealing with.' I'm piecing this together as I go along."

"Okay. I misspoke. I'll rephrase: Why should we think this ghost is related to the Otherness?"

"Maybe it's not. But then again, maybe all the violent deaths in Menelaus Manor somehow created a focus of Otherness. Maybe that focus was concentrated in the fault line beneath the house. When I crossed the threshold I hit a trip wire and . . . boom."

Lyle shook his head. "I still think that little girl's connected to Gia." He turned to her. "Did she look at all familiar to you?"

Gia shook her head. "Not a bit. If she *is* a ghost . . ." She shook her head. "I've never believed in ghosts either, but what else can you call her? If she is one, I think she may have died in the sixties. She looked dressed to ride a horse, so her clothes don't date her, but she kept singing a song—"

" 'I Think We're Alone Now'?" Lyle said.

"Yes! You heard it too?"

"Yesterday. But I didn't see her."

"Well, it's a sixties song—late sixties, I think."

"Nineteen sixty-seven, to be exact," Jack said. "Tommy James and the Shondells on the Roulette label."

Lyle and Charlie stared at him in surprise. Gia wore a wry smile; she was used to this.

Jack shrugged and tapped the side of his head. "Chock full of useless information."

"Not so useless this time," Gia said. "It gives us an idea of when she might have been killed."

"Killed?" Charlie said. "You think someone killed her?"

Gia's face twisted. "You didn't see her. Her chest had been cut open." She swallowed. "Her heart was gone."

"That could be symbolic," Jack said, giving her hand a squeeze.

He wished to hell Gia had never come within miles of Menelaus Manor. This was all Junie Moon's fault. And his for agreeing to drive Junie to her medium. If they'd stayed at that damn party . . .

"After all the blood we just saw?" Lyle said. "If that's symbolism, it's way overboard."

"Tell them about Sunday night," Charlie said.

Lyle looked uncomfortable as he told them about the shape in the shower, the blood-red water flowing into the drain.

A real *Psycho* moment, Jack thought.

He described the writing on the mirror before something shattered it. Then . . .

"I'd seen blood on Charlie's chest on Friday and Saturday nights. Maybe *seen* isn't the right word. Had visions? Hallucinated? But Sunday night was different. I was the one with blood down my front then, and when I pulled up my shirt it looked like my chest had been cut open. I . . ." Lyle looked at his brother. "We both could see my heart beating through the hole."

"Dear God," Gia whispered.

"It lasted only a second, but if whatever's there thought that would scare us off, it was wrong. Sleep's been pretty hard to come by since then, but we're staying. Right, bro?"

Charlie nodded, but Jack didn't pick up a truckload of enthusiasm there.

"You think that's what it's trying to do?" Jack said. "Scare you off?"

"What else? It's sure not trying to make friends. And it doesn't seem to want to hurt us—"

Jack had to laugh. "You damn near drowned less than an hour ago!"

"But I didn't. Maybe I wasn't supposed to. Let's face it, if it wanted to kill me, it had its chance Sunday night. It could've smashed my head instead of my bathroom mirror."

"That's a point," Jack said. "But maybe you're not the one it's interested in. And the question remains: Why now? You've been in that house for almost a year, you said. Why should this thing wait for my arrival on Friday night to start manifesting herself?"

"Not just your arrival," Lyle said. "Gia's too."

Jack looked at him. "You're just not gonna drop that bone, are you?"

Lyle shrugged. "I can't help it. I still think it's connected to Gia."

"Can we stop with the 'it' business?" Gia said. " 'It' is a 'she.' A little girl."

"But do we know that for sure?" Lyle said. "Maybe it can take on any form it wants. Maybe it's chosen to look like a little girl because it knows that's what'll get to you."

Gia blinked. Jack could tell she hadn't considered that possibility. Neither had he. Uneasiness crawled through his gut. Maybe Gia was involved after all.

After a heartbeat's pause, Gia shook her head. "I don't buy that. I think she's limited in what she can do and she's trying to tell us something."

"What?"

"That back in 1967 or thereabouts a little girl was murdered in your house and she's buried in the basement."

Silence at the table, everyone staring at Gia.

She stared back. "What? Look at what we've got." She ticked off her points on her fingers. "A little girl with a hole in her chest, singing a song from 1967, leaving a trail of blood to a basement *full* of blood, that drains away through a hole in the floor. Open your eyes, guys. It's all right there, staring you in the face."

Lyle gave a slow nod. He glanced at Charlie. "I think we need to learn more about our house."

"How we do that?" Charlie said.

"How about that old Greek who sold us the place? I didn't pay much attention at the time, but didn't he go on about how every time the house has changed hands, he's been involved? What was his name? I remember it was a real mouthful."

Charlie grinned. "Konstantin Kristadoulou. Can't forget no mouthful like that."

"Right! First thing tomorrow I'm going to call Mr. Kristadoulou and set up a meeting. Maybe he can shed some light on our ghost."

"Include me in that meeting," Jack told him. "I've got a stake in this too."

More than you can imagine.

"Will do," Lyle said.

Gia leaned forward. "But what about tonight? Where are you sleeping?"

"In my bed."

She shook her head. "Aren't you . . . ?"

"Scared?" He smiled and shrugged. "A little. But I figure it must be—"

"She."

"All right, *she* must be trying to tell us something. Maybe she wants us to do something, then she'll go away. How can I find out what that is if I'm not there?"

Sounded logical enough to Jack, but he thought he spotted something in Lyle's eyes as he spoke. Working on another agenda, perhaps? Jack wondered what it could be.

He'd worry about that later. Right now his first imperative was to escort Gia back to Manhattan and convince her
to stay there. Bad enough to feel that the Otherness had
painted a bull's-eye on his back; the possibility that Gia
might be targeted too dragged a coil of concertina wire
through his gut.

First his sister, then Gia and their unborn child . . . was
that the plan? Crush his spirit—destroy everyone he loved
or mattered to him—before crushing him?

Listen to me. Sound like a raving paranoiac.

Hey, everybody! I'm so important, there's a cosmic
power out to get me and everybody close to me!

But . . . if he had indeed been drafted into the supposed
shadow war, it might be true.

Jack felt the breath leak out of him. He had to find a
way to get himself discharged, even if it was dishonorable.

But first-first-*first*: place Gia out of harm's way.

12

"Like I told you before," Fred Strauss said, his voice halfway to a whisper. "He's a ghost, a fucking ghost."

Eli Bellitto lay in his hospital bed and stared at the flick-
ering polychromatic beacon of the TV screen in his darkened hospital room.

"Who's a ghost?" Adrian said.

Strauss sat at the right foot of the bed, Adrian at the left.
The big man had propelled himself into the room in his
wheelchair. His left knee was braced and straight out before
him. Even in the dim light Eli could see the pair of ugly
purple swellings on his bare scalp. His long arms hung at
his sides, almost touching the floor.

"The guy who clobbered you and stabbed Eli," Strauss

said, his words clipped with impatience. "Haven't you been listening?"

Adrian's short-term memory hadn't quite recovered yet and he'd been having difficulty following Strauss's excuses for coming up empty in his search for their attacker. Even Eli found his repeated questions annoying.

Adrian shook his head. "I have *no* memory of it. I remember having dinner last night, and after that . . . it's all a blank. If it weren't for my knee and this pounding headache, I'd think you both were having me on."

Adrian had regained some of his recent memory—at least now he accepted that this was August instead of July—but he'd made this same statement at least half a dozen times since his arrival. Eli wanted to throw something at him.

I'm the one who's suffered the real damage! he wanted to shout. You just got a knock on the head!

He clenched his teeth as a new gush of magma erupted in his groin. His left hand flailed about, found the PCA button, and pressed it; he prayed he hadn't already used up this hour's morphine allotment.

What a day. An afternoon from hell. A nurse, a three-hundred-pound rhino in white named Horgan had come in and insisted he get up and walk. Eli had refused but the woman would not take no for an answer. She may have been black but she was a Nazi at heart, leading him up and down the hall as he clung to his rolling IV pole, his catheter snaking between his knees, his half-full blood-tinged urine bag dangling from a hook on the pole for all to see. Agony enhanced by humiliation.

And then Dr. Sadiq had visited, telling him that he had to walk *more*, and how tomorrow they'd be removing his catheter—Eli's buttocks clenched at the thought of Nurse Horgan dragging the tube out of him, and that caused another eruption of pain. Dr. Sadiq said he anticipated discharging Eli tomorrow morning.

Not soon enough as far as Eli was concerned. As long as he could take this PCA unit with him.

"In other words," Eli said to Strauss as the morphine took effect, "once we trim away all your excess verbiage, we are left with the simple fact that you've failed us."

The detective spread his hands. "Hey, I can only do so much. It's not like you two've given me a whole lot to work with."

It frightened Eli to know that his attacker was still unidentified.

He knows me, but I don't know him.

He could be in the hospital now, pretending to be visiting someone else, but all the while waiting for Strauss and Adrian to leave so that he can come in and finish the job.

If only they had his name. The Circle could take it from there. With their connections they'd make short work of him.

"Did you bring me his number?" Eli asked Strauss.

"Yeah." He fished a piece of paper out of his pocket. "Got it here."

"Dial it for me."

"You're kidding. It can't be traced and he doesn't—"

"Dial it now!"

Shrugging, Strauss punched the number into the bedside phone and handed Eli the receiver. After four rings, Eli heard a disembodied voice say the client he'd called was not available. He handed the phone back to Strauss.

"Leave the number on the nightstand."

"Waste of time, I tell you. Guy doesn't keep his phone on."

"I'll keep trying. Who knows? I may get lucky."

Eli wasn't sure exactly what he'd say, but the phone number was his only link to the man who'd violated him.

"Hey," Strauss said, pointing to the TV screen. "Isn't that—?"

Eli shushed him and turned up the volume when he recognized the Vietnamese child's face. He missed the introduction as the scene cut to a dark-skinned woman reporter on a crowded sidewalk, a scene obviously shot earlier in the day.

Her name was Philippa Villa and she was doing man-on-the-street interviews about how, in the wake of little Duc Ngo's recent abduction, people thought child molesters should be treated.

Child molesters! Why did everyone assume that the child was going to be sexually molested?

As each bloated visage from Manhattan's multihued lumpen proletariat flashed onto the screen to mouth predictably banal comments about capital punishment being "too good for them," Eli's anger grew. These ignoramuses knew nothing of the Circle's exalted purpose, and were casting them as perverted lowlifes. They were being egged on by this reporter, this Philippa Villa. The Circle had a powerful link within the media. Eli would see to it that this woman's career came to a screeching halt.

He was about to change the channel when the reporter's grinning face filled the screen.

"And if you think the folks we've just seen are tough, you should have heard one woman who did not want to appear on camera. I wrote down what she said: 'The guy who snatched that little boy should be castrated—' "

Eli stifled a moan as he relived the moment when the blade of his own knife sliced into his tenderest flesh.

" 'And after that he should have his hands cut off so he can never touch another child, and then his legs cut off so he can never stalk another child—' "

He saw Strauss lean back, as if trying to distance himself physically as well emotionally from the TV.

" '—and then his tongue ripped out so he can never coax another kid into his car, and his eyes put out so that he can never even look at a child again—' "

He saw Adrian wince and run a trembling hand over his face.

" '—I'd leave his nose so he can breathe in the stink of his rotten body.' "

Eli felt the PCA button crack under his thumb. He hadn't realized he'd been pressing it so hard.

Forget the reporter. Eli now had somebody else he would much rather ruin. If he could find her.

"Did you hear that?" he said to Adrian and Strauss. "Did you hear what that woman said about us?"

"Not *us*," Strauss said. "She knows nothing about The Circle. And besides—"

"But she thinks she does. She thinks she knows our intent. She knows nothing of our purposes and yet feels free to mouth off in public and accuse us of being child molesters. Are we going to stand for this?"

"I don't see that we have much choice," Strauss said.

"There are always choices."

"Really? And what are they here?"

Strauss's unruffled attitude irked Eli. "Find this loud-mouthed woman and teach her a lesson."

"I think you're overreacting, Eli," Strauss said.

"Easy for you to say!" Eli hissed. He wanted to shout but was wary of raising his voice. "You're not the one with the stab wound or the concussion!"

"Finding this woman won't make you feel any better."

"Oh, it will! I guarantee you, it will!"

Eli was well aware that he was overreacting, but he'd been hurt and he was in pain, and Strauss had given him no target for retribution, offered scant hope of providing one in the foreseeable future. Finding and ruining this woman would provide a much-needed outlet for his pent-up fury.

"How am I supposed to find her? She hasn't committed a crime."

"Contact Gregson."

"Gregson's with NBC. This was on—"

"Gregson will know what to do." Eli felt his anger bubbling over. Did he have to lead Strauss by the hand? Did he have to do *everything*? "If you can't find our attacker's name, then get me this woman's name! Do *something*, damn it!"

13

Charlie closed his Bible. Tried to read 'bout the tau cross in Ezechiel 9:4 but it wasn't happening. The words broke up into jumbles soon as they hit his brain.

Maybe it was the music. The jiggly beat of Point of Grace's "Begin With Me" was pumping through his headphones. Righteous lyrics, but the high-gloss arrangement and funky vocals were distracting tonight. He popped them out of his portable CD player and slipped in "Spirit Of The Century" by the Blind Boys Of Alabama. As their traditional harmonies soothed his head, he lay back on his bed, closed his eyes, and prayed for peace.

But no peace tonight. He kept on seeing his brother splashing like a drowning cat in that pool of blood, kept hearing Jack's voice telling 'bout the Otherness . . .

Where was Jesus in all this? Why this happening?

Charlie figured it for a test. But of what?

My faith?

He knew his faith was strong. Powerful. So powerful he wondered how he'd got through his pre-conversion years without it. It was like oxygen now. If someone stole it from him, he knew sure he'd die in minutes.

But what says I'm the target of this test? Maybe it Lyle . . . a test of his faith in nothing.

For as surely as Charlie believed in the healing love of Jesus, so Lyle believed in nothing beyond his five senses. Maybe God was offering Lyle a chance to see how there was more to life than his senses, that life extended beyond the body, that each human body was home to an eternal soul that was gonna be judged when its life on earth was done. Maybe this gonna be Lyle's chance to change, to accept Jesus as his personal savior and see his name written in the Book of Life.

But . . . if this was the work of God, why was He hiding His hand?

Because that the way He wishes it.

Don't go second guessin' the Lord, Charlie reminded himself.

But where did Jack and Gia fit in? Pretty plain that neither of them were saved. Gia had faith in Jack, but in what else?

And Jack? He a mystery. What he'd said the other night about value for value still hung with Charlie. True that. The way things should be, but weren't . . . especially not in how he and Lyle had been earning their daily bread.

Jack's outlook didn't seem to be as earthbound as Lyle's, but his talk of the Otherness and the Ally power, of two cosmic forces in eternal conflict . . . that had Charlie a little shook. Where was God in all that? It didn't even give the God of the Holy Bible the props of being denied. Instead He got bypassed, left and forgotten like an old store by a freeway with no ramp.

And when Charlie had tried to point out that this "Otherness" was just another disguise for Satan, Jack had flipped it 'round, hinting that maybe the idea of Satan had come from awareness of the Otherness.

Charlie rubbed his eyes. He still hadn't answered his question: Who was being tested?

He reopened his Bible. All the answers were here. Have faith and Jesus would guide him to them.

But as for leaving Lyle and breaking up the team, that'd have to wait. Yeah, he promised Reverend Sparks, but if God was gonna go testin' Charlie's faith, he couldn't very well turn his back and geese outta here. And if God testing Lyle, then Charlie wanted to take his brother's back, help him to salvation any way he could. That what brothers was for.

14

Lyle stuck his head into Charlie's room and found him in his usual position, lying on the bed, reading the Bible with gospel playing through his headphones. He waved to catch his attention.

"I'm heading for bed," he said when Charlie took off the headphones.

"Kinda early, yo?"

"Yeah, but there's nothing but that old stuff on the tube. Can't bring myself to watch any more of that."

Charlie held up his Bible. "Gotta extra one if you interested. Great comfort to me, and bro, you look like a dawg who could use some comfort."

Lyle waved him off—not ungently. "Thanks, but I think I'll pass."

"Okay, but you gotta standing offer." Charlie sat up on the edge of his bed. "Strange 'bout the TV. If we think this girl die in the sixties, why's it stuck in the eighties?"

Lyle had been pondering that one too.

"I don't know," he said. "And at the moment I'm too tired to care." He yawned. "You'll be ready to go back to work tomorrow?"

Charlie stared at him. "You gonna be ready to give value for value?"

"What's this? You've switched from quoting scripture to quoting Jack?"

As Lyle started to turn away, Charlie gripped his arm and looked up at him, his eyes searching his face.

"Has what gone down the past few days made you change your mind 'bout a power greater than you?"

Lyle glanced away. An old argument, this one, but now the parameters had changed.

"I'll admit I've encountered a number of phenomena for which I have no rational explanation." He saw Charlie's eyes light and so he hurried on before he could speak. "But that doesn't mean that no rational explanation exists. It simply means that I haven't the information to explain them."

Charlie's face fell. "Ain't you ever givin' in?"

"Surrender to irrationality? Never." He smiled, hoping to soften the impact of his words. "But it has made me afraid of the dark. So I hope you don't mind if I leave a bunch of lights on."

"Go ahead," Charlie said, readjusting his headphones. He held up his Bible. "But this is the only light I need."

Lyle waved and turned away thinking how comforting it must be to believe that the answers to all questions could be found in a single book.

Envying the peace that must bring, he waded down the hall through a sea of turmoil. He'd hidden the uneasiness gnawing at the base of his throat. His home had turned unpredictable, a minefield of dread possibilities. The events of the day had left him jumpy and unsettled, but exhausted as well. Yet the idea of lying down and closing his eyes bordered on the unthinkable.

At least in this house. One night in a motel would do it—allow him a solid eight hours of sleep so he could return in the morning refreshed and ready for anything.

But he was *not* leaving his home.

Lyle glanced at his alarm clock as he entered his bedroom. It read 3:22. Still running backward. The real time was somewhere around 10:30. Lyle realized he was more than exhausted. He didn't feel well. He hoped the blood in that pool hadn't been contaminated . . . blood carried all sorts of diseases these days. But then, it hadn't been real blood, had it. Some sort of psychic or ectoplasmic blood . . .

Listen to me, Lyle thought. I sound like I've been listening to my own jive-ass line so long I'm starting to believe it.

But there'd been nothing jive ass about what happened this afternoon. That had been the furilla, as Charlie liked to say.

He rubbed his skin. He'd taken another shower when they'd got home after dinner, and still didn't feel as if he'd washed off the taint of his blood bath. It seemed as if it had seeped into his skin—no, *through* his skin and into his bloodstream. He felt changed somehow.

The past few days had changed his perspective. Any brightness only served to make the shadows look deeper. So you stepped around them. Trouble was, there seemed to be lots more shadows, so you did a lot more stepping around. Let that get out of hand and pretty soon you spent your whole day stepping around shadows.

Being in a spot where you feared you had only a couple of minutes to live had to change you some. Lyle had been sure he was going to drown in that blood this afternoon. But he hadn't, and he'd emerged from that crimson baptism with a new appreciation for his life, and a determination to make the most of everything he had.

And what he had at the moment was a ghost.

Pretty ironic when he thought about it: A devout skeptic who earns his daily bread by faking the existence of ghosts winds up owning a haunted house. The stuff movies of the week were made of.

But the fact was he'd chosen this house *because* of its morbid history, so if any place had a better-than-average chance of being haunted, it was Menelaus Manor.

So . . . how do we make the most of the situation? If this ghost is a lemon, how do we, as the cliché goes, make lemonade?

The obvious answer had struck Lyle in the restaurant. If these manifestations were truly the doings of the ghost of a child who had been murdered and buried in the house, and if she was trying to tell them something that would bring her killer to justice, or wanted to show them her burial place so forensic science could track down her killer, then she had a willing—no, an *enthusiastic* ally in Lyle Kenton.

Not merely because satisfying her needs offered a good chance that she'd go back to wherever she came from and leave the house in peace . . .

. . . but think of the publicity!

If he could find the body . . . and if the body led the police to her killer . . .

Psychic Ifasen Contacted by Spirit of
Dead Child to Bring her Killer to Justice!

Not a news show or talk show in the world that wouldn't be begging him for an appearance. Hell, even Oprah would want him. But he'd be picky, accepting only the most prestigious venues with the largest viewership. He'd get a book deal, detailing his exploits among the spirits.

And his clientele! Everybody who was anybody would want to see him. He and Charlie would be set for life. They'd charge ten—no, twenty-five K for a private sitting, and have those sitters' limos lined up around the block and backed up all the way across the Triboro Bridge.

It would be like winning a fifty-million-dollar lottery.

With that wonderful fantasy dancing in his head, he stood in the middle of his bedroom and softly called out, "Hello? Anybody there?"

Not that he was expecting a reply, but he had to try to break through this knot of tension winding about him.

A chill rippled over his skin. Was it his imagination or did the temperature just drop? He sensed that he was no longer alone in the room. The degrees continued to fall. He might have welcomed it had he known his air conditioner was behind it. But the unit was off. And this was a different kind of cool . . . clammy, seeping to the bone.

Something was responding to his questions. He spread his arms in a gesture of openness.

"If you've got something to say, I'm lis—"

A drawer in his dresser slammed closed.

Lyle jumped and backed away. As he watched, another drawer slid open, then slammed closed. Then another, and another, faster and faster, harder and harder until Lyle feared they'd splinter and shatter.

Lyle caught movement to his left as Charlie, wide-eyed with his Bible clutched in both hands, edged into the room; he saw his lips move but couldn't hear him over the cacophony.

Then, as suddenly as it began, it stopped.

"What was that all about?" Charlie whispered into the echoing silence.

Lyle rubbed his bare arms against the pervading chill. "I haven't—"

He stopped as he saw a dark line appear in the dust on the dresser top. They could well afford a cleaning service, but didn't like strangers in the house who might see something they shouldn't. So they did the work themselves, but not nearly so often as needed.

Maybe that was going to turn out to be a good thing.

Lyle stepped closer and motioned Charlie to follow him. He pointed to the letters forming slowly in the down of dust.

Where

"Look," he whispered. "Just like on the mirror Sunday night."

is

Charlie pointed to the growing string of letters. "She can sing a song, why don't she talk?"

the

Good question, Lyle thought. He shook his head. He had no answer.

"Look like the spirit writing we fake," Charlie said, "only a thousand times better."

nice

"Because this isn't fake."

Spirit writing . . . all it took was a fake thumb tip equipped with pencil lead, but now he was witnessing the real thing.

The sentence ended with a question mark.

Where is the nice lady?

Lyle heard Charlie breathe, "Gia. You was right. They connected."

"She went home," Lyle said in a voice that was perhaps too loud.

Why?

"She doesn't live here."

Will she be back?

"I don't know. Do you want her to come back? I'm sure she'll come if we ask her."

She is nice

"Yeah, we like her too." He glanced at Charlie. "Who are you?"

Tara

Lyle let out a breath. She had a first name. That was a start, but he needed more.

" 'Tara' what? Do you have a last name?"

Portman

Tara Portman . . . Lyle closed his eyes and balled his fists. Yes!

"Why are you here, Tara? What do you want?"

Mother -

"You want your mother?"

Lyle waited but no answer appeared. He felt the chill drain from the air, the tension uncoil from the room.

"Tara?" he called. Then again, louder. "Tara!"

"She gone," Charlie said. "Don't you feel it?"

Lyle nodded. He did. "Well, at least we know who she is. Or was, rather."

Lyle closed his eyes and realized he wasn't as tense as he'd been a few moments ago. He was no longer dealing with a nameless, violent entity. Knowing the name of the being that had invaded their house made her less threatening. She'd been someone, and something of that someone remained. He could deal with what remained.

He could help her. And she could help him.

"Right," Charlie said. "We got her name. Now what we do with it?"

"First thing we do is get hold of Gia and see if the name Tara Portman means anything to her."

15

"Tara Portman," Gia said, rolling the two names through her brain for maybe the dozenth time. "I've known an occasional Tara and a couple of Portmans, but can't for the life of me recall a Tara Portman."

They'd returned directly from the restaurant in Astoria—no stop at Menelaus Manor per Jack's insistence—and settled down for a movie. Gia had found *Stepmom* on one of the cable movie channels and declared tonight her turn to pick. Jack grumbled and groaned, saying anything but *Stepmom*, but finally gave in. He turned out to be a poor loser, editorializing with gagging and retching sounds at the best parts.

He'd checked his messages before they headed for bed and found an urgent call from Lyle Kenton who'd claimed that the ghost had told them her name.

Lyle had read off what the spirit had written and Jack had copied it down. Staring at the transcription now gave her a chill. A bodiless entity, the ghost of a little dead girl, had mentioned her. She shuddered.

"Well, whoever or whatever it is," Jack said, "it thinks you're nice. At least that's what it says."

Gia was sitting at the kitchen table, the transcription before her. Jack stood beside her, leaning on the table.

"You don't think I'm nice?" she said, looking up at him.

"I *know* you're nice. And you know my agenda. But we know nothing about this thing's."

"Her name is Tara."

"So it says."

Gia sighed. Jack could be so stubborn at times. "Are you going to be difficult about this?"

"If being protective of you translates as difficult, then yes, I'm going to be very difficult about this. I do not trust this thing."

"She seems to want me to come back."

"Oh, no," he said. "That's not going to happen."

"Oh, really?"

Gia knew he was looking out for her, but still she bristled at being told what she could or couldn't do.

"Come on, Gi. Don't be like that. This is the Otherness we're dealing with here. Responsible for the rakoshi. You haven't forgotten them, have you?"

"You know I haven't. But you don't know for sure it's the Otherness."

"No, I don't," he admitted. "But I think the best course is to assume the worst until proven otherwise."

Gia leaned back. "Tara Portman . . . how can we find out about her?"

"Newspapers are the best bet," Jack said. "We can hit the *Times* or one of the other papers tomorrow and search their archives. Start in '67 and work backwards and forwards."

"What about the Internet? We can do that right now."

"The Internet didn't exist back in '67."

"I know. But it can't hurt to try."

Gia led Jack to the townhouse's library where she'd set up the family computer. She and Vicky were starting to use it more and more—Vicky for homework, Gia for reference stills for her paintings. She fired it up, logged onto AOL, and did a Google search for Tara Portman. She got over ten thousand hits, but after glancing at the first half dozen she knew this wasn't going to give her what she needed.

"Try 'missing child,' " Jack suggested.

She typed it in and groaned when the tally bar reported nearly a million hits. But at the top of the list she noticed a number of organizations devoted to finding missing children. A click on one of the links took her to www.abductedchild.org.

She read the organization's mission statement as the rest

of the welcome screen filled in, and was dismayed to learn it had been founded in 1995.

"This isn't going to work. She's been gone too long."

"Probably right." Jack said. "But there's a search button over on the left there. Give it a shot."

She did. The next screen allowed searches by region, by age and physical description, or by name. Gia chose the last. She entered "Portman" in the last name field, "Tara" in the first, and hit enter. The screen blanked, then a color photo began to take shape. Blurry at first, but increasingly sharper as more pixels filled in.

Hair . . . Gia felt her saliva begin to vanish when she saw that the child was blond.

Eyes . . . her breath leaked away as blue eyes came into focus.

Nose . . . lips . . . chin . . .

With a cry, Gia pushed back from the keyboard so hard and fast she might have tipped over if Jack hadn't been behind her.

Jack caught her. "What's wrong?"

"That's . . ." The words clogged in her throat. Her tongue felt like clay. She pointed to the screen. "It's her! That's the child I saw in the house!"

Jack knelt beside her, clutching her hand as he stared at the screen.

"Gia . . . really? No doubt?"

Her voice was a whisper. "None. It's her."

Jack reached for the abandoned mouse and scrolled down the screen.

TARA ANN PORTMAN
Case Type: Nonfamily Abduction
DOB : Feb-17-1979
Height: 5' 4"—135 cm
Weight: 60 lbs—28 kg
Eyes: Blue
Hair: Blond
Parents: Joseph and Dorothy Portman

Circumstances : Tara was last seen in the area of the Kensington Stables in the Kensington section of Brooklyn near Prospect Park after horseback riding.
Date Missing : Aug-16-1988
City of Report: Brooklyn
State of Report: NY
Country of Report: USA
The photo above is how Tara looked the year she was abducted. The photo below is age progressed to age 18. Posted 1997

The age progression showed a strikingly beautiful teen-ager, a classic homecoming queen if Gia had ever seen one.

But Tara Portman never made it to her prom. Gia felt her throat constrict. She never even made it to high school.

"I don't like this," Jack said. "Any of it."

Of course not. What was there to like? But Gia had never known Jack as one for obvious statements.

"What do you mean?"

"Abducted kids. First I get involved with one, now you. It bothers me. Too . . ."

"Coincidental?"

"Right. And you remember what I was told."

Gia nodded. "No more coincidences."

The mere possibility that such a thing might be true sick-ened her.

"You think Tara and Duc might be connected?"

"I don't see how. I mean, there's such a long span be-tween, but then . . . no more coincidences." He shrugged. "Let's see what else we can dig up on her."

The page listed an email contact and three phone num-bers: a toll-free for the Abducted Child network, one for the local Brooklyn precinct, and one for the family.

"Abducted 1988," Jack said. "That doesn't fit with the sixties song, but if that's the girl you saw, we'll worry about the song later."

"That's her."

Gia stared at that nine-year-old face, wondering who

could have a soul so dead that he'd want to do harm to such beauty, such innocence?

"Look," Jack said, pointing to the screen. "Posted in 1997, when she was eighteen. She'd been gone nine years and the family was still looking for her."

"Or looking for closure." She looked at him. "Jack, we've got to do something."

" 'We'? You and the baby are staying far away from Astoria and that house, remember?"

"All right then, you—you or somebody else has got to find her remains and let her family bury her."

"I'll take care of it," he said. "Just promise me you'll stay away from there."

"Look at her, Jack. Look at that face. How could you believe that child could hurt anyone?"

"Something awful happened to 'that child.' Abducted and killed are bad enough, but who knows what was done to her in the time between? She's not an innocent child anymore. She's not even human. And I don't like that she appeared to you and no one else."

"Look what she wrote for the Kentons: 'Mother.' That's me. A mother of one and mother-to-be of another. She wants her mother and I was the closest thing to one in that house."

"Could be," Jack said slowly. "But I still don't like it."

"Jack, if she was looking for her daddy she might have appeared to you."

"Why *isn't* she looking for her daddy?"

"Maybe he'd dead, or her folks were divorced, or maybe she was raised by a single mother."

"Or maybe her daddy's involved."

Gia hated that thought but had to accept it as a possibility.

"None of that matters as much as finding her. We can let the police sort out the rest afterwards."

"I'll handle it," Jack said. "I'll be in touch with Lyle tomorrow and see how far he wants to take this. Maybe I can talk him into tearing up his cellar floor."

"And me?"

"You work on your paintings and whatever else you usually do on a Wednesday."

"Yes, Poppa."

He kissed her cheek. "Please, Gia. Stay safe and stay put."

Gia nodded. "Okay."

But she couldn't take her eyes off the Portman family phone number at the bottom of the screen . . . a 212 exchange . . . right here in Manhattan . . .

IN THE IN-BETWEEN

The being that was Tara Portman floats in the darkness between. She knows who she is, she knows who she was, she knows why she is here, she knows who must die.

But after that death—another death in this place of death—what?

Return to nothingness?

No . . . there must be more. She wants, she needs more.

Knowledge of her old self has awakened memories of the barely blossoming promise of her life before it was ended.

Knowing what she has lost . . . this is agony.

Knowing all that she will never have, never be . . . this is unbearable.

The being that was Tara Portman wants more.

WEDNESDAY

1

"It's called what?" Abe said, frowning down at the froth-filled cup Jack had just placed before him on the counter.

"Chai," Jack said. "They told me at the coffee shop it's very in."

"What is it?"

"Gal said it's an Indian thing."

"Indian as in the subcontinent?

"Right. Told me it was tea with milk, plus sugar and spice and everything nice."

All true. The woman ahead of him at the coffee shop this morning had ordered a chai and he'd asked about it. He'd figured what the hell, try anything once. Anything to give him a break from thinking about Tara Portman and Gia and Duc Ngo, and all the possible interconnections.

"I got you a skinny."

Abe's frown deepened. "A skinny what?"

"It means they use skim milk instead of regular—'cause I know you're watching your waist."

Yeah, Jack thought. Watching it grow.

Abe continued to stare at the cup. It seemed to have mesmerized him. "How do you spell it?"

"C-H-A-I."

Abe shook his head. "You're pronouncing it all wrong." He repeated the word his own way, hardening the "ch" to a raspy sound that originated in the back of his throat. "Like Chaim or Chaya or Chanukah."

"Not according to the girl who sold it to me."

Abe shrugged. "Whatever. And I should be drinking this why?"

"I read where it's the new fave drink of all the cool,

contemporary, contemplative people. I decided I want to be cool, contemporary, and contemplative."

"For that you'll need more than a drink. What's in the other bag you brought in? The one you put on the floor?"

"Never mind that now." Jack lifted his cup. "Let's give it a go. Chai away."

Abe toasted with his. "*Lochai.*"

Jack took a sip, swirled it across tongue, then looked around for a place to spit. Finding none, he swallowed.

Abe's sour expression mirrored Jack's sentiments. "Like an accident in a clove factory."

Jack nodded as he recapped his cup. "Well, now that I've tried chai, I can tell you that I feel cool and contemporary, but I'm also contemplating why anyone would want to drink this stuff."

Abe handed his cup to Jack. "See if you can get a refund. Meanwhile, have you got in that second bag what I hope?"

Jack retrieved the bag from the floor and produced two coffees. "Just in case the chai sucked."

Jack took a quick sip to rinse the chai taste out of his mouth, then settled over the *Post*, flipping the pages in search of a particular name.

"Have you seen any mention of Carl and Elizabeth Foster, or Madame Pomerol?"

"The psychic lady?" Abe shook his head. "Neither of them made the news today."

Jack closed his paper. "Didn't expect anything so soon." He sipped his coffee, grateful for the familiar flavor. "Come up with any ideas on making me a citizen?"

"Nothing yet, but I'm thinking."

He told Abe his idea about assuming a dead man's identity.

Abe shrugged. "As a plan it's got possibilities, but God forbid a long-lost sister should come looking. What do you do then?"

"I improvise."

"Not good. If that plan's going to work, you've got to find a dead man with no friends and no living family."

"Tall order."

Very tall. So tall it was bringing Jack down.

Abe looked at him. "How do you feel about getting out?"

Jack shrugged. "Not sure. Maybe it's time. I've been lucky. I've mined this vein for years without getting myself killed or crippled. Maybe I should take this as a sign to stop stretching my luck and call it quits. I've had a good run, saved a decent amount of money. Maybe it's time to kick back and enjoy the fruits of my labors."

"Before forty? You'll do what with your time?"

"Don't know yet. I'll think of something. Hey, need a stock boy?"

"*Oy!*"

"No? Well then how about you, Abe? How do you feel about me getting out?"

Abe sighed. "With fatherhood looming, it's a good thing. Overdue, even."

The remark took Jack by surprise. This was the last thing he expected to hear from Abe.

"Why do you say that?"

"Because you're mellowing."

Jack laughed. "That chai must be potent stuff. It's affecting your brain. Me? Mellowing? Never."

"You are. You think maybe I'm blind? I've watched it. A slow process, it's been, but it's happening. Ever since you and Gia got back together. Almost a year now, right?"

"A year ago this month."

"You see? I'm right. Before last summer you were a lobster—a spiny lobster."

"And what am I now? A softshell crab?"

"*S'teitsh!* Let me finish. Lobsterman Jack kept to his shell. With all his spines sticking out, people kept their distance. Nobody touched him. Such a hair trigger he had. Now . . ." Abe gave one of his major shrugs, palms turned up, lips turned down. "Now, I should dare say, you've opened a few windows in your shell. You take a longer view. That's the result of the love of a good woman."

Jack smiled. "She's that, all right."

"Until Gia, you never had anyone you cared about. Like a daredevil you were. Completely reckless. Now, you've got someone you want to get back to, someone you know is waiting for you. That changes everything. Makes you more careful."

"I've always been careful. It's essential in my business."

"But you can be too careful," Abe said. "And that's why I'm glad you're getting out. Because having a child will make you way too careful."

"No such thing as too careful."

"In your field of work, there is. I know you, Jack. Once that child is born, it's going to be the center of your world. You'll feel responsible for its welfare and well-being. Beyond responsible. You'll obsess about it. You'll want to be there for it, want to get home safe every night so it shouldn't have to grow up without a father. That's going to push you past too-careful into cautious. Ultimately it's going to make you hesitant in a field where an instant's hesitation can kill you. I'll miss Repairman Jack, but at least Daddyman Jack will still be alive to come around for breakfast, and maybe bring the little one with him."

"You're overstating this just a little bit, don't you think?"

Abe shook his head. "Unless you quit or drastically limit the types of jobs you take on—jobs that will be no fun for you—I don't see you surviving a year after your baby is born."

Jack went silent, thinking about that. Didn't buy it, didn't believe it, but it shook him to know Abe did.

In the long run, though, what did it matter? He was getting out. He was going to become Citizen Jack.

Talk about a bowel-clenching thought.

This life he'd been leading had had more than its share of hair-raising moments, and flying below the radar twenty-four-seven could be exhausting at times, and there were many days he wearied of looking over his shoulder, but damn he loved getting up in the morning without knowing what the day would bring.

Going straight was going to be so strange.

But it would pay the dividend of allowing his child to be able to stand anyplace with anyone and point to him and say, That's my dad.

2

The ride home hadn't been so bad, and getting in and out of the car had been bearable, but the steps . . . even with Adrian helping him, negotiating the narrow staircase up to his apartment above the store was agony.

Finally he was able to ease himself into a recliner, close his eyes, and catch his breath.

Good to be out of the hospital and free of all those tubes—although his belly still quivered at the memory of Nurse Horgan removing his catheter this morning. Good to be back in his home which, in sharp contrast to the cluttered store below, was furnished in a spare, minimalist style with bare walls, naked hardwood floors, and light, spindly furniture. The recliner was a blatant anomaly; a home needed at least one comfortable chair.

"Here. Take this."

Eli looked up and saw Adrian standing before him with a glass of water and two Percocets in his huge hands.

"You're a good man, Adrian. Thank you. How is your leg?"

He flexed his knee. "Much better. But the headaches are terrible. And I still can't remember Monday night. I remember having dinner . . ."

"Yes-yes," Eli said, thinking, Please let's not hear that again. "The doctor said you might never remember what happened. Perhaps you should count yourself lucky you don't."

"I don't feel lucky," Adrian said. He crossed his long arms over his chest and hugged himself. Eli wondered if his hands touched in the back. "I feel scared."

Odd to imagine that such a big man could be frightened. But Adrian wasn't a thug. He had a law degree and assisted Judge Marcus Warren of the New York State Supreme Court.

"You're afraid this man is going to attack us again?"

"I'm not afraid of that. In fact I almost wish he would." Adrian balled his hands into giant fists. "I'd love to make him pay for what he did to me. No, I'm afraid that we won't get the Ceremony done in time . . . you know, before the equinox."

"We will. I haven't missed one for two hundred and six years. I'm not about to start now."

"But what if we don't?"

The possibility spilled acid through Eli's chest. "The consequences for you will be minimal. You'll merely have to start a new cycle of Ceremonies."

"But I've already invested five years."

An initiate had to participate in an unbroken chain of twenty-nine annual cycles before the aging process stopped and invulnerability was conferred. Once the chain was broken, the count went back to zero and had to be started again.

"And that's all you will lose—five years of Ceremonies. Nothing. For me, on the other hand, the consequences will be catastrophic. All the ills, all the injuries, all the aging the Ceremony had shielded me from for the last two centuries will come crashing back at once."

His dying would be long and slow and exquisitely painful. These stab wounds would seem mere pinpricks.

"But after you're gone," Adrian said, "who will perform the Ceremony?"

Eli shook his head. He wanted to ask, Do you ever think of anyone but yourself? But he held his tongue. Adrian was no different from any of the others in the Circle. No more self-centered than myself, Eli supposed.

"No one," Eli said, relishing the growing dismay in Adrian's expression. "Unless the one who attacked us wishes to accept you as an initiate."

Adrian frowned. "I don't understand."

Eli sighed. They'd discussed this already, but Adrian's short-term memory still wasn't up to snuff.

"I believe the one who attacked us is an adept like myself who knows the Ceremony. That is the only way he could harm me."

"Yes," Adrian said. "Yes, I remember."

"But I believe his real purpose is to destroy my Circle. He has a Circle of his own and does not want competition."

"Then I think I should stay here with you," Adrian blurted. "Until you're well enough to protect yourself, that is."

Eli considered the idea and liked it. He could certainly use some assistance for the next few days—he could take care of his dressing changes himself, but help with meals and running errands would be most welcome.

No use appearing too anxious, though. Adrian seemed scared half to death that something would happen to him before the next Ceremony. Nothing wrong with making him sweat a little.

"I don't think so, Adrian," he said. "I'm used to living alone. I don't think I'd do well with constant company."

"I'll stay out of your way. I promise. Just let me stay through the weekend. I'm not going back to court until next week. I can watch over things until then."

Like a puppy dog. Or a huge Great Mastiff, rather. Time to throw him a bone.

"Oh, very well. I suppose I could put up with it for a few days."

"Wonderful! I'll go home, pack a few things, and be back in an hour."

He turned and limped toward the door.

"Wait," Eli said. "Before you go, could you hand me the phone?"

"Of course. Expecting a call?"

"Freddy is supposed to call when he's identified that woman who was quoted on TV last night. I don't want to miss that call." He smiled. "I do hope she's having a nice day, because as soon as I learn her name, her life will go in the shitter."

"I don't like Strauss," Adrian said. "He said things about you last night."

"When?"

"As he was wheeling me back to my room. He said he was beginning to wonder about you, whether you're really as old as you say you are."

"Did he now?" This was interesting.

"He said he did some background on you years ago, and found you were born in the 1940s—I forget the year—to a pair of Italian immigrants."

"Yes, he confronted me with that early on, and I explained to him that it was a false identity. I searched out and contacted a number of poor couples named Bellitto until I found a pair who agreed—for the appropriate sum— to register my name as a home birth. They're dead now and cannot back me up, so I fear you'll just have to trust my word."

"Oh, I do," Adrian said. "Don't get me wrong, I'm just repeating what Strauss told me. He said he could never prove one way or the other whether you were as old as you say you are or just plain crazy—again, his words, not mine. He told me last night that now that you've been wounded, he's starting to lean more toward crazy."

"Is he now," Eli said. "How ungrateful. I believe I shall have to have a word with Freddy."

"Don't tell him I told you."

Eli stared at Adrian. For a bright man he could be so naïve at times.

"Why do you think he said any of this to you? He knew you'd tell me. He *wanted* you to tell me. He's having second thoughts and hopes I will ease his doubts. What he doesn't understand is that I don't care what he thinks. However, his police contacts are valuable to the Circle so I suppose I must confront him and settle this."

"Wait till you're feeling better," Adrian said.

It was so much easier in the old days, Eli thought. I didn't need the Circle. Once a year I'd simply find a wayward child, perform the Ceremony, and go my way. But things have become so complicated these days. With crime detection techniques what they are, one needs backup, connections, networks to safely secure a child year after year.

He needed the Circle as much as the Circle needed him. But they needn't know that.

Eli loosed a drawn-out sigh and rubbed his eyes. "Maybe I should disband the Circle and go it alone. That was how I began . . . alone."

Eli peeked through his fingers to see if his little speech had had the desired effect. The look of horror on Adrian's face confirmed that it had.

"No! Eli, you mustn't even think that! I'll talk to the others. We'll—"

"No. I shall handle it. I'll give it one more chance. Now, you run off and get your things while I make some calls."

After Adrian was gone, Eli leaned back in his recliner and closed his eyes.

. . . he could never prove one way or the other whether you were as old as you say you are or just plain crazy . . .

Sometimes, Eli admitted, I wonder about that myself.

He had memories of his early years in eighteenth-century Italy, his discovery of the Ceremony in a stone vault in Riomaggiore among the Cinque Terre along the Liguorian coast, and then the long trail of hundreds of years and hundreds of sacrificed children, but they were vague, almost as if he'd dreamed them. He wished he could recall more detail.

What if Strauss's suspicions were correct? What if he were no more than a murderous madman trying to turn back the clock, who'd told his mad stories to himself and others so many times he'd come to believe them?

No! Eli slammed his fist against the armrest of the re-

cliner. What was he thinking? He wasn't mad or deluded.
It was the pain, the drugs . . .

. . . the wound . . .

Yes, the wound. There lay the wellspring of his doubts.
He shouldn't have been wounded at all. That was the legacy
of the Ceremony—life and personal impregnability. It
didn't make an adept invulnerable to petty injuries like pap-
ercuts and such. But a stab wound . . . the blade was supposed to glance off the skin.

Unless it was wielded by another adept.

Uneasy, Eli took out the number Strauss had given him
last night and tapped it into the phone. And just like last
night, his attacker was "not available at this time."

Eli broke the connection and simmered. He would put
the number into speed dial and keep calling. The man had
to turn his phone on sometime, and one of those times Eli
would connect. And then they'd talk, and Eli would learn
about his attacker, induce him into a slip of the tongue, and
then he'd have him.

3

Lyle suppressed a yawn as he went through the preliminaries with a new sitter. Not that he was bored talking about
his spirit guide—how could Ifasen feel anything but excitement about communing with his ancient mentor Ogunfiditimi? Lyle was dead tired. He felt as if he'd spent the
night completing an ironman triathlon.

Tara Portman or whatever it was had rested easy last
night after the spirit-writing display. No noises, no blood,
no breakage. Still sleep had eluded Lyle. The mere expectation of noise, blood, or breakage had turned his mattress
into a bed of nails.

Charlie, on the other hand, looked fresh and fully rested this morning. That Bible of his, no doubt.

But Lyle's malaise went beyond fatigue. He couldn't pin it down. Not so much a matter of feeling bad as not feeling *right*. He felt . . . changed. The world looked and felt different. Shadows seemed deeper, lights brighter, sharper, the air felt charged, as if something momentous was in the offing.

He shook it off. He had work to do.

With the Channeling Room repaired, they'd begun rescheduling sittings. Lyle had adjusted the day's appointments to leave room for the meeting with Konstantin Kristadoulou. He'd called the old real estate agent first thing this morning and set up a meeting at one o'clock. He'd left a message for Jack about the time and place.

But that would be this afternoon. This was now, and Lyle wasn't happy with now. Melba Toomey was a far-from-ideal sitter. Lyle blamed his distracted state for allowing her to slip past the screening process. She would not be a good subject at any time, but especially not as the first of the day.

But she'd paid her money for a private sitting and now faced him across the table in her housedress and flower-decked straw hat, dark eyes bright with expectation in her black face.

According to the information on her questionnaire, Melba was fifty-three and cleaned houses for a living. Not at all typical of Ifasen's clientele, and certainly not the social class he was courting.

Lyle cringed at the thought of how long it must have taken her to save enough for a private sitting. But she'd said on her questionnaire that she'd come to him because he was black—didn't say African-American. Black.

Melba Toomey wanted to know if her husband Clarence was alive or dead; and if he was dead, she wanted to speak to him.

Lyle did his utmost to avoid the class of sitter whose concerns deprived him of precious wiggle room. Melba was the worst of that class: Alive or dead . . . was there a more black-or-white, yes-or-no proposition than that? It left him zero wiggle.

He'd have to do a cold reading on Clarence through Melba to try and get a grip on what kind of man Clarence was so as to make a roughly educated guess on whether he might be alive or dead.

I'm going to be sweating for my daily bread this round, he thought.

Lyle had placed two potato-size stones on the table, telling her that they were from Ogunfiditimi's birth place and, because Ogunfiditimi hadn't met her before, it enhanced first-time contact if she kept a good grip on those stones. It also kept her hands where Lyle could see them.

To set the mood—and kill some time—Lyle treated Melba to the histrionics, the table and chair tipping, then settled down to business.

Lyle came out of his pseudo trance and stared at her, watching closely. Her features were slightly fuzzy in the dim red light from overhead, but clear enough to pick up what he needed. Body language, visual cues in a blink of the eyes, a twist of the mouth, a twitch of a cheek . . . Lyle could read them like an old salt reads the sea.

First, some try-ons. She'd mentioned on her questionnaire that Clarence had been missing since June second. He'd start there.

"I'm getting a sense of a state of absence . . . of separation since . . . why does early June keep popping into my head?"

"The second of June!" Melba cried. "That's when I last saw Clarence! He went off to work in the morning and never came home. I haven't seen or heard from him since." She worked a used tissue out of her housedress pocket and dabbed her eyes. "Oh, Lord, you do have the gift, don't you."

Oh, yes, Lyle thought. The gift of remembering what you've forgotten you've told me.

"Please keep your hands on the stones, Melba," he reminded her. "It weakens contact when you remove them."

"Oh, sorry." She placed her hands back on the stones.

Good. Keep them there, he thought.

The last thing he wanted her to do was reach for her pocketbook. Because Charlie, covered head to toe in black, should have crept out of his command center by now and be ready to grab it from where it sat on the floor next to her chair.

"I told the police but I don't think they's doing much to find him. They don't seem the least bit interested."

"They're very busy, Melba," he told her.

Her distress sent a shot of guilt through Lyle. He wasn't going to do any more for her than the cops.

Value for value ... .

He shook it off and formulated another try-on. The first had been just an easy warm-up, to break the ice and gain a smidgen of her confidence. From here it got a little tougher.

Look at her: cleans houses, bargain-rack clothing; he couldn't see Clarence as a corporate exec. She mentioned him going off to work as if it were a routine thing. Good chance he had a steady blue-collar job, maybe union.

Try-on number two ...

"Why do I want to say he worked in a trade?"

"He was an electrician!"

"A loyal union man."

She frowned. "No. He was never in a union."

Whoops, but easy enough to save. "But I get the feeling he *wanted* to be in the union."

"Yes! How did you know! That poor man. He tried so many times but never qualified. He was always talking about how much more money he could be making if he was in the union."

Lyle nodded sagely. "Ah, that was what I was picking up."

Let's see ... blue-collar, frustrated ... maybe Clarence liked to knock back a few after work? And even if he was

a teetotaler or an ex-drinker, the *temptation* to drink offered
a ready fallback.

"I'm getting the impression of a dimly lit place, the smell
of smoke, the clink of glassware . . ."

"Leon's! That awful place! He'd go there after work and
come home reeking of beer. Sometimes he wouldn't come
home till after midnight. We had such terrible fights over
it."

Drunk . . . frustrated . . . go for it, but keep it vague.

"I'm led to say that some harm was done?"

Melba looked away. "He never meant to hurt me. It's
just that sometimes, when I got him real mad after he came
home late, he'd take a swing. He didn't mean nothin' by
it. But now that he's gone . . ." She sobbed and grabbed
the tissue to dab at her eyes again. "I'd rather have him
home late than not at all."

"I'm losing contact!" Lyle said. "The hands! The stones.
Please stay in contact with the stones."

Melba grabbed them again. "I'm sorry. It's just—"

"I understand, but you must hold the stones."

"Got her wallet here," said Charlie's voice in his earpiece. Obviously he'd made it back to his command center
with the pocketbook. *"Picture of her and some fat guy—I
mean, I could be looking at the Notorious B.I.G. here—but
no kid pics."*

Lyle said, "I'm looking for children but . . ."

He left a blank space, hoping she'd fill it in. As with
most sitters, she didn't disappoint.

"We didn't have any. Lord knows we tried but . . ." She
sighed. "It never happened."

"Not much else goin' down here," Charlie said. *"Keys, a
lipstick, hey—beat this: a harmonica. Bet it ain't hers. Good
shot it's her old man's. I'll get the bag back lickity."*

While waiting, Lyle made a few remarks about Clarence's weight problems to bolster further his psychic cred-
ibility. The picture he'd formed of Clarence was that of a
frustrated, money-squeezed, bad-tempered drinker. An answer to a dead-or-alive question on a guy like that had to

lean toward dead. He might have got himself involved in some quick-buck scheme that went wrong, leaving him food for the worms or the fish.

Lyle felt a tap on his leg: Charlie had returned the bag.

Lyle cleared his throat. "Why am I hearing music? It sounds reedy. Could it be a harmonica?"

"Yes! Clarence loved to play the harmonica. People told him he was terrible." Melba smiled. "And he was. He was just awful. But that never stopped him from trying."

"Why do I sense his harmonica nearby?"

She gasped. "I brought one with me! How could you know?"

Preferring to let her provide her own answer to that, Lyle said, "It might facilitate contact if I can touch an object that belongs to the one we seek."

"It's in my handbag." Melba glanced at her hands where they rested on the stones, then back at Lyle. "Do you think I could . . . ?"

"Yes, but one hand only, please."

"We gonna take this poor lady's money, bro?" Charlie asked in his ear. *"She ain't exactly our usual breed of fish."*

Lyle couldn't give him an answer, but the same hesitancy had been nibbling at him throughout the sitting.

He watched Melba free her right hand, pull her handbag up to her lap, and fish out a scratched and dented harmonica with "Hohner Special 20 Marine Band" embossed along the top.

"This was his favorite," she said, pushing it across the table.

Lyle reached toward it, then stopped as warning alarms rang through his nerve ends. Why? Why shouldn't he touch the harmonica?

After a few awkward seconds, with Melba's expression moving toward a puzzled frown, Lyle set his jaw and took hold of the harmonica—

—and cried out as the room did a sudden turn and then disappeared and he was standing in another room, a suite in the Bellagio in Vegas, watching a fat man he knew to be Clarence Toomey snore beside a blonde Lyle knew to be a hooker he'd hired for the night. He knew everything— the half-million-dollar lottery prize Clarence had won and kept secret from his wife until he'd collected the money, how he'd left home and never looked back.

Melba's cry from somewhere in front of him: "What's wrong?"

Charlie in his ear: *"Lyle! What's happenin'?"*

The feel of the harmonica in his hands . . . uncoiling his fingers one by one until . . .

The harmonica dropped onto the table and abruptly Lyle was back in the Channeling Room, looking at Melba who faced him with wide eyes and her hands pressed against her mouth.

"Lyle! Answer me! Are you all right?"

"I'm okay," Lyle said, for Melba's sake as well as his brother's.

But he was anything but okay.

What had just happened? Was it real? Had he truly been looking at Clarence Toomey or imagining it? It had seemed so real, and yet . . . it couldn't be.

Nothing like this had ever happened to him before. He didn't know what to make of it.

"Ifasen?" Melba said. "What happened? Did you see anything? Did you see my Clarence?"

What could he say? Even if he were sure it was true— and he wasn't, not at all—how do you tell a woman that her husband is bedded down in Vegas with a hooker?

"I'm not sure what I saw," Lyle said. Couldn't get much truer than that. He pushed back from the table. "I'm afraid I'm going to have to cut short our session. I . . . I don't feel well." No lie. He felt like hell.

"No, please," Melba said.

"I'm sorry. I will refund your money."

"Mah man!" Charlie said in his ear.

"I don't care about the money," Melba said. "I want my Clarence. How will I find him?"

"The lottery," Lyle said.

She looked at him. "The lottery? I don't understand."

"Neither do I, but that was the message that came through the clearest. Check with the New York State Lottery. Ask them about Clarence. That's all I can tell you."

If she did that, and if Lyle's vision had been real—a big if—she'd learn about Clarence's big win. She could hire someone to track him down, maybe get a piece of whatever was left.

She wanted to find her husband, but success was going to bring her only a load of hurt.

Charlie appeared, looking at him strangely. He had to be bursting with a million questions, but couldn't ask them while Melba was here.

Lyle said, "Kehinde will show you out and return your money. And remember what I told you: Check with the lottery. Do it today."

Melba's expression was troubled. "I don't understand any of this, but at least you tried to help. That's more than the police have done." She held out her hand. "Thank you."

Lyle gripped her hand and stifled a gasp as a whirlwind of sensations blew through him—a brief period of anger, then sadness, then loneliness, all dragging along for a year and a half, maybe more, but certainly less than two, and then darkness—*hungry* darkness that gobbled up Melba and everything around her.

He dropped her hand quickly, as if he'd received a shock. Was that Melba's future? Was that all she had left? Less than two years?

"Good-bye," he said and backed away.

Charlie led her toward the waiting room, giving Lyle an odd look over his shoulder.

"Ifasen is not himself today," he told Melba.

Damn right he's not himself, Lyle thought as uneasiness did a slow crawl down his spine. But who the hell is he?

4

Jack will kill me when he finds out.

Gia stood before the flaking apartment door and hesitated. Against all her better judgment she'd gone back to the abductedchild.org web site and called the family number listed on Tara Portman's page. She'd asked the man who answered if he was related to Tara Portman—he said he was her father—and told him that she was a writer who did freelance work for a number of newspapers. She was planning a series of articles about children who had been missing more than ten years and could he spare a few moments to speak to her?

His answer had been a laconic, Sure, why not? He told her she could stop by any time because he was almost always in.

So now she was standing in the hot, third-floor hallway of a rundown apartment building in the far-West Forties and afraid to take the next step. She'd dressed in a trim, businessy blue suit, the one she usually wore to meetings with art directors, and carried a pad and a tape recorder in her shoulder bag.

She wished she'd asked about Mrs. Portman—was she alive, were they still married, would she be home?

The fact that Tara had written "Mother" with no mention of her father might be significant; might say something about her relationship with her father; might even mean, as Jack had suggested, that he was involved in her disappearance.

But the fact remained that the ghost of Tara Portman had appeared to Gia and Gia alone, and that fact buzzed through her brain like a trapped wasp. She'd have no peace until she learned what Tara Portman wanted. That seemed to center on the mother she'd mentioned.

"Well, I've come this far," she muttered. "Can't stop now."

She knocked on the door. It was opened a moment later by a man in his mid-forties. Tara's blue eyes looked out from his jowly, unshaven face; his heavy frame was squeezed into a dingy T-shirt with yellowed armpits and coffee stains down the front, cut-off shorts, and no shoes. His longish dark blond hair stuck out in all directions.

"What?" he said.

Gia suppressed the urge to run. "I—I'm the reporter who called earlier?"

"Oh, yeah, yeah." He stuck out his hand. "Joe Portman. Come in."

A sour mix of old sweat and older food puckered Gia's nostrils as she stepped through the doorway into the tiny apartment, but she stifled her reaction. Joe Portman hustled around, turning off the TV and picking up scattered clothing from the floor and a sagging couch; he rolled them into a ball and tossed them into a closet.

"Sorry. Didn't expect you so soon." He turned to her. "Coffee?"

"Thanks, no. I just had some."

He dropped onto the couch and indicated the chair next to the TV for her.

"You know," he said, "this is really strange. The other night I was sitting right here, watching the Yankees, when I suddenly thought of Tara."

Gia seated herself carefully. "You don't usually think of her?"

He shrugged. "For too many years she was *all* I thought of. Look where it got me. Now I try not to think of her. My doctor at the clinic tells me let the past be past and get on with my life. I'm learning to do that. But it's slow. And hard."

A thought struck Gia. "What night was it when you had this sudden thought of Tara?"

"It was more than a thought, actually. For an instant, just a fraction of a second, I thought she was in the room. Then the feeling was gone."

"But when?"

He looked at the ceiling. "Let's see . . . the Yanks were playing in Oakland so it was Friday night."

"Late?"

"Pretty. Eleven or so, I'd guess. Why?"

"Just wondering," Gia said, hiding the chill that swept through her.

Joe Portman had sensed his daughter's presence during the earthquake under Menelaus Manor.

"Well, the reason I brought it up is, Friday night I get this feeling about Tara, then this morning you call wanting to do an article about her. Is that synchronicity or what?"

Synchronicity . . . not the kind of word Gia expected from someone who looked like Joe Portman.

"Life is strange sometimes," Gia said.

"That it is." He sighed, then looked at her. "Okay, reporter lady, what can I tell you?"

"Well, maybe we could start with how it happened?"

"The abduction? You can read about that in detail in all the old newspapers."

"But I'd like to hear it from you."

His eyes narrowed, his languid voice sharpened. "You sure you're a writer? You're not a cop, are you?"

"No. Not at all. Why do you ask?"

He leaned back and stared at his hands, folded in his lap. "Because I was a suspect for a while. Dot too."

"Dot is your wife?"

"Dorothy, yeah. Well, she was. Anyway, the cops kept coming up empty and . . . that was the time when stories about satanic cults and ritual abuse were big in the papers . . . so they started looking at us, trying to see if we were into any weird shit. Thank God we weren't or we might have been charged. It's hard to see how things could have worked out any worse, but that definitely would've been worse."

"How did it happen?"

He sighed. "I'll give you the short version." He glanced at her. "Aren't you taking notes?"

How dumb! she thought, reaching into her bag for her cassette recorder.

"I'd like to record this, if that's okay."

"Sure. We lived in Kensington. That's a section of Brooklyn. You know it?"

Gia shook her head. "I didn't grow up in New York."

"Well, it sounds ritzy, but it's not. It's just plain old middle class, nothing special. I worked for Chase here in the city, Dot worked out there as a secretary for the District 20 school board. We did okay. We liked Kensington because it was close to Prospect Park and Green-Wood Cemetery. Believe it or not, we saw the cemetery as a plus. It's a pretty place." He looked down at his hands again. "Maybe if we'd lived somewhere else, Tara would still be with us."

"How did it happen?"

He sighed. "When Tara was eight we took her to Kensington stables up near the parade grounds. You know, so she could see the horses. One ride and she was an instant horse lover. Couldn't keep her away. So we sprung for riding lessons and she was a natural. For a year she rode three days a week—Tuesday and Thursday afternoons, and Saturday morning. On Thursdays she'd have to wait a little while before Dot could pick her up. We told her to stay at the stables—do *not* under any circumstances leave the stables. And for a year it worked out fine. Then one Thursday afternoon Dot arrived to pick her up—right on time, I want you to know—and . . . no Tara." His voice cracked. "We never saw or heard from her again."

"And no witnesses, no clues?"

"Not a single one. We did learn, though, that she hadn't listened to us. Folks at the stable said she used to leave for a few minutes on Thursdays and return with a pretzel— you know, the big kind they sell from the pushcarts. The cops found the pushcart guy who remembered her—said she came by every Thursday afternoon in her riding clothes—but he hadn't seen anything different that day. She bought a pretzel as usual and headed back toward the stable. But she never made it." He punched his thigh. "If only she'd listened."

"What was she like?" Gia said. "What did she like besides horses?"

"You want to know?" he said, pushing himself out of the sofa. "That's easy. I'll let you see for yourself."

He walked around the sofa and motioned Gia to follow. She found him standing over a black trunk with brass fittings. He pulled it a few feet closer to the window and opened the lid.

"There," he said, rising. "Go ahead. Take a look. That's all that's left of my little girl."

Gia knelt and looked but didn't touch. She felt as if she were violating someone, or committing a sacrilege. She saw a stack of unframed photos and forced herself to pick it up and shuffle through them: Shots of Tara at all ages. A beautiful child, even as an infant. She stopped at one with Tara sitting atop a big chestnut mare.

"That was Rhonda, Tara's favorite horse," Portman said, looking over her shoulder.

But Gia was transfixed on Tara's clothing: a red-and-white checked shirt, riding breeches, and boots. Exactly what she'd been wearing at Menelaus Manor.

"Did . . . did she wear riding clothes a lot?"

"That's what she was wearing when she disappeared. In colder weather she'd wear a competition coat and cap. Made her look like the heiress to an English estate. God she loved that horse. Would you believe she'd bake cookies for it? Big thick grainy things. The horse loved them. What a kid."

Gia glanced at Portman and saw the wistful, lost look on his face and knew then he'd had nothing to do with his daughter's death.

She flipped further into the stack and stopped at a photo of Tara beside a trim, good-looking man in his thirties. Their hair and eyes were matching shades of blond and blue. With a start she realized it was her father.

"Yeah, that was me. I was Portman then, now I'm portly man." He patted his gut. "It's all the meds they've got me on. Name an antidepressant and I've tried it. Every one of them gives me these carbohydrate cravings. Plus the only exercise I get is moving around this place." He waved his hand at the tiny apartment. "Which, as you can imagine, isn't much."

"You said you worked for Chase?"

" 'Worked' is right. Not a big job, but a solid one. I made decent money. And I was planning on getting my MBA, but . . . things didn't work out."

Gia flipped to the next picture. Tara standing beside a slim, attractive brunette.

"That was Dorothy," Portman said.

"Her mother."

Portman shook his head. "She took Tara's disappearance harder than I did, which is pretty hard to imagine. They were best buds, those two. Did everything together. Dot never recovered."

Gia was almost afraid to ask. "Where is she now?"

"In a hospital room, hooked up to a feeding tube."

"Oh, no!"

Portman seemed to go on automatic pilot as his eyes unfocused and his voice became mechanical. "Car accident. Happened in 1993, on the fifth anniversary of Tara's disappearance. Ran into a bridge abutment on the LIE. Permanent brain damage. Because of the speed she was going, the insurance company said it was a suicide attempt. Our side said it was an accident. We met somewhere in the middle but it still didn't come near covering her ongoing medical expenses."

"What do you think happened?"

"I don't *know* what happened, but what I *think* is between me and Dot. Anyway, I couldn't afford to pay for all the care she needed—I mean I couldn't lose the house because I had to think of Jimmy who I had to raise all by myself then."

"Jimmy?"

"Flip ahead a few photos. There. That's Jimmy."

Gia saw Tara next to a dark-haired boy with a gap-toothed smile.

"He looks younger."

"By two years. He was five there."

"Where is he now?"

"In rehab. Booze, crack, heroin. You name it." He shook his head. "Our fault, not his."

"Why do you say that?"

"Jimmy was six-and-a-half when Tara disappeared. We forgot about him when that happened. Everything was Tara, Tara, Tara."

"That's understandable."

"Not when you're six. And then seven. And then eight-nine-ten, and your family life is an ongoing wake for your sister. Then at eleven he loses his mother. I'm sure he heard the suicide talk. And to him that meant his mother had abandoned him, that her grief over her dead daughter was greater than her love for her living son. He was too young to understand that maybe she hadn't thought it through, that maybe it was the worst day of her life and some crazy impulse took control."

Gia saw his throat working as he looked away. She couldn't think of anything to say except, You poor man, that poor boy. But that sounded condescending, so she waited in the leaden silence.

Finally Joe Portman sniffed and said, "You know, you can keep hope alive for only so long. When we hit the five-year mark and no Tara, we had to . . . we had to accept the worst. Maybe if I'd been with her more that fifth anniversary day, Dot might have got past it, and she'd still be up and about today. But everything must have looked too black to go on—maybe just for a few minutes or an hour, but that was enough. So now Jimmy was motherless and his father *still* wasn't paying attention to him, what with all that Dot needed." Portman rubbed his face, as if massaging his jowls. "Jimmy's first bust—the first of many—

was at age thirteen for selling marijuana and it was all downhill from there."

Gia felt a growing knot in her chest. The pain this man, this family had been through . . . no wonder he was on medication.

"Then I learned I had to divorce Dot."

"Had to?"

"To save the house and—so I hoped at the time—to save Jimmy, I had to divorce her. That way she'd be without support and could qualify for welfare and be covered by Medicaid. The irony of it is, if I'd waited a couple of years it wouldn't have been necessary."

"You mean they changed the law?"

"No." He smiled, but it was a painful grimace. "I stopped going to work. Jimmy was in a juvenile detention center at the time and I was alone in the house, and I just couldn't get myself out of bed. And if by some miracle I did, I couldn't leave the house. I kept the shades down and the lights off and just sat in the dark, afraid to move. Finally the bank let me go. And then I lost the house, and wound up on welfare and on Medicaid, just like Dot."

Almost numb from the torrent of pain, Gia placed the photos back in the trunk and looked around for something that might elicit happier memories. She picked up a short stack of vinyl record albums. The cover of the first featured a close-up of a cute red-haired girl with a wistful stare.

Gia heard Joe Portman let out a short laugh, not much more than a "Heh."

"Tiffany. Tara's favorite. She played those records endlessly, from the moment she got home."

Gia flipped the top one over. She remembered Tiffany, how she toured shopping malls at the start of her career. What were her hits? She did new versions of old songs. Hadn't she redone an early Beatles tune? Gia scanned through the song list . . .

She gasped.

"What's wrong?" Portman said.

"Oh, nothing." Gia swallowed, trying to moisten her dry

tongue. "It's just that I'd forgotten that Tiffany remade 'I Think We're Alone Now.' "

"Oh, that song!" Portman groaned. "Tara would sing it day and night. She had a great voice, never missed a note, but how many times can you listen to the same song? Drove us crazy! But you know what?" His voice thickened. "I'd give anything in the world—my life—to hear her sing it again. Just once."

If Gia had harbored any subconscious doubts that the entity in Menelaus Manor was Tara Portman, they'd vanished now.

She dug deeper into the trunk and came up with a plush doll she immediately recognized.

"Roger Rabbit!"

Portman reached past her and took the doll. He turned it over in his hands, staring at it with brimming eyes.

"Roger," he whispered. "I almost forgot about you." He gave Gia a quick glance. "I haven't been in here in a while." He sighed. "The movie came out the summer she disappeared. She made me take her three times, and I swear every time she laughed harder than before. Probably would have had to take her a fourth time if . . ."

He handed back the doll.

Gia stared at its wide blue eyes and felt tears begin to slip down her cheeks. She quickly wiped her eyes, but not quickly enough.

"I'll be damned," Portman said.

"What?"

"A reporter with feelings. I can't tell you how many reporters I've talked to since 1988, and you're the first who's ever shown any real emotion."

"Maybe they were more experienced. And maybe this hits a little too close to home for me."

"You've got a daughter?"

Gia nodded. "She's eight . . . and she just discovered Roger Rabbit on video. She loves him."

The tears again. Gia willed them back but they kept flowing. What happened to Tara Portman—plucked out of a happy life and killed or worse. It was too cruel, just . . . too cruel.

"Don't you let her out of your sight," Portman was saying. "Stay on top of her every minute, because you never know . . . you never know."

Terror spiked her. Vicky was far away, at camp. Why on earth had she let her go?

But she couldn't raise Vicky in a bubble. Part of her wanted to, but it wouldn't be fair.

Gia replaced Roger in the trunk and rose to her feet. She felt lightheaded. "I . . . I think I've got enough now."

"You'll send me a copy?" Portman said.

"Sure. If I sell it."

"You'll sell it. You've got heart. I can tell. I want it published. I want Tara's name out there again. I know she's gone. I know she'll never come back. But I don't want her forgotten. She's just a statistic now. I want her to be a name again."

"I'll do my best," Gia said.

She felt terrible about lying to him. There'd never be an article. Scalding guilt propelled her toward the door to escape this hot smelly box where the walls seemed to be closing in.

Portman followed her. "Do you know what Tara might have been, where she could have gone? She could sing, she could play piano, she could ride, she was smart as a whip and she loved life, every moment of it. She had two parents who loved her and a great life ahead of her. But it was all snuffed out." He snapped his fingers. "Just like that. And not by some freak accident, but on purpose. On purpose! And what about Jimmy? Who knows what he could have been? Better than the junkie he is now. And what about me and Dot? We could have grown old together, had grandkids. But that's never going to happen." His voice broke. "You let people know that whoever took my Tara didn't kill just a little girl. He killed a whole family!"

Gia only nodded as she stepped into the hall, unable to push a word past the invisible band that had a death grip on her throat.

5

"So, Freddy," Eli said. "I understand you think I'm crazy."

Strauss had stopped by with news about his investigations—he tended to prefer to report in person than on the phone—but Eli was more interested in straightening out this popinjay vice cop who thought he had all the answers.

Strauss stiffened. "I never—" The wiry cop turned toward Adrian and shot him an angry look. "I see someone's been shooting his mouth off."

"Just as you wanted him to do, am I correct?"

"Listen, you gotta understand—"

"What I understand, Detective Strauss, is that you are a faithless man. I offer you virtual immortality and how am I rewarded? By you whispering behind my back. I'm of half a mind to disband the Circle and continue on by myself, as I used to."

"You can't be serious!" Strauss said. "Just because of a little remark I happened to—"

"More than a little remark! It challenges the integrity of the Circle!"

Eli could tell by Strauss's expression that he didn't want to be held responsible for breaking up the Circle. One could only imagine what the other members would do to him. But a defiant look came over his face. He straightened his narrow shoulders and glared at Eli.

"I ran checks on you, Eli," Strauss said. "Hell, I ran half a dozen on you, from every angle, and nowhere does it say you weren't born in Brooklyn in 1942."

Eli smiled. "I've had centuries of practice hiding my origins. I'm very good at what I do."

"And so am I. And ay, don't think some of the others

ain't thinking the same thing as me. You tell us you've lived this charmed life for over two hundred years, how you're as good as immortal as long as you keep performing the Ceremony, and then some guy strolls up to you and stabs you with your own knife."

"I told you—"

"I know what you told me, but what am I supposed to think? What's anyone supposed to think?"

What indeed? Eli thought.

He had to put a stop to this. Immediately.

He turned to Adrian. "Go to the kitchen and get me one of the carving knives."

Adrian gave him a strange look but did as he was bid and returned with an eight-inch Wüsthof-Trident Culinar carver. It looked small in Adrian's huge hand. Eli took it from him, gripping it by the dull edge of the carbon steel blade, and proffered it to Strauss, stainless-steel handle first.

"Take it."

Strauss looked uncertain. "Why?"

"Just take it and I'll tell you."

The cop hesitated, then reached out and took the knife. "Okay. Now what?"

Eli unbuttoned his shirt and bared his chest. "Now, you stab me."

"Eli!" Adrian cried. "Have you gone crazy?" He turned to Strauss. "Don't listen to him! It's the painkillers! He's not—"

"Et tu, Adrian?" Eli said, feeling a pang of regret. Didn't anyone have faith anymore? "You don't believe me either?"

"Of course I do!" He looked flustered now. "It's just—"

"Do it, Freddy. Do it now. I demand it. And after you see that I'm perfectly all right, you can tell the rest of your faithless crew that *you're* the crazy one, not me!"

Strauss hefted the knife, his gaze flicking back and forth between the blade and Eli's chest. Eli had no fear. He knew he was invulnerable to injury from Strauss or Adrian or anyone else except the mystery man. And this would prove it.

Strauss stepped closer, his lips set in a tight line. Eli closed his eyes . . .

"Don't!" Adrian cried. "Eli, listen to me! What if the man who attacked you interfered with your invulnerability? What if the wounds he inflicted somehow put your powers on hold until they're renewed by another Ceremony?"

"Don't be ridiculous!"

"It's a possibility, isn't it? Nothing like this has ever happened to you before, right? Do you really want to risk it?"

Eli went cold as Adrian's words seeped in. No . . . it couldn't be. It was unprecedented. And yet, so was what happened Monday night. If what Adrian said were true . . .

I have to perform another Ceremony right away! Before the window of this new moon closes!

He glanced at Strauss and noticed a new uncertainty about him.

Do I dare?

Yes. He had to.

"Perhaps you're right, Adrian. But the only way to find out is to see what happens after Freddy stabs me." He looked Strauss in the eye. "Go ahead, Freddy. This will be an experiment."

"Uh-uh," Strauss said, shaking his head and backing away. "Too risky. I'm not experimenting myself into a murder rap."

"Thank God!" Adrian said, and slumped against a wall.

Eli felt exactly the same but couldn't show it. He simply sighed and said, "Perhaps you're right, Adrian. Perhaps we should try to perform the Ceremony as soon as possible."

"But there's no time!" Adrian said. "The Ceremony window is three nights before and after the new moon. That means we have to secure a new lamb—"

"By Friday night," Eli said. "In a way that can't ever be linked back to us." It seemed impossible. But he had to remain calm, and above all, *appear* calm. "We'll ask around the Circle for any good prospects. In the meantime . . ." He turned to Strauss. "Any progress on finding our attacker?"

Strauss shook his head. "Nope. But I did track down that broad who made those comments last night."

"Excellent. So glad to see you contributing something positive for a change. How did you find her?"

"Pretty easy, actually. Gregson got me a copy of the unedited videotape. Seems they had the lady on camera when she said it but she blew off signing the release. Nice looking babe, by the way. We got lucky 'cause the cameraman followed her right to the cab she left in. I got the cab's number, made a few calls, and found out it dropped her off at home."

"Marvelous," Eli said. He'd put this woman on the back burner, but now he was remembering what she'd said and his anger flared anew. "Who is she?"

Strauss pulled out a note pad. "Name's Gia DiLauro. Works as some sort of artist. But things don't add up with her. I ran a check on her state income tax and she doesn't make the kind of money that would put her anywhere near the ultra-tony neighborhood she lives in."

"An artist, hmmm?" Eli said. "Well, we'll find out where she sells her paintings or who she works for and see that her showings and sources of income dry up. That'll be for starters. Then—"

"She's got a kid," Strauss said.

Eli caught his breath. A child. Oh, this was too good to be true.

"Go on."

"It's another of the weird things about her. She's got a daughter she claims as a dependent but the kid's got a different last name: Westphalen. Victoria Westphalen."

"And her age?"

Please say under ten, Eli prayed. Please.

"Eight."

Silence in the room as the three men exchanged glances.

"Eight," Adrian breathed. "That's . . . perfect."

More than perfect, Eli thought. If they could get hold of the child in time, she could become the lamb for the next Ceremony. And her sacrifice would offer the lagniappe of crushing her bitter-tongued mother.

How wonderful. The mere possibility made his blood tingle.

"Find out everything you can about this child, Freddy. Everything. Immediately. We don't have much time."

6

Jack reached the office of Kristadoulou Realtors a little ahead of schedule. Since it was on Steinway Street he'd decided to get a two-fer out of the trip by stopping by his Queens mail drop on the way. He rented boxes in Hoboken and Manhattan as well, but every two weeks they forwarded all his mail to the Astoria drop. With a pair of manila envelopes under his arm, he figured he'd kill the ten minutes to appointment time by checking out the hood.

Kristadoulou Realtors sat in an old stone building in the heart of one of Steinway's most commercial blocks; its windows were filled with photos of properties they had listed. The rest of the street was lined with triple deckers— stores at ground level, two floors of apartments above.

He walked south on the west side, passing little old Greek ladies with shopping bags, lots of guys with black mustaches yammering into cell phones, couples laughing and talking, hardly anyone speaking English.

The businesses were like a poster for ethnic diversity: a storefront touting "Immigration Medical Exams" next to the Kabab Café next to the Nile Deli, then an oriental rug merchant, and something called Islamic Fashion, Inc. A little farther on was the Egyptian Café, the Arab Community

Center, and the Fatima Pediatric Center; farther still was a Colombian bakery and a Chinese Qi Gong center specializing in back and foot rubs.

He crossed the street and turned back north, passing Sissy McGinty's Irish pub, the Rock and Roll Bagel restaurant, an Argentinean steak house, an Egyptian coffee shop right next door to an Italian espresso place. He stopped before the window of an Islamic religious shop offering prayer rugs, incense, and a special clock: "5-Full Azan Talking Alarm Clock—Jumbo Display With 105-Year Calendar." Jack had no idea what any of that meant.

He spotted Lyle getting out of a cab. He looked every inch the African today—blue-and-white batik kaftan, white cotton pants, sandals, and a brightly colored knitted tam. He blended in with the rest of the exotically dressed locals. Jack was the stick-out in his Levis and golf shirt.

"You made it," Lyle said when he spotted Jack. "I wasn't sure if you got my message."

"I got it." He gestured at the surrounding stores. "Do all these folks get along?"

"Pretty much."

"Ought to bring the UN here for a look-see. Find out how they do it."

Lyle only nodded. He didn't look so hot. Even with his eyes hidden behind dark glasses, his face looked strained.

"You okay?"

"Me? Okay? Not even close."

"Uh-oh. What happened?"

Lyle glanced at his watch. "Tell you later. Right now we're due to see Mr. K. But before we go in, I want you to know how I'm going to play this, okay?"

"Sure. This is your show. Shoot."

"I'm going to let *him* think that *I* think the house is haunted."

"Well, it is, isn't it?"

"Yeah, but I don't want him knowing *how* haunted. And no mention of Tara Portman or whatever it's calling itself."

"Tara Portman was a real person," Jack said. "Gia and I looked her up on the Internet last night."

" 'Was'?"

"She was nine when she was abducted in the summer of '88. Never seen again. Her picture matches the girl Gia saw."

"Oh man!" Lyle clapped his hands and grinned. "Oh man, oh man, oh *man*!"

Jack had expected astonishment, or at least a touch of awe or wonder. Not this outright glee.

"Why is this good news?"

"Never mind," Lyle said. "Let's go see the Big K."

Jack wondered what was going on in Lyle's head. He seemed to have developed a personal agenda. That was okay with Jack—he had an agenda of his own. He just hoped they didn't cross each other.

Inside, Konstantin Kristadoulou was expecting them and a secretary led them to a rear office where they met the head man. Jack fully appreciated the 'Big K' remark as Lyle introduced him. They seated themselves in the two rickety chairs on the far side of his desk.

Kristadoulou Realtors looked to be a no-frills operation. Maybe because its owner ate all the frills. At least he looked like he did. Konstantin Kristadoulou dwarfed even Abe in the waistline category. Jack figured he was pushing seventy, but the puffy face and quadruple chins stretched out all the wrinkles, so it was hard to tell. His longish, thinning gray hair was combed straight back to where it flipped up at the collar.

"So," he said, glancing at Jack with his dark, heavy-lidded eyes, then fixing them on Lyle. His voice was lightly accented. "You wish to know about the house you bought, Mr. Kenton. Why is that? No trouble, I hope?"

"We took some damage from the earthquake," Lyle said.

"Serious?"

"Just some minor cracks."

Minor? Jack thought. A cellar floor cracked in half isn't minor.

But he caught a quick glance from Lyle that he read as, Let me handle this.

"The reason I'm here," Lyle went on, "is that we've been hearing strange noises in the house lately. Voices . . . but no one's there."

Kristadoulou nodded. "Lots of people think Menelaus Manor is haunted—not because they've ever witnessed anything, mind you, but because of its history. I hope you remember that I told you all this before you bought it."

Lyle raised his hands. "Absolutely. I'm not here to complain, I'm here to try and understand. I need more in-depth information on the house's history. I mean, if Menelaus Manor 'went wrong' somewhere along the way, I'd like to figure out where. Who knows? Maybe I can fix it."

"'Went wrong,'" Kristadoulou said. "An interesting way of putting it." He leaned back—the only direction his gut would allow—and stared at the ceiling. "Let's see . . . if anything 'went wrong' with the Menelaus house, I'd say it happened during Dmitri's ownership."

"Who's Dmitri?" Jack said.

"Kastor Menelaus's only son. Kastor built the place back in the fifties. That was when Astoria was known as Little Athens, a bit of Hellenic heaven in the heart of New York because of all the Greeks who moved here after the war. I arrived after the house was built but I know something of the family. Dmitri, he was younger than me, so we never socialized, but even if we were the same age, we wouldn't have mixed. A strange one, that Dmitri."

"How strange?" Jack asked. "Strange cults? Strange beliefs?"

Kristadoulou gave him an odd look. "No. I mean he was always keeping to himself. No girlfriends, no boyfriends. If you happened to see him at a restaurant, he was always alone."

Jack had been hoping for some indication of involvement with the Otherness. Or maybe with Sal Roma, or whatever his real name was. He'd also been on the lookout for one of Roma's cutesy anagrams—the last Jack had recognized was "Ms. Aralo"—but Dmitri wasn't one. Not even close.

Lyle said, "Why do you say the house might have gone wrong during Dmitri's ownership?"

"Because of his renovations. Old Kastor died in 1965. Cancer of the pancreas. After Dmitri inherited the place— his mother had died in '61—he came to me for advice. I was working as an agent for another firm then and he wanted me to recommend carpenters and masons to redo his basement. He hired a couple off the list I gave him. I felt somewhat responsible so I stopped in every so often to check on them—make sure they were doing a good job." He shook his head. "Very strange."

Gimme, gimme, gimme, Jack thought. "How so?"

"He was lining the basement with these big granite blocks he'd imported from Romania. He told me they came from what he called 'a place of power,' whatever that means. He said they'd originally been part of an old dilap- idated fortress, but if you ask me, I think they were from a church."

"Why's that?" Lyle said.

"Because some of them were inlaid with crosses."

Jack glanced at Lyle and saw him sitting ramrod straight in his chair.

"Crosses? What kind?"

"Funny you should ask. They weren't regular crosses. They were almost like a capital *T* with the crosspiece brass and the upright nickel."

"Tau," Lyle whispered.

"Exactly!" Kristadoulou said, pointing a knockwurst digit at him. "Like the letter tau. How did you know?"

Lyle's eyes shifted toward Jack. "We've spotted a few around the house. But let me ask you about those blocks with the tau crosses. Do you think they might have come from a Greek Orthodox church?"

Kristadoulou shook his head. "I've traveled a lot, been in many, many Orthodox churches, and I've never seen any crosses like that." Another head shake. "Bad business stealing church stones. It's like asking for trouble. And that's just what Dmitri got."

"You mean his suicide," Jack said, remembering this from when Gia had read to him from Lyle's brochure.

"Yes. He'd just been diagnosed with cancer of the pancreas. He'd seen how his father suffered. I guess he couldn't face that ordeal, so . . ."

"When was that?" Jack asked.

"Nineteen ninety-five, I believe."

Owned the place for thirty years, Jack thought. The span covered the year Tara Portman disappeared. Dmitri had to be involved.

"Dmitri didn't bother to leave a will," Kristadoulou went on, "and that caused problems. With no children or wife, the estate wound up in probate. After years of legal wrangling Menelaus Manor went to one of Dmitri's cousins who wanted nothing to do with it. He called me and told me to sell it as soon as possible."

"And Dr. Singh bought it, right?" Lyle said.

"Only after lots of other potential buyers passed it by. The cellar was the sticking point. All those strange granite blocks I mentioned. And speaking of those blocks, when I inspected the house before putting it on the market, I went down to the cellar and noticed that all the crosses had been removed."

"Any idea why?

"No more idea than why he left a dirt floor."

"Wait," Jack said. "Dirt floor?"

"Yes. Can you imagine? Dmitri went to the expense of importing all those blocks, and then didn't finish the floor."

Maybe because it makes it lots easier to bury things you want no one to see, Jack thought.

"The nephew was unwilling to sink in any money for renovations so we kept lowering the price. Finally a vascular surgeon named Singh bought it for a song."

"A rather short song, as I recall," Lyle said.

Kristadoulou nodded. "He and his wife modernized the interior and refinished the basement with paneling over the granite blocks and a concrete floor. One day he doesn't show up for surgery or his office. Police investigate and find him and his wife in bed with their throats cut."

Jack remembered that too. "Who did it?"

"No one was ever caught. The police didn't even have a suspect. Whoever did it left not a clue."

"No wonder people think it's haunted," Jack said.

Kristadoulou smiled. "It gets worse. The executor of the Singh estate directed me to sell it. I thought, a suicide and a double murder—I'm never going to sell this place now. But lo and behold, this young couple walks in and wants to buy Menelaus Manor."

"In spite of its history?" Jack said. "Or because of it?"

"You must understand," Kristadoulou said, patting his belly. "I didn't delve into the Loms' motivations, because I didn't exactly dwell on the house's history. It was not what you'd call a selling point. I remember Herb, he was the husband, saying that he wasn't the superstitious sort, but it was his wife Sara, a pretty thing, who seemed to be pushing the deal. They were planning on adopting a child and wanted a house for the family to live in. So, I sold it to them." He leaned back again and gazed toward the ceiling. "I wish I hadn't."

This was the point where Gia had refused to read him any more of the house's history, calling it "sick."

"Don't tell me," he said. "Someone slit their throats too?"

"Worse," Kristadoulou said with a grimace of distaste. "They'd been moved in only a short while when the little boy they'd just adopted was found horribly mutilated in the upstairs bedroom."

Jack closed his eyes. Now he understood Gia's reaction. "Any reason given?"

Kristadoulou shook his head. "None. Herbert was found in a daze in the house and later died in the hospital."

" 'Later died'?" Jack said. "What's that mean?"

"That's what I was told," Kristadoulou replied. "I checked with the hospital—he was taken to Downstate

Medical Center—but no one would tell me how he died. They said I wasn't a relative and had no right to know, but I sensed more than ethics involved there. They were afraid."

"Afraid of what?" Jack said.

Kristadoulou shrugged. "Of a lawsuit, perhaps. But I sensed it went deeper than that. I got the feeling it had to do with *how* he died." He raised his hand in a stop gesture. "Don't waste any more breath on Herb Lom. I've told you all I know."

Lyle said, "What about his wife?"

"Sara was never seen or heard from again. As if she vanished from the face of the earth. Or never existed. No one could find a single relative of hers, and Herb left no will, so the house stood vacant for years before it came back to me like an old debt and I had to sell her again. But this time no one wanted her at any price." He smiled and pointed to Lyle. "Until you came along."

Lyle grinned. "I wanted the place *because* of its history."

"But now you're not so happy, is that right?"

"It's not a matter of happy. I'm just trying to get a handle on what might be going on there."

They made small talk for a few more minutes, then thanked Kristadoulou for his time and left.

"Dmitri is a player in this," Jack said as soon as they hit the bright hot sidewalk. "Got to be."

"But he's dead."

"Yeah," Jack said, squinting in the sunlight. He pulled out his shades. "Too bad. Well, what's you're next step?"

"I think I'm going to *de*renovate that basement."

"You mean tear down the paneling to see what's behind?"

Lyle nodded. "And tear up that concrete slab to see what's under it."

"*Who's* under it, you mean."

"Right. Who."

"You'll let me know what you find?"

"Maybe."

"Maybe?"

"Aren't you the guy who said he's the one who kicked this whole thing off?"

"Well . . ."

"Well then maybe you could lend a hand and find out firsthand. You up for that?"

Besides making life miserable for Eli Bellitto and his buddy Adrian Minkin, Jack had no pressing demands on his time for the next few days, but he was curious about something.

"Let's just say we find a child's skeleton under the slab. What then?"

"I call the cops, they bring in their forensics team, and maybe they catch the guy who did it. And then maybe the spook goes back to where it came from."

"And maybe along the way the world hears about Ifasen and his dealings with the ghost of Tara Portman?"

Lyle nodded. "That's a distinct possibility."

Jack had the picture now. "I guess I can give you a day or two of hard labor, but on one condition: If and when you go public, my name is never mentioned."

"You mean Ifasen will have to face the spotlight alone?" Lyle's lips twisted into a wry smile. "It won't be easy, but he'll handle it." The smile faded. "Be a cakewalk compared to some other things."

"Like what?" Jack said, remembering how troubled Lyle had looked before they'd met with Kristadoulou. "What happened at the house?"

"Tell you later." He glanced around at the passersby. "Probably not a good idea for Ifasen to discuss it in public."

"Okay. I guess I can wait. I'll head home and change and see you in the cellar. Give me an hour."

"Great." Lyle straightened as if trying to shrug off a burden. "I'll pick up some picks and ripping bars."

"I'll pick up some beer."

Lyle smiled. "Welcome to the demolition business."

7

"All right, Charles," Reverend Sparks said as he dropped into the chair behind his battered desk.

The springs in the old chair gave out an agonized squeal under his weight. The desk seemed too small for him. In fact the cluttered little office, with its sagging shelves loaded with books and magazines and scribbled drafts of sermons, its walls studded with yellow sticky notes, seemed too small for him as well.

He pointed to the rickety chair on Charlie's side of the desk. "Sit. And tell me what you needed to see me about."

Charlie sat and folded his sweat-slick hands in front of him. "Need advice, Rev."

Did he ever. He and Lyle had had four sittings scheduled for the morning. Lyle started acting throwed off after the first one, then getting further and further off the hinges with the next two, finally eighty-sixin' the fourth and all the others they'd booked for the rest of the afternoon and night. He wouldn't say why, but looked spooked.

Spooked . . . yeah, you got that right. House spooked. Charlie was spooked too.

He'd tried to pry Lyle about what was going down but Lyle clammed, lips tight, eyes somewhere else. No talking to him. Not mad. Scared. Lyle never got scared. Seeing big bro like that had shook Charlie, right down to his toenails.

He'd tried reading scriptures but that hadn't cut it. He needed to talk. So he come to the rev.

"Is it about your brother?"

"Not exactly."

"Then what?"

"I ain't 'xactly sure how to put it. . . ."

The rev let out a sigh. Charlie sensed his impatience.

"A'ight," he said. "It's like this. We allowed to believe in ghosts?"

"Allowed?"

"I mean, are there any teachings 'bout them?"

The rev leaned back and stared at him through his thick rimless glasses. "Why do you ask?"

"Here come the hard part." Charlie took a breath. "Our house is haunted."

The rev continued his stare. "What makes you think that?"

Charlie gave him a quick walkthrough of the spookfest going down at the place.

"So what I'm axing," he said as he tied it up, "is what I do about it?"

"You leave," the rev said, leaning forward and resting his forearms on the desk. "Immediately. Your brother was reason enough to leave before, now you must flee. Do not walk, *run* from that house."

Charlie didn't feature no cut-and-run action, but he was glad the rev wasn't looking at him like he was off the hinges.

"So . . . you believe me."

"Of course I believe you. And after what you've told me about your brother, it's obviously his fault. He has called up this demon."

"Not a demon, Rev. A ghost. She say her name Tara Portman and. . . ."

The rev was slowly shaking his massive head. "There are no such things as ghosts, Charles. Only demons pretending to be ghosts."

"But—"

"The dead do not come back to visit the living. Think about it: The faithful are with Jesus and when you are in the presence of the Lord you want for nothing. You do not miss the living you left behind, no matter how much you loved them in life, because you are basking in the love of

God, you are in the blinding Holy Presence of our Lord
Jesus Christ. Remember Corinthians: 'Eye hath not seen,
nor ear heard, neither have entered into the heart of man,
the things which God hath prepared for them that love
Him.' To abandon that Presence would be ... why, it
would be completely unthinkable."

Charlie nodded. He could get down with that. "A'ight,
then. What about someone who ain't among the faithful?"

"They burn in hellfire, Charles. Oh, the damned would
dearly love to return, every single one of them. They'd give
anything to come back, even for a second, a fraction of a
second, but no matter how much they want to, they cannot.
They aren't allowed. They're in hell for all eternity, and
they must spend every second of forever in torment. 'The
smoke of their torment ascendeth up forever and ever, and
they have no rest day nor night.' "

"Then what—?"

"A demon, Charles." The rev nodded gravely. "You see
the simple logic of it, don't you. An angel wouldn't bear
false witness to the living by pretending to be a dead person
who's returned. Only a demon would engage in such a
fiendish endeavor."

"But why?"

"To seduce the faithful away from the Lord and lead
them onto the path toward eternal damnation. Your brother
attracted the demon, but it is you it is after, Charles." He
stabbed his finger across the table. "You! It lusts after your
fragile soul so that it can serve it to its evil master on a
silver platter!"

The target of supernatural evil ... not me, Charlie
thought, terror rising like a flood tide. Please, Lord, not me.

Charlie jumped as the rev slammed his palm onto his
desktop. "Now will you leave your evil brother?"

"He's—" Charlie cut himself off.

The rev's eyes narrowed. "He's what? Are you going to
tell me again he's not evil—after he's called up a demon?"

He'd been about to say just that. And Lyle didn't call up
no demon. Least not on purpose. He wasn't evil, just off

track. He hadn't seen the light yet. But Charlie knew the
rev wouldn't accept that.

"He's in danger too, Rev. His soul, I mean. Shouldn't
we try to save his soul too?"

"From what you've told me I fear you brother's soul is
lost forever."

"I thought you always said no soul was lost forever long
he still had a chance of accepting Jesus Christ as his personal savior."

The rev's gaze flickered. "Well, that's true, but do you
really believe your brother will do that? Ever?"

Lyle? Not very likely, but. . . .

"Miracles happen, Rev."

He nodded. "Yes, they do. But miracles are the Lord's
province. Leave the miracle of your brother's salvation to
Him and see to your own by leaving that house."

"Yes, Rev."

"Today. Do I have your word on that?"

"Yes, Rev."

But not without Lyle. Charlie wasn't going to leave his
brother in the clutches of no krunk demon.

The rev hoisted himself out of his chair. "Then you better
get to it."

Charlie rose too. "I will." He hesitated. "Um, is Sharleen
round about?"

The rev fixed him with a stern gaze. "I've seen the way
you've been looking at my daughter. And I've seen the way
she's been looking back at you. But I want you to steer
clear of her until you've removed yourself from this evil.
Right now you're at a dangerous crossroads. I want to see
which path you choose before you involve yourself with
Sharleen. Do I make myself clear?"

"Yes." Stung, Charlie backed away. "Very."

Reverend Sparks thought he was a danger to his daughter. He'd have to prove himself worthy. Okay. He'd do that.
Today.

8

"I still don't believe you did it," Jack said.

Gia sipped her green tea and tried to read his expression: Shock? Dismay? Anger? Fear? Maybe a mixture of all.

"I'm fine, Jack. Besides, it wasn't as if I had much choice."

"Of course you had a choice." He'd settled down from his original outburst and now wandered her kitchen, circling the breakfast table with his hands jammed into his jeans pockets. A barely touched beer sat on the table, condensation pooling around its base. "You could have said to yourself, 'Going alone to visit the possibly psycho father of a murdered girl and not telling anyone where I'll be is a dumb idea. Maybe I'll just skip it.'"

"I had to know, Jack. It was going to drive me crazy if I didn't find out about her."

"You could have told me what you were doing."

"You would have thrown a hissy fit, just like you're doing now."

"I don't throw hissy fits. I would have tried to talk you out of it, and if you still insisted I could have gone along as backup."

"Who are you kidding? You've become so superprotective since I told you I was pregnant, you'd have probably locked me in a closet and gone yourself."

"Maybe I'm suddenly superprotective because you're suddenly Repairwoman Jane."

This was getting nowhere. Another sip of her tea—too sweet. She'd overdone the honey.

"Do you want to know what I found out?" she said.

"Yes, I do." He grabbed his beer and quaffed a few inches. "I just wish you hadn't found out the way you did." He sat on the end of the table. "Tell me. Please."

Gia told him about Joe Portman, about Tara's mother and brother and what had befallen them since her abduction. She told him about the day of her disappearance, how she'd been wearing the exact same clothes, how she'd left the stable area to go down the block for a pretzel and was never seen again.

"She did that every Thursday?" Jack said.

Gia nodded. "Why? Is that important?"

"Could be. Means she had an established pattern of behavior. That says to me there's a good chance it wasn't a random snatch. Somebody had been watching her. She'd been marked."

Gia felt a chill. An innocent child, walking the same route every Thursday afternoon, just going for a snack, never realizing she was being stalked. How many pretzel runs had her abductor watched before deciding to pounce?

She rubbed her arms to smooth the gooseflesh. "That's so creepy."

"Because you're dealing with creeps. Just like . . ." His voice drifted off as he frowned.

"What?"

"Just like Bellitto and his buddy. The kid they snatched the other night—"

"Duc."

"Right. He had a pattern too, at least according to his mother. Down the block for ice cream every night around the same time. The kid was already in the store when Bellitto and Minkin arrived and parked outside. They knew he was coming out. They were waiting for him."

"Just like someone was waiting for Tara between the stables and the pretzel cart. A pattern of behavior?"

Jack stared at her. "You mean a pattern of behavior in the abductors of looking for victims with a pattern of behavior?"

"You don't think this Bellitto could be responsible for Tara too, do you?"

"Be a hell of a coincidence if he was."

"But—"

"Yeah. I know." Jack's expression was grim. "No more coincidences."

"I still don't see how such a thing could be."

"Neither do I. Let's face it, just because some crazy old lady said it doesn't mean it's true." He could still hear the old woman's Russian-accented voice as he leaned over Kate's grave. *Is not coincidence. No more coincidences for you.* He shook his head, willing the memory away. "What else did you learn?"

Gia snapped her fingers. "Oh, I learned that the sixties tune was really an eighties tune. Tiffany—"

"Right! Tiffany covered 'I Think We're Alone Now'! How could I have missed that? Especially after she was in *Playboy.*"

"She was? When?"

"Don't remember. Heard it on the radio or something."

"Well, according to her father Tara sang the song all the time. But you know what really creeped me out? She was a Roger Rabbit fan."

Jack didn't exactly go white, but his tan abruptly became three shades paler.

"Jeez."

"What's wrong?"

He told her about the locked display cabinet in Eli Bellitto's shop, how it was filled with kids' knickknacks that he wouldn't part with at any price, and how one of them was a Roger Rabbit key ring.

Gia's skin crawled. "Do you have it with you?"

"No. It's back home. Let's not go jumping to too many conclusions here. Probably sold a million or two Roger Rabbit key rings back in the eighties."

"You could take it to the police and—"

He blinked. "The who?"

"Sorry." What was she thinking? This was Jack. Jack and police didn't mix.

He said, "I wish I had a way to connect Tara and the key ring . . . so I could know for sure. Right now I can only suspect Bellitto."

"Why not take it to the house. See if she reacts."

Jack stared at her. "What a great idea! Why didn't I think of that?"

"Because you're merely Repairman Jack. Only Repairwoman Jane could come up with that."

"Touché," he said with a smile and toasted her with his beer. "You think she'll respond?"

"Only one way to find out. When do we bring it over?"

" 'We'?" He rose, shaking his head. " 'We' are not going back to that house. Oh, no. One half of 'we' stays here while this half goes alone and returns with a vivid eyewitness account of whatever happens."

Gia had expected this. "Not fair. It was my idea."

"We've been over this already, Gi. We don't know this thing's agenda."

"That 'thing' is a little girl, Jack."

"A *dead* little girl."

"But she appeared to me. Not you, not Lyle, not Charlie. Me. That's got to mean something."

"Exactly. But we don't know what. And that's why you shouldn't get within miles of that place. It's got an unhealthy pedigree, even stranger and weirder than what's in Lyle's Menelaus Manor brochure."

Worse than the part about the mutilated child? Gia didn't think that was possible.

"What? That real estate agent told you something, didn't he."

"He told me lots of things, and I'll tell you later, but right now we have to agree that you're staying away from that place."

"But I'm the one she contacted."

"Right. She sent a message and you received it. Now we're going to dig up what might be her grave. If we find her, and she can be linked to Bellitto, you'll have done plenty. You've pointed the way."

"But what if there aren't any clues?"

"Well, then at least she gets a proper burial. And maybe that's what her father will need to kick start his life back into motion."

Gia wasn't concerned with Joe Portman right now. It was Tara who consumed her. Her need was like a noose around Gia's neck, drawing her toward Menelaus Manor. If she didn't yield to it she felt sure it would strangle her.

"She wrote 'Mother,' Jack. I don't think she meant her own mother—Dorothy Portman is brain dead. I think she meant me. It may be twenty-some years since Tara was born, but she's still a child. She's still nine years old and she's frightened. She needs a mother. That's a comfort I can provide."

"How do you comfort a ghost?" Jack said. He slipped his arms around her and pulled her close. She caught the lingering scent of his soap, felt the afternoon stipple of whiskers on his cheeks. "I guess if anyone could, you'd be the one. But tell me: If Vicky were here instead of away at camp, would you be so anxious to go back to that house?"

What was he saying? That this need she felt burning through her veins was simply displaced yearning for her own child? She had to admit it wasn't such a far-fetched notion, but she sensed that the longing within her went beyond that.

"Maybe, maybe not, but—"

"One more question: If Vicky were here, would you take her along?"

That caught her off guard. Her reaction was immediate: Of course not. But she didn't want to voice it.

"That's not the point. Vicky's not here, so—"

Jack tightened his hug. "Gia? Would you?"

She hesitated, then, "All right, no."

"Why not?"

"I'm not sure."

"I am. Because it's an unstable situation, and you wouldn't want to expose Vicky to an unpredictable outcome. Right?"

Gia nodded against his shoulder. "Right."

"Then why expose your second child to that same unstable situation?"

She sighed. Trapped by unassailable logic.

"Please, Gia." He backed away to arm's length. "Stay away. Give me a couple of days to help Lyle find her bones. Then maybe the circumstances won't be so unstable or unpredictable and we can reassess the whole situation."

"Oh, all right," she said. She didn't like it but she'd been backed into a corner. "I suppose a couple of days won't matter."

"Great." He let out a whooshing breath. "That's a relief."

"For you maybe. How about me?"

"What do you mean?"

"Well, if that house is potentially dangerous for me, what about for you?"

Jack smiled. "Did you forget? Danger is my business."

"I'm serious, Jack."

"Okay. I'll check in regularly."

"Leave your phone on in case I need to get in touch."

"Will do." He wriggled it out of his pocket and pressed a button. She heard a beep as it activated. He glanced at the clock. "Got to go. Pick a place for dinner—anyplace but Zen Palate—and I'll tell you all about Konstantin Kristadoulou's history of the Menelaus cellar and the findings of our archeological dig down there."

Gia sighed. All secondhand, but she supposed it would have to do.

"And the key ring," she said. That was what she wanted to know most of all. "You've got to tell me what happens when you cross the threshold with that."

"Yeah," Jack said softly. "That could be very interesting. But how do you top an earthquake?"

9

"*What?*" Lyle said. He couldn't believe what he'd just heard. "You're joking, right? You're pulling my chain, is that it?"

Charlie shook his head as he pulled clothes from his dresser and dumped them on his bed. He concentrated on what he was doing, not making eye contact.

"Nope. This is on the fo' real, bro. I'm geese."

First the craziness this morning with the first three sitters, seeing into their lives, their pasts, their futures—what little there was for each of them. Now this. He felt as if his world was coming apart.

"But you *can't* leave. We're a team. The Kenton brothers have always been a team. Who brung ya, Charlie?"

Finally Charlie looked at him. His eyes glistened with tears. "You think I want to? I don't. We still a team, Lyle, but not in this game, yo. And not in this house."

"What do you mean?"

"I mean we bust outta here together and start all over, givin' value for value, like Jack said."

Jack . . . for a moment Lyle wished he'd never heard of him.

"You mean dump the game?"

"Word. And yo, the way you playin' the game lately, y'know, cancelin' sitters up and down, ain't gonna be a game left, know'm sayin'?"

Lyle winced. Charlie had a point. Lyle had canceled the morning's fourth sitting along with the whole afternoon. He couldn't handle any more. He hadn't told Charlie why.

Should he tell him now? No. It would only reinforce his determination to leave.

"But we don't *know* anything else, Charlie. We'll starve!"

"No way. We two smart guys. We get by."

"Get by? Since when is getting by enough? I want to *make* it, Charlie. So do you."

"Not no more. 'What profit it a man if he gains the whole world but loses his immortal soul?' I wanna save my soul, Lyle. And yours too. That's why I want you to come with me."

"And if I don't?"

"Then I got to roll on my own."

"Roll on your own?" Lyle gave in to a blistering surge of anger. "Why don't you *think* on your own?"

"Say what?"

"This isn't you talking. This is that preacher down that brimstone-breathing, tongue-speaking, snake-handling wacko church you found, right?"

"We don't do no snake handlin'."

"You're such a sucker for these guys. It was the same back in Dearborn when that Reverend What-his-name—"

"Rawlins."

"Right. Reverend Rawlins. He's the guy who told you to boycott the Harry Potter movie."

"That's because it promotes witchcraft."

"How would you know? You never saw it. You never read a line of one of the books. And neither did Rawlins. He got the word from someone else who hadn't read or seen them either. But you all fell in line, marching lockstep against Harry Potter with not a scrap of firsthand knowledge."

Charlie lifted his chin. "Don't gotta do a drive-by to know it's wrong."

"Reading a book to make an informed decision is hardly the same as shooting someone. But you're doing the same thing here. It's this preacher at this new church, right? What's his name?"

"Reverend Sparks."

"It's him, right? He's the one who's put you up to this."

"Didn't put me up to nothin'! He told me this ain't no ghost, it's a demon and it's after our souls!"

A demon? Good thing Lyle hadn't mentioned the morning's strangeness. Charlie would probably think he was possessed and try to drag him off to an exorcism.

"Has he been here, Charlie? Has he seen and heard and experienced what we have? No. Has he sifted all the evidence that points to this being the ghost of a girl murdered back in the eighties? No. He hasn't moved his ass from his church down there in Brooklyn but somehow he's got a lock on what's happening in our house, knows it's not Tara Portman but Beelzebub instead. And you fall right in line and go along." Lyle shook his head, dismayed. "You're a bright guy, bro, but you put your brain on standby whenever one of these ministers opens his mouth."

"Don't have to listen to this." Charlie turned away and returned to emptying his dresser.

Lyle sighed. "No, you don't. But what about that pin on your shirt? WWJD. What Would Jesus Do, right? So why don't you ask yourself that? Would Jesus run out on his brother?"

"Jesus didn't have no brother."

Lyle almost said that some experts thought the apostle James was Jesus' brother, but he wasn't going to get into that now.

"You know what I mean. Would he?"

"Who you to talk 'bout Jesus?"

"Come on, Charlie. Answer me. You know he wouldn't. So how about you putting up with me for two more days?"

"Why?" Charlie didn't look up. "Why should I risk even one more minute?"

"Because I'm your brother. Because we're blood and we're the only family we have. How long've we been a team now?"

He shrugged. "Who knows."

"You know. Tell me."

"A'ight." He looked up, his face a mask of resentment. "Fifteen years."

"Right. And how long've we been in this house?"

" 'Bout a year. So what?"

"So, with all that behind us, why can't you give me two more days?"

"What for? Where's it go? We on a dead-end street, Lyle."

"Maybe not. Think for yourself a moment instead of letting the Reverend Sparks do it for you. Help me dig around that cellar."

"No. Uh-uh. That's the demon's crib."

"Says who? Some guy who's never been here?"

"Reverend Sparks knows about these things."

"But he's not infallible. Only god is infallible, right? So Sparky could be wrong. Go with that a moment. What if he's wrong and what we've experienced here isn't a demon but really the ghost of a murdered child? What if we find her remains and give them back to her folks for a proper burial. Won't that be doing god's work?"

Charlie snorted and looked away. "Yeah, right. You doing God's work."

"Take it a step further: What if those remains lead the cops to her killer and bring him to justice? Won't that be a good thing? Won't that be doing god's work too?"

Lyle wanted to ask Charlie why the hell god would let a child be murdered in the first place, but sensed his brother wavering and didn't want to blow it.

"Two days, Charlie. I bet if Jesus had a wayward brother he'd give him a couple of days if he asked for them."

Charlie shook his head as his lips twisted into a reluctant smile. "Dawg, I hear talk 'bout a silver-tongued devil, and now I see I'm related to him. A'ight. Two days and not a minute more. But this gotta be a two-way deal: Nothin' crackin' by Friday night, I'm geese and you with me. Deal?"

Lyle hesitated. Me too? He hadn't figured on that being part of the deal, but then, he couldn't go on as Ifasen without his brother. And if what had happened this morning was the start of a pattern, he wasn't sure if Ifasen had any future at all, at least in this house. So he could see no downside in agreeing to Charlie's terms.

But they *were* going to find Tara Portman, or what was left of her. He could feel it.

He stuck out his hand.

"Deal."

10

"Mr. Bellitto!" Gertrude cried in her booming voice as Eli stepped through the door. "You should be upstairs resting!"

She was so right. Barbed wire raked across his groin as he shuffled toward the Carrera marble sales counter. He should have stayed put, but he'd been feeling better after lunch and a nap, and so he'd given in to the urge to see his store, examine his stock, peruse the sales book. By the time he'd reached the sidewalk he realized his mistake but by then he was beyond the point of no return: Unable to face, even with Adrian's help, the prospect of turning and challenging the narrow Everest between him and his bed, he'd pushed on.

"Nonsense, Gert." He leaned heavily on his cane as he neared the counter. "I'm fine. But do you think you could bring that stool around front?"

"Of course!" Her tightly pinned-back hair gleamed like polished onyx in the light of the overhead fluorescents. She lifted the stool as if it weighed an ounce or two and bustled her hefty frame out from behind the counter and set it before him. "There."

She gripped one arm and Adrian the other as he eased himself back onto the seat—not sitting, merely leaning. He wiped the cold sweat from his face with his shirtsleeve. The new clerk—what was his name? Kevin? Yes, Kevin—came over, feather duster in hand, and gawked at him.

"I'm so sorry about what happened," he said, and sounded as if he meant it.

But did he really?

Eli hires Kevin and a few days later Eli is stabbed. A connection?

Somehow he doubted it, but it never hurt to examine all possibilities.

Eli suffered through a barrage of questions from his two hirelings about the attack; Adrian gave his spiel about loss of memory, leaving Eli with the task of supplying answers. He tossed off curt, oblique responses until he'd had enough.

"I realize this is our slow season," he said, "but surely you two must have something better to do."

Both immediately buzzed off—Kevin to continue dusting the stock, Gert to continue entering new inventory into the computer. Adrian wandered away, browsing the aisles.

"How are receipts, Gert?" Eli said.

"About what you'd expect." She picked up the black ledger and extended it toward him. "As you said, it's the slow season."

August was always sluggish, and sputtered to a dead stop by Labor Day weekend when the city became a ghost town.

Eli opened the old-fashioned ledger—he preferred seeing handwritten words and numbers on paper rather than a computer screen—and scanned through the day's scant sales. His eyes lit on one item.

"The sturgeon? We sold it?"

He'd had that stuffed monstrosity sitting in the window since he'd opened the shop. He'd started to believe it would be there when he closed the place.

"I not only sold it, I got the tag price for it." Gert beamed proudly. "Can you believe it? After all these years I do believe I'm going to miss that ugly old fish."

Eli flipped back to Tuesday, the day the green clerk had been here alone, literally and figuratively minding the store.

He was almost afraid to look. To his surprise he saw a fairly long list of sales. It seemed Kevin had risen to the occasion. Maybe the boy—

Eli froze as his gaze came to rest on a line that read: *Key chain—$10—Jack*.

No! It's not . . . it can't . . . it's . . .

Gripping the counter for support, Eli levered himself off the stool and began a frantic walk-shuffle toward the rear, toward the display cabinet—*his* display cabinet.

"Mr. Bellitto!" Gert cried behind him. "Be careful. Whatever it is you need, I'll get it for you!"

He ignored Gert, ignored the flashes of pain strobing through his pelvis, and kept moving, leaning on his cane as he rode the desperate edge of panic, trying to stay on this side of it by telling himself that the entry was a mistake, an antique watch fob that that dolt Kevin had mistaken for a key ring.

But urging him past that edge was the memory of the oddly dressed red-haired man who had come in Sunday night and offered him ridiculous sums for a silly trinket. He hadn't given much thought to the incident, writing the man off as someone killing time and playing the dickering game: If it's for sale, find out how low it will go for; if it's not, find out what it will take to make the owner part with it.

But now . . . now the incident loomed large and dark in his brain.

He rounded a corner. The cabinet was in sight. The lock . . . he allowed himself a thin smile . . . the lock, the dear, dear brass padlock was still in place and snapped closed, just like always.

And the key ring, that cartoon rabbit key ring was— Gone!

Eli sagged against the cabinet, gripping the oak frame, sweat from his palm smearing the glass as he stared at the empty spot on the second shelf.

No! He had to be dreaming! This had to be a mistake!

He grabbed the padlock and yanked on it, but it held firm.

The air seemed full of shattered glass, every breath shredding his lungs.

How? How could this be? He had the only key. Objects don't move through solid glass. So how—?

"Mr. Bellitto!" Gert's voice behind him.

"Eli!" Adrian. "What's wrong?"

And then they had him surrounded, Gert, Adrian, and the silent Kevin. Yes . . . Kevin, the weasely, sniveling little shit.

Eli glared at him. "You sold something out of this cabinet, didn't you?"

"What?" Kevin paled and shook his head. "No, I—"

"You did! A key ring with a rabbit! Admit it!"

"Oh, that. Yes. But it couldn't have come from here. I don't have the key."

"It did!" Eli shouted. "You know damn well it came from here! Tell me how you got it out!"

"I didn't!" He looked ready to cry. "The man brought it up to the counter. When I saw that it didn't have a price tag—"

"There!" He raised his cane and shook it in Kevin's face. He wanted to beat his head to a spongy pulp. "Right there that should have told you something! How do you sell something without a price tag? Tell me!"

"I-I-I called you at the hospital about it."

"That's a lie!" He raised the cane higher. He'd do it. He'd kill him, right here and now.

"It's true!" Kevin had tears in his eyes now. "I tried to ask you about it but you said to figure it out for myself and hung up on me."

Eli lowered the cane. Now he remembered.

"That was why you called?"

"Yes!"

Eli cursed himself for not listening.

"What did this man look like? Reddish hair, long in the back?"

Kevin shook his head. "No. He had brown hair. Brown eyes, I think. Very average looking. But he called you by your first name and said you were friends. He even left his name."

Yes, Eli thought sourly. *Jack.* Useless. He knew no one named Jack.

Whoever it was must have picked the lock on the cabinet. But then . . . why pay for it? Why not just walk out with it in his pocket?

Unless he wanted to make sure I knew.

He's taunting me.

Just as his attacker had taunted him before stabbing him.

One man tries to buy the key ring Sunday night, another man attacks me and frees the lamb Monday night, a third man virtually steals the key ring the following morning.

Could they all be the same man?

Eli felt a sheet of ice begin to form along the back of his neck. Just as he stalked the lambs, was someone stalking him?

"Get me upstairs," he said to Adrian. "Immediately."

He had to get to his phone. He had a number he needed to call.

11

Jack approached the Menelaus house warily, the Roger Rabbit key chain tight in his fist. He stepped past the dead bushes onto the front porch and stopped, waiting for something to happen.

After half a minute or so of nothing happening except his feeling a little foolish, he rang the doorbell. When no one answered, he rang it again. Through the screen he heard the faint clank and clatter of banging wood and steel on stone. Sounded like Lyle and Charlie had started without him.

He pulled open the screen door and hesitated, remembering the first time he'd crossed this threshold—the unearthly scream, the earthly tremor. What would happen this time, now that he was holding something that might have belonged to whatever had invaded this house?

Better play it safe, he thought.

He tossed the key chain into the waiting room and stepped back.

No scream, no tremor. Nothing.

Jack stood and watched Roger lie spread-eagle on the floor, grinning and staring at the ceiling.

A little more waiting, accompanied by a lot more nothing.

Disappointment veered toward anger as Jack stepped through the door and snatched the key chain from the floor. He suppressed the urge to turn and drop kick it onto the front lawn. He'd been so damn *sure*.

Ah, well. It was a good try. And he had to admit he was somewhat relieved not to have to face proof that Bellitto was connected to Tara Portman. He'd come to fear coincidences.

He stuffed Roger into a pocket and followed the work noises into the kitchen and down the cellar stairs. Along the way he heard another sound. Music. Jazz. Miles. Something from *Bitches Brew*.

Jack reached the bottom of the steps and stopped to watch the brothers Kenton at work. They'd ditched their shirts and looked surprisingly muscular for a couple of guys in the spook trade. Their black skins glistened from the effort as they pried at the sheets of paneling and hacked at the studs behind them. A ten- or twelve-foot span had been stripped away, exposing dull gray rows of granite block. Neither had any idea he'd arrived.

"Started without me, I see," Jack said.

Lyle jumped and turned, raising his pry bar. He huffed out a breath and lowered it when he recognized Jack.

"Don't do that!" he said. "Not in this house."

"Yo, Jack," Charlie said, waving. " 'S'up?"

"Lots. Gia paid a visit to Tara Portman's father."

"By herself?" Lyle asked.

"Without telling me."

"That girl got game," Charlie said. "She learn anything?"

Jack gave them a brief rundown of what Joe Portman had told Gia.

"So," Lyle said slowly, "the riding clothes she was wearing when Gia saw her match the clothes she was wearing when she was snatched."

"Don't be fooled," Charlie said. "It's not Tara Portman."

Lyle rolled his eyes. "Not this again."

"You won't listen, maybe Jack will. You had your doubts too, right, Jack?"

"Yeah, but . . ." What was he stepping into here?

"I spoke to my minister and he says there are no ghosts, only demons pretending to be ghosts to lure the faithful away from God."

"No worry in my case," Lyle said. "I'm not among the faithful."

"That's because you don't believe in anything," Charlie said with some heat. "Only thing you believe in is your disbelief. Disbelief *is* your religion."

"Maybe it is. I can't help it. I was born with a skeptical mind." He turned to his brother. "Now I ask you, is that fair? If God gives me a skeptical nature and you an accepting one, then you're going to be a believer and I'm not. If belief is a ticket to eternal happiness, I'm definitely handicapped. God gives me a mind capable of asking questions and what?—I'm damned if I use it?"

Charlie's dark eyes were sad. "You just gotta give your heart to Jesus, bro. 'Whosoever believeth in him shall not perish but have everlasting life.' "

"But I can't. That's my point. I'm the type who needs to *know*. I didn't ask to be this way, but that's how it is. I am simply not capable of adjusting my whole existence to accommodate something that must be accepted on faith, on the word of people I've never met, people who've been dead for thousands of years. I can't live like that. It's not me." He shrugged. "Hell, I'm still not sure I believe in this ghost."

"Wait a sec," Jack said. "What's this about not believing in your ghost? Why are you doing this demolition work then?"

He shrugged. "I'm caught between. Certain aspects of this situation don't jibe."

"Like what?"

"Well, like that song, for instance. I heard what sounded like a little girl singing. But how can a ghost sing? Or talk, for that matter?"

"If it can smash mirrors and write in dust, why shouldn't it be able to sing and talk?"

"It's got no vocal cords, and no lungs to push air past them if it did. So how does it make noise?"

Jack thought he knew the answer. "Last I heard, noise is nothing more than vibrating air. If this thing can smash a mirror, I'd think it should be able to vibrate air."

Lyle nodded, grinning. He turned to Charlie. "See? That's what I need. An explanation I can sink my teeth into. Not simply saying 'It's God's will.' That won't cut it."

"It will, bro," Charlie said. "When that final trumpet blows, it will."

"So you believe."

"I know, Lyle."

"That's just it: You *don't* know. And neither do I. Neither of us will ever know until we die."

This was getting a little heavy. Jack walked over to the exposed granite blocks and ran a hand over the stone. Cold. And clammy. He pulled his hand away. For a moment there it felt as if the surface had shifted under his touch. He looked at his hand, then at the stone. Nothing had changed. He tried it again and felt that same strange, squirming sensation.

"Looking for something?" Lyle asked.

"Just checking out these blocks."

As he moved to another stone, he glanced back and noticed Lyle staring at him. More than staring—squinting at him, as if trying to bring him into focus.

"Something wrong?"

Lyle blinked. "No. Nothing."

Jack turned back to the stones. He found one with a cross-shaped pocket and noticed scratch marks in the granite around the depression.

"Didn't the Greek say some of the stones had inlaid crosses?"

"Right," Lyle said, moving closer. "Brass and nickel."

Jack ran a finger over the gouges. "Looks like Dmitri was none too gentle in digging them out."

"Yeah, I noticed those before. I wonder what he did with them?"

"Maybe he used them as grave markers."

"Maybe he wanted to make the place more hospitable to demons," Charlie said. "They can't bear the presence of a cross."

In an effort to head off another argument that wasn't going to settle anything, Jack grabbed a pry bar and held it up.

"What say we take down the rest of the paneling?"

"Why bother?" Charlie said. "Probably just more of the same."

Jack jabbed the straight end of the bar through a section of paneling and felt the tip strike the stone beyond. He reversed the bar, shoved the curved end into the opening, and ripped away a chunk of the laminated wood. Despite the nagging tug of discomfort in his flank, it felt good. Sometimes he liked to break things. Liked it a lot.

"Maybe not. We look hard enough, we might find that some of these blocks aren't mortared like the others. That they slide out and there's some sort of hidey hole behind them. Who knows what we'll find there? Maybe what's left of Tara Portman."

Charlie said, "It's not Tara Portman, I tell you, it's a—"

"Wait." Lyle held up a hand. "Something's happening."

Jack looked around. He hadn't heard anything.

"What?"

"Don't you feel it?"

Jack glanced at Charlie who looked just as confused.

"Feel what?"

Lyle turned in a slow circle. "Something's coming."

Then Jack felt it too. A chill, a sense of *gathering*, as if all the warmth in the room were being sucked into its center to drain away through an invisible black hole there, leaving a steadily growing knot of cold in its place.

Cold stabbed Jack high on his right thigh, so cold it burned. He clutched at the spot and felt a frozen lump in the pocket. The key ring! He clenched his teeth as he dropped to his knees—God, it hurt—and clawed at the pocket, reaching in, trying to grab the key ring but the skin of his fingers stuck to it like a wet tongue to a frozen wrought iron fence. He peeled his fingers away, losing some skin, and yanked at the fabric, pulling it out, inverting the pocket. Finally the Roger Rabbit figure appeared and tumbled toward the floor.

But it never landed. Instead it dipped and then rose and darted toward the center of the cellar. There it hovered in the air. Jack saw a rime of frost form along the figure's limbs, then the head, finally engulfing the trunk.

A high keening wail began to echo the air, growing in pitch and volume as Jack pushed himself back up to his feet. The frost thickened on the Roger Rabbit figure, and Jack thought he heard the plastic creak and crinkle as it became brittle from the intense cold.

Suddenly the wail became a screech of rage as Roger's head snapped off and hurtled across the cellar. It struck one of the granite blocks and shattered into powder that scattered and swirled like drifting snow. Then an arm snapped off and flashed in the opposite direction, just missing Charlie's head. Jack ducked as an arm narrowly missed him.

More pieces flew as the frenzied screech rose in pitch and volume. And then there were no more pieces and yet still the enraged howl rose until Jack had to cover his ears. The sound became a physical thing, battering him until . . .

It stopped.

As suddenly as the sound had begun, silence returned. The sense of *presence* dissipated as well until Jack felt that the cellar was again occupied by just the three of them.

He shook his head to relieve the ringing in his ears. It didn't work.

Lyle and Charlie looked shaken, but Jack felt oddly calm. Deadly calm.

"What the *hell* was that all about?" Lyle said.

"Yeah," Charlie said. "What'd you have in your pocket? Looked like that cartoon rabbit . . ."

"Roger Rabbit."

"Yeah."

Lyle snorted a laugh and shook his head. "Roger Rabbit. Just the sort of thing to drive the average demon into a frenzy."

Charlie took a step toward his brother. "Warning you, Lyle—"

Jack jumped in. "Tara Portman's father told Gia that Tara was a Roger Rabbit fan. I was wondering if that key ring might be hers."

"Judging from what just happened," Lyle said, bending and rubbing his finger through the powdery remains of one of Roger's legs, "I think she answered you with a very big *yes.*"

"That she did," Jack said, nodding. "And she also identified her killer."

But his satisfaction at solving the mystery was marred by the unanswered question of how and why he'd come to be involved.

12

Gia sat in a pew three-quarters back from the altar under
the vaulted ceiling and waited for peace.

She'd taken a slow walk from Sutton Square down to St.
Patrick's Cathedral. She wasn't sure why she'd come,
hadn't consciously headed this way. She'd simply gone for
a walk as a break from painting and found herself on Fifth
Avenue. She ambled past St. Pat's and then doubled back
to visit, hoping to find some of the serenity and inner peace
religion was supposed to bring. So far it remained elusive.

The sense of isolation was welcome, though. Here in this
huge, stone-wrapped space she felt cut off from the bustling
reality just beyond the tall oak doors and insulated from
the need that called to her from that house in Astoria.

She sat alone and watched the gaggles of tourists wandering in and out, the Catholics blessing themselves with
holy water and lighting candles, the rest standing around
and gawking at the gothic arches, the stations of the cross
spaced along the side walls, the larger-than-life statues, the
giant crucifix, the gilded altar.

The images drew Gia back to her years in Our Lady of
Hope grammar school in Ottumwa. Not a particularly Catholic town, but then Iowa wasn't a particularly Catholic
state. There'd been enough Catholic kids to fill the local
church school though, and keep the nuns of the convent
busy as teachers. Of all that black-robed crew, she best
remembered Sister Mary Barbara—known to all the kids
as Sister Mary Barbed-wire. Not because she'd liked the
nun; quite the opposite: she'd scared the hell out of Gia.

Sister Mary Barbed-wire had been the Catholic equiva-
lent of a Baptist hellfire preacher, always harping on the

awful punishments awaiting sinners, all the horrors the God of Love would inflict upon those who disappointed Him. Everlasting suffering for missing mass on Sunday, or failing to make your Easter duty. Little Gia bought the whole package, living in terror of dying with a mortal sin on her soul.

Luckily Our Lady of Hope hadn't had a high school; that allowed Gia to escape to the secular den of iniquity known as the public school system. But she'd still remained a practicing Catholic, attending CCD classes and CYO dances.

Sometime during the eighties, however, she drifted away and never returned. Not that she stopped believing in God. She couldn't buy into atheism, or even agnosticism. God existed, she was sure. She was also pretty sure He didn't care much about what went on here. Maybe He watched, but He certainly didn't act.

To her child's eyes the Old Testament God had appeared stern and imposing; now He seemed like a cranky, petulant adolescent with poor impulse control, creating cataclysms, sending plagues, striking down an entire nation's first-born males. She found the New Testament God much more appealing, but somewhere along the way the whole redemption and damnation thing had stopped making sense to her. You didn't ask to be born but once you were you had to toe the belief line or spend eternity suffering in hell. Easy to believe back in the Old Testament days when He burned bushes, parted seas, and sent commandments on stone tablets. But these days God had become remote, no longer weighing in on human affairs, yet still demanding faith. It didn't seem fair.

Of course, if You're God, You don't have to be fair. You hold all the marbles. What You say goes.

Still . . .

Gia had tried to come back to the church after Vicky was born. A child should have some moral foundation to build on, and the church seemed a tried and true place to start. In the back of her mind too had been the idea that if Gia returned to the fold, God would protect Vicky.

But Gia couldn't make it work. And it was terrifyingly obvious that God did not protect children. They died from brain tumors and leukemias and other cancers, from being run over, shot, electrocuted, dropped from buildings, incinerated in house fires, and in other uncountable, unimaginable ways. Clearly innocence was not enough to earn God's protection.

So where was God?

Did the Born Agains have it right? Jesus was their personal savior who watched their every move and answered their prayers? They prayed to Jesus that their old jalopy would start on a cold morning and if it did they praised Him and gave Him thanks for the rest of the day. Gia couldn't get comfortable with a view of God that turned the Creator of the Universe into some sort of cosmic errand boy for His True Believers. Children were starving, Tara Portmans were being abducted and murdered, political prisoners were being tortured, wives were being abused, but God ignored their pleas for relief in order to answer the True Believers' prayers for good weather on the day of the church picnic. Did that make sense?

Yet when she considered the Born Agains she knew— only a few, but good people who seemed to practice what they preached—and saw their serenity, their inner peace, she envied them. They could say, "Let go, let God," with a true, unshakable confidence that God would take care of them and everything would work out in the end. Gia wanted that tranquillity for herself, craved it, but the ability—perhaps the hubris—to believe she mattered to the Creator of the Universe and could have His ear remained beyond her.

At the other extreme was the God who ignited the Big Bang, then turned His back and walked away, never to be seen again.

Gia sensed the truth lay somewhere between. But where?

And where did Tara Portman fit in all this? Had she come back on her own, or had she been sent back? And why? Why did Gia feel this connection to her?

Gia sighed and rose. Whatever the reasons, she wasn't going to find them here.

She stepped out into the bright afternoon sunshine and headed home. When she reached Sutton Square she ran into Rosa, the Silverman's maid. Their townhouse was two doors down from Gia.

"Did that policeman find you?" Rosa said. She had a broad face and a thick body, and was dressed in her after-work street clothes.

Gia's heart froze. "What policeman?"

"The one who knock on your door little while 'go."

Oh, God! Vicky! Something's happened!

She fumbled in her bag for her keys. "What did he say? What did he want?"

"He ask if you home. He ask if you leave you little girl home alone when you go out."

"What?" She found the keys, singled out the one for the front door. "Did he say why he wanted to know?"

"No. I tol' him no, never. I say little miss away at camp. He ask what camp, I say I don' know."

Gia's knees weakened with relief. For a moment there she'd thought the camp had sent a cop to deliver terrible news about Vicky. But if he hadn't even known she was away . . .

Wait a minute. What was he doing here then? Why was a cop asking about Vicky?

"Rosa, are you sure he was a cop?"

"Oh sure. He have cop car and . . ." She moved her hands up and down the front of her body. "You know . . ."

"Uniform?"

"Uh-huh! Tha's it. All blue. He was cop, yes."

"Did you happen to see his badge number?"

The maid shook her head. "No. I no think to look." She narrowed her eyes. "Now that I think, I don' remember seeing no badge."

"Did he mention me or Vicky by name?"

"No . . . I don' thin' so."

"Thank you, Rosa." Gia missed her first try on inserting

the key, made it on the second. "I'm going to look into this."

Once inside the first thing Gia did was call the camp. No, they hadn't called the NYPD. Vicky and everyone else at the camp were fine.

Next call, her local precinct, the Seventeenth. No, they hadn't had any calls to send someone over to Sutton Square. He might have come from another precinct, but no one could say why.

Gia hung up, relieved that Vicky was safe, but unsettled by anyone, cop or not, asking about her daughter.

Had he been an impostor? No, Rosa had said he'd arrived in a cop car.

Gia thought of Tara Portman. What if Tara had been picked up by a police car? A cop saying her mother had been hurt and he'd take her to her. Vicky would fall for that. Any kid would.

Whoever the cop was, he hadn't learned anything other than the fact that Vicky was away at camp. And he didn't know which camp because Rosa couldn't tell him.

She wanted to call Jack, but what could he do? He was the last person on earth to have an inside line into what the NYPD might be up to.

All she could do was pray that—

Gia frowned. Pray . . . that was what you did when trouble came knocking. Even if you'd lost your faith, old habits died hard.

She'd pray that it was all a mix-up and the cop had the wrong address.

That would do until Jack got home.

13

"Let me see if I've got this sequence down right," Lyle said.

They had just about all the paneling stripped from the wall now, and were working on the bracing studs. They still hadn't found any loose stones. Every one so far had been mortared tight to its neighbors.

Something about these stones gave Jack the creeps. They gave off an alien vibe that made him want to cover them again, hide them from human sight. They didn't belong here, and it almost seemed they knew it and wanted to be back where they'd come from—Romania, wasn't it? The ones that had had their cross inlays ripped out were the worst. The empty pockets looked like dead eye sockets, staring at him.

As they'd worked Jack had told them how he'd come into possession of Tara Portman's key ring—leaving out names, of course, and sidestepping mention of his knife fight with Eli Bellitto.

Lyle began counting off on his fingers. "First you meet Junie Moon, you bring her here, you step across the threshold, and awaken Tara Portman. Two days later someone hires you to watchdog someone he says is his brother but who you later learn is an only child. In the course of guarding the brotherless man you snag a key ring off him which just happens to belong to Tara Portman." He shook his head. "Talk about wheels within wheels."

And no more coincidences, Jack thought glumly, wondering at the purpose behind all this. And why was Gia involved? This whole situation was giving him a very unsettled feeling.

Lyle pried a Frisbee-size remnant of paneling from a two-by-four stud and scaled it onto the growing junk pile at the back end of the cellar.

"But just having Tara's key ring doesn't make this guy her killer. He could have found it on the sidewalk or picked it up at a garage sale."

Jack wondered how much he could tell these two. Since they lived on his side of the law, he decided to trust them with a little more.

"What if I told you that I saw him snatch a kid while I was watchdogging him?"

Charlie gave him a wide-eyed stare. "You frontin' me, right?"

Jack shook his head. "I wish. And if that's not enough, this guy has a whole cabinet full of kids' junk. Like a trophy case."

"Oh, man." Lyle had a queasy look. "Oh, man. What happened to that snatched kid?"

"I unsnatched him."

"Yo! Yo!" Charlie pointed a waggling finger at Jack. "The Vietnamese kid! That was you?"

"I'd rather not say."

"It *was* you!" Charlie grinned. "You a hero, G."

Jack shrugged and turned back to the stud he'd been prying loose from the blocks. Words like "hero" made him uncomfortable. Like "art," it tended to be thrown around a little too easily these days.

"You'd've done the same. Anybody would have." He shifted the talk away from himself. "I'll bet anything there's a link between this guy and the late, great Dmitri Menelaus. If I'm right, I'm afraid we can count on finding more than just Tara Portman's remains down here."

Which would work right into Lyle's PR plans.

Lyle leaned against the wall. "A serial killer." He didn't sound happy.

"More than one," Jack said. "A ring of them maybe. If I can establish a link with Dmitri . . ."

"What then?"

He found a groove between two blocks behind the two-by-four and slipped the pry bar into it. To the squealing accompaniment of protesting nails and the crackle of splintering fir, he wrenched the stud free with a vicious yank.

"A few people are going to wish they'd never been born."

Lyle stared at him. "Someone hire you to do that?"

"No."

Jack still wanted to know who'd hired him to watch Eli Bellitto, but no, no one would be paying him for what was going to happen to Bellitto and his crew.

"Then why're you going after them? I thought you were a pay-or-play guy. Fee for service, and all that. Why the freebie?"

"Because."

"That's not an answer.

"Yeah, it is."

"Praise the Lord!" Charlie said. His eyes glowed like a miniature sun had lit in his head. "Praise the Lord! You see what's goin' down here, don'tcha?"

Lyle said, "I'm almost afraid to hear this."

"Jack, you an instrument of God."

"Yeah?" He'd been called a lot of things since he'd started his fix-it business, but never that.

"True that! The guy hired you to hound this killer? A messenger from God, yo. He point you at the killer so you be there when that little kid need you."

"Really. What about all those other kids this guy's done? The ones like Tara Portman and who knows how many others?"

"Dawg, don't you see? God sent you here to even the score."

"You think so," Jack said.

Lyle laughed. "Hey, that's one ass-backwards god you've got there, bro. Where was he when Tara needed him? I mean, he's not paying attention. If he was, there'd be no score to even. Too little, too late, if you ask me."

Charlie glowered at his brother. "Didn't ask you."

"And what happened to this demon you were talking about?" Lyle said. "First you tell us we've got a demon sent by Satan, and now we've got Jack sent by god. Which is it?"

Jack wanted to tell Lyle to ease up on his brother, but it wasn't his place. What was it with Lyle anyway? He seemed wound as tight as that clock Jack had bought yesterday.

"That's it." Charlie threw down his pry bar. "I'm outta here."

"No way. We have a deal. Two days."

"Yo, I ain't standin' here listenin' to you trash the Lord. Blasphemy wasn't no part of the deal."

Jack watched them, wondering what the hell they were talking about.

Lyle held up his hands. "All right, I'm sorry. My bad. I was out of line. It's been a tough day. Truce, okay?"

"Truce sounds good," Jack said. "Let's keep at this. We've only got a little ways to go before it's all down."

"A'ight," Charlie said. "We keep at it."

"If we're going to do that, can we change the music?" The endless progression of cuts from Miles and Bird and now Coltrane was getting on his nerves.

Lyle frowned. "Don't tell me you don't like 'Trane."

"I guess I'm not cool enough for jazz. Or maybe not smart enough."

"How 'bout Gospel?" Charlie said with a sly grin. "I got a whole collection upstairs."

Jack leaned on the wall. "You know . . . if it's got words and melody, I'm willing."

"Why not a break from music?" Lyle said. "Just the sound of men hard at work."

Jack attacked another stud. "I can handle that."

After a minute or so Jack sensed eyes on the back of his neck and turned to find Lyle doing his stare-squint thing again. This was the third or fourth time he'd caught him.

"Do you find me attractive, Lyle?"

Lyle blinked. "Not at all. You're not my type."

"Then why do you keep staring at me?"

Lyle glanced at Charlie, then back to Jack. "If you must know, I'm trying to bring you into focus."

Jack's turn to blink. "You want to run that by me again?"

"When I look at you you're . . . fuzzy."

"Maybe you ought to invest in some glasses."

"It's not like that. I look at Charlie here and I see him bright and clear. I look at you and your features and most of the rest of you are clear and sharp, but around the edges . . . I don't have a better word for it than *fuzzy*."

Jack had to smile. "Is this a character assessment?"

"It's not funny, man." Lyle's eyes held a haunted look.

"When did it start? I didn't notice you staring at me when we were meeting with the Greek."

"It wasn't happening then. Maybe it's this house. I know it's done some weird shit to me."

"Yo, like what?" Charlie stepped forward, staring at his brother, the animosity of a moment ago giving way to brotherly concern. "This got to do with you canceling all those sittings?"

Lyle nodded, his haunted look growing. "Something's happened to me. I think it was that blood bath yesterday. It . . . did something to me."

"Like what?" Jack said.

"I can see things, know things I have no way and no right to know."

He told them about the morning's sitters, about seeing one woman's runaway husband, about another's lost pet— dead pet, roadkill on Twenty-seventh Street. He couldn't contact another's dead wife; yeah, she was dead but she was *gone*. No messages from beyond her grave.

"It's as if someone or something's playing games with me. Some of the powers I've been faking all these years . . . I really seem to have them now. At least while I'm in this house."

"And I look fuzzy to you." Jack didn't know what to make of that, but he didn't see how it could be good.

Lyle nodded. "Not when we were down at Kristadou-

lou's, but here, in the house . . . yes. There's more. With
the sitters this morning . . . I think I could have handled
what I was seeing and feeling from them if that had been
all. But I was seeing into their futures as well. At least it
felt like I was, but . . ." He shook his head. "I don't know.
What I was seeing didn't seem right or . . . possible."

"You got that right, bro," Charlie said. "Only God can
peep the future."

Again that haunted look in Lyle's eyes. "I hope you're
right, because if what I saw has any validity, there's not
much future left."

"What's that mean?" Jack said.

Lyle shrugged. "Wish I knew. The three sitters today . . .
when I touched them I saw what their lives would be for
the next year and a half or so, and they were each different
up to a certain point, but after that it was all the same:
darkness. And when I say *darkness* here I don't mean just
the absence of light, I mean a cold, hard, *living* blackness
that just seems to gobble them up."

Jack's gut gave a twist as he remembered someone he
loved talking about something very similar, telling him with
her final words about a coming darkness that would soon
"roll over everything," how only a handful of people would
stand in its way, and that he'd be one of them.

Could Lyle's darkness be the same?

"When did you see this happening?"

"Not long," Lyle said. "I got the impression with all three
of them that it happens in less than two years."

"Three random people," Jack said, "all buying it around
the same time, in the same way. Maybe the explanation
could be this new second sight of yours has a limit, or . . ."

"Or one hell of a cataclysm is heading our way."

"Praise God!" Charlie said, his eyes glowing again. "It's
the Rapture! You seen the Rapture! It's like when God
takes the faithful to heaven, leaving the rest behind in the
darkness! Those sitters you touched, Lyle, they ain't been
saved—if they were they wouldn't be foolin' 'round with
no spirit medium. You touched lost souls, Lyle."

"If that's what you want to believe—"

"The End Times! Reverend Sparks been talkin' 'bout all the signs pointin' to the end comin' soon! Praise God, he's right!" He held out his hand. "Here. Touch me, bro."

Lyle didn't actually move, but he seemed to shrink back. "Hey, Charlie, I don't think so. And anyway, I thought you didn't believe in this stuff."

"Who can figure how God works?" Charlie stepped closer. "The Book say the dead'll rise come the End Times. Maybe this is where it starts. Come on, Lyle. Try me."

Jack watched Lyle hesitate, then reach toward his brother's outstretched hand. A shock of alarm shot through him, urging him to warn Lyle off, tell him not to do it. But he bit it back. Lyle and Charlie were brothers. Where was the harm? What could happen?

Lyle's fingers gripped Charlie's in a firm handshake. The two stood staring into each other's eyes.

"Well?" Charlie said.

Lyle's mouth worked, then he let out an anguished cry. His eyes rolled back as he sagged to his knees and started coughing. He clutched at his throat with his free hand as if he were choking.

"Let go!" Jack shouted to Charlie.

"Can't!" Charlie's eyes were wild as he pulled at Lyle's fingers, trying to loosen them. "He crushin' my hand!"

Lyle was kicking and writhing now, looking like a man in his death throes. This was scary as hell. Jack stepped forward, ready to help Charlie break contact, when Lyle suddenly quieted. His rasping breaths stopped for an agonizing moment, then restarted with a cough and a gasp. Finally he released Charlie's hand and slumped the rest of the way to the floor.

Jack bent over him. "Lyle! Lyle, can you hear me?"

Lyle rolled over and opened his eyes. They looked dull, bloodshot. He looked around and blinked as if he'd just stepped out of a cave. His gaze came to rest on his brother standing over him, frozen in shock.

Charlie's voice was very small. "Lyle? You okay?"

"Dumb question," Lyle croaked as he propped himself up on one elbow. "Do I look okay?"

His tongue worked in and out of his mouth as he sat up.

"What's wrong?" Jack said.

"My mouth. Tastes like dirt."

"It bad, ain't it," Charlie said in that same small voice.

Lyle bent his knees and rested his forehead against them. "It started out bad, I can tell you that. It's mostly a blur, but I know for a moment there I felt as if I was suffocating, really and truly choking to death, but then the feeling passed. After that it all became pretty vague and jumbled for a while, but then I came to that same hungry darkness I saw with the others." He looked up at his brother. "But we come through it, the both of us. I mean, it seems like we do because we're still together when it's all over."

"Praise God!" Charlie said, his voice stronger now. "That can only mean you get yourself saved before the Rapture." He lifted his arms and looked up. "God, you are so great and good to have mercy on my brother and I."

Lyle glanced at his brother, sighed, then held out a hand for Jack to help him up.

Jack hesitated. "You sure you want to do that?" Jack was sure he didn't want anyone looking into *his* future. And they could stay out of his past and present too while they were at it.

"You've got a point there." Lyle pushed himself to his feet. He staggered a step when he was fully upright. "Man." He shook his head. "Maybe we'd better call it a day."

"Probably a good idea," Jack said. "We haven't found one loose stone in the whole damn wall. That means tomorrow we start on the floor. Probably should have started there in the first place."

Lyle nodded. "Yeah. If Dmitri was involved with Tara Portman, and maybe more missing kids, I can think of only one reason for a dirt floor all those years."

Jack walked over to the gap in the floor and examined the edge of the concrete.

"Shouldn't be too bad a job. Looks like it's only two

inches thick. You could rent a jackhammer and make short work of it."

Lyle shook his head. "Rather not if I can avoid it. Too much noise. I'm not looking to attract attention."

Jack glanced at him. "Not yet, anyway."

A flat smile. "Right. Not yet. You mind if we try by hand first?"

"Sure. If you think you'll be up for it tomorrow, so will I."

"I'll be up for it. But only till mid-afternoon. I'm speaking to a women's club in Forest Hills tomorrow." He held up a pinky and pursed his lips. "Pre-dinner speaker to the ladies, don't you know."

"Hoping to expand your clientele?"

He sighed. "Yeah. That was the case when I arranged the gig." He glanced at his brother. "Now, maybe I'm just wasting my time." He perked up as he faced Jack, but it seemed to take effort. "Anyway, I'll cancel tomorrow's sittings and we'll start off bright and early. If nothing else, it'll be a good workout."

A good workout . . . right. What would also be good, but far from pleasant, would be finding Tara Portman's remains and putting her to rest. Maybe then Gia would put the little girl behind her. And maybe then Jack could find out what all this meant and why he was involved.

Maybe.

14

Jack loped down Ditmars toward the subway, passing rows of ethnic stores propping up gray-stone triple-decker apartments. Rush hour was in full swing with the sidewalks cramped and the streets stop and go. He turned onto Thirty-first Street and was headed toward the looming elevated N line when his phone rang. He fished it out of his pocket and hit the SEND button.

"Hey, hon. What's up?"

But it wasn't Gia on the other end.

"Am I speaking to *Jack*?" said a faintly accented male voice that cracked his name like a whip.

Jack stopped walking. "Who's this? Who're you calling?"

"I'm calling the one who tried to kill me Monday night. Would that be you, *Jack*?"

Bellitto! How had he got this number? That bothered him, but the scalding fury of realizing he was speaking to Tara Portman's killer engulfed his concern. He looked around, then backed into the doorway of a gyro-souvlaki shop.

"Eli!" Jack said. He felt his lips tightening, pulling back from his teeth. "If I'd wanted to kill you, you'd be making this call from your grave. I didn't recognize your voice. Maybe that's because last time I heard it you were whining like a frightened child. You know what a frightened child sounds like, don't you?"

"Just as you do, I'm sure."

"What's that supposed to mean?"

"Oh, come now, Jack, or whatever your real name is. Don't take me for a fool. I know more about you than you think I do."

Unease blunted Jack's fury. Was Bellitto bluffing? He knew Jack's name—no, wait. Jack had had Eli's clerk write *Jack* next to Tara's key-chain entry in the sale book. That was how he'd got the name. But somehow Eli had found Jack's Tracfone number. What else did he know?

"Such as?"

"I know you're a practitioner."

"Really?" Where was this going? "Of what?"

An instant's hesitation, as if Bellitto was unsure of how much he should say, then, "The Ceremony, of course."

The word meant nothing to Jack, but Bellitto's tone had

loaded it with so much portent he knew he had to play along.

He feigned a gasp of shock. "How . . . how did you know?"

Bellitto laughed softly. "Because I've been a practitioner so much longer than you, so much longer than anyone. And your designs are pathetically transparent."

"Are they now?"

"Yes. You want to take over my Circle."

Jack had no idea what he was talking about but wanted to keep him going, maybe find out what made him tick and use some of that as a point of attack. Because Eli Bellitto was going down. Hard. Only a matter now of when and where.

"I have my own circle, so why would I want yours?"

"Because mine is so much more powerful. I've been performing the Ceremony for hundreds of years and—"

"Wait. Did you say 'hundreds'?"

"Yes. Hundreds. I am two hundred and thirty-two years old."

Jack shook his head. This guy was Froot Loop city.

"I had no idea."

"Now you see what you're up against. My Circle extends into all areas of power and influence. And you want it for yourself, don't you."

"My circle runs pretty deep and wide itself, and—"

The voice hardened. "Yours is nothing! Nothing! You caught me by surprise Monday night, but that won't happen again. I have my Circle casting its net for you. You're clever, but you're no match for me. We have your Tracfone number and soon we'll have your name, and once we have that, you're finished!"

Jack had a pretty good idea of how they'd got his phone number. He'd made only one call since his tête-à-tête with Bellitto, and that had been to 911 to report the kid. EMS would have recorded the number on caller ID. Figuring out from there that it was a Tracfone was no big deal, but to get the number in the first place did indicate a certain amount of suck with officialdom, maybe even the NYPD itself.

Maybe Bellitto wasn't blowing smoke. Maybe he was as well connected as he said.

And maybe he was trying to keep Jack talking instead of the other way around. If his "circle" had a couple of tracking cars riding around, tracing this call, could they triangulate on Jack's position and move in?

Lucky for him he was far from home.

Jack stepped away from the building and rejoined the pedestrian flow toward the elevated tracks. He'd keep the call going for a while longer, then step on a train and zoom away.

"What's the matter?" Bellitto said. "Cat got your tongue?"

Jack forced a laugh. "How typically unoriginal. You haven't a clue as to who I am or what I'm up to. And you never will. Your time is finished, Eli. Time for a new generation to take over. Step aside or die."

"Never! The Ceremony is mine! I don't know how you found out about it, but no Johnny-Come-Lately is going to usurp my power!"

Johnny-Come-Lately? Usurp? This guy was too much.

But this Ceremony he was ranting about . . . Jack had a sick feeling it might involve killing children. If he was right, maybe he could turn it on its head to give Bellitto a swift kick in his already cut-up balls.

"The old original recipe Ceremony might be yours, Eli, but I've done my own variation on it. The Ceremony, Version two-point-oh, is all mine."

"What?" An uncertain note here. "What are you talking about?"

"I've *reversed* the Ceremony, Eli."

"I don't understand."

"I can bring them back."

"What? Nonsense! That's impossible!"

"Is it? That was me in the store on Sunday trying to buy the Roger Rabbit key ring."

"You? But . . . but why would you want it?"

"Not me. I didn't want it. Tara wanted it."

"Who?"

"Tara Portman." Jack swore he heard a sharp intake of breath on the other end. "You remember her, don't you. The pretty little nine-year-old blonde you snatched by the Kensington riding stables back in eighty-eight." Jack fought to keep the growing rage out of his voice. Had to sound cool, play it like someone as sick as the guy on the other end of the line. "She's back, and she wanted her key ring. So I went and got it for her. Tara's back, Eli. And is she ever pissed."

With that Jack broke the connection and gave the OFF button a vicious jab, damn near punching it out the back side of the phone as he cut the power.

Chew on *that* for the rest of the night, scumbag.

15

"Slow down." Eli said, peering through the passenger window into the growing darkness. "It's just a little ways ahead. Number seven-thirty-five."

Adrian had the wheel of Eli's Mercedes, a black 1990 sedan. Despite its age its mileage was low. Eli used it infrequently and only for short trips. He preferred this old classic for its room and comfort and lines. The new models held no appeal for him.

Eli's wounds were feeling much better tonight, but not well enough to drive. Moving his leg back and forth to work the brake and gas pedals would flare his pain, so he'd given Adrian the keys. Adrian was still having some trouble with his knee, but fortunately it was his left that had been injured, so he could still drive.

Just as well that Eli had a physical excuse for not driving, for he wasn't up to it emotionally either. Not tonight. Too rattled, too distracted ... why, in his present mood, he might very well drive into oncoming traffic without realizing until it was too late.

But he couldn't let Adrian and Strauss see his unease, his uncertainty. He had never been in a situation like this, and found this inexplicable turn of events almost overwhelming. Everything had been going so well for so long, and now ...

Initially he'd been delighted to make contact with his attacker, the mysterious "Jack." He'd called with the intention of shaking him up, of letting him know that he hadn't got away clean with his vicious, underhanded act, that he was being hunted and would be found.

Instead, it had been Eli who had been left shaken.

The man knew that he'd abducted Tara Portman, knew that the key ring had been hers. How? He didn't believe for a second that the Ceremony could be reversed, and yet ... how did the man know about Tara?

The questions had plagued Eli until he'd given into a yearning to return to the house where the Portman child had died. Just for a look ...

"I still think this is a lousy, stupid idea," said Strauss from where he slouched in the rear seat. "Lousy because this whole deal could be a trick to get us to come back to this place, which we're doing. And stupid because Tara Portman ain't back and she ain't never coming back. Did we or did we not cut up her heart and eat it? No way that kid is back and looking for her key ring."

Eli winced at Strauss's casual mention of these Ceremony details. They were never to be spoken.

"First of all," Eli said, "we are not going back to Dmitri's house, we are simply driving by. Just another car passing on the street. As for the other matter, I fully agree that Tara Portman cannot be back, but we must find out how this man knows about her."

"Easy," Strauss said, the edge still on his voice. He

leaned forward and jutted his head over the back of the front seat. His breath reeked of garlic. "Somebody talked."

"No one talked," Eli said. "I've spoken to our other members, all ten of them, since this afternoon. No one has been kidnapped and tortured into a confession. Everyone is fine and looking forward to the next Ceremony. And think about it: If someone did talk, why talk about Tara Portman? Why not last year's lamb, or the year before? Tara Portman was ages ago."

"Perhaps," Adrian said. He'd been strangely silent all day. "But she was the first lamb we sacrificed in Dmitri's house."

"You're right," Eli said. "And oddly enough, I found myself thinking about Tara Portman just the other night."

That was why he'd been so shocked when the stranger had mentioned her name. It had to be a coincidence, but what a strange one.

"Really?" Adrian said. "Out of so many lambs, why her?"

"I've been asking myself that same question since my talk with our attacker this afternoon."

"Maybe it was because this mystery man tried to buy the key ring."

"No, that wasn't it. At the time I'd forgotten who that key ring belonged to. To tell the truth, I doubt I could match many of the little souvenirs in that cabinet to their original owners. And besides, I'd thought of Tara Portman days before."

"When?" Strauss said.

"Friday night."

He remembered he'd been reading in bed, deep into Proust's *Remembrance of Things Past*, and feeling drowsy, when suddenly she leaped into his mind. The briefest flash of her face, calm in the repose of deep anesthesia, and then her thin pale etherized body, still and supine on the table, awaiting the caress of Eli's knife. As quickly as the memories had come, they fled. Eli had written them off as random reminiscences, triggered perhaps by Proust's prose.

"There's the house now," Adrian said.

They lapsed into silence as they glided past Menelaus Manor. The lights were on. Who was home?

With a pang of melancholy Eli experienced a Proustian moment, caught up in a swirl of memories of Dmitri Menelaus, the brilliant, driven, tortured man he had brought into the Circle back in the eighties.

Dmitri had started off as just another customer in Eli's shop, but soon proved himself a man with a connoisseur's eye for the rare and arcane. He began to suggest sources where Eli might order rarer and stranger objects. As he and Eli got to know each other socially, Dmitri told of how he'd traveled the world investigating what he termed "places of power." He'd been to the usual locales—the Mayan temples of Chichen Itza in Yucatan, Macchu Picchu in the Andes, the tree-strangled temples of Angkor Wat in Cambodia—but had found them dead and cold. Whatever power they'd once held had been leached away by time and tourists. Along the way he'd heard tales of other places, secret places, and had also searched them out, all to no avail.

But then came whispers that fired his imagination, tales of an old stone keep in an obscure alpine pass in Romania, an ancient fortress that once had housed unspeakable evil. No one could give him the exact location of the pass, but by collecting and comparing notes based on the whispers, Dmitri narrowed his search to an area where these tales appeared to converge. He followed old trails through steep gorges, fully expecting this search to end as had so many others over the years, in despair and disappointment.

But this time was different. He found the fortress in a ravine near the ruins of a peasant village. As soon as he stepped through a gap in its crumbling foundation and let its walls enfold him, he knew his search had ended.

Immediately he'd arranged for a quantity of its loosened stones to be shipped back to the States and installed in his basement. He said the stones had absorbed the power of the old keep and now he had some of it for himself. His own home was now a place of power.

Eventually Eli learned the reason for Dmitri's obsession with these matters: He was terrified that he would die of pancreatic cancer like his father. He'd watched the man rot from the inside out and had sworn that would never happen to him.

Eli knew a better way to protect him, far better and more reliable than importing stones from Old World forts. Slowly, slyly, he felt out Dmitri about how far he'd be willing to go to protect himself from his father's fate. When he'd ascertained that there was nothing Dmitri would not do, no lengths to which he would not go, he introduced Dmitri to the Circle. He became Eli's twelfth disciple.

Dmitri quickly evolved into Eli's right-hand man, for Eli sensed that his motives were pure. For too many members of the Circle, Eli suspected that the abducted children and what was done to them were almost as important as the Ceremony and the immortality they'd eventually gain from it. They might be men in high places, but he sensed their motives were low. Year after year he'd seen the lascivious light in their eyes as the deeply anesthetized lamb was stripped naked upon the ceremonial table. It had disturbed Eli so deeply that he'd begun leaving the lambs fully clothed, baring only the minimum amount of flesh necessary to slit open the chest and remove the still beating heart. None of the Circle looked away during the bloody procedure. Some went so far as to suggest that the lamb be strapped down and conscious during the Ceremony.

How dare they? The Ceremony was to be performed without pain to the lamb. That would debase the ritual. The point was not pain but to gain life everlasting. The annual death of a child was an unfortunate but necessary price that had to be paid.

How lamentable that he had to ally himself with such

creatures, but in these increasingly Big Brotherish times, he needed their power and influence to safeguard the Ceremony and guarantee its annual performance.

But Dmitri was different. His focus was on the end, not the means. He soon became an indispensable member, especially once the Ceremony was moved to the basement of his home. It was perfect. The stones did indeed resonate with a strange power, and the dirt floor was a perfect resting place for the lambs. Disposing of a body, even once a year, had always been a perilous chore.

Eli would be performing the Ceremony at Menelaus Manor to this day were Dmitri still alive. But his doctors discovered that he had his father's cancer—too early to be helped by medical science, and too early to be saved by the Ceremony, for Dmitri had participated in nowhere near the twenty-nine he needed for immortality and invulnerability.

Unable to face the same agonizing death as his father, he'd seated himself on the dirt floor of his cellar and put a bullet through his head. What a loss . . . a terrible, terrible loss. Dmitri had been like a son to Eli. He still mourned his passing.

"I wonder who's living there now?" Adrian said as he drove on.

"I checked that out already," Strauss said. "Couple of brothers named Kenton. Bought it a year ago."

Eli felt a surge of excitement. Could they have tracked down his nemesis? "Do you think one of them could be our 'Jack'?"

"Doubt it. I ain't got much in the way of contacts here in the one-fourteen, but I did learn that not only are these two guys brothers, but they're also *brothers*—if you know what I mean."

Excitement dipped toward disappointment. "They're black?"

" 'S'what I'm told. You said your attacker was white. No chance you could be wrong?"

"I wouldn't know," Adrian said. "I can't remember. The last thing I remem—"

"He was white," Eli said, jumping in before Adrian could launch into his litany. "So that leaves them out."

"Who knows?" Strauss said. "A guy who can raise Tara Portman from the dead can maybe turn himself white too."

Eli was about to tell Strauss that this wasn't a joking matter when Adrian spoke.

"I don't care who they are as long as they don't dig up the cellar."

The remark brought silence to the car. That had been the great fear after Dmitri's death: the new owners would excavate the cellar. Eli had wanted a member of the Circle to buy the place so they could go on using it, but no one wanted his name connected with a house that held the remains of eight murdered children.

"The possibility of that is so small," Eli said, "I've ceased to worry about it. Step back and consider it objectively. How many homeowners, no matter how extensively they renovate a home, tear up their cellar floor?"

"Virtually none," Adrian said.

Strauss said, "Just lucky for us the people who bought it poured a cement floor over the dirt down there."

"It didn't bring them much luck, though," Eli said.

Strauss barked a laugh. "Yeah! Two slit throats and still nobody has a clue. If you don't close a murder in forty-eight hours, chances are you'll never close it. It's been years for that one. Guess by now you could call it a perfect crime."

Eli had been shocked when he'd read about the dead couple, and worried that the crime scene investigation might venture too deeply into the cellar.

And then there'd been the mutilation of the little boy adopted by the next owners. Eli had begun to wonder if a combination of the Ceremony and those strange stones lining the basement could somehow have laid a curse on the place.

"The other thing I'm worried about," said Adrian, "is that key ring."

"So am I, Eli." Strauss tapped Eli on the shoulder. "It connects you to the girl, and you can be connected to me. That's not good. Not good at all."

Adrian stopped at a red light. He continued to stare straight ahead as he spoke. "I've had nightmares about something like this happening because of that trophy cabinet of yours, sitting out there in your store for all to see. I always thought it was risky and . . . and arrogant as well."

Eli stared at him. Had he just heard correctly? Had Adrian, so deferential despite his size and strength, actually dared to call him arrogant? He must be furious, and very frightened.

Arrogant? Eli couldn't dredge up any anger. Adrian was right. Displaying the trophy cabinet had been arrogant and even foolhardy, but not half as arrogant and foolhardy as what Eli had done on Saturday.

Maybe the impetus had been the unbidden thoughts of Tara Portman the night before, perhaps it was nothing more than mere ennui, but whatever the reason, Eli had yielded to an urge to flaunt his invulnerability. So on Saturday afternoon he had told someone that he had killed hundreds of children, and that another would die with the next new moon, all but daring him to do something about it.

Eli permitted himself a fleeting smile. Adrian would shit his pants if Eli told him.

Instead Eli said, "Be that as it may, the trophy cabinet had nothing to do with our current predicament."

Strauss leaned back and returned to his slouch in the rear seat. "Maybe it did and maybe it didn't, but it was a bad idea all around. That kind of in-your-face shit threatens us all. Maybe you don't care, but we do."

"I sympathize, and I'll try to take your feelings into account in the future," Eli said. If the Circle had a future.

They lapsed again into silence as the car moved into traffic, then Adrian cleared his throat.

"Eli, am I the only one bothered by you thinking of Tara

Portman for no good reason on Friday night, and then this stranger popping into your shop on Sunday to try and buy the key ring? Then someone—possibly the same man—attacks us Monday night, and steals Tara's key ring on Tuesday. And today he claims that Tara is 'back'—whatever that means. Could he have brought her back on Friday night?"

"She's not back!" Eli said, his voice rising of its own accord.

"Then why, of all possible lambs, did you think of Tara Portman?"

"What time was this?" Strauss said, leaning forward again and refouling the air of the front seat with his breath. "That you thought of her, I mean."

"I don't know. I wasn't watching the time. Late, I'd say."

"You know what else happened late Friday night? The earthquake."

Eli remembered reading something about that. "I didn't feel a thing."

"But locals around here did. The paper said it was centered in Astoria."

"Dear God," Adrian whispered.

"Oh, come now," Eli said. "You can't seriously believe one has anything to do with the other. That's absurd!"

But was it? Eli felt an Arctic chill blow through the chambers of his heart. He couldn't let on how deeply the scenario Adrian and Strauss were describing disturbed him. It only heightened his feelings of being at the mercy of chance as well as the forces of nature itself.

"Perhaps it is," Adrian said. "But you can't help wondering, can you."

No, Eli thought. You can't.

He realized the only thing that would assuage this mounting malaise and uncertainty was another Ceremony to bulwark his defenses.

"For the moment," he said, "let's turn away from lambs of the past and focus on a lamb for the present." He glanced at Strauss. "Any progress in the matter of Ms. DiLauro's child, Freddy?"

"Some. I spent a little time watching her place today." He laughed. "I was wearing my old blues—they still fit me, y'know—and I waltzed them up to her door after I seen her leave her place alone. I figured if the kid was there, I'd pull the old your-mommy's-been-hurt routine, but she wasn't home. Learned from a neighbor's maid that she's away at camp."

"Really?" Eli said. He felt a surge of hope.

"Why are you fixated on her?" Adrian said. "We can snatch a child anywhere—"

"We've succeeded in lasting this long because we don't take chances. This situation has interesting possibilities. Think: A child disappears from a camp in the woods and the first thing everyone assumes is that she wandered off. They waste precious time beating the bushes for her when all the while she could be miles away, unconscious, in a car speeding toward the city . . ."

"Yes," Adrian said, nodding. "I see. Which camp?"

"That's the problem. This maid didn't know."

Adrian groaned. "Do you know how many summer camps there are in the tri-state area? We'll never find her."

Eli's mood sank. Adrian was right. There were hundreds, maybe thousands.

Strauss slapped the back of the front seat. "Never say never, my friend. I'm working a few angles. I've already recruited Williamson. He'll be full speed on the trail of little Victoria Westphalen tomorrow."

Wesley Williamson was a longtime member of the Circle and deputy director of the state banking commission. Eli didn't know how he could help, but he'd leave that to Strauss.

"He'd better hurry. If we don't complete the Ceremony by midnight Friday, we'll have to wait until next month."

Eli couldn't bear the thought of spending a whole month in his current state. Not just the fear and uncertainty, but the vulnerability, which was so much worse. His nameless enemy would have all that time to move against him.

"I'm doing my best, okay? This is short notice, but we'll get her. So sharpen up your knife for Friday night."

IN THE
IN-BETWEEN

The entity that was Tara Portman floats in darkness and frustration. The one she was sent for has stayed away. She has something Tara wants, something Tara desperately needs.

She must find a way to bring her here. She thinks she knows a way. Tara touched her while she was here, perhaps she can touch her in another way, beyond these walls. Touch her and make her return.

And then what? What will happen to Tara after her purpose is finished? Will she be returned to nothingness? Anything, even this half-existence, is better than that.

Stay here. Yes ... but not alone. She does not want to stay here alone ...

THURSDAY

1

Break time.

Jack glanced at the clock above the Kentons' kitchen sink: 10:15. Was that all? Seemed as if they'd been working a lot longer than two hours. He sipped his Gatorade and considered the progress they'd made.

When he'd arrived, Lyle and Charlie had already started chipping away at the concrete along the edges of the crack. If there'd been a gap in the earth below after the quake, it was gone. Just a groove in the dirt now. Jack had brought along some blues CDs as a compromise between his kind of music and the Kentons'. He heard no objections when he put on a Jimmy Reed disk, so he picked up a pickax and joined in, swinging in time to the beat, chain-gang style.

He started off stiff and achy. Yesterday he'd worked muscles he rarely used and they awoke today tight and cranky; but ten minutes of swinging the pick loosened them up.

Two hours later they'd widened the gap to maybe four feet. Slow, hard work. And hot. The cellar had started out cool but the heat thrown off by the exertions of three bodies soon raised the temperature. Like a sauna down there now. Jack could see he was going to need lots of Gatorade before the day was through, and lots of lager after.

He and Lyle sat and sipped at the kitchen table in their damp T-shirts. The faint breeze through the windows and open back door carried little cooling power. Charlie had grabbed a paper and a donut and retreated to the shade of the backyard with the morning paper. He'd said little all morning.

"Something wrong with Charlie?"

Lyle's eyes gave away nothing. "Why do you ask?"

"Pretty quiet."

"He's just going through a phase. Not your worry."

Right. Not Jack's business why the brothers Kenton weren't getting along. But he liked these two, and it bothered him.

He dropped the subject. He lifted the front of his T-shirt and wiped his face. "Ever hear of air-conditioning?"

"Not much use when the windows and doors won't stay closed."

"Still?"

Lyle nodded. "Still. If I close them they don't reopen as fast as they used to, but eventually they do."

"Tara, you think?"

Another nod. "I get the feeling she's trapped here. She wants to get out—maybe she keeps trying—but can't."

Just then Charlie burst through the door, waving the morning paper. "Yo, Jack! Peep this!" He had the *Post* folded back and then in half, commuter style. He dropped it on the table and pointed to a headline. "Is this you, dawg? This yo' setup?"

Jack picked up the paper. Lyle came around and peered over his shoulder.

SHE SHOULD'VE KNOWN BETTER

Elizabeth Foster, better known as psychic advisor Madame Pomerol, has had her second brush with the NYPD in one week. Just last Sunday morning she and her husband Carl were found wandering the financial district unclothed; but the charges are more serious this time: the Federal government is involved. Foster and her husband Carl were picked up yesterday afternoon trying to pass phony hundred-dollar bills at La Belle Boutique on Madison Avenue. The Treasury Department is investigating.

But things get worse. A search of their Upper East Side apartment—also known as "Madame Pomerol's

Temple of Eternal Wisdom"—not only turned up
thousands more of the funny money, but provided in-
disputable evidence that this particular psychic medium is little more than a scam artist.

Jack had to grin as the article went on to describe the
eavesdropping devices found in her waiting room, the electronic ear pieces hidden in her hats, the monitors, the trap-
doors, and most damning of all, the files on her clients, filled
with xeroxes of driver licenses, Social Security cards, bank
statements, and notes containing more than a few scathing
comments about their weaknesses, predilections, and obses-
sions. As a result, the Manhattan DA was preparing to add
charges of fraud and conspiracy to defraud to the federal
counterfeiting rap.

"They're done!" Lyle cried. "Gone! Fried! Fini! Madame
Pomerol will be reading palms for cigarettes in either Rik-
ers or a federal pen! Is this your fix?"

"I do believe it is."

"The queer? How'd you manage that? You plant it on
them?"

"Trade secret, I'm afraid."

"You done it, G!" Charlie said, grinning for the first time
all morning. "You nailed her!"

Jack shrugged. "Sometimes things go according to plan,
sometimes they don't. This one did."

He stared at the article, basking in the sunny sensation
of a job well done. He'd set the Fosters up for a fall and
had known they'd tumble sooner or later. He was glad it
turned out to be sooner.

The big *if* in this particular fix-it had been how they
handled their cash. Did they deposit it and write checks, or
spend it? Jack had banked on the latter. With a good cash
flow—real cash, not checks and charges—that they probably didn't declare, they'd tend to pay for things in cash to
leave less of a money trail should the IRS come sniffing.

Lyle clapped Jack on the shoulder. "Remind me never

to get on your wrong side, Jack. You are *not* a man to mess
with!"

If Jack had his way, Eli Bellitto would soon feel the
same, only worse. Much, much worse.

As they all headed back down to the cellar, Jack sensed
a better mood than when they'd started the break. They
retrieved the pickaxes and renewed their combined attack
on the concrete slab, tossing the broken chunks onto the
pile of paneling.

By midday they'd broken up half the slab. After a quick
lunch of juicy gyros at a Greek deli up on Ditmars, they
returned to work.

"You know what?" Lyle said as he surveyed the rubble
that had once been a basement. "I think two of us should
start digging in the dirt while the other keeps after the concrete."

Jack kicked at the hard packed, red-brown soil. Not a
hell of a lot softer than the concrete.

"You mean, start looking for Tara."

"Right. The sooner we find her, the sooner we can stop
pretending to be day laborers and go back to being gentle-
men of leisure."

"How will we know it's her?"

Lyle stared at the dirt. "You still think she's got company
down there?"

"I'd bet on it."

"Well, we'll cross that bridge whenever." Lyle looked up
at Jack. "You game to dig a little dirt?"

"Not exactly my idea of a fun treasure hunt," Jack said,
"but I'll give it a go."

Lyle turned to his brother. "How about you, Charlie? Dirt
or 'crete?"

Charlie shrugged. "I'll stick with the slab."

"Okay. We'll rotate around if anybody wants to switch."
He leaned toward Jack and spoke in a stage whisper. "And
if you should happen to find the remains of the Missing
Link while you're digging, don't let Charlie know. He
doesn't believe in evolution and it would upset him."

Charlie said, "Step off, Lyle."

My sentiments exactly, Jack thought.

Lyle grabbed the shovel and jammed the spade into the dirt. "Well, it's true, isn't it. You believe the universe was created in six days, right?"

"That what it say in the Bible, so that what I believe."

"So did Bishop Usher, who ran down all the dates in the Bible and the ages of all people mentioned. According to his calculations, the earth was created on October 26, 4004 BC." He tossed a shovel full of dirt aside and struck a pensive pose. "I wonder if that was A.M. or P.M.? Anyway, seems to me the earth's packed an awful lot of growth and development into six thousand years."

Jack grabbed a shovel. "Fascinating. Let's dig."

"That what it say, then that what I believe. We talkin' the word of God, yo."

"Are we?" Lyle raised a finger. "Well, I've got a few words of my own—"

Oh, no, Jack thought. They're off.

"Hey, what is all this?" he said, cutting in. "I didn't always pay my bills doing fix-its. I've done landscaping and worked with nonunion wrecking crews, and all I ever heard guys talk about was booze and broads. But you two—what is it with you guys, anyway?"

Lyle grinned. "Maybe it's because Charlie doesn't drink and we've both been celibate far too long."

"Ay, yo, how 'bout you, Jack?" Charlie said. "What you believe?"

"About what?" he said, although he knew exactly what.

Lyle said, "Faith, god. All that."

That was a little too personal for Jack. He didn't even tell anyone his last name, so he wasn't about to discuss religion with a couple of guys he hadn't known a week. Besides, it wasn't a subject he gave much thought to. In his world, the unseeable and unknowable simply hadn't much mattered.

Until lately.

"I'm pretty much for whatever gets you through the day,

as long as you don't start insisting it's the way everyone
should get through the day."

"That ain't tellin' nothin'."

"Okay, then, I can tell you that whatever I did believe
has been pretty much turned upside down in the past few
months."

Lyle looked at him. "All that stuff you told us about the
Otherness?"

Jack nodded.

"Here's my problem," Lyle said. "I have just as much
trouble believing in your Otherness as I do in Charlie's
personal God."

"How about Tara Portman?" Jack said. "And what's been
going on in this house? That's not hearsay. You've been
here. It's your own experience."

Lyle's cheeks puffed as he let out a breath. "Yeah, I
know. This is terra nova for me. I never believed in ghosts
or life after death, or even the soul. I assumed when you
died you were gone forever. Now . . . I'm not so sure."

Jack said, "Then maybe we should stop jawing and dig
up this terra nova."

Lyle laughed. "Excellent idea!"

The Best of Muddy Waters was in the boombox tray. Jack
turned up "Mannish Boy" loud enough to make conversation a chore, then went to work.

By late afternoon, with another Gatorade break somewhere in the middle, they'd pocked the surface of the dirt
with holes but hadn't come across a single bone.

"We've only been going down three feet or so," Lyle
said. "Maybe that's not deep enough."

Jack leaned on his shovel. "Hate to think they went the
full traditional six."

"Might have. Especially if they wanted to be sure of not
having any telltale odors. Which means we have to go
down six."

Jack's T-shirt was soaked. He looked around. The pile
of smashed paneling and broken concrete already took up

one end of the cellar. They'd added some of the dirt to it, but they'd be running out of room soon.

"You're talking a lot of dirt."

"Tell me about it. Look, I know it's been a long day, but I'd like to keep after this."

"There's always tomorrow," Jack said.

Charlie stopped digging and looked at his brother. "No there ain't."

Jack opened his mouth but Lyle cut him off.

"Don't ask. Look, why don't we take another break and see if we can come up with a systematic way of going about finding her."

Jack glanced at his watch. "I've got an errand to run, but I should be back in an hour and a half or so."

"I'm going to have to bail soon myself. That Forest Hills women's club thing."

"That's right," Charlie said. "Everybody run off and leave baby brother to do all the work."

Jack laughed. "I'll be back to help out as soon as I can."

"Where're you off to?" Lyle said.

"To make sure the last piece of the Tara Portman puzzle fits where I think it does."

2

As Jack rode the N train back to Manhattan he debated stopping off at his place or Gia's and taking a shower. He damn sure needed one. By the time he reached the decision point at Fifty-ninth Street, he decided it would take too much time. He stayed on the train as it turned downtown.

When he reached SoHo he made a quick pass by Bellitto's store and noted the sturgeon was no longer in the window. Too bad; he'd kind of liked it. Took a peek through the glass of the door and saw the older woman with the jet-black hair helping a customer. She was the one he wanted to talk to. He'd got the impression she'd grown old with the store. But Kevin was there too, behind the counter.

He moved on, frustrated.

Damn. He'd hoped this would be the kid's day off. No sign of Bellitto or the gorilla-armed Minkin though, which was good. Doubted they'd recognize him after their encounter in the dark, but didn't want to take the chance. This was primarily an information-gathering trip, with maybe a little cage-rattling bonus thrown in. He knew he'd eventually have to deal with those two before they zeroed in on another kid. But Bellitto was laid up for the present, so Jack had some time to plan his course.

Jack found a shady doorway with a view of the front of the shop and waited, watching the shadows lengthen and the traffic thicken. Evening was edging into the picture and he didn't have all that much time, but there was always a chance Kevin would clock out or make a Starbucks run. He needed to talk to the lady alone. If he couldn't do it face to face, he'd try the phone, but that would be settling for second best.

He thought about what Gia had told him about the mystery cop from the unknown precinct. He didn't like anyone, maybe cops especially, knocking on Gia's door and asking the whereabouts of her daughter. Nobody's damn business but Gia's. And Jack's too, sometimes.

He pulled out his Tracfone and called her to see if the cop had stopped back. She said no. All quiet on the East Side. He told her they hadn't found anything yet at Menelaus Manor and not to wait dinner for him—he'd be late tonight. She sounded tired. She hadn't been sleeping well. He told her to take a nap and she said she might just do that.

After saying good-bye, Jack turned off the phone. Didn't want Bellitto calling him again. Let him wonder. Let him stew.

Jack's patience finally was rewarded by the sight of Kevin stepping out and hurrying down the sidewalk. Didn't know how long he'd be gone so Jack hustled over to the shop.

"Yes, sir?" the woman behind the counter boomed as he entered. She had a mannish build, with broad shoulders and a hefty frame. Above her Richard Belzer face her black hair looked spit shined. She eyed his sweat-stained T-shirt, dirty jeans, and grimy hands with poorly disguised disdain. Obviously he didn't look like a typical Shurio Coppe customer.

Knew I should have showered, he thought.

He decided to adopt a personality to go with the look. He rounded his shoulders and made only the briefest eye contact.

"Um . . ."

"Are you looking to *buy* something, sir?"

"Uh, well, no, y'see," he said in a meek, faltering voice, "I was kinda like wondering if—"

Jack heard the bell on the door tinkle behind him and turned to see a big no-neck guy with outlandishly long arms limp through. Adrian Minkin, in the flesh. Jack tensed and looked away as he approached.

"Eli wants the book again," Minkin said as he brushed past Jack and stepped to the counter.

He wore black slacks and a long-sleeve white dress shirt.

The woman made a face. "That's the third time already," she said. "Why doesn't he just call down?"

Minkin leaned on the counter, just a couple of feet away, giving Jack his first close-up look at Minkin's hands in good light. Massive, with wiry black hair crawling all the way out to the third knuckle on the long thick fingers.

"You know how he is, Gert." Minkin leaned closer and lowered his voice. "He's very tense, waiting for a call, plus I think he's bored out of his mind."

"Bad combination," Gert said, handing him a black ledger. "Just get it back to me as soon as he's finished."

"Will do."

When he turned he came face to face with Jack. He stopped and stared for a few heartbeats that seemed to stretch into minutes. Jack met his cold blue eyes, looking for signs of recognition and readying to make a move the instant he saw the first hint. But Minkin only blinked, nodded, and moved on.

"Sorry for the interruption, sir," Gert said. "What can I help you with? Looking for anything in particular?"

"Yes, well, I . . ." Jack shuffled closer to the counter, killing time until he heard the bell chime and the door close behind Minkin. He glanced over his shoulder to make sure he was gone, but he made it into a timid gesture. "I'm looking for Mr. Menelaus. Mr. Dmitri Menelaus."

Gert blinked. "Mr. Menelaus? What would you want with him?"

Jack wished she'd cut her volume. Wouldn't be surprised if Bellitto and Minkin could hear her upstairs.

"I, um, did some masonry work for him some years ago, y'know, in his cellar, and he said I should meet him here."

Gert's eyes narrowed. "Did he now? And when was this?"

"Oh, um, just this morning, on the phone."

"This morning? Oh, I doubt that very much. He's been dead for years."

"Get out! You're lying!"

"Sir, I do not lie. He was a regular customer. He and the owner were quite close."

"I figured that."

Jack took a deep breath and let it out. There it was. The final link between the Menelaus house, Tara Portman, and Eli Bellitto.

Gert shook her head. "Tragic the way he died."

"Not tragic at all," Jack said, dropping out of character. "I'm pretty sure it was long overdue."

Gert's eyes widened as she straightened her wide shoulders. "What?"

Jack turned and strode for the door. "Thanks lady. Tell Eli I was asking after Dmitri."

"You know Mr. Bellitto? Who are you?"

"Just tell him. He'll know."

Jack hit the sidewalk and headed straight for the subway.

3

"This is not to be borne!"

Eli slammed the phone down. He could barely speak. The brazenness of the man! The absolute gall!

"What is it?" Adrian said, hovering.

"It was him! The mysterious 'Jack'! He was just in the shop asking Gert about Dmitri!"

Adrian gaped at him. "Just now? Then I saw him. I looked right at him and didn't recognize him. But then of course I wouldn't recognize him since I still don't remember what happened Monday night. The last thing I remem—"

"What did he look like?"

"Like . . . like a common laborer. He was dirty and he smelled sweaty. I can't believe—"

"Believe it! He said he'd had a call from Dmitri telling him to meet him in the shop."

Adrian paled. "But Dmitri's dead."

Eli glanced at him. What had always impressed him most about Adrian, besides his size, was his swift mind; but since those blows to his head his mental functions seemed to have slowed to a walk.

"I'm well aware of that. He's just trying to rattle us." Though Eli said us, he meant *me*. "He wants to keep us off balance."

"But why?"

Suddenly Eli saw it all, comprehended the mystery man's plan in all its terrible simplicity.

"He wants to prevent us from performing the Ceremony during this cycle. That will put terrible pressure on us because we'll have to complete the Ceremony during the next cycle, the last new moon before the equinox, or . . ."

His words dried up as he contemplated the consequences.

Adrian was staring at him. "Or what? What will happen?"

"To you? Nothing much. Your string of Ceremonies will be broken and you'll have to go back and start at one again."

Adrian groaned. "Oh, God, no."

"But for me it will be much, much worse. If I fail, all the diseases and traumas I've been shielded from for the past two centuries will rush upon me and crush me."

Terror squeezed his shuddering heart in a cold fist. He'd die slowly and in unimaginable agony. And then the interloper would be free to take over the Circle.

That was why this Jack hadn't killed him Monday night. He wanted Eli to suffer a month of pain and anxiety before a horrible death.

"And to think I was *that* close!" Adrian gritted through clenched teeth. "If only I'd known I'd have . . ." He balled his hands before him, crushing huge fistfuls of air.

"He won't win!" Eli cried. "He thinks that by stealing our lamb he's sabotaged our Ceremony for this cycle. He can't know about the DiLauro woman's child—we didn't know ourselves until yesterday. We can still beat him."

He snatched up the phone, punched in Strauss's beeper number, and left a message to call back. The phone rang minutes later.

"Progress?" Eli snapped as soon as he recognized Strauss's voice.

"Some. Not moving as fast as I'd like. What's wrong?"

He filled Strauss in on the mystery man's latest stunt without getting into his theory of what the man was planning. "What's the hold-up? What are you doing?"

"I'm not sure I want to say," Strauss said. "With all this guy seems to know, how can we be sure your line's not tapped?"

Eli felt his chest tighten. The possibility had never occurred to him.

"Can you check the line?"

"Yeah, but not today. We got some situations here that won't allow me to get down there till late tonight."

Not good enough. Eli needed to know now. Then he had an idea.

"Fax it to me."

"What?"

"You heard me. Jot it down or type it out. Be as oblique as you wish—I'll understand—and fax it. You destroy the original, I'll burn the copy at this end, and no one but we will know."

A pause on the other end, then, "All right. That might work. Just make sure you burn it right off."

"I'll have the matches ready."

He gave Strauss his personal fax number, then hung up. Twelve minutes later the machine rang, then started printing out a brief, scrawled message.

Our financial friend got the ladys checking account records but no check written to a camp. Looking into credit cards but that takes longer. Will know by tonight and fax results ASAP.
BURN THIS!

Strauss, ever paranoid, hadn't signed it.

Eli handed it to Adrian. "Find some matches and do what the man says."

Checking accounts and credit cards . . . how clever. Why comb through the rosters of a thousand summer camps looking for a particular child when you can use the mother's own records to find out. Big Brother certainly had his drawbacks, but in this instance, he could be a Godsend.

Eli felt better. They'd know the lamb's location by tonight and could then determine the best way to acquire her.
If all went well, by dawn she would be theirs.

4

Lyle struck a pose on the bottom cellar step. He'd shaved,
showered, and donned his black silk suit. Ifasen was ready
for Forest Hills.

"How do I look?"

Charlie glanced up from his digging. "All G'd up like a
wolf huntin' him some sheep."

"Thanks loads."

Not at all the image Lyle wanted to cut, but he knew
Charlie's perception was tinted toward the cynical where
he was concerned.

Lyle said, "Jack called. He's been delayed. He's going
to grab a bite before he comes back. Why don't you take
a break till he gets here. I should be back shortly after that
and then the three of us can give it a couple more hours."

Charlie shook his head. "Nuh-uh. Told you I'd give you
two days and that's what I'm doin'. Don't want you sayin'
I shorted you. You go. I'll keep workin'."

"Charlie—"

"Go, man. I find somethin', I call you. We find nathan
by midnight, we gone, right? That was the deal, right?
Right?"

Lyle sighed. "Right."

He realized he should have rescheduled his women's
club talk, or canceled it altogether. What good was wooing
new sitters, no matter how well-heeled, if he wasn't going
to be in business after tonight? He never should have struck

that deal with Charlie, or at least should have insisted on three days instead of two.

Cool it with the negativity, he told himself. We're going to find Tara tonight. I know it.

And then these Forest Hills ladies would be cat fighting to book sittings with him.

5

The foil-wrapped sandwich was cool under Jack's arm as he stepped into Julio's. The after-work crowd was building and smoke hung thick in the air. As Jack headed for one of the rear tables he waved to Julio and flicked his thumb above his fist in a pop-me-one gesture.

A minute later Julio plunked an open Rolling Rock long neck onto the table and stood watching as Jack unrolled his sub from the greasy foil. A vinegary odor seeped into the air. He'd swung into Costin's mom and pop on the next block and grabbed it on the run from the cooler; a pre-fab construction of spongy bread filled with sliced meat by-products topped with a cheeseoid substance that had never been within a hundred miles of a cow. But it was fast and promised to fill the void.

"Hey, meng, people see you they gonna think this some kinda bring-your-own-food place."

Jack took a long pull on the beer. Damn, that tasted good. He'd stopped home to shower and change. A clean pair of jeans, a fresh shirt—an Allman Bros. concert T he'd picked up at a secondhand store—and he felt halfway to a new man, ready to dig again.

"Nobody's watching and I'm too hungry and too short on time to deal with those wings and other finger foods you serve."

The little man bristled and flexed his considerable biceps. "Hey, we serve the best food money can fry."

"Your message said you had something for me?"

As Julio fished an envelope out of his back pocket, Jack bit into his sandwich. A pasty texture that tasted like oil and vinegar. Swell. At least he wouldn't be hungry when he finished.

"Old guy drop it off this morning." He ran the envelope under his nose. "Mmm. Smells like money."

"Old guy?"

"Yeah. He meet you here Sunday."

Jack almost choked on his sandwich as he came half out of his seat, looking around. "He still here?"

"Nah." Julio snapped his fingers. "He come and go like that. Like he don' wanna be seen."

"Shit!"

"You lookin' for him?"

"Yeah. Big time."

"He short you?"

Jack opened the envelope and flipped through the bills. The amount looked about right.

"No. But he owes me some answers."

Like why he hired me and why he lied about who he is. Probably never know now.

Jack spotted a slip of yellow paper among the bills. He pulled it out, unfolded it, and read the handwritten note.

Thanks for taking care of my brother.
Edward

Was he mocking him or sincere? Jack couldn't tell. Despite his frustration he resisted the urge to ball up the note and fling it across the room. Instead he refolded it and put it back in the envelope.

"Y'know," Julio said. "I think Barney recognized him. I think I hear him say something like, 'My-my-my, look who's here.' Or son'thing like that."

"Barney?" Jack scanned the room. He usually hung at the bar with Lou. "Where is he?"

"Working. Night shift this week. He be back in the morning."

"Then so will I." Jack shoved the remains of the sub into his mouth, washed it down with the rest of the beer, then rose.

"Gotta run. Don't let Barney leave before I get here tomorrow. Feed him, buy him drinks on me, whatever you have to do to keep him here till I arrive."

Jack headed for the street. Time to dig again. He felt a certain amount of satisfaction. Two more questions left: Was Tara Portman truly buried beneath Menelaus Manor, and who had hired him to watch Eli Bellitto? By this time tomorrow he expected to know the answers to both.

6

Even through the heavy beat of Point of Grace's music Charlie heard the noise. He stopped digging. From upstairs. A slamming, banging sound, like some rhythm-impaired giant beating the house with a two-by-four.

He dropped his shovel and scrambled up the steps. He reached the kitchen in time to see the windows shut themselves with a bang. Then the back door slammed closed.

For one panicky moment Charlie thought he might be locked in. He jumped for the knob, gave it a pull, and it swung open. He let out a relieved breath. When he released he knob, the door swung shut again.

How 'bout that? Whatever used to want everything open must've had a change of heart. Now it want everything closed up tight.

Well, not everything, he thought as he checked the front

room. The windows were down, but the front door stood open. He pushed it closed but it unlatched itself and swung open again.

Weird how this sorta thing had spooked him a couple days ago but was just everyday stuff now. Showed you can get used to 'most anything.

Charlie wondered why this door was left open while everything else shut up tight, then decided, no matter. After tonight it wasn't his worry. Lyle's neither.

He went back to the cellar and the hole he'd been digging. He'd got down maybe four feet and so far he'd come up with the same as all the other holes: nathan. He figured on giving this one another foot or so before calling it quits.

As the shovel bit into the dirt, the music stopped.

"You're getting warm."

Charlie yelped in terror at the sound of the little-girl voice behind him. He dropped his shovel and snapped around so quick his feet got tangled and he sprawled onto his back.

"No!" he cried as he lay in the cool dirt and looked up at the blond girl in riding clothes standing over him. He knew who she was and what was pretending to be her. "Demon! Sweet Jesus, save me!"

"From me?" she said, smiling and twirling a strand of her golden hair. "Don't be silly."

"Stay away!"

Charlie's heart was a boot kicking inside his chest. He dug in his heels and palms and scrabbled away like a backward crab.

The little girl's face crinkled up and her blue eyes danced as she giggled. Her laugh was sweet and musical. "You look funny!"

"You can't fool me! I know what you are!"

She stepped closer. "You do?"

Charlie kept backing away, and then he banged his dome against a wall and that was it. Nowhere to go.

"You—you a demon!"

She laughed again. "Now you're really being silly!"

His mind screamed, What do I do? What do I *do*?

He couldn't think. He hadn't expected this, wasn't prepared, never believed that the demon would appear to him. Shoulda listened to the rev, shoulda took his advice and packed his gear and geesed.

Pray! Of course! Words from the Twenty-third Psalm jumped into his brain.

He raised his voice. " 'Yea, though I walk through the valley of death I shall fear no evil. Thy rod and thy staff they—' "

" 'Valley of death'," she said, looking around and nodding. "Yes. That's where we are." She pointed to the hole he'd been digging. "You're only seven inches from my head. If you keep digging you'll find me."

Charlie slashed the air with his hand. "No! You can't fool me! You're not Tara Portman!"

The child frowned. "Then why are you digging?"

The question took Charlie by surprise. Why *was* he digging? Because he'd made a deal with Lyle. And because . . .

"Because Tara Portman may be buried here, but you're not her."

Her blue eyes turned cold. "Oh, but I am. And I'm not the only one down here. There." She pointed to a hole Jack had dug half a dozen feet to Charlie's left. "Another foot deeper and you'd have found Jerry Schwartz. He was only seven. Right where you're sitting, five feet down, is Rose Howard. She was nine, like me."

Charlie wanted to jump off the spot but couldn't bring himself to move.

Suddenly she disappeared, but immediately flashed back into view in a far corner.

"Jason Moskowski is here."

Charlie blinked and she was in another corner of the cellar.

"Carrie Martin is here."

She flashed to three more locations, naming another child

each time. And with each name her eyes grew icier and the cellar colder.

Suddenly she was in front of him, not three feet away.

"Eight of us," she said, her voice barely above a whisper.

Lord forgive him, he was starting to buy her line. Maybe the rev was wrong. Maybe this wasn't no demon. Maybe this was the furilla ghost of a murdered child.

Or maybe that was just what the demon, kin to the Father of Lies, wanted him to believe.

Real cold in here now. His puffing breaths were smoking the air. He rubbed his bare arms. His sweaty T-shirt was freezing his spine. He saw his sweatshirt balled up by the junk pile.

He rose uncertainly. "I'm gonna get my shirt, okay?"

"Why are you asking me?" she said.

Good question. She hadn't threatened him or nothin', but just seeing her had turned him into a scrub.

He grabbed the hoodie and pulled it on. Better, but still cold.

"You want us to find your body and the others. That it, ain't it? That why you back, right?"

She shook her head.

"Then why?" Sudden fear slammed Charlie like a truck. "You want my soul!"

She laughed like that was such a wack idea, but the sweet sound didn't match up with her ice eyes.

Charlie's hand brushed against the pin on his shirt. He looked down at it. WWJD—what *would* Jesus do in a case like this?

Simple: He'd tell this spook or demon to get back where it belonged. But Charlie didn't have Jesus' power. Still . . . it was worth a try.

"Go back where you came from!" he cried.

The little girl blinked. "But I don't know where I came from."

That shocked him. "Lie! You were in heaven or hell, one or the other! You gotta know!"

She shook her head. "I don't remember."

Maybe she was telling the truth, maybe she was lying, but Charlie wasn't hangin' around to find out. If she wouldn't go, then he would. Right up those stairs. That was what Jesus would say: Highside evil. Don't even give it the time of day.

He started to step around her but she flashed out of sight and reappeared by the cellar stairs.

"You can't leave. Not yet."

"Why not?"

"You might ruin things."

He could make a run at her, but what then? Could he knock her down? If she was a real kid, no problem. Couldn't be more than seventy pounds soaking wet. But she wasn't. Was there even anything there to knock aside? Or would he pass right through her—or her through him? That would put her inside him. He couldn't handle that. What if she stayed in?

Charlie shuddered and backed off a step. This little girl had him down and whipped. Couldn't scrap a lick against her.

"What you want with me?" He didn't like the way his voice sounded—all high up and scrub whiny.

She stared at him. "With you? Nothing."

"Then—?"

She raised a hand and his voice died. He tried to speak but couldn't make a sound.

"Quiet now. I'm waiting for someone else, and I don't want you scaring her away."

Point of Grace's vocals blared to life again.

7

Gia hears the voices as soon as she steps through the door. Children's voices, whimpering, sobbing . . . lost sounds that tear at her heart. She recognizes the waiting room of Menelaus Manor but the voices are coming from the second floor. She rushes up the stairs and finds herself in a long hall lined with doors. Eight of them. The voices are louder here, and grow louder still as she moves down the hall. All the doors but one are open and as she passes each she sees a child, a boy or a girl, standing alone in the center of an empty room, sobbing. Some cry out for their mommies. Pressure builds in Gia's throat as she tries to enter the rooms to comfort them, but she can't stop. She must keep moving down the hall toward the closed door at its end. She stops before it and reaches for the knob, but before she touches it the door slams open and there's Tara Portman, the front of her blouse all bloody and her eyes wide with fear, and she's screaming, "Help! Help! Someone's hurt! You've got to come! Come now! NOW!"

Gia awoke with a start and the word *NOW!* echoing through her head. She looked around the darkening bedroom. Through the window she saw that the sun was down and twilight fading fast.

A nap. She hadn't slept well last night. She'd kept waking from dreams, remembering little of them except that they were disturbing. Being pregnant probably added to the fatigue. But as tired as she'd felt all afternoon, she'd fought Jack's suggestion of a nap until she could barely keep her eyes open. Finally she'd allowed herself a quick lie-down on the bed, just for a few minutes . . . She'd just had another disturbing dream. What had it been about? She seemed to remember something about Menelaus—

Gia lunged to her feet as it all rushed back to her: Tara's terrified face as she screamed about someone being hurt and how Gia had to come now. *Now!*

"Jack!"

A bolt of alarm shot through her chest as she ran downstairs through the dark house to the kitchen where she had Jack's cell phone number magneted to the refrigerator door. She found it, dialed, but was told by a mechanical voice that he wasn't available. She flipped on a light, grabbed her pocketbook, and dumped it onto the counter. She rummaged through the mess until she found the Ifasen brochure she'd picked up at Menelaus Manor. She punched in the number and hung on through the rings until the Kentons' voice mail picked up. She hung up without leaving a message.

Gia didn't know if someone was really hurt or if the dream had been nothing more than that, but she had this awful feeling that something must be wrong. Whatever the case, she couldn't simply sit here. She knew she'd promised to stay away, but if Jack was hurt she wanted to be there; if he wasn't, she could hang out and visit for a while. Promise or no promise, she was heading for Menelaus Manor. Now.

She picked up the phone again and called for a cab.

8

Giving in to an impulse to stop in at Gia's, Jack stepped off the N train at the Fifty-ninth Street station and walked over to Sutton Square. He hadn't seen her all day.

He had a key but he knocked anyway. And knocked again when she didn't answer. Odd. He saw lights on in-

side. He used his key and entered. When he saw that the
alarm was armed he knew Gia wasn't home. He punched
in the code and stood in the foyer wondering where she
could be. He'd told her he wouldn't make dinner so maybe
she'd gone out by herself. But dinner alone in a restaurant
. . . that wasn't Gia.

He stepped down the hall to the kitchen to see if she'd
left him a note but stopped cold when he found one of
Lyle's Ifasen brochures on the counter instead.

Aw, no. She'd promised she'd stay away from that place.
Had she . . . ?

He picked up the phone, hit REDIAL, and eventually heard
Lyle's outgoing message.

That was it. She was heading for Menelaus Manor. Could
be there already.

Jack dashed for the front door. He didn't like this. Gia
wouldn't break a promise without a damn good reason.
Something was very wrong.

9

Gia hesitated when she saw a shadowy form standing halfway down the walk to the Kentons' front door. The sky
was moonless but the house was lit up like they were
throwing a party. The figure was too small for Jack or Lyle
or Charlie.

Then she spotted the dog.

Oh, no, Gia thought. Not her again.

"Please stay away," the woman said in a voice at once
rapid-fire and lilting. In the faint wash of light from the
house Gia could see she wore an orange sari tonight. Her
nostril ring had been replaced by a tiny jeweled stud. "I

have warned you before but you did not heed. This time you must listen."

Gia's annoyance got the better of her as she edged past. She needed to be in that house, not out here listening to a woman who probably wasn't all there.

"What's your problem? Why are you telling me this?"

Her silver-ringed fingers twisted the long braid hanging over her shoulder. "Because that house is dangerous for you."

"So you've said, but nothing's happened."

The woman's black eyes bore into her. "If you won't think of yourself, think of the baby you carry."

Gia stumbled back a step, shaken. "What?" How could she know? "Who *are* you?"

"I'm your mother." She spoke flatly, as if stating the obvious. "A mother knows these things."

That clinched it. Gia's mother was in Iowa and this woman was crazy. She had her going for a moment with that remark about the baby . . . a wild lucky guess.

"Thank you for your concern," she said, backing away toward the house. Never confront a crazy person. "But I've really got to get inside."

The woman stepped closer. "Oh, please," she said, her voice thick with anguish. She clutched her braid with both hands now, twisting it back and forth. She seemed genuinely upset. "Don't go in there. Not tonight."

Gia slowed her retreat as something within her cried out to listen. But she couldn't stay out here when Jack was inside, possibly hurt. She forced herself to turn and run up the steps to the porch. The front door stood open. Without knocking she hurried inside and closed it behind her and felt . . .

. . . welcome.

How odd. Almost as if the house were overjoyed to see her. But that wasn't possible. Just relief from escaping that crazy woman.

"Hello?" she called. "Jack? Lyle? Charlie?"

Then Gia heard the music. She couldn't catch the words

but it sounded upbeat and soulful. And it was coming from the cellar. She hurried down the steps but stopped when she saw the devastation. It looked like a bomb had gone off—the paneling and concrete floor had been torn to pieces and scattered; random holes had been dug into the dirt beneath.

And then she saw Charlie, huddled against the far wall. He looked terrified and was gesturing to her. His mouth worked, forming words, but he wasn't speaking. What was he trying to tell her? He looked crazy. First the Indian lady, now Charlie. Had everyone gone mad?

"Charlie? Where's Jack?"

The music stopped. And with that Charlie started to speak.

"Gia!" He pointed to her left. "She—it's here!"

Gia stepped into the cellar and gasped when she noticed the little girl.

"Tara?" After visiting her father, seeing her photo collection, hearing her story, Gia felt as if she knew this child. "It's really you, isn't it."

She nodded her blond head. "Hello, mother."

Mother? There seemed to be a lot of confusion about that going around.

"No, I'm not your mother."

"Oh, I know."

"Then why—?"

Charlie pushed away from the wall and edged closer. "Get out, Gia! She been waiting on you."

"That's okay, Charlie." Despite the cellar's cool dampness, Gia felt warm and welcome. "I'm not afraid. Where's Jack?"

"He and Lyle left me here alone." He pointed to Tara. "Then that showed up."

"My mother . . ." Tara frowned. "She doesn't think about me anymore."

"That's because she can't, honey. She—"

"I know." The words came out flat, with no feeling.

Charlie had reached her side now. He gripped her arm

with a cold, trembling hand. His voice sounded ragged, barely above a whisper.

"We gotta get outta here. If she let us."

Gia looked at Tara. "You're not holding us here, are you?"

The child smiled wistfully. "I'd like the mother to stay for a while."

"Not right!" Charlie said. "Dead and living don't mix!"

"Why don't you go," Gia said. "I'll stay."

"Nuh-uh." Charlie shook his head. "Not without you, I ain't. This is bad—*she* bad. Can't you feel it?"

Gia felt sorry for him. He was so frightened he was shaking. Oddly, she felt perfectly calm. Hard to believe she was talking to the ghost of a murdered child and didn't feel the least bit afraid. Because she knew this poor lost soul, understood what she needed.

"I'll be fine."

He shook his head again. "We both go or we both stay."

"Tell you what." She took Charlie's arm and led him toward the steps. "We'll both go up and then I'll come back down, just for a few minutes."

But as they reached the steps Gia stopped—not because she wanted to, but because something was blocking her way. An invisible wall.

With a chill of foreboding she turned. "Tara?"

"You can't go," Tara said with a pout. "I need the mother to stay."

That's the heart of it, Gia thought. She wants a mother—*needs* a mother.

She felt the nurturer within her responding, reaching out to quell that need. But she had to be realistic here.

Gia spoke softly, slowly. "Look, Tara, I know you want your mother, but she can't come. I can't take her place, but if there's something I can—"

Tara shook her head. "No. You don't understand. I don't want a mother."

Gia stared at her, baffled. "Then what—?"

And then everything changed. A wave of cold slammed

through the air as Tara's expression shifted from sweet innocence to rage. She bared her teeth.

"I want to *be* a mother."

The earth suddenly gave way under Gia's feet. She screamed as she and Charlie tumbled into the black pit that opened beneath them.

10

As soon as Lyle stepped out of the taxi he sensed something was wrong.

Then he saw someone running toward him along the sidewalk. He tensed, ready to jump back into the cab until he recognized Jack.

"Hey, Jack. What's the hurry?"

Jack stopped before him, puffing, but not too heavily. "Gia. I think she's here."

"Why would—?" He stopped himself. "Never mind. Let's go see."

As they walked toward the house Lyle said, "You run all the way from Manhattan?"

"Just from the subway."

"Why didn't you take a cab?"

"Subway's faster this hour."

Lyle looked at Jack and noticed that his outline was no longer blurred. Maybe his strange new awareness was gone, or maybe it only worked in the house. But the nearer Lyle drew to the house, the stronger the sense of wrongness. He couldn't place his finger on it until—

"I'll be damned!" He stopped, staring.

Jack stopped beside him. "What?"

"The windows . . . the doors . . . they're closed!" He laughed. "This is great! We can put on the AC now."

"I don't like it," Jack said, moving again.

"Why not? Maybe it means whatever's been there has gone home."

"I doubt it."

Lyle followed Jack, saw him go to step up onto the front porch, then fall back.

"What the—?"

Lyle came up beside him. "What happened? Slip?"

And then Lyle could go no further. He stared at his foot, stranded in midair halfway to the first porch step. A chill ran down his back as he kicked his shoe forward, putting some weight behind it, but it didn't get any farther than before.

"Oh, man!" he said as icy fingers clawed his gut. "Oh, man, oh, man, oh, man! What's this shit?"

"I don't know," Jack said.

He threw a punch at the air but his fist came to a screaming halt in midair. Lyle tried the same. Pain shot through his shoulder as his hand stopped short at about the same plane as Jack's.

It wasn't like hitting a wall. It wasn't like hitting anything. No impact. His hand simply . . . stopped. And no matter how hard he pushed it wouldn't advance a millimeter farther.

Lyle glanced at Jack and saw him backing up, searching the ground. He bent, came up with a rock, and threw it. Lyle watched it arc toward the house, then stop in midair and drop to the ground.

With a guttural roar Jack hurled himself at the front steps, only to stop short and stagger back.

"Easy, Jack."

"Gia's in there!"

"You don't know that."

"I do! Damn! This is what Tara was after all along—to get Gia alone in there."

"But she's not alone. Char—" Lyle's heart tripped, skipped a beat. "Oh, shit. Charlie's in there too. What do you think's happening?"

"Don't know, but it can't be good if she's got the place sealed up." He started for the side of the house. "Let's see if this goes all the way around."

It did. They circled the house, punching at its windows and rear door, throwing rocks at it. Anyone seeing them had to think they were drunk and locked out. They called for Gia and Charlie, but no one answered.

Then they came to the garage—and walked right in. But they couldn't reach the door from the garage to the house.

Lyle leaned against the impenetrable air and felt sick. This couldn't be—*shouldn't* be. What was happening to the world?

"Jack . . ."

His face was reddening with the effort of trying to force a broom handle through the barrier. "Gets to you, doesn't it. Down is up, up is down, immutable laws get broken, things you always thought impossible aren't." With a grunt of frustration he tossed the broom across the garage. "Welcome to my world."

Lyle spotted a ladder leaning against the wall. "Hey, if we can't get through it, maybe we can get over it."

"Do not waste your time," said a woman's voice. "You cannot."

Lyle turned and saw a Hindu woman in an orange sari. Her dark eyes, and those of the big German shepherd standing beside her, were on Jack.

"Why not?" Lyle said.

"Because it goes up far."

"How far?" Jack said,

"Forever."

Who was this lady? Where'd she come from?

"How do you know so much about this?" Lyle asked.

"I know."

The way she said it, Lyle believed her.

"You've got to do better than that," Jack said.

He took a step toward her but stopped when the dog growled.

Her eyes flashed at him. "Have I not warned you about

this house and its dangers for you and your woman? Have I not? And neither of you listened!"

Why didn't I know about this? Lyle thought.

"Yeah, you did. And obviously we should have. So what? I-told-you-so doesn't solve the problem. If you know so much, what's going on in there?"

"Your woman and her baby are in grave danger."

Baby? Was Gia pregnant? Lyle saw Jack blanch. He looked frightened, something Lyle hadn't thought possible.

"How do—? Never mind. What kind of danger? Why?"

"The *why* does not matter because the *why* has changed. But the danger is mortal."

Lyle's mouth went dry. "Charlie too?"

She didn't look at him. "Anyone in that house now is in danger."

How could she know all this—any of it? She could be wrong or just plain crazy.

Jack seemed to have bought it. He was turning in a circle, his hands raised and balled into fists. He looked ready to explode.

"Got to be a way in. Got to!"

The woman's eyes remained fixed on Jack. She paid Lyle no more heed than a piece of furniture.

"You cannot break in, and no one inside can break out. You must be *allowed* in or out."

"Allowed? How do we arrange that?"

"I do not know for certain. Perhaps by offering the entity something she wants more than your woman."

Jack said nothing, just stood and stared at the woman.

"Name it," Lyle told her. This was Charlie, his brother at risk here too. The sky was the limit. "Whatever it is we can use to trade, name it and we'll do our damnedest to get it."

"It's not an it," Jack said. He started for the door with a strange light in his eyes, almost like glee, yet disturbingly malevolent. It made Lyle want to back away. "It's a he. And I know who. Let's go."

Lyle had a sudden inspiration as to who that "he" might be and was very glad he was not him.

11

"You all right?" Charlie said from where he sprawled next to her.

Gia had landed on her left leg harder than her right and it hurt. She pulled it under her and tried to stand, leaning against the dirt wall at her back for support. It held.

"I think so." She brushed off her jeans. "How about you?"

Charlie stood easily. "Fine."

Light filtered down from above. Gia looked up. She could see the panels of the cellar ceiling, but all around her was dirt. She and Charlie had dropped into a well-like pit maybe a dozen feet deep and half that across.

She fought a surge of panic as the walls seemed to tilt toward her and move in. She closed her eyes and clenched her teeth to let the moment pass. She'd never been claustrophobic, but she'd never been tossed into an oubliette before either.

"Tara?" she called. Her fear-dry throat made it sound more like a croak than a name. "Tara!"

No reply.

"Tara, why are you doing this to us? We never hurt you. We can help bring your killer to justice. Please let us out!"

Only silence from above.

Gia's heart pounded as she ran her hands over the smooth circular wall. The dirt was hard packed, with no ridges or depressions for handholds.

She glanced at Charlie. His wild-eyed gaze darted up and around and back. He licked his lips as he placed his sneakered right foot against the wall, then stretched out his arms and placed both hands against the opposite side. When he raised his left foot and put it next to his right, he was arched across the pit. Now he started inching his hands and feet upward toward light and freedom.

But after half a foot or so his hands slipped off the wall and he fell, landing on all fours like a cat. Without a word he tried again, with the same result.

He stood and leaned against the wall, head back, eyes closed, breathing hard.

"Lord, give me the strength for this, I pray you. Please."

He tried again and this time advanced maybe a foot before falling. He sat hunched against the wall, knees up, head down, the picture of dejection.

"If the walls was just one foot closer—half a foot, even—I could slam it. I know I could."

"It's okay," Gia said softly. "You gave it your best shot."

"Not good enough." He stood and looked at her. "We trapped."

Gia glanced up and thought about standing on Charlie's shoulders. But even then she'd be short of the upper rim.

"Maybe Tara will get us out when she's ready."

"When's that gonna be? And why we down here anyway?"

Gia shrugged. "I don't know. Maybe she just wanted us out of the way."

"That don't make no sense."

Gia had to agree, but did a ghost have to make sense? Look at what she'd said before the ground opened up: *I want to* be *a mother.* What did that mean? How could she be a mother? She was dead. But that wouldn't stop her from wanting what she couldn't have, Gia supposed.

"At least we're not hurt." She pointed to her shoulder bag lying on the dirt floor. She'd dropped it when they fell. "And we won't go hungry because I have a couple of power bars in my—" She dropped to her knees beside the bag as she remembered. "Oh, God. My cell phone!"

She rummaged through the jumbled contents and pulled out the phone, but when she turned it on, nothing happened. No light, no beep, no power.

"Damn, it's dead."

Charlie knelt beside her. "Like I said. We trapped. She wouldn't let us up the steps and I bet she ain't lettin' nobody down. All we got left is prayer."

"And hope that Jack figures out I'm here." Gia cursed herself for not leaving him a note, but she thought she was going *to* him. "Once he knows, he'll get us out."

Charlie looked at her. "You say that like it a done deal."

"In a way it is. He's inventive and relentless and he won't quit on me. Ever." The simple truth of that was a balm on her nerves.

"That ain't no done deal. That's just a hope."

Gia smiled. "No . . . it's faith." She looked around at the high dirt walls. "But we ought to be trying *something* to get ourselves out." She reached out and touched the pin on Charlie's sweatshirt. "wwjd. Not a bad idea in a situation like this."

"True that. What Would Jesus Do?"

"I was thinking more along the lines of What Would Jack Do?" A thought occurred to her. "Where's Lyle, by the way?"

"Out mackin' some ladies group. Shoulda been back by now."

"I'd guess you can count on him doing what he can to get you out of here as well, right? WWLD—What Would Lyle Do?"

Charlie looked away. "Anything he could. He never let me down before, not 'bout to start now." Gia heard a catch in his voice. "More'n he can say for me."

"I don't understand."

"Long story."

"I think we've got time."

He shook his head and looked ashamed. "Nuh-uh."

As Charlie folded his hands and bowed his head to pray, Gia scanned the walls again looking for something, anything. She remembered Jack asking her once if she wanted to take up wall climbing. She'd laughed him off. The last thing she wanted to do with her spare time was cling to a wall like a bug. Now she wished she'd taken him up on it. Not that this wall offered much in the way of handholds, but at least—

What was that?

She spotted something shiny up on the wall. There. About six inches or so above her head. Keeping her eyes fixed on the spot, she reached up and touched it. Something hard stuck in the dirt. It felt metallic. She dug her fingernails into the dirt around it, clearing some away, but it was too hard.

"Charlie? I've found something."

He was beside her in a flash. "What? Where?"

"It's some kind of metal."

Charlie's extra height put him at eye level with it. "Look like brass or copper. Probably just scrap from when the place built."

"Let's dig it out. Who knows? Maybe it's something we can use."

"A'ight. Let's see."

As Charlie dug with his hands, Gia knelt and dug into her shoulder bag again. Finally she found it.

"Here," she said, holding up a metal nail file. "Try this."

He took it and began stabbing at the dirt, loosening it and then digging it out with his fingers. Soon it became clear that they'd found some sort of metal bar. When he'd exposed enough of it, Charlie grabbed the end and began wiggling it back and forth.

"Here we go!" he said as dirt began flying everywhere. "We got it now!"

Suddenly it came free and he stumbled back, falling against the opposite wall. He shook off the dirt and held up what he'd unearthed.

Gia gasped. "A cross!"

A cross with no top piece worth mentioning. Exactly like the crosses left on the wall after the whirlpool had receded. This one's crosspiece was slightly bent and twisted and looked like nickel or silver; the upright was brass, or something that looked very much like it.

Charlie stared at it. "Gotta be one of the tau crosses from the blocks in the wall. They musta buried them after they pried them out. But we found one!" He held it high. "It's a sign!"

"It's a digging tool!"

"Dig? I think we deep enough already."

"Not down—in. We can use this to dig footholds and handholds so we can climb out of here."

Charlie grinned. "Why didn't I think of that?" He gripped the base and swung the cross at the wall. The cross-piece dug in and sent dirt flying. "Oh, yeah! We on our way. We beat this ghost yet."

12

"Shit!" Jack rose and stepped back from the door. "Latch won't budge. We'll have to do this the hard way."

The hard way? Lyle had thought they were already doing it the hard way. Here he was standing in his socks on a rooftop in SoHo while the guy he was with tried to break into the building below. He felt exposed, as if he were on an open-air stage. At least there was no moon, but plenty of light leaked in from the city around them. All someone had to do was look out a window in one of the higher buildings nearby and see them trying to jimmy the lock on the roof door. A 911 call would get them arrested for criminal trespass, attempted B and E, and who knew what else.

Still, better to be caught now than after they'd picked up what they'd come for; kidnapping was a capital offense.

Half an hour ago Jack had left Lyle at a bar named Julio's; he'd returned a few minutes later in a different set of clothes and carrying a gym bag that clinked and rattled with the metallic sound of tools. They'd driven here in Jack's

car and parked outside. Jack had stood across the street
from the building and studied it for a few minutes, then
moved on. Half a block down they'd sneaked up a fire
escape and traveled across three other roofs to reach this
one. Sure, easy for Jack; he was dressed for this sort of
thing. Lyle was still in a dress shirt and suit pants—and
black leather shoes no less. Jack had made him take them
off when they reached this particular roof.

So, if what they'd been doing was the easy way, what
was the hard way?

Jack lifted his jersey and began unwinding a length of
nylon cord from around his waist. Where'd that come
from?

He handed Lyle the free end of the rope and whispered,
"Tie this to that vent pipe over there."

Lyle was more used to giving orders than taking them,
but this was Jack's show, so he deferred to his expertise.
Jack seemed to know what he was doing. With somebody
else this sortie might have turned into a male-bonding experience, but Jack had changed after leaving the house. He
went silent and into himself. The easygoing manner had
fallen away, replaced by cool crisp efficiency behind an
impenetrable hardshell exterior. A man on a mission, determined to bring home the goods at whatever cost. Lyle
found him a little scary. As if he'd locked all the gentler
human emotions in a small back room, leaving his dark and
raw side unfettered.

"Tie why?"

"I'm going over the side."

Lyle's chest tightened. He stepped to the parapet and
peeked over. He stood atop a three-story building. Falling
from here would be like jumping out a fourth-story window. A surge of vertigo gripped him and threatened to pull
him over, but he hung on until the spinning passed. He
expected to see a brick wall; instead he saw smooth beveled
surfaces and ornate columns.

He turned back to Jack. "You're crazy. There's nothing
to hold on to."

"Yeah. These old ironclads can be a bitch."

Lyle felt a seismic tremor start from his center and pulse out to his extremities.

"I don't think I can do this, Jack." Actually he was absolutely positive he could not go over that ledge.

Jack gave him a hard look. "You backing out on me?"

"No, it's just . . . heights. I'm—"

"You thought you were going over that wall?" He shook his head. "Not a chance. You're here to watch the rope and make sure that pipe doesn't start to bend."

Lyle sighed with relief. That he could do.

Jack pulled on a pair of work gloves and took the rope from Lyle. He tied it around a steel pipe jutting vertically from the roof, tested the knot, glided to the parapet, and sat on the edge.

"How do we know this guy's even home?"

"We don't. But the third floor—where I assume the bedrooms would be—is dark. The second floor is all lit up and a television is on."

"How can you tell?"

Jack looked impatient. "Different kind of light. And besides, he hasn't been very mobile since our last meeting." He glanced down. "Here's the plan . . ."

Lyle listened, nodded a few times, then helped Jack ease over the edge. Shifting his attention between Jack and the vent pipe, Lyle watched him ease down the iron facade and stop next to the window directly below. Further down, Lyle saw passing cars and strolling pedestrians.

Please don't look up.

Jack placed a foot on the ledge and eased up the window. Great. It was unlocked. But then, who locks a third-story window? Especially in summer.

Jack disappeared through the opening and seconds later the free end of the rope sailed back out. Lyle quickly hauled it up and untied the other end from the pipe. He coiled the rope as he padded back to the roof door, then shoved it into Jack's gym bag. As instructed, he pulled on a pair of latex gloves and was ready and waiting when Jack opened the door from the inside.

As Jack exchanged his work gloves for a latex pair, he whispered, "Here's where it could get dicey. If Bellitto's alone, we're golden. But if that big guy I told you about is here . . ."

He reached into the bag and pulled out a pistol with a dark matte finish. Lyle didn't know much about guns, but he knew a semi-automatic when he saw one, and assumed it was a 9 mm. And he knew that fat cylinder stuck on the end of the barrel was a silencer.

The sight of it, and the casual way Jack handled it, made him queasy.

It had seemed like such a good idea back at the house, a simple, straightforward plan: Trade Tara's killer for Charlie and Gia. But the farther they'd traveled from the sur-reality of Menelaus Manor into the reassuring hard reality of Manhattan, the more the idea of kidnapping a child mur-derer—*suspected* child murderer; they had no real proof—from his own apartment seemed downright insane.

And now . . . a gun.

Lyle swallowed. "You're not really going to use that, are you?"

Jack's voice was flat. "I'll use whatever I have to. He's no good to us dead, so I want him alive, if that's what you're worried about. But I'll do what needs to be done to get him." His cold dark eyes, the ones that had seemed such a mild brown this morning, bored into Lyle. "Maybe you should wait here."

"No." That was Charlie trapped in that house back there. His brother. His blood. Lyle would help Jack and worry about law and morality later. "I've come this far. I'm in."

Jack nodded once. "Want the Glock?"

Glock? Oh, the gun.

"I'd better not."

"Well, no way you're going in empty-handed."

He reached back into the gym bag and came up with something Lyle recognized: a black leather sap.

"Comfortable with this?"

Lyle could only nod. He wasn't comfortable at all, and doubted he could crack that weighted end against anybody's skull, no matter who they were, but he took the heavy thing and stuck it in his pocket.

Next Jack pulled out a roll of duct tape and began tearing off strips, some long, some short. These he stuck to the front of his jersey.

Then they were ready. Jack worked the slide on his pistol, picked up the bag, and started down the stairwell.

"Hey, wait," Lyle whispered as something occurred to him. "Shouldn't we be wearing masks? You know, like stockings or something?"

"Why?"

The reason was so obvious he was surprised Jack hadn't thought of it. He seemed to have thought of everything else.

"So this guy doesn't see our faces."

"Why should we care?"

"Because what if Tara doesn't want to trade? Then we're left with a guy we've kidnapped who knows what we look like. He can go to the cops—"

"He won't be going to the cops."

"Why? Because he's a child killer and he's got more to hide than we do? Maybe. But we're taking him to *my* house, not yours. He'll know where *I* live, not—"

"Won't matter what he knows."

"It'll matter to me, damn it."

Jack looked at him, his eyes colder and darker than ever, and spoke very slowly. "It . . . won't . . . matter."

The full meaning of the words struck Lyle like a runaway D train.

"Hey, listen, Jack, I don't think I want to be part of—"

Jack turned away. "You won't be. Not your problem. Come on. Let's bag this mutant."

Jack started down the stairs. Lyle held back, weighted down by the cold lump of lead that had formed in his stomach. But the thought of Charlie spurred him to follow.

At the bottom of the stairwell they entered a dark hallway

lined with a number of doors, all closed. No light seeped around them. Cooler here. Air-conditioning doing its job. The smell of fried onions in the air. Light filtered up from a stairway at its far end, and with it the sound of canned laughter—a sit-com on the TV.

Jack handed the bag to Lyle and moved toward the stairs with his pistol before him. Lyle followed. At the top step he motioned Lyle to wait, then he descended the stairs one at a time with excruciating slowness, keeping his sneakered feet against the wall at the very edge of each tread. He reached the bottom and disappeared for a moment, then returned to motion Lyle down. Walking in his socks—his noisy leather-soled shoes were stowed in the gym bag— Lyle followed Jack's example, staying near the wall end of the treads.

At the bottom he looked around. They stood in a small, spare dining room. Dinner plates still cluttered the mahogany table. The kitchen to the left, and another room beside it; Lyle guessed from the glowing computer screen that it was some sort of office. The living room lay to the right; the TV sounds came from there.

Lyle jumped as a phone rang in the office. He looked to Jack to see what to do but Jack was already moving like a cat toward the living room. He reached the entrance at the same time another man dressed in gray suit pants and a white shirt with French cuffs came out. He was older, a six-footer with pale skin and dark receding hair, and he was moving carefully, as if movement was uncomfortable. This had to be the man they'd come for, the Eli Bellitto Jack had told him about.

Jack shoved the silencer under the man's chin and grabbed a handful of hair at the back of his head, yanking it back to expose his throat.

"Hello, Eli," he said in a low, harsh voice. "Molest any little boys today?"

Lyle didn't think he'd ever seen anyone more terrified. The man looked ready to collapse from shock and fear as Jack backed him into the living room.

"W-what? How—?"

Lyle, still carrying the gym bag, followed at a distance. In the living room a big Sony—a thirty-something-incher— was playing a *Seinfeld* rerun.

"Down! On the floor!"

Bellitto's face twisted in pain as Jack kicked the back of his knees, sending him down to a praying position.

"No! Please! I'm hurt!"

The *Seinfeld* audience laughed.

"That's the least of your worries," Jack said, his voice still low.

He pushed Bellitto face down on the bare hardwood floor, then half straddled him, pressing a knee into the small of his back. Bellitto groaned in pain.

Lyle kept reminding himself that this creep had killed Tara Portman and who knew how many other kids, and that Jack was closer to this situation than he—after all, he'd seen the guy snatch a kid firsthand. He was playing rough, but if anyone deserved it . . .

Jack pulled a short strip of duct tape from his shirt and slapped it over the man's mouth. Then he looked up at Lyle.

"Over here."

Lyle hesitated, then approached. Jack handed him the pistol.

He winked at Lyle. "He tries anything cute, shoot him in the ass."

The *Seinfeld* audience laughed again.

"Yeah." Lyle cleared his throat. His saliva felt like glue. "Sure thing. Which cheek?"

Jack smiled—a quick one, the first Lyle had seen to-night—and gave him a thumbs up. Then he pulled Bel-litto's arms back and used the longer strips of tape to bind his hands. He stood and held out his hand; Lyle gladly returned him the pistol.

"One down." Jack looked around. "Maybe one more to go. Maybe not."

Lyle hoped not. Barely thirty seconds had passed since

the phone ring, but in that brief period he knew he'd gone from flimflam man to class-A or -B felon. He wasn't made for the rough-and-tumble scene, for guns and violence. It had him shaking from his fingernails to his spine.

Jack gestured with his pistol toward Bellitto. "Help me get him up."

They each grabbed the trussed man under an arm and lifted him into a soft, cream-colored chair. Bellitto winced in pain but Jack seemed unmoved.

Lyle grabbed his shoes from the gym bag and slipped them on. No further need for stealth that he could see, and it felt good to have something on his feet again besides socks.

"Anybody else here, Eli?"

When Bellitto didn't respond Jack leaned close, grabbed his hair, and pulled his head up so that they were nose to nose.

"Where's your buddy Minkin? Is he around? You can nod or shake, Eli. *Now*."

Bellitto shook his head.

"You expecting him or anyone soon?"

Another head shake.

Jack shoved him back. "Right. Like I'd believe you." He turned to Lyle. "Get out your sap and stay close to him. He tries to get up, clock him down."

Lyle didn't want to be left alone here with this man. "Where're you going?"

"To check the other rooms. Just to be sure. I've got this bad feeling Minkin's hiding someplace, maybe upstairs. I don't want to leave him behind if he's here. And while I'm at it, I'll see if I can find something to wrap up this garbage." He looked around the bare living room. "Jeez, Eli. You ever hear of a rug?"

As Jack stalked away, pistol at ready, Lyle pulled the sap from his pocket and took a position behind Bellitto where he wouldn't have to see his cold eyes. He was glad the man's mouth was taped so he couldn't talk or plead. Did he have any idea this was his last night alive?

Suddenly Lyle heard a hoarse cry—Jack's voice—echo from the other end of the house.

Oh, shit, what now?

He tightened his sweaty grip on the handle of the sap as his heartbeat lunged into triple time. Damn, he should have taken that gun when Jack offered it.

And then Jack flew into the room, face white, teeth bared, the pistol in one hand, a sheet of paper in the other.

Lyle cringed at the look in his eyes. He hadn't thought a human could look like that—like death itself.

He jumped back as Jack backhanded the pistol across Bellitto's head and held the paper before him.

"What *is* this? Who sent it?" He dropped the sheet into Bellitto's lap and ripped the tape from his mouth, then he lowered the pistol till the muzzle was poised over one of the man's legs. "*Now*, Bellitto, or I start sending your knees to hell, one piece at a time till I hear what I want!"

13

"Much as I'd like to see Jack," Charlie said, "I hope he don't pop in right now. This might be just a leetle hard to explain."

Gia laughed. "I wouldn't even bother. I'd just get on his case about what took him so long."

Gia's feet rested in a foothold about four feet off the floor of their prison and her arm ached as she dug a new hole above her head in the dirt wall. Charlie was behind and below her, holding her in place by pushing against the backs of her upper thighs. He'd dug out the first four holes in record time—the ability to do something to help them out had galvanized him into a digging machine—stretching as far as he could for the last; then it was Gia's turn. Somebody needed to use the foot- and handholds to dig the next ones. Since she was smaller and lighter, it was easier for Charlie to hold her up.

"God, this dirt is hard."

She kept her eyes closed and her face averted to avoid the loose earth that rained down as she stabbed the cross into the wall. She was covered with dirt; her short blond hair was especially full of it; she felt gritty and grimy, but she kept jabbing away. They were making progress, they were getting out.

The cross clunked against something in the hole. Another swing, another clunk, with very little dirt falling out.

"Uh-oh. I think I'm up against a rock."

"You got it deep enough for a foot yet?"

Gia gauged the opening to be three inches deep, tops. "Not yet."

"See if you can dig around it."

"What if it's too big?"

She felt Charlie shift behind her.

"Here. Stand on my shoulders and see if you can get a look. If it too big we shift the hole to one side. If it ain't, see if you can yank it out."

"You're sure?"

"Do it. Just don't go droppin' it on my dome."

Clinging to the shallow depression she'd been digging, Gia lifted one hesitant foot onto Charlie's shoulder, then the other. Straightening her knees, she raised her head to the level of the hole and looked in—

—to find the empty sockets of a child's skull staring back at her.

Gia let out a scream of shock and revulsion and lurched back. She lost her grip and started to fall. Terrified, she flailed her arms about but could find nothing to hold on to. Somehow Charlie managed to catch her and save her from injury.

"What's wrong?"

Gia sobbed. "A child's skeleton. Maybe Tara herself. I hate this!" she shouted, letting the tears flow. She thought of Vicky, how except for luck that might have been her skull. "This shouldn't happen to anyone, especially not a child!" She wiped at her tears and the back of her hand came away muddy. "What kind of monster—?"

The ground shook then. Just a little, but enough to bring her around.

Charlie was turning, looking up at the surrounding walls. "You feel that?"

Gia nodded. "I sure—"

A section of the wall near the top broke free then and tumbled onto them. Gia coughed and gagged as she inhaled a cloud of dirt. Another load of earth landed on her back, knocking her to her knees.

"It's collapsing! We'll be buried!"

The cascade continued as Charlie grabbed her arm and pulled her to her feet. "Keep moving your legs! Stay on top of it as it falls!"

It was like being under a dirt waterfall, but Gia saw what he meant. As long as too much didn't fall at once, they had a chance of—

She cried out as something cold wrapped around her ankle. She looked down and saw a small hand, ghostly pale, clutching her. She tried to tug away but couldn't break free. The little fingers held fast, like a steel manacle.

Charlie gave a shout. Gia turned to see a similar hand gripping his foot. The dirt was starting to pile up around them and his expression was frantic as he tried to yank free.

"It's Tara!"

Charlie stared at her. "Why? We never did nothin' to her."

"Tara!" Gia cried, still trying to pull free from the relentless grip on her ankle. "Tara, stop it! We're not your enemy!"

She still clutched the cross. In desperation she swung it at the little hand, striking it just above the wrist. It sliced through the ghost flesh with no more resistance than air, and then . . .

The hand disappeared. She was free.

"Charlie! The cross! It breaks her grip!"

Charlie's ankle was buried. Gia crouched beside him and dug through the dirt till she saw the hand. She rammed the cross against it and the hand disappeared.

"Praise Jesus!" Charlie cried as he jumped away from the spot where he'd been held. "Nothing can stand against the power of His cross!"

But just then she felt another hand grab her left ankle, and still another grab her right. She glanced at Charlie and saw that a pair of arms had snaked out of the wall to trap his lower legs.

The dirtfall doubled in volume.

Gia didn't hesitate. She slashed at one little hand and then the other. As soon as their grip was broken she lurched across the pit to help Charlie. She slipped and the weight of the falling dirt knocked her flat. For one panic-seared moment she thought she'd never get up, but she forced herself to her feet and reached Charlie's side. Choking and gasping, she slashed at the hands. But no sooner was he free than they both were gripped again—by three or four hands each this time.

"She's like a hydra!" Gia shouted as she cut at the new hands—hers and Charlie's—but new ones appeared as soon as she severed the old ones.

"Don't know 'bout no hydras," Charlie said, his voice thick. "But I don't see us gettin' outta this alive. Leastways not together."

Gia glanced at him. His expression looked stricken, as if he were about to cry.

"It's okay, Charlie. We'll make it. We've just got to keep—"

His expression hardened, as if he'd come to a decision. He stuck out his hand. "Gimme the cross."

"I'm doing okay with it."

"No, you ain't." He grabbed her arm. His eyes had a strange look. "Not nearly. Gimme."

"Charlie? What are you doing?" Gia leaned away from him but he was stronger and had a longer reach. He caught hold of the cross and ripped it from her grasp. "Charlie!"

Without a word he bent and began hacking at the hands imprisoning her left leg. As soon as that was free, he grabbed it, lifted it, and placed her foot on his back. Then he went to work on her right leg. When that was free, he lifted her and placed her on the dirt which had now piled to above his knees.

As soon as Gia hit the dirt, new arms emerged like snakes and grabbed her. Charlie immediately went to work on these.

The dirtfall redoubled. Gia could barely see him.

"What about you?" Her throat constricted as she realized what he was up to. "Charlie, you've got to get your feet free!"

"Too late," he said without looking up. He was waist deep in the dirt and kept hacking away at the new hands as soon as they sprouted, allowing Gia to stay atop the rising level of dirt. "Can't get to 'em."

"You can if you do it now! We can both make it."

He shook his head. "Nuh-uh. Then we both be in the same sinkin' boat."

"No!" Gia couldn't, wouldn't let this happen. She began clawing at the dirt around his waist. "We'll take turns! We'll—"

A ghost hand shot up from the loose earth, gripping her wrist and jerking her down. She cried out as her face hit the dirt.

Charlie slashed at the hand, freeing her, then roughly shoved her back.

"See? See?" He was looking at her now and she could see tears in his eyes. His lips trembled as he spoke. "I know what I'm doin', okay? But I don't wanna do it for nothin'! Let it mean somethin', huh?"

"But Charlie—"

At that moment the dirtfall stopped.

Gia looked up, looked around, looked at Charlie. It had ceased as suddenly and mysteriously as it had started. Why?

"Praise the Lord!" Charlie sagged forward. The dirt had

piled up to the lower part of his chest. He cradled his head on his arms and spoke toward the ground. "He's delivered us from evil!"

Just then Gia felt the dirt shift under her, felt it change, become finer, grainier. It began to move, surging and flowing like thick fluid.

And rising.

"Oh, no!" Gia cried. "What's happening?"

Charlie straightened and began slashing at the soil as it rose to his armpits.

"Don't know! Please, God, stop it! Stop it!"

The dirt, though dry, was lapping at him like water, swallowing him, but Gia remained afloat, buoyed on the grainy swells. She cried out and grabbed his free hand, tugging on it, trying to pull him up to her level but he was anchored fast below.

As the soil reached his neck his wide terrified eyes found her, held her, pierced her. "Oh, please, oh, please, Lord, I don't wanna die!"

And then the dirt swirled into his open mouth and he coughed and choked and gagged and writhed, stretching his neck. Gia, crying and whimpering with terror, tugged on his arm but couldn't budge him. The dirt rose past his mouth and into his nostrils, and his eyes were wider, bulging, pleading, and then with a final surge the loose earth rose and engulfed his head, leaving only his raised arm in sight.

Gia screamed and dug at the dirt, frantically pawing at it like a dog as she tried to clear it away from his face.

"Charlie! Charlie, hang on!"

But it was like trying to dig through soup. It flowed around and through her fingers and immediately filled back in behind her hands. She could feel his face, touch his hair but couldn't clear away enough to see him. If only she had a hose or a pipe, something to feed him air until—

Suddenly Charlie's other hand broke the surface, still holding the cross. She grabbed the wrist and pulled, throwing her back into it, but nothing! Nothing!

And then as she gripped him she felt agonal tremors radiate through his arms and spread to his hands, saw the fingers straighten, stiffen, drop the cross, claw the air for an instant, then fall limp and still, twitch, then go still once more, and not move again.

"No!" Grief spilled through Gia like acid. She'd met Charlie only twice before and yet he'd given his life for her. She knelt and clutched his cooling hands and cried out in a long, drawn-out wail that trailed off into sobs. "No!"

"I'm sorry." Tara's voice.

Gia looked up. What had been a pit was now a smooth, shallow depression in the earth. Tara stood half a dozen feet away, staring at her, looking as sweet and innocent as ever, but not looking sorry at all.

"Why? This was a good man! He never hurt you or anyone else! How could you kill him?"

Tara stepped closer, her eyes fixed on Gia—not on her face, but her abdomen.

"Because he'd only be in the way."

Gia's grief chilled, sliding toward unease. "In the way . . . of what?"

"Of what happens next."

Crystals of ice formed in Gia's veins as she rose unsteadily to her feet.

"I don't understand."

Tara smiled. "Your baby becomes my baby."

14

"No-don't-please!" Bellitto cried, squirming in the chair as Jack pressed the tip of the silencer over his left knee. He stared down at the sheet of paper in his lap. "Please! I've never seen that before in my life!"

"Lie!"

"No! I swear!"

"Read it now then. You've got ten seconds."

The darkness within Jack pounded on the bars of its cage to be set free and let it pull the trigger and blow this puke's kneecap into the floor. But he held it back. Bellitto wasn't exactly a spring chicken. Didn't want to lose him to a heart attack or stroke.

Almost had a heart attack himself a moment ago when he'd walked into the office at the other end of the apartment. A small room, no place for a guy Minkin's size to hide, but Jack had checked the storage closet anyway. Empty. On his way out of the room he happened to glance at the sheet of paper lying in the fax machine's tray. His gaze skittered off the handwritten lines as he passed, and he was stepping through the door when one of the words he'd seen snagged in his brain, caught like a sheet of newspaper in a fence.

. . . Westphalen . . .

With a cry of alarm he'd leaped back to the machine, snatched up the sheet, and read:

Success! The ladys Visa records show a hefty charge to something called Pint-Size Picassos which turns out to be a summer camp right outside Monticello. I checked and the Westphalen package is there. All it needs is to be picked up and we're in business. A. can handle the job no sweat.

BURN THIS!

Jack read it again, then a third time, still not believing . . . Westphalen . . . Pint-Size Picassos . . . that was Vicky. Bellitto and his gang had their sights on Vicky!

How? Why? They couldn't possibly know Vicky's connection to him—they didn't know who he was!

Or did they?

He needed some answers.

Bellitto looked up from the note. "I don't know what this

is! I've never seen it before! It must be a mistake!"

"That does it." Pressed the silencer muzzle deeper into Bellitto's knee.

"Jesus, Jack!" Lyle, standing behind Bellitto, staring with wide, sick-scared eyes.

"Hey, I'm reasonable." Didn't want to get into gunplay here and now. Once it got started you never knew where it would take you. But he had to *know*. Had a feeling Bellitto was just a nudge away from opening up. "I'll let him choose which knee first."

Bellitto tried to squirm away. "No! Please! You must believe I've never seen it! Check the time at the top! It just came in! The fax had just rung and I was on my way to check it when you stopped me."

Grabbed the sheet and handed it to Lyle—didn't want to take his eyes off Bellitto. "True?"

Lyle squinted at the tiny print, then nodded. "Yeah. Transmission time was a couple of minutes ago." He dropped the note back onto Bellitto's lap. "Why are you all worked up about a package?"

All right. So Bellitto hadn't seen it. That didn't mean he didn't know anything about it. Jack raised the pistol and placed the muzzle over Bellitto's heart.

"Vicky Westphalen—what's she to you?"

Didn't expect Bellitto's reaction—his expression registered genuine shock. He glanced down at the sheet again.

Jack remembered then that Vicky's first name wasn't mentioned in the message. And Bellitto looked confused, as if trying to figure out how Jack knew it.

He doesn't know she's connected to me!

Then how the hell—?

Lyle leaned forward, looking at the message again over Bellitto's shoulder. "You mean this is about a kid? A kid you know?" He groaned in revulsion. "This is sick, man! This is really sick!"

Jack was thinking about how there'd be no more coincidences in his life and how this had pushed way beyond sick into vile and ugly.

And then he remembered the cop sniffing around Gia's place, asking about Vicky. Part of Eli's "circle"?

One way to find out.

He waved the fax in front of Bellitto. "This is from your cop friend, isn't it."

Bellitto stiffened and stared at Jack. His eyes answered.

"I know your whole circle, Eli."

Not quite, but the others were secondary. Especially now. He grabbed the tape and slammed it back over Bellitto's mouth.

"I've got to go."

Lyle blinked. "Go? Where?"

"The Catskills. Got to get to that camp and make sure Vicky's all right."

What if this wasn't the only machine this fax went to? Bellitto had talked about his "circle." That could mean any number in addition to Minkin. That was who the "A." probably referred to: Adrian Minkin. He could have received the same fax. Could be on his way now. Maybe picking up fellow members as he goes, like this cop, a whole crew of pervs stalking Vicky.

"You don't have to go!" Lyle said, sounding frantic. "You can call!"

"I know I can, but that's not enough."

He'd call right now, tell the camp Vicky's been threatened, to keep watch on her and not release her to anyone but her mother. Then he'd go up there and sit guard in the woods to make sure no one screwed up.

"But what about this guy? What do we do with him?"

"I'll help you load him into the car. You take him to the house and make the trade. Tell Gia to meet me at the camp and we'll bring Vicky home together." Caught Bellitto staring at him with puzzled eyes. Leaned closer to give him something to think about. "Yeah, that's right, Eli. We're trading you to Tara Portman for someone else." At least Jack hoped they were. "She's waiting at your old buddy Dmitri's house. Got something real special cooked up for you."

That ought to loosen his sphincters.

Now . . . find a phone. He'd seen one in that little office.

"Be right back," he told Lyle as he started away. He jabbed a finger toward Bellitto. "Don't let him budge an inch."

Lyle nodded. "All right, but hurry. We don't know how much time we've got."

Jack was halfway across the dining room when he heard a sound, caught a blur of motion from the stairs to his left. His guard was down but he managed to raise his hands fast enough and far enough to put the pistol between his head and the fireplace poker swung by a gorilla of a man. The gun spun away through the air. Jack stumbled back, knocking into the dining room table, scattering plates and utensils, then rolled to the side to dodge another two-handed poker swipe from Adrian Minkin.

15

Gia clutched her abdomen as the horror of what Tara wanted seeped through.

"My baby? No . . . you can't mean that."

Tara nodded and started floating toward her. "I do. I want that baby. I need that baby."

"No!"

Gia spotted the cross that had fallen from Charlie's hand. She stooped, grabbed it, held it up. She couldn't believe she was doing this. Like playing a scene from one of those corny old vampire movies Jack liked to watch.

Tara stopped. "Put that down."

"You're afraid! Afraid of the cross!"

"I'm not afraid of anything!" she said a little too quickly. "It's just . . ."

"Just what?"

"It's just that the crosses that were in these stones stayed too close to the wrong thing for a little too long. Centuries too long. They absorbed some."

"What does that mean? Absorbed what?"

Tara shook her head. "I don't know. Poison."

"Poison for you, maybe, but churches aren't poison to me."

"Church?" Tara's brow furrowed. "What makes you think that was in a church? It lined the wall of what you might call a prison."

Gia didn't understand, but at least she had a weapon, or at least a defense. She took a couple of deep breaths and tried to calm herself. She was only partly successful.

Gia took a step toward the stairs. "I'm leaving now. I'm going up those steps and out the front door."

And never coming back. Dear God, why hadn't she listened to Jack and stayed away from here?

Tara shook her head. "No, you're not."

Her calm confidence shook Gia, but she kept up a bold front.

"Watch me."

Keeping the cross straight-armed before her, she sidled to her right toward the stairs. Tara watched her calmly, making no move to halt her. When Gia reached the steps she stopped—she could go no further. As before, something like an invisible wall of cotton was blocking her. She thrust out the cross—that went through fine, but no matter how hard she pushed after it, she couldn't follow.

She turned and gasped when she saw Tara directly behind her. She held up the cross and Tara backed away.

"Let's be fair," the child said. "You can have other babies. I can't have any. Ever. Let me take yours and—"

"Don't even think about it! You're not even ten years old! What could—?"

"I'd be in my twenties now!" Anger distorted her features. "I want a child! I can't have one of my own, so I'll adopt yours!"

"How?" Gia cried. "This is insane!"

"No. Not insane. Very simple. If the baby dies here, within these walls, among these stones, she'll stay here. I can keep her."

"But she's not yours!"

Tara's voice rose to a scream that shook the earth beneath Gia's feet. "I DON'T CARE!"

Gia was finding it harder and harder to breathe. Tara . . . the shifting dirt . . . Charlie . . . the granite blocks . . . the strange cross in her hand . . . her baby . . .

"Tara, this isn't you."

The child face contorted. "What do you know about me? Nothing!"

"I talked to your father."

"He gave up on me, just like my mother."

"No! Your mother—"

"I know about my mother. She gave up first!"

Gia tried to think of a way to reach her. If not through her family, then what?

"Tara, you were loved. I saw the family pictures. You with your horse—"

A quick smile. "Rhonda."

"—and your brother."

A frown. "Little brat. What a loser he turned out to be."

"Tara, how can you be like this?" Every humane impulse and emotion seemed to have leached out of her. "Losing you destroyed their lives. That's how important you were. I can't believe you mean this."

"Believe it!" Cold rage disfigured her features. "I was ripped from my life and brought down here to this place where I was surrounded by thirteen men. One of them cut out my still-beating heart while the rest watched."

Gia's free hand flew to her mouth. "Oh, dear God!"

"Not one of them moved to stop him." Her tone was frigid, flat. "No one came to save me. After that they sliced my heart into thirteen pieces and ate them."

The horror of it pushed bile to the back of Gia's throat. "And you were awake . . . through it all?"

"No. I was drugged. But I know what was done. So don't tell me what's me and what's not. You may think you know me but you don't. I was a happy girl. I had my whole life ahead of me, endless opportunities. Now I have none."

"I'm sorry, Tara. But still . . ."

"The Tara you saw in those pictures is dead. Long dead. She died under that knife." She pulled open her blouse to reveal the empty bloody cavity of her chest. "The new Tara is heartless!"

Gia stumbled back a step. "But I never hurt you. Why do you want to hurt me?"

"I don't. I don't care about you. *It* wants you dead."

"It? What it?" All Gia could think of was Jack's Otherness.

"I don't know. I only know it brought me back to kill you."

Kill her . . . dear God, someone, something wanted her dead.

"Why?" What had she ever done?

"I don't know and I don't care. I'd be happy to leave you alive just for spite. All I want is your baby."

"But you tried to kill me, bury me like . . . like Charlie."

Gia bit back a sob. Oh, God, poor Charlie.

"I did. But then I realized that if you die here with your baby, you'll keep it. I'll never have it then."

"But the baby's just a clump of cells now. What would you do with—?"

"It would be *mine!* I would have something of my own then! I have nothing now!" Tara inched closer. Her voice edged toward a whine. "Come on, pretty lady. You can have another. Just let me reach inside you and squeeze, just once. You won't feel a thing. Then you can go."

Her hand darted forward but Gia slashed at it with the cross and Tara snatched it back.

"It's not fair!" Tara screamed. "You can have all the children you want and you won't give me one! I hate you!" She stepped back and cooled her mood like turning a switch. "All right. You won't put down that cross? Fine. I know a way to take it from you."

Tara disappeared, then popped into view a dozen feet away. Gia stood tense and ready, holding the cross before her, watching for a trick. Then she noticed movement to her left . . . Charlie's hands jutting up from the dirt . . . limp and cold and splayed when she'd left them . . . the fingers twitching now . . . stretching, clenching . . . rising from the earth . . .

16

Lyle jumped at what sounded like the cry of an enraged animal from the adjoining room. He heard the dining room table go over and then saw Jack fighting off a huge man swinging a poker. He glanced at the sap in his hand. He could help. In fact he damned well better help.

As Lyle started toward the fight, Bellitto shot out a leg and caught his ankle. Lyle stumbled but before he could regain his balance, Bellitto kicked him in the leg. Lyle went down and felt a blaze of pain in his back. Another kick. But how—?

He looked around and saw that Bellitto was up, standing over him, his face suffused with rage. Muffled screeches pushed against the tape across his mouth, air whistled through the flared nostrils above it.

He aimed another kick, at Lyle's stomach this time, but Lyle rolled and took it on his flank, groaning with the pain. He swore he heard a rib crack.

The next kick was aimed at Lyle's head and connected. The room went into a spin . . .

◈

"You!" Minkin screeched though his bared and clenched teeth. "You don't know how I've prayed for this moment!"

Jack's back pressed hard against the floor. The edge of a broken plate cut into his shoulder blade as Minkin straddled him, his huge hands wrapped around Jack's throat, thick thumbs trying to crush his larynx.

Jerk. Allowed himself to be distracted by the fax. The surprise attack plus his lack of conditioning over the past month had left him at a disadvantage. Managed to kick the poker out of Minkin's grasp, but during the close-in fighting that followed, the big man had put his greater size to full advantage.

Hoped his neck muscles held out. So far they'd resisted the pressure from Minkin's thumbs, but weren't going to outlast him. Kicked and twisted but the bigger man had him trapped under his weight. His Glock was out of sight, couldn't get to the Spyderco in his pocket or reach the backup .38 strapped to his ankle.

Vaguely aware of thuds, shouts, scuffling from the other room. Lyle?

Head felt swollen, as if about to explode. Running out of air. Minkin wasn't. Bastard had air to spare.

"So . . . this is the thief who strikes in the dark from behind . . . who cut up Eli and robbed me of a piece of my memory . . . this is the tough guy who thought he'd kill Eli and take over the Circle." He grinned. "You're not so tough. In fact, you're a puny piece of shit!"

Tried to peel the fingers away but couldn't get any leverage on them. Jabbed his own thumbs toward Minkin's eyes—kept the nails extra long for just this sort of situation—but his reach fell short.

Minkin laughed. "That won't work, little man."

Needed help. Where the hell was Lyle?

Shaking off the pain and dizziness, Lyle did the only thing he could: roll away.

But Bellitto followed. Though his hands were still taped behind his back he didn't need them. His feet were more than making up for them, landing one vicious kick after another. Lyle tried to use his sap against the flying feet but couldn't put any meaningful force behind his swings.

In desperation he pivoted on his hip and lashed out with a kick of his own. It caught Bellitto on the calf and that slowed him. Buoyed by this tiny victory, Lyle kicked again, harder this time. His heel connected with Bellitto's shin.

As the man stumbled back Lyle struggled to his hands and knees—Christ, he hurt all over—and lunged. He got a grip on one of Bellitto's ankles and yanked it up.

With no hands to use for balance Bellitto went down hard. Lyle was up and over him then. He still had the sap and didn't hesitate. Bellitto raised his head, Lyle knocked it down. It stayed down.

Lyle stood over the semi-conscious man and looked at the sap in his hand. He'd wondered if he'd be able to use it on a fellow human being. No problem. Of course, Bellitto didn't necessarily qualify as a fellow human being.

Then he heard a taunting voice from the next room. It wasn't Jack's. Hefting the sap, he left Bellitto and moved toward the dining room.

"You should see your face," Minkin said. "A lovely shade of purple."

Jack had given up trying to reach Minkin's face or shake him off. Neck muscles were giving out, dark spots clustering on the periphery of his vision, multiplying . . .

Flailed his hands about on the surrounding floor looking for something, anything to use as a weapon.

"Oh, and by the way . . . here's something to take with you into the Great Beyond. I was listening . . . I heard you . . . it appears you know the DiLauro woman and her little girl . . . you even know the lamb's first name. What a coincidence . . . what a lovely coincidence. Eli never lets me play with the lambs before they're sacrificed, but I'm going to make an exception with this one. Oh, yes, I'm going to have great fun with your little friend 'Vicky' before she's sacrificed."

Strength just about shot. Groping fingers of right hand touch something. A handle. Knife? Please, a knife, even a butter knife. No. A fork. Still . . . grab tip of handle with fingertips.

Light fading. Raise left hand to claw weakly at Minkin's face. Not even close.

"That the best you can do?" Minkin laughed and brought his face closer so that Jack's fingertips brushed his cheek. "Here, pussy-man. I've got an itch. Scratch right there."

Right hand up and jabbing the tines into Minkin's left eye.

"Aah! Aah! Aah!"

Abruptly the pressure let up and Jack could breathe again. Vision cleared as he choked down lungfuls of air. Minkin loomed above, still straddling him, making sounds of pain and shock as his big hands fluttered like Mothra-class butterflies around the fork protruding from his eyeball, afraid to touch it, afraid to leave it there.

Jack levered up and slammed the flat of his palm against the handle and felt the tines scrape against the bone at the back of the socket.

Minkin screamed and fell backward off Jack to land on the floor on his back, writhing, retching, kicking. To the side Lyle stood with a sick look on his face, the sap slack in his hand.

"Oh man," he said. "Oh man, oh man, oh man!"

Jack forced himself to his feet and staggered toward the living room. He could still feel Minkin's thumbs on his throat. His skull throbbed between the bolts of pain lancing though it.

"Go—" His voice came out a harsh whisper, barely audible even to him. He motioned Lyle closer. "Go upstairs. Find a rug. You can't find a rug get a sheet or a blanket. Move. We've wasted too much time."

Lyle ran up the steps. Jack found his pistol and dragged himself into the living room. His flank felt damp. He looked and saw blood starting to ooze through his shirt from the knife wound. No pain though. It was all concentrated from the neck up.

Bellitto lay on his side, groaning. Jack spotted the fax, grabbed it, read it again.

Burn this? Not yet.

He shoved it into his pocket.

"A." wouldn't be picking up anyone tonight. And Bellitto?

Jack found he still had a length of duct tape stuck to the front of his shirt. He used it to bind Bellitto's feet.

Glanced at his watch. Had to get moving. This trip had taken far too long.

Gia . . .

Hang on, babe. I'm coming.

Lyle hurried in carrying a summer blanket. They stretched it out next to Bellitto and rolled him up in it like a burrito.

The plan was to carry him downstairs; Lyle would bring the car up to the front door where they'd dump him in the trunk and steam back to Astoria.

As they carried Bellitto through the dining room, Jack saw Minkin on his hands and knees, the fork still protruding from his left eye, blood coating his cheek as he made "Unh-unh-unh!" noises like a hog in heat. His good eye found Jack and he bared his teeth.

Minkin's taunts about Vicky when he had him down flashed through Jack's brain. The darkness flowed out of its cage and suffused him, taking over. Nobody threatened his Vicky like that. Nobody.

Even with the clock riding him like a heavy-handed jockey, he was compelled to waste a few seconds here. He dropped Bellitto's legs and stalked toward Minkin.

"Gonna 'play with the lamb,' huh?" His voice still wasn't back yet. Sounded grating, ugly, like a board dragging on concrete. "Gonna have 'great fun' with my 'little friend

Vicky before she's sacrificed,' right? Not a chance, pal. Not tonight, not tomorrow, not ever."

With that he lashed out with his foot. The heel connected with the protruding end of the fork, crunching the tines through the back of the eye socket and deep into Minkin's brain.

He heard Lyle cry out in shock behind him but Adrian Minkin, would-be player with lambs, made no sound. He looked like he was screaming as he straightened up on his knees, then shot to standing, mouth open impossibly wide, displaying his perfect teeth. His arms spasmed out from his sides and he flopped backward, landing on the back of his head. For a few heartbeats his body bent into an impossible arch with only his heels and head touching the floor.

Jack watched impassively, feeling nothing beyond satisfaction that here was one less threat in the world to Vicky and others like her.

Finally Adrian Minkin went limp and still. Completely still. No breath stirred his chest.

Jack turned to find Lyle gaping at him wide-eyed and slack-jawed.

"Oh, shit, Jack! Oh man! What—?"

"I know. Just when you were starting to think I was kind of a nice guy. Almost cuddly, right?"

"No, I—"

"Stop gawking." He picked up Bellitto's legs. "We've got to lug this garbage out and get rolling. And hope to hell we're not too late."

17

"Charlie?"

Gia backed against the cold granite blocks and watched with horrid fascination as Charlie began to pull himself from the loose earth that had smothered him moments before. It might have been a cause for rejoicing if Charlie were alive, but as soon as his head emerged Gia knew it wasn't Charlie, only his shell. His face was slack, expressionless; and his eyes—dirt clung to the lids, to the eyes themselves, and he never blinked.

He crawled from the earth and rose shakily to his feet. As he took an unsteady step toward Gia she pressed herself back against the stones, wishing she could seep between them.

"Charlie, no. Please!"

He stopped, his dead eyes fixed somewhere above and beyond her.

Tara, standing to the rear and to the side during his resurrection, glided forward now, silent, but her expression furious as she glared at Charlie's corpse.

Charlie shook his head.

Gia watched, holding her breath as she sensed a silent battle of wills.

Tara bared her teeth and loosed a frustrated screech.

Again Charlie shook his head. Then his corpse turned and walked unsteadily to the far side of the cellar where it lowered itself against the wall and slumped into a sitting position, immobile, staring at its lap.

"He won't do it," Gia breathed, more to herself than to Tara.

There was too much of a good man left inside to allow his body do Tara's bidding.

Tara turned to her, eyes blazing. "This is so unfair!"

"You talk about fair? What's fair about you taking my baby?"

Her face screwed up. She looked as if she were about to cry. "Because you've got everything and I've got nothing!"

Gia's felt an instant of pity. Yes, she did have everything, or pretty close to everything she wanted or needed from life, things Tara never had a chance at and never would. But that didn't mean Tara had a call on the new life within her.

"I'm sorry, Tara. I really mean that. And if I could undo what was done to you, I would. But that's not in my power."

"The baby," Tara said. "Just give me the baby and you can go."

"No." Gia pressed her back against the wall again and raised the cross, holding it between them. "Let you kill my baby? You ask the impossible. I won't. I can't. Never."

Tara stared at her a moment, then stepped back. She disappeared, then flashed into view at the center of the cellar. She said nothing, simply stared at Gia from afar.

Gia lowered the cross and glanced toward the steps. Were they still blocked by that invisible wall? Should she try—?

Then she felt something cold loop around her right forearm—the arm holding the cross. She looked and saw one of the ghost hands clutching her in its iron grip. She started to reach around with her left hand to take the cross but that arm was trapped before it moved.

And now Tara was directly before her, smirking. "I don't know why I didn't think of this before. It's so much easier."

Gia cried out and struggled to break free, trying to angle the cross up so it would touch the ghost hand trapping her right arm, but her wrist wouldn't bend far enough.

"Easy now," Tara said in a soft tone as she leaned closer.

"Hold still. This won't hurt. You won't feel a thing, I promise you."

Two more ghost arms whipped around Gia's thighs, imprisoning them.

"Tara, no! Please! Don't do this!"

Tara said nothing. Her eyes were bright, her expression rapt as she reached her right hand toward Gia's belly.

Trapped, immobilized, Gia writhed with horror and loathing as the fingertips slipped through the waistband of her jeans. She screamed with the piercing cold as they entered her skin.

"Just a little further," Tara whispered. "Just a little squeeze, a tiny pinch, and it will all be—"

She stopped and cocked her head as if listening to something. She stepped back, removing her hand from Gia's belly, still listening.

"Yes," Tara whispered, nodding as a smile tugged at the corners of her mouth.

Gia couldn't hear who Tara was listening to, but she knew it could be only one person.

Jack.

She sobbed and dropped to her knees as the ghost hands released her.

"Oh, yes!" Tara shouted.

Gia glanced up and shuddered at the pure malevolence in the hideous grin that split Tara's child face.

18

"Do you hear me, Tara?" Lyle shouted at the closed door. "A trade! Your killer for Gia and Charlie!"

Can't be too late, Jack thought, refusing to think the unthinkable as he watched and waited for a sign that Tara had accepted the deal. Can't.

He'd have been doing the shouting if his voice had been up to it.

He and Lyle stood in the garage with Bellitto propped between them. They'd backed in the Crown Vic, closed the garage doors, and hauled him from the trunk. Jack had freed his feet but left his hands and mouth taped. The creep was fully awake now, looking scared, but not yet a hundred percent alert.

Jack felt a good long way from a hundred percent himself. Weak. Sick. Head still throbbed. Throat swollen. Stomach roiled with acid from the adrenaline come-down. On the way over from Manhattan Lyle had told him to look in the mirror. He wished he hadn't. His throat was ringed with purpling bruises, the white of his left eye was mostly bright red from a ruptured vessel, and his face was speckled with countless tiny red hemorrhages. He looked like he'd botched a try at hanging himself.

"Test the door," Jack said. His voice had cleared a little but not much. "Maybe the wall is down."

Jack kept a tight grip on Bellitto's arm as Lyle stepped to the door, reached toward the knob, but stopped well short.

He turned back to Jack. "Still there. I'll try calling her again."

Lyle had laid out the deal twice already. Jack couldn't see what good a third try would do. If Tara was around to listen, she'd have heard it the first time.

A winter chill of despair began to seep through his chest. Gia . . . he couldn't lose her . . . but what else could he do?

The door swung open.

"Yes!" Lyle said and returned to the threshold. But when he tried to step across he stopped. He turned to Jack with a baffled expression. "It's still blocked."

"Maybe for us," Jack said, hoping he was right. "But maybe someone else will slip right through and be welcomed with open arms."

Lyle nodded. "Worth a try."

Bellitto began to struggle, kicking, twisting, making terrified pleading noises behind the tape.

"How're you feeling, Eli?" Jack rasped through his teeth
as Lyle took the other arm and they started dragging him
forward. "Helpless? Scared out of your mind? No one to
turn to for help? All hope gone? Good. It's just a little of
what those kids felt when you and your pal Minkin dragged
them into your car. Like it?" Bellitto's wide, panicky eyes
said it all. "Didn't think so. But whether we work this deal
or not isn't going to make a hell of a lot of difference to
you. No matter what happens, you don't see tomorrow."

"I've got a problem with this," Lyle said as they neared
the door. "What if he does go through? We don't exactly
have a deal with Tara. She could stiff us or . . ."

Jack knew what he was getting at: It might already be
too late.

"Don't like it either," Jack said. "But we have to chance
it. She holds all the cards."

What if this doesn't work? he wondered. What then? He
was out of options.

He glanced around. That Indian woman, the one who
seemed to know everything—where was she now when he
needed her? Hadn't seen her or her dog since he and Lyle
had left for Manhattan.

Bellitto's legs went limp as they reached the threshold
and he sagged in their grip.

"Passive resistance won't cut it here, Eli." Jack looked
at Lyle. "Grab the back of his belt."

Lyle did and together they gave Eli Bellitto an old-
fashioned heave-ho toward the door.

Jack half expected him to bounce back at them but he
sailed through and sprawled in the short hallway.

"You were right!" Lyle cried.

Jack tried to follow but met with the same impenetrable
resistance as before. He leaned there, clawing at the thick
air that wouldn't let him pass.

Please, Tara, he thought. Don't welch on us. We did our

part. You've got the guy who killed you. Now you've got to do your part.

On the other side of the invisible divide, Jack watched Bellitto regain his feet. Somehow, in the course of the heave-ho, the tape on his wrists had loosened. He struggled with it, frantically working his arms behind him until his hands came free. He then pulled the tape from his face and lunged toward Jack and the door. Jack cocked a fist, ready to smash him back but he never got close. He slammed against the divide and staggered back.

At that instant a little girl appeared behind him. Jack had seen her picture only once on the Internet site but recognized her immediately.

Tara Portman.

Jack saw her mouth work but heard nothing. Bellitto whirled toward her, then spun back. Jack knew from the horrified expression on his face that Bellitto recognized her. He hurled himself at the doorway but once again was halted inches from Jack. His mouth worked, screaming no doubt, as his fingers clawed the impenetrable air between then. Jack heard nothing and felt less.

"Sometimes, Eli," he whispered, "what goes around comes around. Not nearly as often as it should on its own, but sometimes we can help it along. That's why I'm here."

Behind him Tara smiled, her face a malicious mask of incandescent glee, then winked out of sight.

The next thing Jack knew, Bellitto was falling backward, arms flailing, then landing on his back and being dragged by some force Jack couldn't see. He slid kicking and screaming down the hallway and out of sight.

Jack and Lyle leaned on the barrier, waiting.

"Come on, Tara," he whispered. "We did our part. Time to do yours. Don't let us down. We—"

Then Jack saw movement in the hallway. Someone coming their way. Bellitto? How had he got away?

No. Someone else. His pain and despair vanished as he recognized Gia—but Gia as he had never seen her. Hair, clothes, and hands coated with dirt, face muddy from the tears streaming down her cheeks. Her eyes looked wild as she stumbled his way, picking up speed and rushing toward him with outstretched arms when she saw him.

Don't! he wanted to shout. She might run into the divide and hurt herself.

But she leaped at the threshold and flew into his arms and then he had her, he had her, he had her, arms locked around her, spinning her around, absorbing her quaking sobs, unable to speak past the fist-sized lump in his throat.

They held each other, Gia's feet not touching the floor, and would have stayed that way much longer if not for Lyle's question.

"Where's Charlie? Where's my brother?"

Aw no, Jack thought, looking around and seeing only the three of them. Don't tell me . . . not Charlie . . .

Gia slumped against Jack and reached out a hand to Lyle. Between sobs she told him about she and Charlie falling into a pit, how the sides began to collapse, and how Charlie had sacrificed himself to save her.

"Charlie?" Lyle whispered, his face slack, stricken. "Charlie's dead?"

His features tightened as tears began to slide down his cheeks. He stumbled toward the door but still couldn't enter. He leaned against the resisting air and pounded on silent nothing, sobbing, calling his brother's name.

FRIDAY

1

Jack let Gia sleep in as he got up early, intending to run back to Astoria to see what he could do for Lyle. But a quick listen to the news changed his plans. "The Horror in Astoria" was all over the radio. He flipped on the TV and that was all any of the local newsheads could talk about.

Gia came down in a light yellow terry cloth robe, looking tired and worn but so much better after a shower and some sleep.

He kissed her and held her and said, "I was hoping you'd sleep in."

"I woke up and started thinking about last night." She shuddered against him. "How can I sleep when I remember how Charlie—?" She bit her lip and shook her head. Then she looked up at him and touched his throat. "This still looks sore. And that eye . . ."

"I'll be fine."

He'd told her about trading Bellitto for her and Charlie and how one of Bellitto's friends had tried to choke him, but had decided against mentioning the fax that had targeted Vicky. She'd already had enough shocks to her system.

She stiffened and pointed to the TV. "Say, isn't that—?"

"Yeah. Menelaus Manor. Looks like Lyle called the cops."

Jack surfed from channel to channel until he found a newshead with the good grace to summarize the developing story.

"For those of you just tuning in, here's what we know so far. At 1:37 A.M. this morning the police received an emergency call from Lyle Kenton, owner of the house in Astoria you see pictured here, saying that he'd returned

*home after a night out to find his brother Charles dead in
a ditch they'd been digging in their cellar. The ditch had
apparently collapsed and smothered him.*

*"Why were they digging a ditch in their cellar? you ask.
Good question. Here's where the story veers into the Twilight Zone. Lyle Kenton claims to be a spirit medium who
'practices' under the name Ifasen. He states he and his
brother were contacted by a spirit who called herself 'Tara
Portman' and claimed she had been murdered and buried
in the basement by a previous owner. For the past few days,
Lyle and Charles had been digging up the cellar, trying to
find her remains. Last night their excavation collapsed,
trapping Charles. When the police arrived, Lyle had dug
his brother out but it was too late.*

*"If that were the whole story it would be sensational
enough. But it gets stranger. The police did a little digging
themselves and have so far unearthed the skeletons of two
children. They are looking for more.*

*"The police want to make it very clear that Mr. Kenton
is not a suspect. He has lived in the house less than a year
and the remains found in the cellar so far appear to have
been there much longer.*

"Back to you, Chet . . ."

Jack surfed on, looking for mention of Eli Bellitto, but
his name never came up. Where was he? What had Tara
done with him? He hoped it hadn't ended quickly for him.

He clicked off the set. "The barrier must have come
down some time after we left."

"Poor Lyle," Gia said. "I feel so bad that we left him to
deal with this alone."

The three of them had waited together for the barrier to
fall, but after an hour or so, Gia started to get the chills
and shakes. Jack had needed to get her home and offered
Lyle a bed for the night. Lyle told them go, he'd wait here.
Jack promised to come back in the morning.

"Alone is the only way he can deal with it. We can't
show our faces—at least I can't. And no reason you should.
We can't add anything."

"We could be there for him. He and his brother seemed so close."

"They had their differences, I can tell you that, but there was a bond there, beyond blood. They'd been through a lot together."

"I'm glad he called in the police, though. They'll find the rest of the bodies. Then the families of those poor children will be able to bury what's left of them and have some closure."

Her gaze seemed to drift.

"Thinking of Tara's father?"

She nodded. "I wonder if burying Tara will change things for him and his son." She sighed. "Somehow I doubt it. I think they've been pushed too far off track to get back on."

"I've got an idea," Jack said. "Why don't we get out of town, say, drive up to Monticello and visit Vicky at camp?"

"But she's coming home tomorrow."

Jack knew that, but from the brightening of Gia's expression he could tell she loved the idea. After her ordeal with Tara, seeing her little girl would be just the tonic she needed.

"Even better. You and I can find a motel, stay over tonight, take her out for breakfast in the morning at this neat old-fashioned diner I know, then we'll drive her back ourselves. It'll be fun."

Gia smiled. "Okay. I think I'd like that. When do we leave?"

Jack repressed a sigh of relief. He'd been looking for a way to get up to Vicky's camp without alarming Gia. This was it. Last night, when Gia was in the shower, he'd made a couple of calls, one of them an anonymous tip to the camp warning them that one of the children—he didn't name the child—was in danger of being abducted in a custody dispute. He placed the same call to the Monticello police department, suggesting extra patrols around the camp.

With its leader dead, Bellitto's circle was a snake without a head. But even so, it wasn't enough for Jack. He wouldn't rest easy until he'd seen Vicky and placed her under *his* protection.

Gia too. She'd told Jack what Tara had said: *It wants you dead.* Who knew if Tara was telling the truth, but Jack had to assume she was. "It" could only mean the Otherness. What was it trying to do? Wipe out everyone he cared about?

That gut-wrenching thought had kept him awake most of the night. How do you fight something you can't see, that works so far behind the scenes you can never reach it?

The only thing he could think of was to circle the wagons and keep Gia and Vicky close by.

"You pack up some things while I run a few errands, and we'll get going soon as I get back. Make a day of it."

"What kind of errands?" she said, serious again.

"Just a stop by Julio's. Need to check out something with one of the regulars."

2

Jack sipped coffee at the bar and watched the TV while he waited for Barney to show. He'd put on a gray turtleneck to hide the bruises on his throat and wore sunglasses despite the bar's dim interior. Made it hard to see what was happening on the TV. Everyone around him, including Julio, was glued to the on-the-scene reports from what was being called "the house of horror."

He thought about Lyle and wondered how he was dealing with his brother's death. It left him alone for the first time in his life. Jack knew alone. He'd handled it, but he probably had a better tolerance for it than others. He wondered about Lyle's tolerance. He was tough. He'd done all right last night. Hadn't liked it, but he'd hung in there.

He'd be all right.

Bellitto. Lots more questions about him beyond where the hell he was.

Hell . . . yeah, if it existed, he'd be a charter member.

He'd said he was hundreds of years old and didn't seem to be lying. Could that be true? Not likely. Maybe he'd just thought he was telling the truth. Told himself he was that old for so long he'd come to believe it.

Still, Jack wondered where Tara had taken him. Down through the dirt and into the fault line? Someplace where she could toy with him for the longest time without being disturbed?

That was all right with Jack. The longer the better.

And then the question of Edward, Eli's ersatz brother. Early last night Jack had wanted to wring his neck; by the end of the evening he'd wanted to thank him. If Edward hadn't put him onto Eli, Adrian might have got to Vicky . . .

His mind refused to go there.

A familiar face popped through the door then and bellied up to the bar about three stools down.

"Barney!" Jack called, waving. "Sit over here. I'll buy you one."

Barney grinned and hurried over. "Never turn down a man who's in a buying mood, I always say."

He'd just got off work and needed a shave. The essence of his grimy Willie Nelson T-shirt gave advance notice of his approach and he had pretty much the quantity and quality of teeth you'd expect in a Willie fan.

"What're you having?"

"A shot of Johnny Walker Red and a pint of Heinie."

Jack nodded to Julio who laughed. "Ay, meng, what happen to your usual Ol' Smuggler an' eight-ounce Bud."

"That's when I'm buying." Barney turned to Jack. "To what do I owe this generosity?"

"Julio tells me you recognized an older gent dropping off an envelope for me the other day."

Barney took a quick sip of his Scotch. "That was no gent, that was a priest."

Jack hadn't been expecting that one. "You mean as in Catholic priest."

"Right. That was Father Ed from St. Joseph's. You thinking of converting, Jack?"

"Not this month." Ed . . . well at least he hadn't lied about his first name. "You're sure it was this priest?"

"Course I'm sure. St. Joe's was my church back when I used to live down in Alphabet City. Father Edward Halloran's the pastor. Least he used to be. You mean you don't know who he is and he's leaving an envelope for you?" Grinning he lowered his voice and leaned closer. "What was it? A message from the Vatican? The Pope got a problem he needs fixed?"

Jack gave him a hard look. "How'd you know? You been reading my mail?"

Barney stiffened. "Hey, no, Jack. I wouldn't—" He stopped, then broke into another spotty grin. "You rat! Almost had me there!"

Jack slipped off the stool and clapped Barney on the back. "Thanks for the tip, my man." He waved to Julio. "Another round for Barney on my tab."

"Hey, thanks, Jack. You oughta stick around so I can buy you one."

"Some other time. Barn. Gotta go to church."

3

Jack found St. Joseph's church on a Lower East Side street, mid block between rows of sagging tenements. He took an immediate liking to the old Gothic, granite-block building with her twin crocketed spires and large rose window. Could have done with a good power washing though. A convent sat to her left, the smaller rectory to the right.

Jack knocked on the rectory door. A thin elderly woman in a smudged apron answered. When he asked to see Father Ed she tried to tell him that he didn't have any appointments till the afternoon. Refusing to be put off he said to tell the good father that Jack—just Jack—was here.

That did the trick.

Father Edward Halloran—the Edward who'd hired Jack to watch his "brother" Eli—greeted him in his cramped little office with a mixture of warmth and wariness.

"I should have known you'd be finding me," he said as he offered his hand.

Jack shook it, not exactly sure what he was feeling. Looking at Edward in his Roman collar and hearing that thick brogue, he felt as if he'd walked onto the set of *Going My Way*. Any moment now Bing Crosby would waltz through the door. Still he'd lied to Jack. Big time.

"I thought priests were supposed to tell the truth."

"They are." The little man slipped behind his desk and pointed to a chair for Jack. "And I did."

Jack remained standing. "You told me your last name was Bellitto, Father Halloran."

"Never. Those words never passed me lips."

"You said Eli Bellitto was your brother. Same thing."

Father Ed gave him a cherubic smile. "The Lord says all men are brothers, don't you know."

"Can we cut the word games?" Jack leaned on the desk and stared at the priest. "I'm not here to cause you trouble. I just want to know what this was all about. How did you know Eli Bellitto was going to snatch a kid?"

Father Ed glanced past Jack, as if to make sure the door was closed, then sighed. He swiveled in his seat and stared off to his left.

"He told me."

"Why? Did you know him?"

The priest's head snapped around. " 'Did'?"

"Let's not get into that. Why did he tell you?"

"I don't know. Last Saturday I was hearing confessions next door when this man enters the booth and starts telling me he has killed hundreds of children and wants absolution."

"You believed him?"

The priest shrugged. "One is after hearing many strange things in the confessional. I took him on his word and told him to receive absolution he must be turning himself in to the authorities. He laughed and said he couldn't do that. In fact, he was going to kill another child in the following week under the dark of the moon. And then he left."

"How did you know he was Eli Bellitto?"

"I followed him," he said, looking a little ashamed. "I didn't know if he was deluded or telling the truth. Either way he was certainly daft. I left the confessional, removed my collar, and trailed him to his store. It wasn't far. But as I stood outside his shop I thought of a third possibility: perhaps he was after having some grudge against the church and trying to see if he could make a priest compromise the holy privilege of the Sacrament of Confession. I needed a way of protecting the Church and protecting any child he might harm. I thought of you."

"Me? How does a priest even know about me?"

"One of my parishioners once confessed to me about hiring you."

"Confessed? You mean I'm a sin?" Jack didn't know whether to be offended or pleased. "Who was it?"

"I can't be telling you that, of course."

"Oh, yeah. I guess not."

He decided being a sin was kind of cool.

"Someone was after being hurt as a result of my parishioner hiring you and the lad was afraid he'd sinned. So anyway, I went and bought one of those little disposable cameras and took Mr. Bellitto's picture when he came out. I learned what I could about him—not much, I'm afraid—then called you." Father Ed leaned forward. "Tell me now, would it be true what he said about killing children?"

"It would be," Jack said. "I don't know about the hundreds he told you about, but yeah, more than one. Many more."

Father Ed gasped and crossed himself. "Saints preserve us."

"You hear about that house in Astoria this morning? He was part of that."

"Then I did the right thing. But why was he telling me? Why did he confess?"

"Arrogance, I guess. He kept trophies from his victims on display in his shop. I gather he thought he was some sort of superior being and liked to flaunt it."

"Hubris." The priest shook his head. "Sometimes we can be thankful for it, I suppose." He glanced at Jack. "And where would Mr. Bellitto be now?"

"Gone."

"Gone where?"

"Not sure. Just . . . gone. And don't worry. He won't be coming back. Ever."

Father Ed took a deep breath. "Like my parishioner, I'm feeling I might have a need to confess. Would that be true?"

Jack shrugged. "Not my call."

"How about you? Would you be needing to confess?"

"I don't think so. I had it on the authority of a good man that I was doing God's work."

EPILOGUE

When Jack arrived at Menelaus Manor two weeks later, Lyle was in the yard watching a landscaper replace the dead foundation plantings. He greeted Jack warmly with a two-handed handshake.

"Jack, how are you? Come on in."

Jack followed him inside to the kitchen where Lyle popped the tops on a couple of Miller Genuine Drafts.

Jack lifted his can. "To Charlie."

He'd died saving Gia's life. Jack would be drinking toasts to him indefinitely.

"Amen to that." After each took a long pull, Lyle said, "How's Gia?"

"Still shaken up, but she's handling it. Having Vicky back has helped a lot."

"And the baby?"

Jack grinned. "Fine."

Gia had had a sonogram two days ago. Too early to tell the sex, but everything was as it should be. What a relief that had been.

But he still hadn't figured out how he was going to become the baby's legal father.

"I'm really glad you could come over, Jack."

"Glad to make it." He meant that. "Would have been by sooner but for all the company you've had."

In the weeks since Charlie's death, the police, using some sort of ground sonar, had recovered eight bodies from the cellar. They were sure they'd found them all. Sweeps of the surrounding grounds had yielded nothing.

Lyle smiled. "Yeah, well, the cops finished up. At last. I've finally got my house back."

"Not that you would've been home much anyway."

During the past week Lyle had been a ubiquitous presence on the tube. Every talk show, from *Today* and *GMA* in the morning to *Oprah* in the afternoon, to the *Rose-Leno-Letterman-O'Brien* axis at night, had had him on.

"Yeah, I guess I've been doing a bit of traveling, haven't I."

"You're good on the tube." True. Came across as a very personable, likable guy. "You ought to have your own show."

He laughed. "Been offered two already." His smile faded. "But I might have to broadcast from jail if they link me to Adrian Minkin."

Minkin's body had been found the following day when clerks from Bellitto's store came looking for him.

"They won't. We left that place clean."

Lyle shook his head. "What a night. I still can't believe I was there. Did you hear the latest? Eli Bellitto is a possible suspect."

"Speaking of Eli," Jack said. "Where is he?"

"I have no idea. Not a trace of him in the house."

"So he just vanished, body and all?"

"Tara has him."

Jack was struck by the certainty in his tone.

"Hope she's having fun with him."

Lyle nodded. "She is. Oh, she is."

Again that certainty. "How about visits from Tara?"

"Not a one. She's gone for good." Lyle frowned. "But Bellitto's circle of child killers is still around. I wish there was a way to give them a share of their leader's fate."

"I've taken care of that," Jack said.

"How?"

"Made a call that night to a pair of brothers I know." The Mikulski brothers. Jack saw no reason Lyle needed to know their name. "Told them Bellitto's address and that I'd left the door open. They called me the next day. Said they paid a visit, went through his files, stole his computer's hard drive. Lots of interesting stuff there, including names and addresses of Eli's ring."

"Are they detectives?"

"No." Jack didn't know the Mikulskis' story, and figured he could live without knowing it. "But they've got a thing for pedophiles."

"A thing?"

"Yeah." Jack leaned against the counter and took another sip. "They're very serious about this. They know my word's good, but even so they won't take it. They'll check out the guys on Eli's list themselves—watch them, break in and toss their digs. Once they're satisfied someone's the real deal, they'll make their move. People will start to disappear."

"You mean, they'll kill them?"

"Eventually."

"Eventually?"

"Yeah. Eventually they'll die. Long after they want to."

Lyle rotated his shoulders, as if shaking off a chill. "What else have you been up to?"

"Still trying to figure out the whats and whys of what happened here. Especially Tara telling Gia that something wants her dead."

"I've been chewing on that one too. It has to be the Otherness you told us about."

"I thought you couldn't buy into that."

Lyle looked at him. "I buy into a whole lot more than I used to. You said this Otherness feels it's got a score to settle with you. The best I can figure it is maybe it can't strike at you directly. Maybe something's guarding your back. So it tries to strike at you indirectly, through the people you love."

Jack had wondered about that. Kate was gone, and the Otherness probably deserved the rap for that. And if things had gone differently two weeks ago, Gia, Vicky, and his unborn child would be gone too.

Lyle sipped and said, "Let's take Tara at her word: The Otherness brought her back to get Gia. She was certainly playing to Gia all along. But somewhere along the line Tara developed her own agenda. I guess the Otherness can't always fine-tune the forces it sets into motion."

"But what about Bellitto? The day after the earthquake when we assume Tara returned, he decides to taunt a priest with his past killings and the one he's planning for the following week."

"Not entirely out of character."

"But he chooses a priest that just happens to have heard of me through that same confessional."

Lyle shrugged. "Strange, isn't it. Stranger than I ever could have imagined. Maybe the Otherness isn't the only force operating here. What about that Indian lady who popped into the garage and knew all about what was going on? What side is she playing for?"

"Her own, for all I know. You seen her since?"

"Not a trace. Used to see her walking her dog past the house a lot, but not once since that night."

Jack had been wondering about the Indian lady. Something about her reminded him of another woman who'd popped up a few months ago with her own set of dire warnings, then vanished. She'd had a dog too, but she'd been older and had sounded Russian.

What's happened to my life? Jack thought. He wanted to scream the question. Bad enough that something seemed to be moving him around a cosmic chessboard, but Gia and Vicky . . . they were noncombatants . . . they shouldn't be involved.

But then, maybe there were no noncombatants in this conflict.

"What's the answer then?"

"Wish I knew," Lyle said. "We seem to be at the mercy of unknown forces. All we can do is go with the flow and fight like hell to keep our heads above water."

" 'We'?"

"Yes. All of us. Remember that coming darkness I told you I saw? Well, it's still coming."

Jack didn't want to mention to Lyle that he'd claimed to

see himself and his brother still together after the darkness was over.

"Where do you plan to ride it out? Back in Michigan?"

Lyle shook his head. "No way. I'm staying right here and doing my thing."

"Without Charlie?"

"That's what I wanted to see you about. Come back to the Channeling Room."

Jack followed him but stopped on the threshold when he saw the coffin—a simple pine box—in the middle of the floor.

"Is that . . . ?"

Lyle nodded. "Charlie. The autopsy confirmed that he died of smothering, so the police finally released his body. I had it delivered here. Ostensibly to have a wake and ship it back to Michigan, but I'm going to bury Charlie in the cellar. I'd like your help."

The request jolted Jack. "What? I mean, of course I'll help but—"

"It's what Charlie wants. He wants to stay here."

"He does?" Had Lyle lost it? "How do you know?"

"He told me."

"Really."

Lyle laughed. "You should see your face, man! You think the cheese has slid off my cracker, don't you." He looked around. "Charlie? Look who's come to see you. Say hello!"

Jack listened, expecting a trick, but heard nothing. He did notice Charlie's coffin begin to move. He watched it rise into the air, stop with its base four feet off the floor, do a 360-degree turn, then lower back to the carpet.

"Pretty good," Jack said. "How'd you work it?"

"It's not a trick, Jack." He walked over to the seance table and pointed to the Tarot deck sitting there. "The night after Charlie died I was sitting here, mourning him, when the tarot deck flipped itself over, fanned itself out, and the Hermit card rose in the air and hung right in front of my

face. The Hermit. That was Charlie's card. That was what
he'd started calling himself."

And then the deck did just as Lyle had described, leaving
the Hermit card floating not six inches from Jack's nose.

Jack snatched the card out of the air, inspecting it for
invisible thread. He found none.

"Got to hand it to you, Lyle. That's excellent."

"Not a trick. I swear, Jack." He had tears in his eyes.
"Charlie's back. I mean, he never really left. Come look."

He took Jack's arm and led him into what had been Charlie's control room. It was nearly empty. "When the police
started digging around in the basement, I figured it was only
a matter of time before they moved upstairs to check things
out. I remembered what had happened to Madame Pomerol
after they searched her place and didn't want that happening here. So I started dismantling Charlie's equipment. Just
as well, since we won't be needing it."

Jack heard a chime and turned. The old temple bell that
Charlie had carried around to collect the envelopes on
Jack's first visit was floating toward him through the air.

"I have powers in this house, Jack, and I'm going to use
them. I'm dropping the Ifasen role and just playing myself.
Charlie will still be backing me up—but only on the condition that we give value for value. So that's what we'll
do. No tricks, no bullshit."

A deck of tarot cards lifted off the round séance table
and sprayed itself at Jack.

Lyle laughed. "The Kenton brothers are still a team, Jack.
But now we're the real deal. The only real deal in town."

Look for

MIDNIGHT MASS

Available now
from Tom Doherty Associates

Part One

Opus Dei

1

ZEV ...

Gasping in horror and revulsion, Zev Wolpin stumbled away from St. Anthony's church. He stretched his arms out before him, reaching into the dark for something, anything to support him before he fell.

Leaves slapped his face, twigs tugged at his graying beard as he plowed into foliage. His bike ... where was his bike? He thought he'd left it in a clump of bushes, but obviously not this clump. Had to find it, had to get away from this place. But the dark made him disoriented ... the dark, and what he'd just witnessed.

He'd heard whispers, stories he couldn't, wouldn't believe, so he'd come to see for himself, to prove them wrong. Instead ...

Zev bent at the waist and retched. Nothing but a bubble of bile and acid came up, searing the back of his throat.

The whispers were only partly true. The truth was worse. The truth was unspeakable.

He straightened and looked around in the darkness. Wan light from the crescent moon in the cloud-streaked sky made the shadows deeper, and Zev feared the shadows. Then he spotted a curving glint of light from the chrome on his bike's front wheel. He ran to it, yanked it by the handlebars from its hiding place, and hopped on.

His aging knees protested as he pedaled away along dark and silent streets lined with dark and silent houses, heading south when he should have been going west, but *away* was all that mattered now.

Lakewood was a small town, maybe ten miles from the Atlantic Ocean; a place where the Rockefeller family was said to have vacationed. So it didn't matter much if he headed south or north, he wouldn't be far from the place he now called home. The town was once home to fifty thousand or more before the undead came. Now he'd be surprised if there were a thousand left. He'd heard it was the same all up and down the East Coast.

The exertion helped clear his mind. He had to be careful. Prudent he hadn't been. In fact he'd been downright reckless tonight, venturing out after sundown and sneaking up on St. Anthony's. *Shmuck!* What had he been thinking? He prayed he didn't pay for it with his life. Or worse.

He shuddered at the thought of ending up the victim in a ceremony like the one he'd witnessed tonight. He had to find temporary shelter until dawn. Even then he wouldn't be safe, but at least there wouldn't be so many shadows.

The blue serge suit coat that had once fit rather snugly now hung loose on his half-starved frame and flapped behind him as he rode. He'd had to punch new holes in his belt to hold up the pants. He'd complained so often about not being able to lose weight. Nothing to it, really. Simply don't eat.

His ever-hungry stomach rumbled. How could it think of food after what he'd just seen?

A shadow passed over him.

A blast of cold dread banished any concern about his next meal. His aging neck protested as he glanced up at the sky, praying to see a cloud near the moon. But the glowing crescent sat alone in a clear patch of night.

No! Please! He increased his speed, his legs working like pistons against the pedals. Not a flying one!

Zev heard something like a laugh above and behind him. He ducked, all but pressing his face to the handlebars. Something swooped by, clawing at the back of his coat as it passed. Its grip slipped but the glancing impact was enough to disrupt Zev's balance. His front wheel wobbled, the bike tipped to the left and hit the curb, sending him flying.

Zev landed hard on his left shoulder, his lungs emptying

with a grunt. His momentum carried him onto his back.
What he saw circling above him made him forget his pain.
He rolled over and struggled to his feet. He instinctively
checked the yarmulke clipped to his thinning gray hair, then
gripped the cross dangling from a string around his neck.
That might save him in close quarters, but not from a creature that could swoop down from any angle. He felt like a
field mouse under the cold gaze of a hawk.

He started running. He didn't know where he was going
but knew he had to move. The bike was no good. He
needed a tight space where his back was protected and
he could use the cross to keep his attacker at bay. One of
these houses, maybe. A basement, even a sewer drain—
anyplace but out here in the open where—

"Here! Over here!"

A woman's voice, calling in a stage whisper to his left.
Zev looked across an overgrown lawn, saw only a large
tree, a pine of some sort with branches almost brushing the
ground.

"Quick! In the tree!"

A trap maybe. A team this could be—a winged one driving prey into the arms of another on the ground. He'd never
heard of anything like it, but that meant nothing.

A glance over his shoulder showed him that the creature
had half folded its wings and was diving his way from
above. No choice now. Zev veered left for the tree and
whatever waited within its shadowed branches.

He was almost there when the woman's voice shouted,
"Down!"

Zev obeyed, diving for the grass. He heard a hiss of rage,
felt the wind from the creature's wings as it hurtled past
no more than a foot or two above him. He lurched back to
his feet and staggered forward. Pale hands reached from the
branches and pulled him into the shadows.

"Are you all right?" the woman said.

He couldn't see her—she was a shadow among the
shadows—but her voice sounded young.

"Yes. No. If you mean am I hurt, no."

But all right? No, he was not all right. Never again would he be all right.

"Good." She grabbed his hands and pressed them against a tree limb. "Hold onto this branch. Steady it while I try to break it. Quick, before it makes another pass."

The dead branch sat chest high and felt about half an inch in diameter. With Zev steadying it, the woman threw her weight hard against it. The wood snapped with a loud crack.

"What are you—?"

She shushed him. "It's coming back."

She moved to the edge of the trees, carrying the branch with her. Zev watched her, silhouetted against the moonlit lawn. Average height, short dark hair were all he gained about her looks. He saw her crouch, then hurl her branch like a spear at the creature as it swooped by on another pass. She missed and high-pitched derisive laughter trailed into the sky.

She returned to Zev, stopped on the other side of the broken branch, and patted the front of his shirt. She pulled him close and whispered in his ear.

"Your cross—tuck it away."

"No! It will—"

"Do as I say. They can see in the dark. And try to look frightened."

Try? Who had to try?

She put an arm around him to hold him close, keeping the branch between them.

Another whisper: "Pull out that cross when I tell you."

Zev had no idea what she was up to but had nowhere else to turn, so . . .

Her grip on him tightened. "Here it comes. Ready . . ."

Zev could see it now, a dark splotch among the shadows of the branches, wings spread, gliding in low, arms stretched out before it.

". . . ready . . ."

Suddenly it folded its wings and shot at them like a missile.

"Now!"

As Zev pulled out the cross he felt the woman shove him away. He lost his balance and tumbled back, saw her fall in the other direction, felt a clawed hand grip his shoulder, heard the creature's screech of triumph rise into a wail of shock and agony as it slammed against the trunk of the tree.

Zev regained his feet amid the frantic and furious struggling of the hissing creature. Its charging attack had opened a passage through the branches, lightening the shadows. As he ducked its thrashing wings he realized it had impaled itself on the broken branch. It flopped back and forth like a speared fish, then pushed away from the trunk, trying to dislodge itself from the wood that had pierced its chest.

Zev turned to run. Now was his chance to get away from this thing. But what of the woman? He couldn't abandon her.

He spotted her standing behind the creature. She'd hiked up her already short skirt and kicked at the thing's back, shoving it further onto the branch. The creature howled and thrashed, and in its struggles broke the branch off the trunk with a gunshot crack.

Free now, it whirled and staggered out into the moonlight. Its wings flapped but couldn't seem to lift it. Perhaps ten feet beyond the branches it dropped to its knees. The woman was right behind it, giving it another kick. It rolled onto its back, clawing at the wooden shaft that jutted two or three feet from its chest. Its movements were weaker now, its wings lay crumpled beneath it. Howling and writhing in agony, it gripped the branch and started to slide it out of its chest.

"No, you don't!" the woman cried.

She gripped the upper end, shoving it back down and leaning on it to hold it in place.

"This is for Bern!" she screamed, naked fury rawing her voice. "This is what you made me do to her! How does it feel? How does it *feel*?"

For an instant Zev wondered who was more frightening,

this screeching woman or the struggling monster she held pinned to the earth.

The creature clawed and kicked at her, almost knocking her over. He had to help. If that thing got free . . .

Mouth dry, heart pounding, Zev forced himself from the shadows and added his own weight to the branch. He felt it punch deeper into the thing's chest. Then a sickening scrape as it thrust past ribs and into the ground beneath.

The creature's struggles became abruptly feebler. He saw now that it was a female. It might have been beautiful once, but the sickly pallor and the bared fangs robbed it of any attractiveness.

Finally it shuddered and lay still. Zev watched in amazement as its wings shriveled and disappeared.

"Gevalt!" he whispered, although he didn't know why. "You did it! You killed one!"

He'd heard they could be killed—all the old folk tales said they could be—but he'd never actually seen one die, never even met anyone who had.

It was *good* to know they could be killed.

"*We* did." She finally released her grip on the branch but her gaze remained locked on the creature. "If you have a soul," she said, "may God have mercy on it."

What was this? Like a harpy, she screeches, then she blesses the thing. A madwoman, this was.

She faced him. "I'm sorry for my outburst. I . . . it's just . . ." She seemed to lose her train of thought, as if something had distracted her. "Anyway, thank you for the help."

"You saved my life, young lady. It's me who should be thanking."

She was staring at him. "You're Rabbi Wolpin, aren't you."

Shock stole his voice for a few heartbeats. She knew him?

"Why . . . yes. But I don't recognize . . ."

She laughed. A bitter sound. "Please, God, I hope not."

He could see her now. Nothing familiar about her features, no particular style to her short dark hair. He noticed a tiny crescent scar on the right side of her chin. Heavy on the eye make–up—very heavy. A tight red sweater and even tighter short black skirt hid little of her slim body. And were those fishnet stockings?

A prostitute? In these times? Such a thing he never would have dreamed. But then he remembered hearing of women selling themselves to get food and favors.

"So, you know me how?"

She shrugged. "I used to see you with Father Cahill."

"Joe Cahill," Zev said, feeling a burst of warmth at the mention of his friend's name. "I was just over at his church. I saw . . ." The words choked off.

"I know. I've—" She waved her hand before her face. "She's starting to stink already. Must be an older one."

Zev looked down and saw that the creature was already in an advanced state of rot.

"We'd better get out of here," the woman said, backing away. "They seem to know when one of their kind dies. Get your bike and meet me by the tree."

Zev continued to stare at the corpse. "Are they always so hard to kill?"

"I don't think the branch went all the way through the heart at first."

"Nu? You've done this before?"

Her expression was bleak as she looked at him. "Let's not talk about it."

When Zev wheeled his bike back to the tree he found her standing beside a child's red wagon, an old-fashioned Radio Flyer. A book bag emblazoned with *St. Anthony's School* lay in the wagon. He hadn't noticed either earlier. She must have had them hidden among the branches.

She said, "You mentioned you were at St. Anthony's. Why?"

"To see if what I'd heard was true." The urge to retch gripped Zev again. "To think that was Father Cahill's church."

"He wasn't the pastor."

"Not in name, maybe, but they were his flock. He was the glue that held them together. Someone should tell him what's going on."

"Oh, yes. That would be wonderful. But nobody knows where he is, or if he's even alive."

"I do."

Her hand shot out and gripped his arm, squeezing. "He's alive?"

"Yes," Zev said, taken aback by her intensity. "At least I think so."

Her grip tightened. "Where?"

He wondered if he'd made a mistake telling her. He tried not to sound evasive. "A retreat house. Have I been there? No. But it's near the beach, I'm told."

True enough, and he knew the address. After Joe had been moved out of St. Anthony's rectory to the retreat house, he and Zev still shared many phone conversations. At least until the creatures came. Then the phones stopped working and Zev's time became devoted more to survival than to keeping up with old friends.

"You've got to find him! You've got to tell him! He'll come back when he finds out and he'll make them pay!"

"A *mensch*, he is, I agree, but only one man."

"No! Many of his parishioners are still alive, but they're afraid. They're defeated. But if Father Joe came back, they'd have hope. They'd see that it wasn't over. They'd regain the will to fight."

"Like you?"

"I'm different," she said, the fervor slipping from her voice. "I never lost the will to fight. But my circumstances are special."

"How?"

"It's not important. *I'm* not important. But Father Joe is. Find him, Rabbi Wolpin. Don't put it off. Find him tomorrow and tell him. When he hears what they've done to his church he'll come back and teach them a lesson they'll never forget!"

Zev didn't know about that, but it would be good to see

his young friend again. Searching him out would be a mitzvah for St. Anthony's, but might be good for Zev as well. It might offer some shape to his life . . . a life that had devolved to mere existence, an endless, mind-numbing round of searching for food and shelter while avoiding the creatures by night and the human slime who did their bidding during the day.

"All right," Zev said. "I'll try to find him. I won't promise to bring him back, because such a decision will not be mine to make. But I promise to look for him."

"Tomorrow?"

"First light. And who should I say sent me?"

The woman turned away and shook her head. "No one."

"You won't tell me your name?"

"It's not important."

"But you seem to know him."

"Once, yes." Her voice grew thick. "But he wouldn't recognize me now."

"You can be so sure?"

She nodded. "I've fallen too far away. There's no coming back for me, I'm afraid."

She'd been through something terrible, this one. So had everyone who was still alive, including Zev, but her experience, whatever it was, had made her a little meshugeh. More than a little, maybe.

She started walking away, looking almost silly dragging that little red wagon behind her.

"Wait . . ."

"Just find him," she said without turning. "And don't mention me."

She stepped into the shadows and was gone from sight, with only the squeaks of the wagon wheels as proof that she hadn't evaporated.

Father Joe Cahill and a prostitute? Zev couldn't believe it. But even if it were true, it was far less serious than what Joe had been accused of.

Maybe she hadn't sold herself in the old days. Maybe it was something she had to do to survive in these new and

terrible times. Whatever the truth, he blessed her for being
here to help him tonight.

But who is she? he wondered. Or perhaps more importantly, who *was* she.